SHERWOOD ROGUE

(INCLUDES THE FICKLE UNIVERSE COMPANION STORY, LEAVING SHERWOOD)

KRISTI CRAMER

Amazon ASIN: B079HR3SMC

Paperback ISBN: 978-0-9862105-9-4

Editor: Kim Young, Kim's Fiction Editing

Cover Designer: Christian Bentulan, Covers by Christian

Interior Formatting: Marissa Honeycutt, Marissa's Design Corner

www.kristicramerbooks.com

SHERWOOD ROGUE

CHAPTER
ONE

Oregon Cascades—1985

Hiking high up on my mountain, the melting snow slushed beneath my feet and the sky arced like a dome of crystal blue above my head. I stopped often to inhale deeply, savoring the crisp air of the brisk day.

Spring had erupted in full glory, and it was a perfect day to be outside.

Cabin fever had driven me out when the walls of my uncle's cabin closed in on me with every caged step I took, and the rank smell of wood smoke and the fish I'd fried last Tuesday made me long for fresh air. I'd read every book, completed every crossword and word find, assembled each of the three puzzles more than twice.

When the weather finally cleared, I'd packed my survival gear into my carryall, picked up my bow, and went out to burn off some nervous energy.

I felt like a child again, playing my lonely make-believe on the hill behind the school. Sometimes I had played Maid Marian, sneaking away to see my friends in the forest. But more often I was the outlaw Robin Hood, King of Sherwood Forest. Nothing and no one was safe from the bite of my arrows!

I smiled at the memories, but I was no longer a child. I had survived another winter alone in the mountains.

On a high knoll, the forest below stretching away on all sides, I raised my arms above my head and shouted a challenge to the universe.

"I'm here! I'm alive!"

My words echoed back to me from the next ridge, an affirmation, an acceptance of the metaphorical gauntlet I'd thrown down.

In one fluid motion, I nocked an arrow to my bow, took aim at a rotten stump, and let it fly.

Well, I wasn't Robin Hood, but I was getting better. Despite its warped condition, the arrow actually hit the stump. My arrows gave conspicuous evidence of my miss-and-hit method of learning archery—miss the mark and hit the rock or tree, only to bend the aluminum during retrieval. Sometimes I was happy just to be able to draw the big compound bow, but my marksmanship had served well enough to feed me this winter.

My arrow had lodged deep in the stump. I got a good grip and pulled . . . and a bright flash of light hit me right between the eyes. The arrow vanished from my hands and I lost my balance, falling backwards to land smartly on my ass in the slush. I gasped, both in pain and at the sight before my eyes.

To my left and right, the knoll was still cloaked in wet snow, but in front of me a shimmering light formed a doorway. Through that doorway were trees—deciduous trees in full summer green.

I struggled to my feet, gaping at the sight. The stump and my arrow were gone. Oak and birch spread their branches in front of me. I squeezed my eyes shut and opened them again, but the forest was still there, like a mirage in the cold mountain air.

Reaching out, I passed my hand into the light, marveling as it enveloped my fingers. A tingling sensation ran up my arm and into my head, like a voice calling to me through my blood. Without thinking, I stepped forward, through the light.

A sound like a clap of thunder assaulted my ears and I staggered as I spun around. The light was gone. The knoll was gone. The forest was strange and quiet around me, and I fought the urge to run.

Run where? I didn't know where the hell I was.

Cursing, I turned in a circle, trying to get a handle on what had happened, then clutched my head against the wave of dizziness that washed over me.

Where am I?

Fear leapt into my throat, but I clamped down on it, shutting away all the questions spinning in my mind.

Survival came first.

I took off my pack and rummaged through it with shaking hands until I found my packet of hunting broadheads. I removed all the dull practice tips from my arrows and screwed in the sharp, wicked hunting barbs. Every fiber of my soul screamed danger, and if I could shoot it, I would.

I packed everything away again, taking a moment to check the survival knife strapped to the calf of my left leg. Turning to the trunk of the nearest tree, a tall alder, I used the knife to cut away a deep swath of bark. I wanted to make a reconnaissance of the area and marking where I started seemed like a good idea . . . just in case the "door" came back.

Upon closer inspection of my surroundings, I saw a break in the ferns and shrubs close by. I edged over and discovered it was a road running from the northeast to the southwest. The weeds choking it on either side had overgrown so badly it couldn't have seen a car in years. I squatted and traced the outline of a footprint that looked days old, maybe older.

A deep breath let me taste evening on the air, and long rays from the westering sun slanting through the trees confirmed I had better look for shelter before nightfall. The sky was clear, but I knew the weather could easily take a turn for the worse, and trying to make camp after dark was never wise.

In the near distance, I caught sight of a sign and a faint inter-secting track that was little more than a game trail. Keeping to the edge of the road, I moved closer.

The arm pointing down the track had some scratches in it that I couldn't make any sense of. I moved in front so I could see the other two directions.

LINCOLN, it read, pointing the way I had been going.

NOTTINGHAM, the other direction read, a self-important flourish to the carved letters.

"No way," I whispered.

I stared at the sign for a long moment, the thoughts I had been suppressing whirling in my head. "This has to be a dream. I fell asleep in the woods and I'm dreaming."

The words sounded hollow, even to my own ears. "Well, if I'm dreaming, I'll wake up." I laughed a little, feeling silly. "If I'm not, I'll go to Nottingham."

I rubbed savagely at my eyes, then opened them to find myself still standing in the road talking to myself. Was I awake then? Or merely dreaming? I had proven nothing to the skeptic in me, though the dreamer in me sent my heart soaring. With a foolish grin on my face, I turned around . . . and stopped dead in my tracks.

Four men stood spread out across the road, blocking my path. Two had quarterstaffs. One had a bow, nocked and half-drawn. The other had a sword, which was sheathed.

The bushes rustled behind me and I turned my head. Six men lined up across the road, all with bows or swords.

Bows and swords?

Squashing a rising panic, I nocked an arrow to my bow and half-drew, not quite ready to shoot one of them before they could shoot me. They were definitely menacing, but not exactly threatening. My action caused two of the men with swords to draw.

"Hold, friend," a tall man said, stepping forward.

His accent surprised me. He sounded like someone from one of those period BBC reenactment shows my mother had loved to watch.

Were they from some kind of LARP troupe? A cult? They wore clothes made of leather or rough linen, wide belts over long tunics and close-fitting pants, not to mention every one of them carried a weapon of some kind—all aimed at me.

"Get back," I growled, lifting my bow to draw on him.

The man chuckled but obliged, taking one step back. "The puppy barks," he said. Someone laughed.

"I bite, too," I said under my breath.

"Come now, lad," another said from behind me. I whirled to face him, aiming for his heart. "We only want your money, not your life." He had an accent, too, thick enough I struggled to follow the words.

Then I laughed. He thought I was a boy! "You're thieves!" It wasn't an accusation. I was simply stating a fact. Who were these men? Thieves? Dressed like that? Armed with authentic-looking weapons? It was no longer a question of where I was: it was more like *when?* At this point, it seemed anything was possible.

"We are," said another, behind me again. I turned to face the new speaker—a short, skinny, blond-haired fellow. "But if you're caught with that bow . . . ."

I aimed for his heart in turn. "Look, just let me pass."

"Give us your money," said someone behind me. I turned to face him, realizing they were closing in.

"I know what you're trying to do. It won't work." I searched their faces, looking for the leader. I spotted him right off. He was a short, stocky man with broad shoulders who wore authority like a comfortable coat. I shifted my aim to him.

"Come any closer," I said, trying to sound tough, "and your leader dies." If my bluff didn't work, I prayed my aim would be true.

"You would be dead, too, lad." He spoke in a soft voice, but the words slapped me in the face. My fingers began to tremble and I almost loosed my arrow in sheer panic as it dawned on me that this was real. I wasn't in control.

I lowered my bow, easing tension on the string. I wasn't ready to die yet. Not in Sherwood Forest with a chance at something miraculous right in front of me. I was beginning to get an idea about these outlaws, but couldn't let myself think about the absurdity of my assessment.

"You're absolutely right." My tone was too high to sound assured, and I cleared my throat. "I have news for you, though. I have no money. Not even a penny."

"I'll be the judge of that," the short man said, walking over to me. The other men relaxed their bowstrings but eyed me warily, as though I were going to try and take as many of them as I could along with me to hell. I chuckled, slowly removing my pack. I gathered the arrows I had dropped—I had no quiver—and the man gave them to one of the bowmen, who looked at them in disbelief.

"I have no money. Look for yourself." I stood aside as the short man knelt to investigate my pack. He searched through my supplies —blanket, dried food, canteen, fire-starting kit, rope, tarp, first aid kit. He didn't pull out any money, but he did remove my small knife and high tops.

He clipped the knife to his belt, then grasped a shoe and looked at it curiously as he stood.

"It's a shoe," I said.

"I can see that," he said mildly. "It's the material that interests me. And your pack and gear . . . . They're finely made." He fingered the sleeve of my wool jacket. "Where are you from?"

Finely made? They were just Goodwill finds, nylon and wool, but machine made. All their clothes looked like homespun. "That depends on where, exactly, I am right now," I answered. "I—"

One of the men came up behind me and slipped my survival knife from its leg sheath. "Hey!" I snatched at it, but he held it away from me while another man half-drew his sword. "Okay, take it. But I want it back."

"David," the man with my knife said. "Come look at this." He showed the short man the compass at the hilt of my knife, then gave it to him.

David shook it, then brought it over to me. "What's this?"

"It's a compass. It shows directions. See. It points north. May I please have it back?"

David checked the compass and glanced up at the sun, making his own determination, then looked at me. "You're from Asia, aren't you? They have things like this there. What are you doing in England?"

"I'm traveling." I let his guess slide. They wouldn't know anything about where I was from. I was beginning to have an inkling of who these people were, and where . . . or rather, when I was. My common sense warred with the bizarre notion insistently nagging my thoughts.

"Funny, you don't look like an Asian. You've been to Asia then. You're not from England, though. You don't talk right. Where are you from?"

"When did you ever see an Asian, David?" asked a smooth-faced man whose black hair stood out among the blonds and browns of the others.

"Quiet, Mark. My brother told me. He says they're dark. This boy's fair. Leave off." I was surprised at how defensive David became with the simple question. Then I saw the nasty smirk on the other man's face.

"All right," the one called Mark said, nodding. "But what are we going to do with him? He hasn't got any money."

Ignoring him, I looked at David. "I'm from Italy," I lied. The words were out of my mouth before I realized what I was saying. I thought of taking it back, telling them I was from America, but decided to ride with my initial instinct. Something told me my instincts weren't wrong this time, and it didn't matter whether they believed me. I somehow doubted any of them had ever seen or heard an Italian before, much less an American. "My grandfather was an English sailor. I wanted to see his mother country."

They were all silent, most of them looking at David. Others seemed to be contemplating the truth of my story. I stayed quiet, waiting.

"Aren't Italians dark, too?" someone asked softly. "How can he be Italian if he's fair?" Others nodded in agreement.

"I said I've an English grandfather. I inherited his blond hair and blue eyes," I explained. That much was true.

A part of my mind weighed all the elements of my surroundings, cataloging accents, dialects, clothing . . . . I wasn't sure what year it was. It certainly wasn't the twentieth century. Their clothing and weapons suggested it was somewhere around the reign of Henry II, or his son, Richard the Lionheart. I swallowed in a dry throat, excitement rising in my chest.

These could be the men of Robin Hood.

I knew the legends, the folklore surrounding Robin Hood. As a child, I had dreamed of being an outlaw in Sherwood Forest. I sent up a prayer to God that these men were from Robin's group. Partly because it would be a dream come true, and partly because if I were wrong, I might be dead in a few moments.

David was silent, staring at the ground. He tugged at the whiskers on his chin and I wondered what was going through his mind.

"It's getting late, David of Doncaster," I said, making a wild guess. David of Doncaster was Robin Hood's best wrestler. When his head snapped up, I knew I was right. "Take me to Robin Hood."

Someone gasped as David's eyes went wide. Some of the men

drew knives, long and wicked, better than swords for fighting in close quarters. Once again, I was in the danger zone. I held up my hands, palms out, to remind them I was unarmed.

"What did you say?" David asked me, speaking slowly.

"He's a spy." Mark took one long step closer to me and set the blade of his knife against my throat. "He's come to find out where we live, then he'll go tell the sheriff."

"Hah!" I exclaimed, then felt the knife bite into my neck. I suppressed the urge to wince in pain as blood began to trickle down. "Look, everyone in England knows of the outlaws in Sherwood Forest. I've been here long enough to have heard of Robin Hood and some of his men—including David of Doncaster." Their reaction surprised me. Surely they knew they were notorious. I wondered if I had blown it. Maybe they'd only been in the forest for a short time.

A blond man muttered something to his neighbor, who laughed. David silenced him with a swift gesture. "Why do you want to see Robin?" he asked, gesturing for Mark to put his knife away.

"Perhaps I want to join with him, to take my oath and serve him for good or ill." I grinned, rubbing at the cut on my neck. Salt from the sweat of my palms stung. "It would be far better than marching across the rest of England. Vagrants like me don't get much respect." I paused a moment, wondering if someone would call my bluff.

I had fallen into the role I created and felt comfortable in it. It didn't matter if I didn't know how I came to be where I was. I was here, so I'd deal with it. "Well?" I asked.

"Give him back his knife," David said, and it was returned to me. He gestured to me with a nod, indicating I should come with them.

I shouldered my pack and received my arrows from the bowman who had held them all the while. He gave me a strange look, then shook his head. I had no quiver, and with the hunting tips on, I couldn't put them in my pack as usual, so I carried them. I slung my bow across my back. I was surprised no one had questioned it. There was no way any of them had seen a compound bow before.

"Let's go then," said David, gesturing for me to start walking along the road toward Nottingham. The men moved to follow.

I had been right about Robin Hood. I started to smile, but the implications hit me. Robin Hood? How on earth . . . ? Not only had I gone through space, but time as well. The thought made my blood run cold as my initial adrenaline spike wore off.

What's happening? What am I doing here?

The thoughts kept returning to my mind as we walked. Again, I wondered if it wasn't all just a dream, but everything was so . . . real.

WE STAYED on the road for a while, then cut up into the woods to head west by northwest. I moved noisily through the underbrush, though I could hardly hear my companions. They were quiet as falling sunlight, while I was a spring windstorm.

Finally, we came to a clearing and I saw men moving around. A deer roasted in a huge fire pit, while men set up tables and brought out dishes. I stopped at the edge of the clearing to look around, taking in the scene. David kept walking, as did most of the others, but Mark and two others waited behind me. I saw the dull flash of a knife as one of them moved.

In a sweeping glance, I took a quick head count. A little over forty, including the ones in David's group. Not as many men as legends said.

"Well, Little Italian," Mark said, stepping up beside me. "What do you think?"

"I have a name," I said, not looking at him. My gaze landed on a man standing by the fire pit, talking with David.

"I don't care," Mark sneered.

His attitude reminded me of the bullies from school, and I struggled to ignore his insulting manner. I'd been out of school for four years, but the urge to fight back was still strong—and would not do here.

"Is that Robin Hood talking with David of Doncaster?" I gestured with my chin. David pointed my way, and the man looked at me and nodded.

"Aye, that's him, boy. Look, he wants you. You'd best go, Little Italian."

When Robin beckoned to me, Mark's attitude was forgotten.

I moved slowly across the clearing, afraid of meeting the man who was such a major figure in my childhood fantasies. The man who would decide my fate.

I stopped about a yard away from him and dropped to one knee, my eyes focused on his worn, soft leather boots. I cleared my throat, trying to find my voice. "Master Robin Hood."

"Get up," Robin said, his voice a mixture of command and kindness. A voice one could not easily disobey.

I looked up, then stood.

Robin Hood.

I didn't know what I'd been expecting, but the man before me certainly wasn't what I had imagined. He had a kind face, laugh lines at the corners of his eyes. The eyes themselves were so deep blue, they looked black in this light. He had a small, sharp nose and a mouth that seemed generous with its smiles. His chin sported a blondish three-day beard, and a moustache of the same color grew above his upper lip. Blond hair fell to his shoulders in waves splashing against the faded red of his jerkin.

But more than physical appearance, the man had a charismatic presence demanding blind faith. He made me feel I would go to hell and back for him if he asked.

I could see why Robin Hood had gained a following such as legends were made of, and why he was such a feared fellow in his time. If the others felt like I did . . . then this man commanded a company of men who would do anything he asked—and the ruling class had every reason to be afraid.

Robin looked me over, then stepped closer. When his gaze locked on mine, my knees felt like they would turn to water at any moment. His presence was strong, just like the fire behind his eyes. I was drowning in him while he looked into my soul, and I tried not to quake in my boots.

When he broke our gaze, I still felt his presence, but it wasn't as strong. He knew what he was doing, knew exactly what his stare could do. Released from that intensity, I didn't need to worry about falling any more.

"I am Robin Hood," he said. "Who are you?"

"Kay," I answered.

"Just Kay? Nothing more?"

"Just Kay."

"David tells me you're from Italy."

"That's what I told him, sir."

"*Are* you from Italy, lad?" he asked, looking me straight in the eye.

I cleared my throat. "No, sir." How could I lie to Robin Hood? "I'm from America." I attempted a smile. "I didn't think David would know where it was." I looked steadily back into Robin's eyes. I was surprised when he broke the gaze first, glancing at David, then back to me.

"I've never heard of America. Is it far from England?"

"Very. It's west, over the sea. Many days of travel away." I dropped my gaze to the ground, unsure of my footing on this subject. "Please, sir. I don't want to talk of my home. It is as lost to me as I am to it. I want to be a part of your band, be your faithful servant." I looked up quickly, then made a low bow.

Robin Hood shook his head and laughed. His laughter sounded like a hunting horn playing bright notes on a crisp morning. "All right, boy. You'll have your trial time, and I'll be your judge. You understand?"

"I do."

"Then you'll excuse me." He left me standing there, stunned, next to the fire pit.

I watched after him. "What do I do now?" I murmured, running my hand along my bowstring.

"Hello," said a voice at my shoulder. I turned to see a man smiling at me. He was tall and looked strong, but his face was kind. Curly brown hair framed his smiling blue eyes. "I'm Much. Come on. Let me show you where you can put your pack. Robin forgets things like that. Here. I'll carry your bow and arrows for you." He stooped a little—he was a good deal taller than my 5'6"—and took my bow from me. I handed over my arrows.

"I don't have a quiver for them yet," I apologized.

Much shrugged. "We'll remedy that." He looked at my bow with a curious eye, but didn't say anything.

He led me to a place off to one side of the clearing, pointing out other packs hidden under the fern and underbrush. He waited for me to settle mine behind a bush, then he fingered the strings of my bow.

"This is a strange bow. I've never seen its like. Why does it have three strings?"

I hesitated a moment, worried about what would happen if the compound bow was invented earlier than history related, then decided to tell him.

"It's a bow we have where I came from. It's called 'compound.' It's new to you because we don't yet trade with eastern countries. Look. The long string goes through the pulley system to amplify the velocity and power behind the arrow, while also making it easier to hold at full draw." He blinked at me, and I realized he didn't have a clue what I was talking about. "Try it. Just don't loose without an arrow."

I took my arrows from him and he lifted the bow. I saw the muscles in his bare arms working as he drew. The string dragged at his pull until it reached a certain point, then the tension broke and he was holding at full drawn, recovering from the sudden lack of resistance. He had almost ripped the string off its pulleys. Letting it back slowly, he tested the strength, feeling how the pull increased as he released the tension.

"Do you see?"

"Yes!" said Much, a twinkle of excitement in his light blue eyes.

"Then someone who is not as strong, like me, can still hold it at full drawn and shoot with power. Unfortunately, I'm not a very good marksman."

Much looked down at the arrows in my hand. "It'd be a wonder if you could hit anything with those."

"I know, but they're all I could get a hold of."

"Are the shafts made of metal? I've never heard of anyone doing that. It's not very practical." He took an arrow from me. "They're light enough, though. What's the flight made of? Not real feathers, that's sure. This place, America, must be a strange place to live."

I shrugged. "It's not so special. I like it here better," I told him, realizing it was the truth. I already felt much more at home here than I had in my uncle's cabin.

Much smiled at me, and I decided I liked him.

It was full dark by then, and someone called out that the food was ready. Much showed me to the long table set up in the clearing, and the food was served. It was decent. Not exotic or spicy, but good in the way only meals cooked over an open fire are.

As I ate, I listened to the conversations. The men told stories even I could tell were outrageous. I laughed and smiled, almost in shock. Nothing like this had ever crossed my mind as a possibility before. It was like a dream, but so vivid with energy, emotion, and life, it had to be real.

"Hey, Little Italian," Mark said, coming up behind me to fill my cup with ale. "Enjoy your night of rest because tomorrow you've been assigned to clean the plate. All by yourself. That gives you something to look forward to, doesn't it?" He laughed and gave my arm a shake, spilling ale down my front. Then he moved away to fill more cups.

I brushed half-heartedly at my shirt, looking at Much. "He doesn't like me, does he?" I whispered. Mark's voice had held an icy edge that belied the smile on his face.

"Who? Mark?" Much asked around a mouthful of food. He swallowed and wiped his mouth with the back of his hand. "He doesn't like many people. He's vicious. The only person who really tolerates him is Scarlet. They have history from before the Greenwood. Mark respects Scarlet like he respects nobody else but Robin, who mostly ignores him." Much glanced around the table, then called out, "Eric! Let's have some of that bread!"

A loaf of bread came sailing through the air, straight at me. I caught the hard loaf with my left hand and surrendered it to Much. "Nice catch," he said, then turned to look back down table. "Eric?! Where's your manners?!"

"Sorry, Much. I lost my head for a moment."

"And your aim!" Much cried in mock rage. "You could have disabled the lad!"

A roar of laughter went around the table. I picked out Eric so I could attach his name to his face.

It was hard to get used to, having all these men addressing me as if I were a boy. That would have never happened at home. Granted, I was flat-chested and neither my features nor my voice were strikingly feminine, but my hair was too long for a boy's. Shoulder-length and straight was not "in" for boys in the small town closest to my home. Here, it was natural. I just hoped I wouldn't be found out before I had a chance to prove myself. If they knew, they would send me packing . . . or worse.

While the legends I grew up with painted a picture of merry rascals who lived by a chivalrous code, the reality was by no means clear. I wasn't at all certain these men wouldn't take me off, rape me, and leave me in the forest if they knew I was a woman. I heard Phillip and Warren, who sat on my other side, boast about a girl they knew in the village, how she had played hard to get until Warren had "taken her behind the barn."

So I kept my secret and my peace on the subject and watched the goings on around me with an eye toward determining just how different this world was from the tales of Robin's Merry Men.

"Listen, Kay," said Much, leaning toward me. "Tomorrow, I'll show you how to make some decent arrows and we'll see how well you shoot." I nodded, my mouth full of venison. "Do you know swordplay?"

I swallowed. "I'm afraid not. I've never had enough money to buy a sword."

"What about a quarterstaff? Can you use one of those?"

"I've never tried." I dipped some bread into the soup to soften it up, then took a big bite.

"Well then, Kay, I'll teach you."

The offer surprised me, and I hurried to swallow. "Thank you."

"Don't mention it. If I teach you, I won't have to do some of the nastier duties for a while, though that's not the main reason I'm helping you."

"No? What is?"

"I like you. And a man's got to be able to take care of himself in this group. Not that others won't, if you're in a bind. Sometime, though, you might find yourself in a fix with no one around to help you out of it."

CHAPTER
TWO

I lay in the nearly complete darkness of the forest. It was early morning, the moon making fanciful patterns in the treetops. I had dropped off early, unused to drinking ale with my meals, but I woke when things calmed down, the men went to sleep, and the quiet began to settle.

The stillness of the forest sank into my bones while I gazed up through the trees at familiar constellations in unfamiliar places. The stars looked so close in the pristine air.

Unable to get back to sleep, I got up in the hopes of talking to the man on watch. When no one was at the fire when I got there, I wondered where he had gone.

I found out when I felt cold steel at my neck. I froze.

"Aye," a voice whispered at my ear. Warm, bad breath stirred my hair. "Don't move. Who are you?"

"It's Kay."

"Kay? That's right." The knife slid away from my throat, making a subtle threat with an implied cut. I knew it would still be poised, ready. "You're the new one."

"Yeah."

A figure came around to my right where the fire lit his features. He was one of the few men whose name I didn't know.

"What are you doing up? You're not for the watch, are you?" I heard the suspicion in his voice, and it worried me that I couldn't see his knife.

"No. I couldn't sleep. I was looking for some company. It's too . . . still."

I heard a faint breath of laughter. "Some say your conscience keeps you awake out here."

There was no right response to that statement, so I took it as a joke, pushing the jibe right back at him. "Did yours?"

The man grinned. "I couldn't sleep the first night out here under the trees."

"When was that?"

"Quite some time ago. Sit down," he offered. I sat on a piece of firewood. The man sat next to me, close enough for quiet conversation, but not so close as to be within arm's reach. I wondered what his name was, but when he didn't offer it, I was curious to see if I could figure out who he was without asking.

"I heard you're from Italy." The man flipped his knife in little circles, catching it by the hilt, even when he turned to look at me.

"Really? Who told you that?"

"Someone I know. He calls you Little Italian. It suits you, I think."

I chuckled. "You do? Why?" I picked up a twig and broke it up in my hands, throwing the pieces one by one into the fire. Flames flickered and jumped.

"You aren't an English lad, for sure." His eyes watched my every move.

"I'm not from Italy."

"Oh?"

"Yeah. But if you like the name, well . . . . I've been called worse."

I watched him out of the corner of my eye. He was a handsome man. He had brownish hair, a hawk-like nose, and eyes that reflected the fire, as though they were flames themselves. I felt my cheeks warm at the thought of that gaze laying my thoughts bare, and looked back into the fire.

"Who do you think will get the crown?" I asked, struck with the need to know who was king. If John were already on the throne, Robin didn't have much longer to be happy in the Greenwood.

He glanced at me in surprise. "It's a little early to be hatching new kings with Richard only coronated last year."

"Isn't Richard at war?" I asked, struggling to remember my English history. Richard reigned for how many years?

"Well, if Richard gets himself killed crusading, John, the plotting knave, will take the throne. Some say there's a bastard son, but if that's true, he won't live long after Richard dies."

"That's too bad."

"I know. Quite a selection we have, isn't it? A snake on the throne, or a bloody fool who'll get himself killed fighting Saracens."

"Tell me about the war in Palestine." I turned to him. "Have you been there?"

"Aye." He paused a moment, his eyes closed. The knife he held loosely in his hand jumped at some reflex, perhaps a memory. "It's like hell. Fields trampled down to mud or burned. Peasants lying slaughtered in the streets, bodies left for the ravens and jackals. Hunger and disease everywhere. I was there some three years ago, yet those images still burn in my memory."

He paused again, his voice dropping to little more than a whisper. "I was commanding a troop of my father's men. Half of us were wiped out by some foreign disease, and the rest . . . ." He swallowed. "We were attacked by Saracens in a desert valley. It was a trap. Only three of us got out alive. I'd hardly been there two months, but I'd seen enough death to make me sick. So much destruction . . . . I was wounded in that attack, so they let me go home." He fell silent.

I knew I'd opened an old wound that had nothing to do with blood and body parts. He stared into the fire, seemingly unaware I was still there.

"I'm sorry. I didn't mean to stir up old memories better left sleeping," I told him.

Slowly, he turned to me and shrugged. "No matter. I still think of those days a lot. That's why I take night watch. I can't sleep in the evening, but by the time my relief comes, I'm ready to drop."

I yawned, trying too late to cover it.

"Speaking of being ready to drop, you look as if you ought to be getting some sleep. The second day is always the hardest."

As if his words were a cue, fatigue overwhelmed me. Standing, I nodded. "I enjoyed talking to you this evening," I said, waiting to see if he would drop me his name.

"Sleep well, Little Italian," he said, turning to throw another bit of wood onto the fire.

I made my way back to my blanket and climbed beneath it, asleep before I could count to twenty-five.

I dreamed I stood on a high cliff looking out over the scene of a battle. Tiny figures ran at each other, swinging broadswords and screaming battle cries. I winced at the cries of the dying. Then a foot pushed me over the edge of the cliff and I fell headlong into the frenzy.

Gasping, I rolled over, awake.

Much looked down at me and smiled, the early morning sunlight making a nimbus of his hair and dazzling my eyes.

"Was it a good dream?" he asked.

"No, no, no! That's not the way you do it. Look. This way. Keep from bending the feathers over with the thread or you'll have an unbalanced spin. The feathers need to *be* straight to fly straight! Now. Try again."

I had been trying to make an arrow all morning. It was nearly noon and Much's patience was wearing thin. I tried again, fingers fumbling with the tools. Finally, I got it right, though it was a shoddy job. The shaft lay straight and true, but the feathers were rumpled and crooked from rough handling. The thing yet lacked a tip.

"Good!" said Much. I smiled in relief at the accomplishment. "Now, the tip is the easiest part." He showed me how to slide the flat, wedge-shaped end of the tip into a slot at the end of the arrow. The tip looked like a big, flat triangle balanced on top of a smaller one, both shaped from the same piece of metal and very sharp. From there, he took a bit of wet leather thong and strapped the tip to the arrow. The width of the small end kept it in place while the leather, shrinking as it dried, would hold it tight. Much undid it and gave it to me. "Here, you try. Remember to center the blade to keep the balance even."

I duplicated his actions, only slower, fastening it together carefully.

"You did it! Your first arrow!" He swatted me on the back. "This one won't fly well on account of its feathers, but if you practice, you'll get better."

He gathered up his few tools as I put out the fire we had used to straighten the shaft.

"You'll have to get your own tools. Once you've been with us a while, you can see about trading for them. Come on. Let's go eat. After lunch, I'll teach you some tricks at quarterstaff."

"Anything other than arrow making," I said, glad to put the experience behind me. Arrow making was tedious and hard. I wasn't even convinced a wooden shaft would hold up to the velocity my bow could bring to bear on it, though my bow was only set at about forty-five pounds. That was an experiment for another day.

I hoped I could get away without having to spend much more time at this activity. I would have to find some other way to contribute.

When we reached the clearing, it was nearly empty. Only a few souls sat scattered, eating cold stirabout and drinking ale. As I had at breakfast, I looked around for the man I had spoken to last night, but he was nowhere in sight.

As we ate, Much told me what we were going to do next. "There's a good-sized clearing by the river near where some oak saplings grow. I'll size you up for a staff. Not many people go there, so no one will see it if you dust my shirt for me."

"I wager I'll be dunked in the river before that happens," I said, and Much laughed.

"You'll get knocked down—into the river or the dirt—more than once, if I have any say in the matter. Avoiding pain is one of the best incentives to learning to fight well."

Out by the river, the sun shone brightly, almost too warm. Much sized me up, then picked a stout sapling and showed me how to cut off all the branches and trim it down to my size. Once done with that, he demonstrated the proper hold. Then he picked up his own staff.

"Ready?"

I took a deep breath. "As I'll ever be."

"Then defend yourself."

His first swing was slow. I blocked it easily, noting the way he held his hands and the way he moved. He nodded, swinging again slowly, telling me the best ways to block and stopping when I didn't do it right. He showed how to judge what his moves would be by the way his body moved, and that was part of learning how to attack.

Now *this* was the kind of learning I liked.

As we continued, he stopped telling me what to do and kept going if I did it wrong. He let me feel the knocks he aimed at me, giving me incentive to learn quicker. He got faster, the blows coming stronger.

I had been in fights before, had felt many a mean knock, but I'd never fought staffs with a man. Much's strength went beyond anything I had ever encountered, even in one of my dad's drunken rages. Yet he was holding back.

I could have laughed at the thought that popped into my head. With all the blows and accompanying pain I felt, I knew I wasn't in a dream. Normal dreams didn't hurt like this.

Distracted, my guard slipped, and Much delivered a tap on my head that sent me sprawling over the bank and into the river.

I came up sputtering, coughing and disoriented by the blow, and tried to find the river bottom with my feet. It was all I could do to stay afloat. Finally, my feet found purchase, and my sight cleared enough to see a staff wavering in front of me. Much called for me to take it. I reached out and grabbed it.

"Come on in!" I cried, yanking as hard as I could. "The water's wonderful."

I heard the splash as Much went in. I looked around for my staff and swam for it, then pulled myself up onto the bank, soon joined by Much. We lay there, laughing.

"I guess I should have seen that coming," he said after a while. "Like you should have blocked that strike." He lay with his eyes closed against the sunlight, and I envied his ability to relax so completely. I was too busy trying to find a position that wouldn't display my . . . feminine assets.

"You're right," I replied. "And I regret the error."

Much chuckled without opening his eyes. I shifted and leaned out over the water, gazing at my reflection. The image wavered, distorted. My tawny hair looked brown, and my blue eyes made dark hollows in my reflected face. My nose, however, was still too small, and my mouth still quirked up on one side when I was happy. Yes, I could see how one might mistake me for a boy. I dropped a blade of grass onto my reflection. It broke the surface, made its ripples, and floated away on the soft current.

I wondered what effect my appearance in the past would have on the events to come. Would my ripples change anything?

"Oh," I said, after a while. "What a way to cool down."

"Aye," agreed Much. "Now, let's dry off properly, shall we? You still need more practice."

I sighed and stood, picking up my staff. As soon as Much was on his feet, I attacked, surprising him into action. I used most of the same moves he had used on me, pressing the advantage I had gained by surprise.

Twice, I got past his guard to give him a good rap on the ribs. Then I pulled a nasty trick, playing my staff across his fingers. He dropped his staff in surprise and pain, looking at my staff wavering before his face.

"You're a fast learner," he said with a slow smile as he straightened.

"I have to be. I'm not nearly as strong as you, so I have to use my wits or surprise to protect myself." I plucked experimentally at my clothes. "One more bout? I'm not quite dry."

Much nodded, still smiling, and picked up his staff.

"Do you remember I said I'd be tossed in the river before I ever dusted your shirt?" I wiggled my eyebrows at him, feeling cocky.

"I remember. But you haven't dusted me yet. Guard up." He raised his staff.

"Aye," I said doggedly. "But I will."

This time, Much attacked first. He held nothing back. I blocked what I could, taking the other blows—like a man. I even got through a couple times to rap him on the ribs and leg. For a long while, we fought, neither touching the other except for our staffs. The only other sounds were our labored breathing and an occasional grunt at an unexpectedly strong blow.

At last, something over my shoulder distracted Much for a

moment. I took advantage of his lapse and tripped him up. The move sent him sprawling backwards, head over heels.

I turned around to see what had caught his attention, but nothing moved in the forest. I frowned. I was missing something.

Much sat up, shaking his head as though to clear it. "By our Lady, that was a good throw. I'd say you dusted me good." He picked up his staff and stood, brushing off his shirt and trousers. I thought his face was flushed from more than his exertion, though he wouldn't meet my eyes.

"It's about time for supper," he said at last and led the way back to the clearing, limping a little. "Ah . . . . I'll ache in the morning for that one," he muttered.

I smiled, hefting my staff. I knew I could throw him. I just had to watch for the right opportunity.

WE WERE LATE FOR DINNER. Everyone was already seated and eating, but they paid little attention as we set our staffs against a tree. I quietly took a seat at the table, while Much made a great show of climbing over the bench with a groan, his hand on his back. His ploy worked.

"What's the matter, Much?" Edward called. "You look like you've been run over by a horse."

Much looked over at me. I said nothing, so he gestured to me and growled, "I was."

Edward and a few of the others laughed. "He's got some potential then, eh?"

"Some?! The boy threw me like a doll, and I didn't even see it coming!"

This brought a general burst of laughter. Much's ears turned pink and I smiled, but didn't dare laugh with them. His self-sacrifice in order to boost my status deserved more than my rubbing it in.

"I hope the little Italian isn't too tired to clean the plate!" a familiar voice called out. I turned to see Mark staring at me, the challenge in his eyes obvious. When I met his gaze, his lip curled in a harsh smile before he drained his cup of ale.

I smiled, lifting my cup to him. I wasn't about to let him ride my nerves and spoil my good mood. It would be time to do the dishes soon enough, and my humor would slide downhill fast enough then.

As it was, it took an hour to clean the dishes. Everyone else sat in the clearing, talking or having wrestling matches. Alone by the small stream, I scrubbed on wooden bowls, mugs, and copper plates with a coarse, damp cloth, whistling a soft tune to keep my mind off the task.

My muscles ached as I went through the motions of washing, but I had to smile at the memory of the day. I had actually thrown Much the Miller's Son, a legend!

I wiped my hands on the moss and started putting the clean plates back into the basket, admiring the simple workmanship of the utensils and dishes.

I was about to lift the basket when I heard someone moving through the brush. It could have been the soft step of a wild animal or the wind, but I didn't think so. I dropped into a crouch, drawing my knife and searching the thicket for the intruder.

The man from the watch fire came through, looking at me without surprise. "Good evening," he said, splashing across the stream. "Is there any food left?"

I sheathed my knife. "If you want to wait here, I'll bring you some bread and ale. There's no meat left, I'm afraid. You look tired."

"I am, lad." He sat down as I stooped to pick up the basket and carried it back to the area that served as a kitchen.

The firelight from the main clearing leapt, making shadows dance across the ground and trees around me. The vision was surreal, though there was no longer any doubt in my mind that I was, indeed, in twelfth-century England.

When I returned with a loaf of bread and a cup of ale, the man had his boots off, soaking his feet in the brook. I sat next to him, setting the loaf and cup between us. He looked up at me gratefully and began tearing bites off the loaf, stuffing them into his mouth.

I watched him, curious to hear where he had been, but not willing to ask. A man's business was his own to tell or not if he chooses. Who was I to question an outlaw? He caught me staring and read the question behind my eyes.

"I've been to see Tuck," he said, swallowing. He held a finger to his lips briefly. "I wasn't supposed to go. Robin doesn't like any of us to leave alone. But he's my friend, see. He keeps up with the news of my father's land, and I like to hear what's going on."

"Ah." I tried again to figure out who this man was. Did he have any part in the stories I read in my youth?

"Well?" he said after a moment, looking at me expectantly.

"What?" I asked, snapping out of my thoughts.

"What did you learn today?"

"I made my first arrow, but it won't fly."

He chuckled. "That's all right. Most of mine don't. I've never had the patience for it. Anything else?"

"I started learning how to use a quarterstaff." I waited for his comment, but he just nodded. "Much said I did quite well," I added, trying to goad him into asking. It worked.

"He did, did he?"

"Well, not in so many words, but I did throw him."

"Did you?" There was genuine surprise in his voice. "Now there's a trick. I'd give a silver penny to have seen that. Did you dust him good?"

I shrugged. "He's limping."

"By our Lady, you must be stronger than you look."

I shook my head and smiled, glad of his approval. "Not yet."

The man emptied his cup and I got up to refill it, but when I came back, he was gone. I shrugged and sat down on the moss to drink the ale myself, listening to the murmur of the stream and the voices of the men in the clearing.

I woke at the sound of a footfall and looked up to see Much standing over me.

"There you are, lad. I've been looking for you. Mark said you'd run off to the sheriff."

"Well, I didn't, did I?" I grumped, rubbing my eyes. "I've been here, sleeping. I got tired after doing all those dishes, so I came here with a cup of ale."

Much sat down beside me and rubbed his forehead.

"You're supposed to watch me, aren't you?" I asked, sitting up.

"What?"

"Robin asked you to watch me, make sure Mark isn't right."

Much sighed. "You mustn't take it personally. All our new ones get watched. We can't take any chances."

"I understand, though you make enough noise to wake the dead."

Much laughed. "The sheriff's men are afraid to come into the forest at night. Dreadful things happen to foresters who brave Sherwood's shadows. They're usually found along the high road in the morning, frightened out of their wits. If they're found at all."

I digested that information, deciding it was best not to comment. I went back to my earlier thought. "But we're friends, aren't we? You're not just being chummy because you have to stick to me like a leech?"

"No. You're all right, Kay. Anyway, if I didn't like you, would I have told everyone that you threw me at the river today?"

"No, I don't believe you would have." I smiled.

"What you did this afternoon was unusual. Not many people can just pick up a quarterstaff one day and throw an old hand like me. I'm good." He smiled, gazing off into the trees. "I even beat Little John once."

"Something behind me distracted you. That's how I threw you."

Much raised an eyebrow. "I only glanced away for a moment. You've got quick wits to catch that and use it."

"You should watch your concentration, especially when fighting a smaller opponent. I've always been quick to find an opening to finish a fight."

"Aye. Well, I'll work on that." He winked as he stood up. "Come on. It's time to get some sleep.

"Much, what distracted you?"

He looked down and blushed. "Stutely was watching."

I furrowed my brow. "Was he? I looked, but I didn't see anyone."

"You had better learn to see, my boy. He was there." Much tapped my forehead between my eyes, then strode back to the clearing.

I washed out the cup and brought it back to the kitchen, then went to my blanket and curled up. I fell asleep soundly while the men in the clearing still chattered, but when they went to sleep, I woke up to the stillness.

I sat up, disoriented for a moment, feeling as though something was missing. Then I saw a figure moving around the watch fire and remembered I wasn't at home, might never be home again. The thought wasn't all that disturbing.

Getting up quietly, I went to the fire and sat down, soon joined by the man.

"'Lo," I said. He grunted in answer.

We sat together in silence for a while. I thought about what he had said earlier about his father's land. It was a puzzle, but I felt I should know how the pieces fit.

"Do you mind if I ask you a question?" I asked.

Prodding the fire with a stick, he made sparks fly. "I don't mind."

"It's rather personal." He didn't respond. "You don't have to answer."

He sighed heavily. His gaze was on the fire, but I could tell he was alert to the sounds, or absence of them, around him. "I know."

I raised my eyebrows, then asked, "Your father was a landowner, right?"

"Yes."

"Then how did it come about that you are an outlaw?"

He turned to me and our gazes locked. His eyes lit like fire for a few moments, then the flames sank low. He didn't answer, just turned away.

We sat silently for a few moments, then I picked up a twig and snapped it in two before throwing it into the hungry fire and climbing to my feet.

From my blanket, I watched the figure sitting by the fire, unmoving.

CHAPTER

THREE

In the morning, I woke to Robin's hand on my shoulder. He raised a finger to his lips and beckoned me to follow him out of the camp. We walked through the forest and emerged at the river downstream from where Much and I had fought.

Still bleary-eyed with sleep, I rubbed my face, trying to wake up. Robin was silent, so I watched the water, drowsy, not really thinking about who stood beside me. I wished I could strip off my clothes and wash myself in the pre-dawn freshness, but thoughts of bathing vanished when I remembered where I was.

I waited for Robin to speak first, afraid to ask why I was with him, worrying more with each moment that passed.

"Much tells me you have quite a hand for the quarterstaff," he said at last. He sat on the riverbank and motioned for me to join him.

"He told me that, too," I agreed, still wary as I settled beside him.

"He said you caught him looking away, played him up on it, and threw him."

"I did."

"You don't sound like you're too proud of it." He threw stems of long grass into the river, watching them float away.

"It's not my nature to be proud, sir." He was after something. I could tell.

"You should be. It's been a long time since anyone has thrown Much, except John."

"I was lucky."

"But you can see people's weaknesses, know how to get behind someone's guard. That takes a good eye and a sharp mind. Use it."

I looked at him keenly for a moment, different thoughts crossing my mind. "You didn't bring me out here to talk about quarterstaffs and fights."

"Like I said, a sharp mind." Robin looked at me. I shifted my gaze away from his, unused to hearing compliments. "No, I didn't. Some of my men are a bit concerned about your background. I won't mention any names, but they're not sure about my decision to let you join us. I'm curious about you myself."

"So you want to hear all of it." I sighed. I knew I couldn't go on forever without telling someone. But how much should I reveal? "If I tell you," I said, still debating where I should draw the line, "and hide nothing, I would rather you didn't share it with any of your men. I will abide by your decision."

"You have my word." His tone suggested he was intrigued.

"That's all I ask. First, I must ask a question."

"Yes?"

"What do you think about women?"

"What?!"

"Do you believe women should be allowed to do what they set their minds to, or should they only bear children and keep homes?"

Robin thought for a moment, looking at me with that probing stare of his.

"It depends on what they set their minds to," he said carefully, watching. "Why do you ask?" I knew at that point he had a good idea why and was only waiting to hear it.

I took a deep breath. "Because I am a woman."

Robin's stare intensified. I wanted to shrink away from his gaze and hide somewhere, but I held out, staring back at him. I couldn't back down. Not this time. There was too much to lose.

The look on his face was hard to read. I saw disbelief, but I couldn't tell if he was angry or not. After a long moment, my stomach growled, breaking the tension. He looked away, gazing out over the river.

"Tell me why you are here."

I looked down at the ground, forming the words in my head. "I am here because I've always dreamed of being here. My dream came true. I am a woman, yes, but there is more. What I have to say sounds impossible, but it is the truth." I hadn't decided to tell him all of it until that moment. "I come from a land called America, as I said. You haven't heard of it because it hasn't been discovered yet. I come from the future, Robin."

I looked up to see his reaction to my words, but his face was a mask as he looked out over the river. "Continue," he said, his voice hard.

I didn't stop to think of a story. This time, I spoke from my heart. "In my world, *Robin Hood*, I am an outcast." I emphasized the name his outlawry had given him, hoping he would see some common thread to bind our lives together. "I don't fit anywhere. I live in the mountains and come down twice a year for supplies. I spend the rest of my time hunting, learning to survive. I am alone because no one wants to understand me and be my friend. In my world, I am a very lonely person . . . .

"But here, in this world, in this time, I finally feel like a whole person. Except for the fate of being female, I might have been born in this time to be what I could be here. But I am from the future. And why not? Stranger things have happened. Man has walked on the moon. He flies in metal birds that weigh tens of thousands of pounds. He splits atoms. He can speak to someone thousands of miles away. Why not fall through a door in time? If you could see what the future is like, Robin, my being here would not surprise you.

"And you . . . . In my time, you are a legend in storybooks my mother read to me. I dreamt of joining your men and working my way to fame like yours. To experience the reality—" I broke off my rambling with a sigh and gathered my thoughts.

"I have dreamt so well, it has become reality for me. I can't tell you how I come to be here—I don't know myself—but here I am."

I didn't voice my greatest fear. *Maybe I am still at home, in a coma. Or maybe I'm dead.*

It would be a cruel cosmic joke if I woke up now when all I wanted was to stay.

I waited for his response, unsure what would happen next. I had let my nerves do some of the talking and didn't know if I had said too much . . . or too little. I wanted so much for him to believe me.

Robin turned to look at me, his face flushed. "You are jesting, trying to distract me from the fact you are a woman."

"No, sir," I insisted. "As impossible as it seems, I'm telling the truth."

His stare intensified, stripping away any chance I had of misleading him. I could almost feel him flipping through pages of information in my mind as he judged my every reaction. "Then you are a witch?"

I jumped at the implication. "No!"

"But to come as you have said, there must have been strong magic."

"I don't have magic, Robin, but it must be magic that sent me here. It must have been the challenge. Yes. That's as good an explanation as any."

"What do you mean?" He eyed me with suspicion.

I blushed slightly. "I was standing there, on the knoll, burning inside with spring fever. I had been thinking of you and yelled out that I was there, that I was alive . . . ." The feelings of that moment came back. In retrospect, I thought myself extreme, my challenge quite foolish. If the answer hadn't been to send me through time . . . . "And then I was here. I don't want to leave." *I'll be more careful when next I dare the universe to notice me*, I added silently.

"Magic is strong, Kay. Never underestimate the power of wishes. Or perhaps someone here called you. But as you say, you are here."

Nodding, I held my breath, not daring to speak.

"And because you have told me the truth, you may stay. I don't understand it, but I believe it is truth." His eyes glazed over for a moment. "I have so many questions about my . . . ." He shook his head. "Your secret will remain with me. But because you are a woman, I would test your strength."

"How, sir?" I blurted, relieved and anxious all at once.

"I would cross staffs with you." He smiled.

MUCH PUSHED his way through the ring of men forming in the clearing. I followed in his wake, and the gap closed behind me. It was late afternoon, close to dinnertime, but everyone had gathered to witness this match.

I entered the ring behind Much and stood uncertainly, waiting for Robin. *He could have made this a private match,* I thought. *Just the two of us, without everyone watching.*

Much slapped me on the back and stepped away. I clutched my staff, knuckles white, and wished Robin would hurry.

The men across the ring from me parted and Robin stepped through, pausing a moment to size me up, then held his staff at the ready. I raised mine in salute and we moved toward each other.

He attacked, fast, and the men cheered, distracting me. Taking a few hard blows to the ribs, I got myself together and parried. I tried to keep my defense close, making him work to get at me.

"Come on!" somebody yelled. "Fight, you!"

I defended myself, observing Robin's form, judging his skill, feeling his strength. Ignoring the crowd, I concentrated on keeping up my guard, hoping for an opportunity to strike.

Finally, Robin slipped up on a feint and I caught him off balance. The fight turned so swiftly, it was a moment before the crowd realized it. But Robin knew. I drove at him, pushing him back across ground I had so recently given up. The crowd grew silent. There was no sound save the rapping of our staffs. I landed some good blows as I drove him across the ring.

Someone shouted angrily as I cuffed Robin on the shoulder and ribs.

Retaliating on my second blow, he cut across my recovery to give me a good knock on the leg. I limped back a couple of steps, lost my balance, and retreated under the onslaught of his attack. The men cheered.

He laid down several blows on my staff in rapid succession, then feinted a blow to my head. I moved to block, but he brought his staff down and swept my legs out from under me, propelling me into the crowd.

Reeling, I staggered backwards, but several hands lifted me up. Somebody said, "Get in there, Little Italian."

I recognized the voice of the night watchman as they pushed me back into the ring.

I stood, waiting for Robin to advance. He leaned on his staff, chuckling as he caught his breath. I took in deep, ragged gulps of air, trying to ease my raging heart.

Robin advanced on me and I circled, waiting for him to pounce.

He swung his staff. I blocked it, then he rained blows on me like a waterfall. I was back on the defensive, only able to slip in a couple blows behind his guard, slamming him in the stomach and ribs, but I got hit far more than I hit. Sweat bled down my face and stung my eyes, and as the moments went on, I found it harder and harder to fill my lungs with air.

Desperate for a breather, I slid my staff down from a lock and gave his wrist a sharp rap, disarming him. His staff fell to the ground. I backed off, clutching my side.

Robin panted, laughing and rubbing his wrist. He took a moment to catch his breath before he picked up his staff. I nearly sat down, my head spinning from his last attack.

The crowd waited in tense silence.

When Robin approached again, I stood up straight, forcing back my pain. I attacked before he had a chance to and for a few moments, I held him. I thumped him on the shoulder, bringing my staff down to poke his ribs as he staggered back a pace. He fell to one knee and I backed off, thinking it would be a moment before he got up.

Robin caught me off guard then, springing up quickly to give me three raps in the gut before I could raise my staff.

I doubled over to protect my stomach, and when I raised my staff, he brought his down, knocking me flat to the dirt at his feet. He stepped back a pace, allowing me to get up, then he cracked me across the cheek, sending me reeling into the crowd. I fell among them and lay still a moment.

When I tried to get up, my legs would not obey. The men, silent and staring, moved away from me as Robin stepped forward, offering me his hand. I took it and struggled up, clutching my staff and preparing to go again.

"Hold," said Robin. "I don't believe we need to go another round. I've seen enough."

Feeling myself listing to one side, I staggered to regain my balance. I knew I should understand what he just said, but my thoughts would not focus. I had only been beaten so badly once before . . . when my dad put me in the hospital. I ached all over. It would be worse in the morning, after I stiffened up in sleep.

I became aware of the men murmuring around me. "Well," someone called, "does he stay?"

Robin turned toward the voice. "Yes, Andrew. He stays."

"But we don't know anything about the boy!" shouted Mark.

"I do. He stays."

That was it. They would accept Robin's declaration and they would accept me . . . to various degrees. I just had to live up to my tag of "boy."

Slowly, the crowd dispersed, talking energetically about the fight. Much came forward to take my staff from me, wrapping his arm around my waist to give me support. "You took some beating. I'd not want to be in your boots right now."

"I don't want to be in them, either." I clutched my head, feeling tender spots where I knew bruises would appear by morning.

"You fought well, Kay," said Robin, rubbing at his ribs a little. He winked at me. "You do have talent. For a beginner. Practice!" he admonished, then turned his attention to Evan of Chester, who tugged on his sleeve. They walked to the edge of the clearing together.

"Unbelievable," I moaned. "Did I even wind him?"

Much laughed, shaking me gently. "He has been doing this a while longer than you, Kay."

I sagged in his grip. "I could use a soak in a hot tub right now," I said, feeling my tender ribs protesting with each breath I took. I looked around, surprised to see people lighting torches. It wasn't dark yet, but the shadows were long and dinner was late in coming.

"I know of a warm spring not far from here," said Much. "I'll take you there tomorrow. It's too far to travel tonight."

"Great." I grimaced. "Help me find somewhere to sit."

Supper came and went in a blur. Thankfully, I fell asleep early, but I didn't sleep long. Despite my aches, or perhaps because of them, I woke when the night became quiet.

After lying still a while, wondering if I had any ibuprofen in my pack, I sat up stiffly and looked toward the watch fire. The watchman made a stoic silhouette and got me thinking about things left unsaid in our earlier conversation. After a moment, I eased to my feet and slowly walked over to sit next to him. My mouth ached, so I didn't speak, just stared into the fire.

"Oi, you're making a habit of this, aren't you?" he asked, standing up to throw a piece of wood onto the fire. I nodded as he sat down again. "That was some fight this afternoon," he said after a moment, then chuckled. "I didn't think you were going to get up after that last fall."

"I didn't, either," I said. I stuck a finger into my mouth, testing for loose teeth.

"Someone told me you'd never used a quarterstaff before yesterday," he said. I nodded, still not looking at him. "That took a lot to stand up to Robin and get beaten while everybody watched."

I didn't say anything, not knowing how to respond to that. I had only done what Robin demanded so I could stay in the forest. The pause stretched on for long moments while I held my hands out to the fire for warmth.

"You're strong," he said softly. "My father would have liked you."

"Your father?" I asked, turning to look at him. I still wanted to know how he had become an outlaw, but I wasn't going to ask him again.

"Yes, my father." He smiled slightly. "He was a good, strong man, but he got old too soon."

"You cared a lot about your father?"

"Aye. I respected him . . . ." His voice trailed off and he frowned. Moments later, he began talking so softly I almost couldn't hear him. "When I got back from Palestine, I found that my father had been charged with treason—for helping Prince John with his rebellion. I knew it was a lie. My father hated the prince." The man cracked his knuckles angrily, then he gathered himself together. "Any road, he lost his lands to a neighboring Norman lord, the man who had set him up. When I came back, he was living only by the 'grace' of that bastard, and I couldn't do anything about it. My hands were tied. You can't help a traitor.

"One day, about a year later, I caught the bastard talking down to my father, pushing him around, and I cuffed the rat upside the head." The man gave a derisive snort of laughter, glancing sidewise at me. "The old spade died. I must have broken his neck. I had to leave. I couldn't stay around to be hanged . . . ." He fell silent.

After a moment, I sighed. "Do you miss it? Your life at home?" I asked.

The man looked at me again, not quite smiling. "Not much. It wasn't romantic like you're thinking, boy. It was a hard life, like any other. Because my family is Saxon, we were constantly waging a war of control with the Normans. We had to work very hard to keep our lodge, and when my father lost his lands, things got worse. In the end, I think death was kinder."

"How did—" I stopped. It wasn't my place to ask.

"How did he die?" The man pulled at his lower lip and frowned. "He was accused as an accomplice to murder and was hanged." I closed my eyes against the pain and anger written on his face. "If I'd 'a been there, I'd have cracked some heads!"

I couldn't think of anything to say, so I laid a hand on his shoulder. We sat in silence for a long time before I got up and went to my blanket.

When I finally fell into a restless sleep, snatches of dreams teased my memories, prompts telling me I was missing something important.

I saw a wounded man in the frenzy of a battle, then coming home to an unfriendly household. I couldn't see his face. Someone killed, a man running. Red. A meeting between two men who called each other cousin, as nobles do.

Red . . . . Scarlet.

I WOKE UP IN PAIN. My right arm was trapped beneath my body by the awkward position I was in, and my whole body ached. Gently freeing my arm, I sat up and looked around.

Only a few people were awake and moving. The sun wasn't even up yet, and the low light lent an eerie quality to the quiet of the camp. The trees seemed to lean forward, wisps of phantom-like fog gliding among them.

To shake off the spooky aura, I tried some stretching exercises and was able to loosen up a little. I took a brisk walk, trying to get my body working again, and found myself at the river, where I splashed cool water onto my face, then sat down to watch the sun rise.

Through the trees, the sky changed from a cold navy blue to a lighter, softer, warmer blue, then gold, as the rising sun lit up the thin fog. When the gold turned white, I knew the sun was up.

Birdsong filled the air as the whole forest stirred, getting ready for the day.

I got up with a meadowlark's song and headed back to the clearing to get some breakfast.

Much met me halfway.

"Kay! There you are. I went to wake you, but the watch said you'd gone to the river, so I came to look for you."

"Are you still keeping an eye on me? Did I get the snot beat out of me for nothing?" I snapped, still tired and grouchy because of my bruises. I immediately regretted my tone. "I'm sorry. That was uncalled for."

"That's all right, Kay. But I'm not your guard, just your guardian to help you get used to the camp. I came looking for you because we were going to go to the warm springs today."

"Oh yeah," I said sheepishly. Because I couldn't think of anything intelligent to say, I simply followed Much back to the clearing.

"Good morning, Patrick," I said to the keeper of the stores as Much and I picked up a loaf and some cheese for lunch at the springs. Much grabbed an extra loaf of bread to eat on the way.

Other men were doing the same, and the clearing started emptying down to its daytime numbers. Almost all the outlaws left during the day. It was easier to avoid foresters when everyone split up into smaller groups.

"That was bonny fighting you did yesterday," Patrick said, grinning. "Sure and I wouldn't want to be wearing Robin's mark, like you do." He nodded at my face. I touched my left cheek gingerly, feeling the bruise. "It's a beauty, let me tell you."

I half-smiled at him, my left side too stiff to lift. "I can see it without a mirror, Patrick."

Much and I departed, him telling me how to place my feet so I made no mark in passing. To my surprise and pleasure, his technique made my step quiet as a deer. We followed no path. Paths lead to something, and even a forester would think to follow a path he had never seen before.

When we got to the road, I turned to him. "Is it really that bad, Much?" I asked, touching my cheek. I had been afraid to look at the rest of my body, fearful of what I might find, but everyone could see my face. "I mean, I don't want to attract attention."

"Don't worry about it. If we pass anyone, they'll think you're my boy and I sometimes rough you up. Whenever anyone passes us, you walk a little behind me. If it's a noble, don't look up at him. They take that as insolence."

I frowned. "What if someone recognizes you?"

"Shouldn't happen here, but if it does . . . sorry to say . . . you're on your own."

"Then I hope you're right." I knew if Much left me, I would either get hopelessly lost in the forest or arrested and hung for associating with outlaws.

We walked for an hour down a road that twisted lazily through the forest, dipping into dells and climbing gentle hills. Then we struck off on a faint path heading into the forest. Fifteen minutes later, we came upon a large spring, the water steaming in the coolness of the morning. Sunlight slanted through the trees and into the hollow, making shifting, dappled patterns on the water of the pools and inviting me to strip.

I stopped short. I had forgotten that this man thought I was a boy. How was I to explain I wasn't? I looked at Much, who was already starting to take off his clothes.

I opened my mouth to tell him, make up something, then just started to undress. That was the only way I could think of to broach the subject. Not subtle, but effective.

"This is going to be great," said Much as I pulled my shirt over my head. My eyes were covered, but I could tell when he turned around. "I used to come here all—"

I whipped off the shirt and looked at him. Slack-jawed, he stared at my breasts.

"Much—" I began.

"By our Lady! All this time! A girl?!" He was torn between suspicion and laughter. Suspicion won out. "What are you up to? Are you a spy then? Does Robin know?" His questions were rapid, his eyes searching the ground for the knife that lay on his discarded shirt. He reached for it, then stood, ready for anything.

"Of course Robin knows, Much! Why do you think we fought yesterday? He wanted to make sure I'm strong enough to carry my weight."

"But women can't—" Much began insistently.

"Where I come from, women *do*. I'm no spy. Do you think the sheriff would send a girl to find you? I told Robin everything. Now, you have to trust his judgment until you can make your own."

"A woman!" He shook his head, looking at me coolly, already passing judgment.

I had to jar him. "Much, who threw you two days ago? Look at me. Really look." I glanced down and pointed to the purple-and-blue bruises showing vividly against the white skin over my ribs. "Who took a beating from Robin Hood yesterday? Took it as well as any man, I might add. I can handle myself, can't I? I'm not what you're thinking, Much."

"Aye, you're no regular woman," he agreed, looking thoughtful. "But why didn't you say anything when David came across you?"

"He assumed I was a boy. I was outnumbered. I wasn't going to tell him he was wrong." I tossed down my shirt. "Besides, if you were David, would you have taken me to Robin if I'd told you I was female? I want to be where I have been these last few days. I don't want anything to change, which is why it must remain a secret—at least until I've had a chance to prove myself."

"I understand," said Much, and I really believed he did. An amused look replaced the indignation on his face, and he tipped back his head and laughed. "A woman, and she threw me. *Me!*"

He roared with laughter for a few moments, and like a contagion, I found myself laughing with him. His laughter slowly subsiding, he tried to say more. "You sure . . . had me fooled. Me, the best staff in England, and . . . and Kay the novice throws me! Imagine! Much thrown by a woman! You know I won't say a thing!" he exclaimed, then swiftly finished undressing.

Too late, I averted my eyes from his very male body. When he caught me looking, I felt my cheeks flame.

"Come on. Boy or woman, you still need to soak in this water." He sauntered over the tumbled rocks and slid into the pool.

Suddenly feeling very awkward, I struggled out of the rest of my clothes, leaving them where they fell. Much had already submerged himself by the time I waded into the steaming water.

"Just what the doctor ordered," I said with a sigh, as Much shook wet hair out of his eyes. I made my way into the middle of the spring and ducked my head under the surface.

When I came up, I felt Much's fingers brush against my shoulder. My eyes flew open, stinging from the sulfur in the water. I backed away from him. "What?" I asked, unreasonably frightened by the funny look on his face.

"Easy," he said, coming closer. "I just want to touch you. That's all."

"Well, don't. You give me goose bumps when you do that." At his touch, all the hairs on my arms and the back of my neck had risen.

"That's good," he said, casually caressing my shoulder again. I backed away once more. "Don't you like it? Don't you want to—"

"No!" I said. "I've never . . . I mean, I don't . . . !" I knew he was talking about sex, making love. "That's for married people and lovers. We're not either."

"That could change," he said, smiling until I climbed out of the water. "Where are you going?"

"Much, please don't." I picked through my clothes until I found my tank top and underwear and put them on. "I'm sorry if I teased you or led you on. I won't let it happen again. I didn't come out here to . . . you know. I came here to soak, and that's all." I stood on the edge of the pool, looking down at him and shivering in the chilly morning air.

Much looked surprised. "Most girls like it," he said. "Most will even go out of their way to attract my attention."

"I can see why they would, Much. I really can. But I'm not most girls."

"Aye, that's true." He shrugged, playful again. "I've been wrong before. It was one of the reasons I was outlawed. I thought a lady was after my attention, but one kiss and she told the lordling she wanted to make jealous. It worked remarkably well. What was a miller's son to do but run?" He winked at me. "I don't see you playing such games, but I've learned my lesson, lady. I daresay you'd make a man feel the error of his ways if he got it in his head to try and force you."

"Is it safe to come back into the water then?" I asked, smiling a little, though still not entirely convinced.

"Quite safe. I'm on my best behavior." He made a short bow to me, so I had to laugh. I walked back into the water, but I left my shirt and underwear on.

We stayed at the spring for the better part of the day, alternately soaking and basking in the warm sun. We didn't talk much, just enjoyed the quiet and each other's company.

As we dressed to leave, I said, "I'm glad I didn't lose you." I laced up my boots, watching him from the corner of my eyes. I wasn't sure I hadn't alienated him.

"What do you mean?" Much glanced up from tying the lacings of his shirt.

"We're friends. If that had changed, Much, I don't think I'd be very happy here. You could have rejected me."

"I'll keep you around." Much winked at me, smiling in that charming way he had. "If only until you change your mind. And I'll keep your secret, just to save myself the competition. We're friends, Kay. I like you."

"Good. I hate to keep this a secret from the rest, but I'd hate to be sent packing even more."

"Robin wouldn't—" Much protested.

"No, Robin wouldn't want to, but he might have to. What about the rest? You spoke of competition. I don't think Robin would permit silly cockfights over a woman. I don't see what there is to fight about—except the obvious, of course."

I tried to ignore Much's vulgar pantomime, but my cheeks flamed. I decided I needed to change the subject.

"But more than that, I know people. If they get it in their heads that they don't want me around, I might as well be gone for all the easier they will make it." I spoke from experience, like school or dealing with my uncle. He had made my life unbearable until I got away from him.

I started up the trail to the road. "But if I proved I was worthy, more than just taking a beating from Robin, it would be easier to accept."

"'Just taking a beating from Robin . . . ,'" Much echoed, laughing as he followed me.

I pursed my lips. "You know what I mean. That fight didn't matter one bit to some of them. It just proved I'm dumb enough to take a few hits."

"You're too hard on yourself," he said, coming up to walk beside me. He put a hand on my shoulder in friendship.

"It's better to know you have enemies than to blindly assume you don't." I blew out a breath. "Listen, can I tell you a little about myself?"

"You don't have to. That's part of what's nice about living out here. Nobody will ask what you were before. You can keep those secrets to yourself."

We had reached the road and were making pretty good speed back to camp. "Secrets are lonely things, Much. This isn't a secret. I want you, my friend, to understand why I want to stay here in Sherwood."

"I would like to hear what makes a woman want to stay out here," Much admitted, smiling at me sheepishly.

"It's not a pretty story," I said in warning. "My father was an alcoholic—a drunk. He abused my mother and me. I used to escape the beatings by running away into the hills near my house. Some of the happiest moments of my life were spent in the forest. When my father found out, he beat me so badly, he knocked me unconscious for ten minutes, then threatened to kill me if I ran off again. It terrified me, and it was a long time before I could think about leaving. Then my mother got sick, so I stayed. When I was twelve, he died, and my mother died the following summer. My uncle Jim took me in after that, but I got into trouble at school for fighting."

"What is school?" Much asked.

"School? It's a place where children go to learn things, like how to read, write, and work numbers."

His eyes widened. "Like the nobles? You're noble?"

"No, Much, I'm not. In America, all children go to school."

Much accepted that with the ease of an uninformed man. "But

why did you get into trouble for fighting? When there are lots of children, there is always fighting."

"They have to control the children, keep us from fighting, or we wouldn't learn anything."

"Why did you fight then?"

I laughed at his many questions. "I went to an all-girl boarding school and things were very political. When the tough girls kept trying to take my money, I fought them. The school threw me out and I had to take my lessons at home. My uncle wasn't too happy about that. We had words often.

"Finally, I found out about the cabin and talked my uncle into letting me stay there. I learned how to survive in the woods, taught myself how to shoot a bow and hunt. I stayed there for three years, until I found myself traveling to England."

"Why did you come to Sherwood?"

"It was a spontaneous thing, Much. It was spring and I had to get out of my cabin. Before I knew it, I was on my way. I'm glad I came. So, you see, there's really no reason for me to go back."

CHAPTER
FOUR

I sat up in the darkness, shaking off the last bit of sleep. Supper was ready for serving, and the mouth-watering smell of fresh bread and roasted meat must have woken me. I stood up and stretched, muscles feeling much looser after soaking all day, then walked to the table to sit next to Much.

Upon returning from the warm spring, I had fallen asleep and no one had bothered to keep me awake.

"Try to stay with us." Much laughed, putting his hand on my shoulder.

"It was a long day, Much. Too relaxing. That makes me more tired than working all day." A huge yawn followed my words as I looked around at all the men talking excitedly. "What's up? Why's supper so late tonight?"

"It's Mid-Summer's Eve! There'll be a feast, and the fires will be lit. It's a special night for you, too."

I looked at him, seeing anticipation and excitement in his eyes. "Why?"

"You'll see."

Men passed food around, but no one touched anything on their plates. They all looked at Robin expectantly, so I did, too. Robin sat, smiling, waiting for everyone to quiet down.

Soon, the only sounds were the pitch torches crackling from

their brackets in the trees. A huge stack of firewood stood in the clearing, ready for the flame.

I knew there was history about this ceremonial feast. They lit the fires and danced. The fire symbolized life and fertility. If you leapt through the flames, it was good luck. In ancient times, the tribal chieftain took on the identity of the god to perform the rituals of the evening and bless the people, the crops, and the beasts, but I didn't know if they still practiced that now. I sat back, excited by this unexpected activity.

Robin stood. "Tonight," he said, "is Mid-Summer's Eve. In the tradition of our people, we light the fire, dance, and sing. Tonight, we celebrate our freedom. Freedom we have fought for, worked for, traveled for. Freedom some have died for. Tonight, we celebrate the mid-summer fires. We laugh at the past, or cry, and hope for tomorrow." Robin looked around the table, his eyes dark and solemn. "Tonight, we celebrate Mid-Summer's Eve."

He returned to his seat, and I wondered at his demeanor. I'd thought this was a festive time.

"John," he said, gesturing to the giant of a man sitting beside him. Little John got up and walked around the table. I watched him, surprised when he stopped behind me.

"Stand up!" John said when I didn't move. I stood, stepping over the bench. "Come with me."

Bewildered, I glanced at Much, who shooed me off. I followed John back up the table.

Robin turned on his bench and gestured for me to kneel. Glancing around at the seated men, I saw them craning their necks to get a good look at what was happening. I knelt before Robin and lowered my gaze to stare at his feet.

"Look at me," he whispered, and I raised my eyes to his. He drew his sword, took my hands, and put them on the blade.

He spoke in a loud, clear voice. "You come to me, asking me to accept your oath. Is there any reason I should?"

"None, sir," I answered, sensing the ritual in his words. He wanted to hear more. Though I had no lines, I continued. "Save a desire to serve you to my last breath."

Robin smiled in approval. "Do you swear then, by our Lady and by my sword, that you will abide by my rules and serve me for the good of the brotherhood?"

"I swear," I said. The moment brought back childhood reflexes, so I crossed myself.

"Then tonight, we also celebrate a new brother!" he announced. His words had a hint of laughter behind them, and I smiled. I was now a "brother" of his people.

Robin slid his thumb along the blade of his sword and a line of blood appeared. He nodded to me, and I did the same, forcing myself not to wince. My blood flowed into my palm.

We clasped hands, thumbs inside. I broke our gaze to look down at our hands, blood oozing out between our fingers.

I squeezed his hand and looked into his eyes again, tears of joy brimming in mine.

Robin's men cheered as he turned to hold up his bloodied hand.

"Now we number four and fifty!" he called, pulling me up to stand with him.

Little John stepped forward and slapped me on the back, nearly knocking me over, then he clasped my hand, smearing my blood on his. "Good to have you, Kay!"

Will Stutely, Robin's second lieutenant, was next, with Much pressing forward to be after him. Each man in the group came by and clasped my hand, until everyone in the band had my blood on them. Some of them scowled as they said my name, and I knew I still had some work to do. Especially with Mark, one of the last to come up, reluctant and sullen.

The very last to come through the line was the night watchman. He came up and clasped my hand warmly.

"Congratulations, Little Italian," he said with a smile. I realized I still did not know his name, but he turned away before I could ask him.

Adam of Lincoln came forward with a bowl, and Robin stuck his thumb in, smearing a dark, smelly paste onto the cut his sword had made. When Adam held the bowl out to me, I looked into it, but it didn't look like anything I was familiar with. I glanced at Robin.

He smiled and nodded his assurance. "It's to heal the cut."

I stuck in my thumb, wincing at the sting as I smeared the mixture on.

Everyone went back to their seats but did not sit. I found my way back to Much's side, grinning like a fool.

"You're one of us now," he said, grinning as much as I was.

Then, to my surprise, I heard women's laughter. Some twelve unlikely-looking "ladies" came into the clearing. They made themselves at home with the men who whooped and called to them. Now I knew what the excitement was really for!

Each woman attached herself to a man or two, then everyone gathered around the heap of firewood as all torches were extinguished. As men and women chanted the ancient words of the lighting of the fire, Adam and Matthew, following the age-old formula, took turns sawing at the fire drill. Finally, after what seemed like ages, a spark caught and began to glow. Adam carefully nursed it to a flame and lit a torch. The chanting erupted into a howl of primal joy as Robin took the torch and plunged it into the wood. The fire sprang to life, the sacred rite confirming another prosperous year. Everyone cheered and the festivities began.

The feast started late and lasted most of the night. Men leapt and cavorted around the fire and through it, the women gyrating around it. They sang the ancient songs and got roaring drunk, and we ate better than we would all year.

On this night, we didn't worry about making noise. There would be many such parties in Sherwood on Mid-Summer's Eve. The sheriff couldn't stop people from celebrating in the forest. This ceremony was older than the Normans, older than the Saxons. It was as old as the forest we danced in, so we practiced no caution on this night.

About midnight, my head heavy and spinning from more than just the dance, I flung myself out of the dance ring and staggered to the table to get another drink. As I sloshed more ale into a cup, I saw two figures sitting at the edge of the torchlight, holding hands. I leaned against the table to steady my gaze and squinted to focus better. The red jerkin told me one was Robin, but the woman—it had to be a woman—would not get any clearer than a brownish blur in the shape of a woman's dress. Her lily-white hands shone in the torchlight as she reached up to touch Robin's face.

Someone bumped into me and I reached behind me to grab a handful of shirt, turning to find myself holding onto Much.

"Whozzat?"

"Where?" Much, not much better off, squinted his eyes and peered into the trees.

I stabbed my cup in Robin's direction, spilling ale across the table. "There, wi' Robin."

"With Robin? Mus' be th' lady."

"A lady? Here?"

"Yez. Hiz sssweetheart. Marian."

"Oh, yeah. Tha's right. Marian. How silly of me not to'v know."

I let go of Much's shirt and we both fell to the ground in a mass of giggles. It took forever to sort out our limbs and climb to our feet again.

"Ah god, Much. 'Ere she comes agin. Hide me."

I grabbed him, pulling him around between us as Amelia came looking for me again. The woman wouldn't take no for an answer, and I hoped she was at least as drunk as me and wouldn't discover my hiding spot. I listened to Much head her off, but my gaze caught the image of Robin and Marian sitting together.

There, I thought with surprising solemnity. *That is the stuff legends are made of.*

Adam appeared out of nowhere, grabbed my hand and whirled me back into the dance chain.

Scant hours before dawn, the last man staggered drunkenly to his blanket. Only the watch remained.

Well . . . and me.

I sat at a bench by the table, dribbling ale along the blade of my knife, watching it in the firelight. I couldn't sleep earlier. I was too happy. But when everyone was either in their blankets, passed out, or wrapped up with a woman, my mood turned melancholy.

I stared at the table littered with the cold remains of the feast and overturned cups. The whole scene, complete with me sitting alone at the table, turned my thoughts in a sad direction. I thought about being alone, about how I hadn't fit in all my life, and wondered if I really belonged with these people. I certainly felt comfortable enough with them, like maybe my problem at home had simply been that I'd been born too late.

When the bench moved beside me, I looked up to see the first watch sitting down next to me. I smiled, my head wobbling on my neck. I had to concentrate to steady it.

"Quite a feast," I slurred.

"Aye," he said, filling a cup with ale and handing it to me. He filled another for himself. "I'd say I put on some weight this night." He patted his stomach, which definitely strained at his belt. As I watched, he belched and the bulk of it sank down.

"Me, too," I said, wishing it were that easy for me to get rid of extra bulges.

"You?! I watched you. You ate like a mouse!"

"You must know some hungry mice," I countered, drinking the ale he'd given me. His chuckle turned into a laugh when I tried to grasp his shoulder and missed. But I had something on my mind, so I persisted. "I'm sorry if I made you remember something you didn't want to last night."

"Don't be a fool. If I hadn't wanted to, I wouldn't have told you."

"No," I said, perhaps a little drunk. "I feel like I forced you to talk to me. I want to make it up to you."

"How?" He smiled indulgently.

"I'll tell you something about me. Something painful."

"All right." He knew I would not have accepted a refusal.

"I hated my father," I told him. Ever since I had spoken to Much earlier, this was on my mind. I was just drunk enough to tell this man the things I hadn't told Much. "He was a mean old coot. When he got drunk, he used my mother as a punching bag, and I hated him for it. He would hit me, too, when I wasn't quick enough to get out of the way, but I never gave him the satisfaction of seeing me cry." My shoulders jerked involuntarily, dodging the memory of his blows.

"One night, on his way home from a bar, there was an accident and he was killed." I paused for a long time, remembering the flashing police lights and the officer telling my mother that Daddy had driven underneath a semi-trailer.

I looked up at him. "I was twelve years old. Ever since I could remember, I'd been thinking of ways to kill him. When he finally did die, it shocked me. He was really dead, and I realized it wasn't hate I felt for him, but anger—at what he did to my mother, to me, to himself." I put my hand to my head to slow the spinning and steady myself.

"I still couldn't cry. My mother, who had always sworn she loved him more than herself, couldn't cry, either. She had long since run out of tears." I fell silent, taking another sip of ale, pondering how I still couldn't feel the pain of that loss, only a slow-burning anger.

The man looked at me curiously. "What am I supposed to say to that?"

"I dunno." I sniffed into my cup. "Just thought I'd tell you."

He took away my cup and helped me stand, giving me a tolerant smile. "Go to sleep."

I staggered a few steps toward my blanket, then turned around. "I don't even know your name," I said. I hadn't planned on saying that. I was waiting until he told me of his own free will. Of course, being a bit tipsy, I forgot.

"I thought you knew." By then, I couldn't see anything beyond the tip of my nose, which was in perfect focus, but he sounded surprised.

"I don't," I said, swaying.

"Scarlet. Will Scarlet."

His name was nearly drowned out as my ears started to ring. "Of course," I murmured. "What an idiot I've been." In slow motion, the world tipped as I swayed, and it seemed the ground rose up to meet me as I fell.

Vaguely, I felt myself lifted, but I don't remember being put down.

I woke late in the morning, my head pounding. At the group of bushes that served as the kitchen, I begged a bit of bread off Patrick, who looked worse off than I. He made a vague comment about my bruises, saying a poor, beaten child like myself should at least eat.

I retreated to the river to eat there, drinking from my water bag and humming a tune. The morning air had cooled my headache, and I took my boots off to trail my feet in the water, enjoying the sunshine. My body felt nearly free of its aches and pains, though

Patrick had reminded me I was still bruised. By his reckoning, I would be for days.

Softly, I began to sing the country song I'd been humming. "Snow falls in winter, and the sun shines in May. And when the leaves start falling, you'll be on your way. Oh Carolina!"

I stopped singing when I heard someone coming upriver toward me. I loosened my knife in its sheath and waited.

It was Much, looking rumpled and pleased with himself. It didn't look like he had suffered at all by rescuing me from Amelia.

"There you are! I'm always looking all over for you. We must make you some arrows. You'll need them to practice."

"For what?"

"For hunting mostly, but Robin's talking about taking you with us on a trip out. You know what that means, don't you?"

"We rob from the rich to give to the poor!" I cried, waving my bread in the air above my head.

"Exactly," said Much, smiling. "And if you're lucky, you might get yourself a halfway decent sword."

"I might?"

"Aye. But you have to help bring in the quarry, or else you only get a carrier's wage—a small portion of what we take."

"I see."

"Come on then!" Much hauled me to my feet. "Let's make those arrows."

"All right already." I pulled away from him so I could tug on my boots and throw some of my bread into the water for the fish. Stuffing the rest into my mouth, I followed Much. "So much for a peaceful morning," I muttered, though my ire was half-hearted, at best. I was going to be a real outlaw soon!

"CAN YOU BELIEVE IT!" a voice called out.

It was no voice I knew, so I whistled the warning. The group scattered into the trees, vanishing into cool shadows. I "vanished," too, running off the road and crouching behind a tree. It had taken weeks of practice, but I'd finally learned the outlaws' knack of instant invisibility. From my new perspective, it wasn't magical, but before I learned how, it seemed as though my companions could appear and disappear at will.

The voice again, laughing, accompanied the distant jingle of a harness.

I nocked an arrow to my bow and waited. From around the bend, two horsemen rode, escorted by two armed foot soldiers. The riders—laughing and fussing over a falcon perched on the younger man's wrist—were lords, riding out to hunt. Catching a glimpse of a fat purse hanging at the side of the older man, I smiled. A fair choice of game.

I leveled my bow at one of the foot soldiers. If he found a target to loose his crossbow bolt at, he would at least have an arrow of mine in him. I had been practicing and was quite accurate now that I had good, straight arrows specially crafted from oak of slightly larger diameter to withstand the impact my bow could generate— though it was probably an unneeded precaution. English longbows were every bit as powerful as my compound bow. Perhaps even more so, since I didn't have my bow tuned to the highest draw strength.

Robin gave the signal and we rushed out, encircling the men on the road. The horses spooked, rearing up, and for a moment, it was all the riders could do to control them. The young man controlled his horse with his knees as he fought to keep the falcon calm.

One of the foot soldiers let fly a bolt. It whizzed by the head of Edmond the Jew—missing him by a mere inch, he swore later.

Little John knocked the man down and smashed the crossbow over his knee, then stood looming over him. "None of that now."

The horses pranced in circles, nearly trampling the downed soldier.

Robin stepped forward. "My lords," he said, bowing low. "You must excuse this rude interruption, but this is a toll road today. Will you pay the fee?"

"This is an outrage!" the old man blustered, fighting to control his horse. The more he yanked on the reins, the more the beast plunged and danced, setting the other off again.

"That it is, but you'll pay!" said John.

"I know your faces. When the sheriff hears of this, he'll hunt down every last one of you himself!"

"Do you think he hasn't tried?" asked David of Doncaster, grinning, his sword held high.

"Father," said the younger man, deftly controlling his horse and the falcon at the same time. "We have plenty of gold, but these men obviously don't have any. Don't you think—"

"Close your mouth, boy! These men are thieves! You give in to them once and they'll never let you rest!"

"You misjudge us, milord," Richard Donaldson said in his deep voice. "We ask only for what you can afford to pay. Show us your purse!"

"Never!" The old man charged the ring, but the horse turned aside before the swords, throwing its rider.

Dropping my bow, I caught the reins of the plunging horse, soothing it until it calmed. Ears forward, it lipped my fingers and listened to my crooning voice while I stroked its muzzle. Richard and Edmond sprang forward to help the man to his feet.

He sputtered indignantly, but seeing how vulnerable a position he was in, he handed over his purse. Little John laid out a cloth and quickly counted out the money. Of the ninety pounds in the purse, John withheld forty pounds as a "toll."

The man angrily dusted off his clothes, then stepped up to his horse and looked at me holding the reins. I bowed low, like I had seen Robin do. He nodded back stiffly. Edmond the Jew helped him mount while I held the horse still. As soon as he was up, I bent to retrieve my bow.

When John gave him back his purse, he weighed it in his hand and felt how much remained. "Perhaps . . . ," the old man said. "Perhaps I have misjudged you—some."

Robin gestured for the circle to part, letting the riders through. "And a good day to you, milord!" he called after them, chasing them with a laugh.

The disarmed foot soldiers followed the riders, turning to glare at us once they were a good distance away. We laughed and waved cheerfully. When they turned to look again, we were gone.

"YOUR FIRST ROBBERY?" Will Scarlet asked, smiling at me from across the fire.

"Yeah." I had just told him about it. "They aren't all that easy, are they?"

"No. Lots of times, someone gets hurt, even killed. Mostly soldiers, occasionally a noble, rarely a brother. But we don't lose men often." Will spoke of "we," the brotherhood, of which I was now a part. I had just completed my second month in Robin's band.

"It was scary," I confessed. "I don't know what I would have done if there had been any fighting."

"You've never been in a fight then?"

I chuckled. "Not with swords and arrows." I held out my hands, closed them into fists. "These I know. I can fight with these."

"Small as you are?" Will asked, teasing.

"Yeah, small as I am." I changed the subject, not wanting to come any closer to my size and perhaps why I was so small. "Much said I might have gotten a sword today. Why didn't we take the young lord's sword? It was pretty enough."

"We only take weapons from the dead," Will explained. "Or when we are in danger. To take a sword from a man while he lives would be shameful for him and dishonorable for us. The dead feel no shame." He paused. "What do you want with a sword anyway?"

"I want to learn to use one." I looked up into the cloudy night sky, listening to someone's snores. The sky grumbled, threatening rain.

"Really?" he asked, amused. "And who is going to teach you?"

I shrugged. "Much, I guess."

"Much?! Now that would be a sight."

"Yeah?"

"Aye." He snorted. "Much may be good with a quarterstaff, but he doesn't know anything about swords."

"Oh, and you do?" I asked, not able to pass up that remark.

"Aye, I do," Scarlet answered smoothly, unruffled by my jibe. "I'm good, too. One of Robin's best."

There was nothing I could say to that. A piece of wood settled in the fire, sending sparks skyward. Flames grew bright for a moment before returning to a steady glow. An idea came to me.

"Would you teach me?"

Will arched his eyebrows in surprise. "Me?"

"Yeah, you." The more I thought about it, the more the idea appealed to me.

"Why would I want to teach you?" he asked. I knew he was playing a game. It annoyed me, but I would have to play along to get anything out of him.

"Why not?" I asked carefully, not wanting to let on how important this was. Everyone in the camp had a rudimentary knowledge of swords. Everyone but me. "I thought we were friends. Don't friends teach their friends?"

"I suppose they do." He scratched the back of his neck. "What would you teach me in return?"

I thought a moment. "I could teach you Spanish." I had learned in school when I was fourteen. I was rusty, but I thought it would come back to me if I were to try and teach it.

"Why would I want to know how to speak Spanish? Anyway, where did you learn it?"

"A friend taught me." I grinned. "Don't you run across any Spaniards here?"

"Not often."

"Okay. What about French?" I didn't know French, but I wanted to hear his answer.

"I know French," he said, trying to hide a wry grin. I should have known. He was a noble, and though he was good Saxon stock, most nobles were Norman. And Normans spoke French.

"Oh. I suppose you already know how to read, too." I sighed, irritated at this game.

"Aye. My father taught me. But I don't do much reading out here. What else do you know?"

"I don't think anything I know is going to be useful to you, Scarlet." I swatted angrily at a moth hovering in front of my face.

"I guess you'll have to find someone else to teach you then."

I turned to him, a sharp retort on my lips, but when I saw his smile, the retort died in the making.

"Little Italian," he said. "There *are* things you can teach me. I will teach you."

"There are? You will?" I was almost afraid he was still teasing me. I really did want to learn to use a sword.

"Aye." He turned away from me to listen to the night, holding up a hand to keep me quiet a moment. Then, satisfied by what he heard, or didn't hear, he continued. "I spoke to Much about you while you were gone today. He said you have sharp eyes and will let a person know when you see a weakness. Can you do that for me?" He winked. "Just until I think of a better favor."

I laughed with relief, taking his words for their face value. "My eyes are at your service."

"Good. Your lessons begin tomorrow. Sleep now."

I grinned at him. "Goodnight, Will." I got up and went to my blanket.

Sleep came swiftly, along with a growl of thunder in the distance and a whisper of a breeze picking up in the trees.

CHAPTER
FIVE

Rain pelting my face woke me. After a few futile moments of trying to sleep longer, I got up for some bread and goat's milk. It had taken me a while to get used to goat's milk, but it now tasted no different than my memory of cow's milk.

Nibbling on the hard bread, I went back to my blanket to put it and my few belongings into my pack, then covered it with a leather skin borrowed from Richard of Newcastle-under-Lyme to keep it dry. I sat down under the shelter of an elm to eat the rest of my breakfast.

Looking around at the others, I wondered how they could sleep. Watching, I saw many of them stir, pulling blankets over their heads.

I sighed, drinking my milk. The rain wasn't coming down hard, but I sure couldn't sleep through it.

By and by, Will walked over. Breaking off a piece of the bread he held, he chewed on it, dropping down to squat beside me. "You're up early," he commented.

"It's raining," I said, as if that explained the world. "Don't you ever sleep?"

"Not when it rains," he answered. "I don't see how they do it." He gestured to the rest of the men. "I could sleep through a tree falling on my head, but not rain. They hardly even stir."

He munched on his bread and I drank my milk, companionable in our silence.

"Are you ready to learn the sword today?" he asked, and stuffed the last of his bread into his mouth.

"As ready as I'll ever be."

He stood. "Then wait here. I need to get some things."

I waited. A few moments later, he came back with two swords and a bundle, then we headed to the river.

"I'd teach you to fight with two swords," said Scarlet as we walked, "but it would be better to learn that from Frederick the Norman. He's a master at it, if you can talk him into teaching you. From me, you'll learn with one."

We went to the same spot where Much and I had fought. The river caught and absorbed raindrops, imprinting momentary craters on its surface and raising drops of water that danced to the rhythm of the rain. The wet grass smelled of earth. The leaves of the trees had turned a deeper green, like the grass.

I drew in a deep breath. "What a beautiful day," I said, wandering in a semi-circle, looking around at everything.

"Right." He tossed down the bundle and handed me a sword. I noted that the blade had been blunted. These were training weapons. "Beautiful or not, we've got work to do. Now, pay attention. You hold a sword like this." He demonstrated. I knew when I was being patronized, but I paid attention. I had been looking forward to this.

Scarlet showed me a few basic blocks, correcting my grip and stance. He took a few swings at me so I could use them.

"Remember," he told me, "this is no play at quarterstaff. I'm not looking forward to having my fingers cut off if you try to disarm me that way." He sarcastically reminded me of the trick I had used to disarm Robin. "If you need to rest, just ask me to stop. We're not enemies."

I nodded, ready for more.

He showed me another block, then swung at me again and again, forcing me to block as he'd shown me.

"You'll learn only defense today," he told me, still swinging. "That's most important. If you can't block a blow, you're dead. If you get knocked down with a quarterstaff, chances are you can get back up. You don't often get that chance in swordplay."

I lost my concentration for a moment and Will's sword stopped inches away from my ear.

"Pay attention," he snapped. "It's called swordplay, but there's nothing playful about it." He moved his sword away.

"Sorry," I said, getting ready for another strike.

"You will be if you don't keep your mind on the lesson." He paused, considering me with an intense expression that stirred a thrill of excitement in my blood. "I've seen what you can do with a staff, and you'll do well with a sword, if you really want it. My teacher told me anything that keeps you alive is a good move. You only fail if you're dead."

A wicked twinkle flashed in his eyes. "Let me show you a trick I learned the hard way. If your opponent is agile and you overreach yourself, you are extremely vulnerable. If this happens, and it will, you could roll forward, like this." Will executed a somersault that amazed me, jumping back to his feet in an instant. "The trick is to hold your sword just so," he said, demonstrating, "to avoid slicing your hand or your own throat."

"I can't do that!" I protested, wondering what I had just gotten myself into.

Will smiled viciously. "You will be able to by the time I'm through with you! Now!" He swung his sword at me and roared, "Block!"

Will clearly enjoyed mastery with his chosen weapon. He also clearly loved the strategy and skill involved in swordplay. Though undoubtedly impatient with my bungling maneuvers, he took the time to make sure I made the countermoves correctly. He explained the reason behind the motion and demonstrated, with speed and accuracy, how the move should be made.

Before mid-morning, I knew it would be a long time before I had learned enough to match him in a fight.

We stopped for a break at noon, soaked with rain and sweat. As I pushed wet hair out of my eyes, Scarlet unwrapped the bundle he had brought along. He revealed a soggy loaf of bread and dried venison strips. Activity had sharpened my appetite. I could have eaten anything.

As we ate, we talked about his experiences learning sword fighting and my progress, and he quizzed me on moves and theory.

By the time we got a drink from the river, the rain was coming down in torrents. We picked up our swords again.

"Now," said Will, standing at the ready. "I'm going to see how well you've learned what I've taught you so far. I'm the enemy. I won't tell you what I'm doing. Use that sharp mind of yours and don't let up. I won't unless you ask me."

I nodded and he swung.

When he said he was the enemy, I hadn't thought much of it. But now, as we fought, I could have sworn he really wanted to kill me. I knew if I fought one whit less than my ability, I would at least get a nasty scratch.

I blocked blows and threw off thrusts, soon sweating, despite the rain. Wisps of steam rose off both our bodies as we fought our way back and forth across the clearing. Always falling back, I would slip beneath his arms or around his reach when I ran out of places to go. I couldn't let him corner me, and Will had taught me how to escape that early on.

Some of my blocks were ill placed as I began to tire, and I finally called a halt.

"Good," he said, thrusting the tip of his sword into the ground. "You're not unwilling to stop. I taught a fellow once who was so stubborn, I lopped off his hand at the wrist. An accident, but all because he wouldn't stop."

"That was . . . foolish," I panted, resting the point of my sword on the ground. The anecdote was no doubt meant to impress the danger upon me, but I thought of how close some of those last blows had come.

"Aye." Will nodded solemnly, but the twinkle in his eye suggested that perhaps he was exaggerating.

The sun chose that moment to come out from behind the clouds, and for a few moments, rising steam enveloped us. I laughed as Will disappeared from my view. I stepped toward him, nearly tripping over him before I discovered he'd sat down.

I sat beside him on the bank, watching the rising steam turn the world ethereal.

"You've done well," he said after a while. "You've still got offense to learn, and that's more work, but I tried some attacks calling for moves I didn't teach you, and you made them tolerably well. Of course, I was holding back."

"It sure didn't feel like it." I leaned back to let the sunshine sink into my body, tipping my face to the light. I could easily have stretched out in the wet grass to sleep. "Ouch!"

"What?" asked Will, sitting up at my unexpected cry.

I leaned forward, rubbing my cramped right arm. "My arm feels like a block of stone and my shoulder hurts. I guess I'm not used to using my arm like that."

"Here." Will shifted. "Turn around."

I turned my back to him and he began to massage my shoulder and arm. Relaxing under his probing fingers, I got that prickling, rising/sinking sensation telling me my body wanted to sleep. Tempted to lean back into his arms and oblige it, I stopped myself. I needed to act like a boy—to shape up—but it felt so good.

My spine tingled as Will spoke, closer than I expected. "I know something about you," he whispered. My eyes snapped open and I tried to turn toward him. "No. Don't look at me." He continued massaging my shoulder. "I know you're hiding something, and I know what it is."

I sat rigid beneath his gentle hands. After a moment, he stopped.

"Little Italian, did you think you could hide what you were forever?"

He knows I'm a woman, I thought, groaning inwardly. *How many others know?* Bracing myself for the shame of being thrown out of Robin's band, or worse, I straightened my shoulders.

"I know you're a noble. Your father is a very important person somewhere. You weren't happy living the life of nobility, so you left your father—"

"My father is dead!" I said. This time, I did turn around.

"All right. Your mother. You defied her and came here to join us out of spite. But you can't hide your learning and your gentle speech—"

"Is that really what you think?" I was relieved he hadn't guessed the truth, but I had a feeling this might be worse.

"Yes." A half-smile I couldn't read came to his lips.

"Who else thinks this . . . theory is true?"

"Nobody I know of," he answered, his smile deepening.

"Good, because it's nowhere near the mark." If others thought this, too, they could laugh me right out of Sherwood Forest. There were other former aristocrats among us, but crime or misfortune had outlawed them. Not petty spite or boredom.

"It's not true?" he asked, sounding vaguely surprised, but the smile hadn't gone away. What *was* he smiling about?

"None of it. My father was a barkeep before he died. My mother, who is also dead, taught the children."

"Oh." He finally stopped smiling, then nodded. "That explains your learning and your manners. But it doesn't explain why you're here."

"Doesn't it? I have no family, no better place to be." That was down to the bone truth, and I wondered if that really was the reason I was here.

Will smiled in understanding. "Yes, I suppose that's a good enough reason to be here."

"Yeah, it is. But Will—" I stopped. What had I been about to say?

"What, Kay?"

I shrugged. He would find out eventually, and I liked this fellow for what he was—a man. How could I expect him to like me the same way?

"Will, there's something I think I should tell you."

"Go on." He smiled again, but I ignored it.

I took a deep breath, getting my nerve up to make this admission. "I'm taking a chance by telling you this. But I want you to know. I'm a woman."

Looking at his face when I said it, I thought he was angry. Nothing showed. No emotion, just that stupid smile.

"Will . . . ," I began, trying to think of something to say that would remedy this gross blunder I had made.

"I know," he said, the idiot smile breaking into a grin.

"What?!" It was my turn to be surprised.

"I know you're a woman," he said. Laughter bubbling up, he pointed at me. My face must have registered my astonishment.

"How? How long?!" I asked, batting at his hand. Had he told someone like Mark, who would tell everyone else?

"I guessed on Mid-Summer's Eve." I remembered that he had carried me to my blanket. "I didn't know for sure. Before now, it was just a guess. Don't worry. I didn't say anything."

"And you don't want me to leave?" I asked, incredulous.

"No. We need you here." He pointed to the ground. "It's not such a big deal. There have been women with Robin before, and I don't mean the whores. Two women have spent time out here."

"Where are they now?" I asked, wondering why Robin hadn't said anything.

He shrugged. "They left for reasons of their own. But you . . . . There will be no trouble with you staying. I like you."

I was startled by his candid admission. But something else bothered me. "So I don't have to prove I'm worthy before I admit I'm female?"

Will looked thoughtful. "I wouldn't just skip back and tell everyone. Most of them will figure it out eventually and understand your silence. Those who don't will need the reassurance that you're up to standard. So keep your secret a while longer." He smiled, and to my supreme embarrassment, I blushed.

"You like me?" I had to ask, feeling like a schoolgirl again. "I mean, you really don't want me to leave?"

"Really," he answered, pretending he didn't notice my response. "How's your arm?"

"What? Oh, better."

"Good. Do you want to go for a swim?"

"But it's raining again."

"So? We can't get much wetter than we already are. Come on!" He was already up and stripping.

I shrugged and took off my clothes, but remembering Much's reaction, I left my tank top and underwear on.

WHEN WE GOT BACK to camp, the clatter of plates seemed muted by the mist of the falling rain. The whole atmosphere of the clearing was desultory, melancholy. The men looked tired, or maybe it was just because of the rain. I got the impression no one had left the camp all day.

As soon as Will and I entered the clearing, he went to speak with Stephen of the Norfolk, leaving me alone. I went to the table, looking around for Much. Feeling a tap on my shoulder, I turned around, smiling.

"Hi!" I said.

"You're cheerful today. Where have you been?" Much sounded sullen, not really looking at me.

My smile falling, I answered, "I went to the river with Scarlet. He was teaching me to sword fight."

"Oh, really?" He seemed disinterested. I wanted to ask what was wrong, but he moved down to a vacant seat.

"Yeah," I said, following him. We sat down as the meal was passed around.

Then I caught the underlying mood of the brotherhood. It was like a live wire running beneath the melancholic, lazy mood. Something had happened. Something I had missed.

I turned to Much and whispered, "What happened today?"

He answered just as quietly. "The sheriff's men were out. Because of the robbery yesterday, I warrant. Hugh of Lancaster and Gilbert Whitehand were hunting when the soldiers surprised them down by the Leaford road. Hugh caught a bolt in the foot. Robin and Edward the Red are seeing to him now."

"And?"

"And I don't know. The bolt wasn't treated, that's sure, but we don't yet know if he'll ever walk right again."

I hissed between my teeth. That was bad. A man needed speed to live out here. I lowered my voice even further. "Everyone is so tense."

"That's because some wanted to mobilize everyone to go after the soldiers and make them pay for what they'd done. Robin said no, and there was an argument. He said he'd take care of it and that put an end to it. But some aren't satisfied. They've been plotting around while Robin's been inside."

"Oh." Then Much's last statement made me blink. "Inside? Where?" I hadn't seen any buildings around.

"The cave. It's off in the trees, over there." He gestured to the north end of the clearing. "That's where Robin, Little John, and Will Stutely sleep. The extra weapons, money, and food are—" Much clamped his lips together, as if he'd said too much.

I watched him for a moment, disturbed by his reaction. I thought he trusted me, but now he wouldn't meet my eye. I put a hand on his arm and squeezed, and when he looked up at last, his smile was sheepish.

"It's not you. There was just no reason to tell you sooner."

I smiled to show him I understood, and I did. But it served to knock me down a few notches, and left me wondering how many more secrets I wasn't privy to.

We were eating when Robin and a red-haired man came to the table, and everyone grew quiet. "He's sleeping," Robin said.

A murmur ran around the table. Someone called out, "Well, what are we going to do about it?"

Robin raised his hand before the shouting got out of control. "It's been seen to."

"What? How?" several people shouted.

Much got a thoughtful look on his face. "What have you done?" he asked softly. Only I could have heard him in the uproar. His voice had a hint of laughter on the edge, tempered with concern.

He looked at me. I raised my eyebrows in mute response.

Before Robin could give an answer, three men came into the clearing, laughing. Silence fell as they walked to the table. It was Will Stutely, David of Doncaster, and Edmond the Jew.

"Well?" Robin asked.

"We caught up with them all right," David said with a laugh. "We scattered them and took their captain. We tied him up by his heels near Nottingham town, alongside the road."

"Stripped naked," Edmond said, chuckling.

The men laughed.

"Is Hugh well avenged then?" Robin asked, looking around the table.

"Aye!" the men cheered, except a few who muttered into their ale cups. This turn of events did not please some.

We finished the meal in our usual robust nature, but the tension didn't completely go away. I watched the men around me, trying to see what exactly was going on.

After Peter and David of York cleared the table, Much and I sat on a bench at one side of the clearing. I saw Mark of Leicester and a group of men gathered across the clearing. They looked subdued, but I caught several glances in my direction and in Robin's and wondered what was afoot.

Wrapping my fingers around a mug of ale, I talked quietly with Much, telling him some anecdotes about my past. He didn't know about my being from the future, so I was careful with what I included in my stories. We often spoke, and in return for my tales, he would always share a story of his own.

I often worried about creating a paradox by telling Much about the future. Time could be stable enough not to be affected by things I might say, but I couldn't be sure, so I made my stories very commonplace.

A short time after dinner, I saw Robin get up to go back to the cave to see about Hugh.

Listening to Much talk about an ancient Roman city he had once seen up north, I took a sip of ale, watching the ground at my feet. A pair of leather boots came into my line of sight and stopped in front of me. Others made a semi-circle behind them.

I looked up to see Mark standing there, looking down at me. Seven or eight men stood behind him.

"Get up."

I didn't move, not sure what was going on.

"Get up," he repeated.

"Why?" asked Much, putting a hand on my wrist to keep me seated. Glancing at him, I saw his mouth set in a thin line of displeasure. He shook his head at me. "Don't do it."

"Stay out of this, Much." Mark didn't even spare him a glance. "Get . . . up!" His hands made quick lifting motions and I stood, setting my cup of ale on the bench. "Traitor!" he said and spit in my face.

With deliberate motions, I wiped the spittle off with my shirt-sleeve, hearing Much's angry exclamation. The blood in my veins had turned to ice and my hands balled into fists. If Mark was looking to wind me up, he was doing just fine.

"Easy, Kay." Much rose from his seat, only to have Albert of

Trent and Jerod Longfingers grab hold of him from behind to keep him back. "He's talking rubbish."

Mark and I faced each other, only inches between us. He pushed me, but I stood my ground. Much didn't want me to fight back, but I'd about had enough.

"You filthy Italian," he said with venom, poking his finger into my chest. "*You* went and told the sheriff where Hugh and Gilbert were hunting, so that—"

"What?" I slapped his hand away and pushed my face closer to his. "I was with Scarlet all day."

"With Scarlet, eh? Well, where is he now?" Mark shoved me again. I shoved back, not willing to let him accuse me like this.

"He left me when we got here."

"I saw him—" began Much.

Mark gestured at Much. "Quiet him."

Jerod thumped him viciously in the back of the neck and Much slumped. They let him fall to the ground.

I moved for him, but Mark stepped into my path. "You'll pay for what you did to Hugh."

"How can I?" I said, my voice rising with anger. "I haven't done anything! Ask Scarlet!"

Mark pushed me back a step. "I'll ask him . . . after I'm through with you."

"Whatcha gonna do then?" I put my hands on my hips, cautioning myself to keep control of my temper. I wasn't in any position to get into a fight, especially with Much lying on the ground, unconscious. Mark's accusations were bad enough. I didn't need to compound it by brawling with him.

His face contorted. Too late, I realized what he intended. I couldn't block his punch, and he knocked me back across the bench, toppling it and my ale as I fell hard onto the wet ground.

"Get up!" he said, his voice hoarse with anger.

I lurched to my feet, feeling my jaw, and turned around into Mark's swinging fist. This time when I hit the ground, I didn't get right up.

Taking his punches without fighting back was the hardest thing I had ever done. It was like my father all over again, but I was stronger now. I wanted to leap up and dive on him, smash my fist into his face. But he had his men and his greater strength behind him, and fighting against such uneven odds would be a foolish gesture. I looked up at him from where I lay.

"Do you feel better yet?" I asked sharply.

"Not yet. Get up!"

I climbed to my feet. "I haven't done any—" He swung. I tried to stay up, but he kicked me in the stomach and I doubled over, falling as he struck me again.

"Mark!" I heard Robin's voice as if from a distance. Then someone helped me to my feet. Through a red haze, I saw Robin holding onto Mark's shoulder. "What are you doing?!"

"He betrayed us, Robin!" Mark said. "He told the sheriff where Hugh and Gilbert were!"

Robin shot a quick glance at me, then looked back at Mark. "Do you have proof?"

"I don't need any! I know!"

Robin looked at me again, unsure. That uncertainty hurt me far more than any punch Mark could throw.

"He was with me, Robin." Will stood behind me, hands under my arms, helping me stand. "We were at the river. I was with him all morning and most of the afternoon. Then we came back here and he was with Much. There was no time for him to tell the sheriff."

Robin relaxed visibly, but Mark shot me a look of pure hatred.

Will patted me on the shoulder and my sight cleared enough to see everyone looking at me. Some with pity, some with shame, still others with hostility. I looked around for Much and saw him sitting with Kenneth of Richmond, holding a damp cloth to his neck.

"Mark," said Robin. "I can't have you—"

"Robin," I interrupted. "Please. These people don't know me. He has every reason to think the way he does, and I've done nothing to prove him wrong. Let it rest."

"Right." Robin was more than ready to let the matter drop.

"Look, you." Mark pointed at me. "I don't need you to defend me. I still think you're a spy!" He glared at me, his face red with shame, eyes wide with anger.

"I know you do." I turned away. Nothing I could say to him would change his mind.

THE RAIN DAMPENED SPIRITS, so things broke up early that night. No one was in the mood for having a good time after everything that had happened that day.

One by one, the perimeter guards came back to summon their replacements, who vanished into the damp night. There were always some men at various points around the camp, keeping watch. I had spent a few long days and cold nights in a tree myself.

But this night, Will and I sat beside the fire, talking.

"I don't know what to do about him, Will. Mark just won't accept me. Anything I say, he takes as a lie. Anything I do, he twists to make it treachery." I scowled at my hands, as if I could unbend Mark's stubborn mind with them.

"Little Italian, just stay away from him. You want to earn his trust, but Mark isn't like that. He makes quick, harsh judgments. He's stubborn. Poor attitude is the least of his sins."

"He makes me so mad. God, I wanted to hit him back."

"Why didn't you?"

"Much warned me not to fight him, and there were eight of them. I have enough sense to know when I'm outnumbered."

"If it had been just Mark?"

"There would have been a real fight."

Scarlet shook his head. "Look, he's trouble, so just stay away. All right?"

"For the good of the brotherhood?" I asked, sighing.

"Something like that."

"I'll stay away from him then." Pushing wet hair out of my face, I chewed on my lower lip thoughtfully. "Will?"

"Mmm?"

"Do you think I should tell the others?"

He turned to look at me. "Tell them what?"

"About me. I mean, I sit here expecting them all to trust me, but they don't know anything about me." I leaned toward him intently. "You call me Little Italian for fun. Do you know Mark actually thinks I'm from Italy?"

Will ignored my question. "Robin trusts you."

"Does he? You saw the way he looked when Mark accused me.

He believed him until you spoke up. Much believes me, but he's still not sure how far he can trust me. What about you?"

Will stared into the heart of the fire. "What I think hardly matters."

"But it does . . . to me. I need to know if there is someone in this group who really trusts me, Will."

He said nothing for a moment. "Robin trusts you, Kay." He very pointedly abandoned his pet name for me. "The others will come around."

I pushed on. "Even so, Robin's trust isn't enough for some of them. Didn't today prove that? Some of those men were ready to go against him just for the revenge of a wounded foot. Tempers were on edge." He turned to me, a blank look on his face. "Don't tell me you didn't see it. You'd be a blind man if you couldn't."

"Here now!" Scarlet chose to take offense at that remark.

"Sorry, but either I'm imagining things or something is seriously wrong. I don't believe it's just me. If someone is ready to risk the brotherhood for a foot, there's something—"

"You really take your oath seriously, don't you?" Will interrupted.

"Don't you?" I countered.

"Yes, but not like you." He pointed at me with a calloused finger. "You're concerned about people having trust in you. You're almost feverish about it. Then you turn around and, in the same breath, point at a major weakness of the brotherhood without getting an answer to any of your questions."

"Ah, hell. I'm not important, Will Scarlet. We are. All of us."

"You're right," he said softly.

We sat in silence for a long while, each thinking our own thoughts, then Will spoke quietly. "Kay, I do trust you."

He went on, as if he hadn't made that admission. "It's something that's been going on for a long time. Mark's a rebel. You've already noticed that, I'm sure. He only trusts two people in this world. Robin Hood and me. We were mates when we were young. Lately, though, he's been stirring up some of the men, getting them to disagree with what Robin says. He's nearly broken his oath." He paused, thoughtful.

"Something has to be done, but Robin just won't see it. He insists Mark must bring it up to him. Robin is a brilliant leader and a strong, kind man, but there are some people he just can't see through. It will be a frigid day in Avalon before those two talk it out. Swords will be bared first." Will fell silent, staring into the fire.

"I need to think," I told him, putting my hand on his shoulder. "I'll see you in the morning."

"Goodnight, Kay."

Something had to be done about Mark, or the whole of Robin's band might fall apart.

But it doesn't happen, I thought, lying awake under my blanket. *I know that for a fact. The band stays together until Richard . . . . But how do I know if they stay together because of something I do?*

The dampness gave my churning thoughts just enough charge so that when the rain stopped during the night, I was awake to appreciate it.

CHAPTER

SIX

I cy wind howled across the opening of the cave as I entered, a shiver slithering across my shoulders and down to my navel. Backing away from the windbreak, I turned and warmed myself by the fire. Hugh of Lancaster hobbled up from the back of the cave to sit beside me.

"Hugh," I greeted him.

"Kay."

"How is Scarlet?" I tried to mask the concern in my voice.

"Resting. The fever's left him. He should be on his feet in a week or so."

"Good." I sighed.

It was past the middle of a hard winter. We had retreated to an old haunt—five caves in a cliffside. We needed protection from the cold and a place for those who had fallen ill with sweating sickness —what I knew as influenza—to get better.

Will had caught it a week ago and had been in bed since. Hugh took care of him and the others, having learned some of the healing craft from the old woman who had taken care of his foot. That, combined with what I knew of the sickness, meant we hadn't lost any men to it . . . yet.

I came to see Scarlet every day. Between that and our talks on cures, Hugh and I had become friends.

"How are the others?" I asked.

"Jack of Nottingham still has the fever. John Ainsley got up and walked about this morning, but the other two and Will are resting." As if in answer, Kenneth of Richmond broke into a fit of coughing. Hugh got up to ease him.

"You've done an excellent job, Hugh," I said when he came back.

"I was afraid we'd lose some of them. So far, Luck has been on our side."

"That she has," I agreed.

Hugh was a superstitious one. He believed in all kinds of demons and personalities. I think he liked me because I never said he was foolish to believe in those things. I wasn't particularly super-stitious myself, but who knew if some of those personalities were real or not? After all, I still did not have an explanation for my pres-ence in this time.

I went to the back of the cave where the ill men slept. Jack moaned softly in his sleep, delirious. Sweat glistened on his fore-head. Kneeling next to him, I dabbed at his face with a cool cloth. He woke to my touch, his feverish eyes searching mine as he grasped my hand at the wrist, holding on with more strength than I would have thought a sick man could manage.

"I'm not dying, am I?" he asked, intense.

I covered his hand with mine. "Not if I can help it."

He sighed and let go. "Kay, I'm trusting you."

"I'm glad." But he had closed his eyes as the fever took him back into delirium. I dabbed his face again and sat a moment, holding his hand to feel his pulse. It was a little fast from the fever, but the rush of blood through his veins felt reassuring against my fingers. He was going to be all right.

I got up and went around the fire. Scarlet lay awake, watching me.

"Good day. I presume it is day, though I don't know for sure." Huddled in the blankets against the cold, the only part of him visible was his head.

"It's evening," I said quietly, resisting the urge to stroke his hair. "How are you feeling?"

"Tired. I'm so tired, Kay. I feel like I've carried a buck the length and breadth of Sherwood. Hugh says the worst is over, though. If it doesn't come back, I'll be up and around soon."

"He's right."

A particularly nasty gust of wind shrieked across the mouth of the cave, rattling the windbreak. I turned, startled. "I wish this storm would let up."

I looked back down at Will. He was asleep. I brushed a strand of damp hair from his forehead before I realized what I was doing. Snatching my hand back, I sat, watching his face.

"Kay?" a voice said at my shoulder. I looked up to see Will Stutely standing just behind me. "Robin wants to see you."

"Right." I stood up. Stutley turned to the fire to warm himself.

As I climbed the rope ladder to Robin's cave, darkness engulfed me. That was just as well. I didn't want to see the tree branches tossing wildly in the fierce gale or the ground so far below. The wind tore at me as I climbed, trying to pluck me off the rope, the rocks heavy with ice. Several times, I had to stop and hold on for dear life, praying the bucking rope would not break.

Coming as it had on the heels of a rainstorm, the dry, frigid wind had frozen everything it touched, then sapped the moisture from the very air, leaving it cracking with static charge. I imagined that if I stayed outside long enough, I would either blow away or disappear in a puff of electric shock.

By the time I reached Robin's cave, which was the highest one, my fingers were numb with cold. I climbed in past the windbreak and pressed through the crowded space. I asked one of the widow's sons where he was, and the man pointed me in the right direction.

Most of the men were eating and talking. As I passed, I made greetings to the ones I knew best. Almost everyone stayed in this cave, keeping warm.

Of the five caves, our people only used three. Robin's cave, the largest, was always crowded, especially at mealtimes. There wasn't much to eat, but even outlaws felt a need to be social in the dark of winter. The press of bodies was too much for me, though, so I spent more time in the other caves than in the sweaty stink of this one.

Finally catching sight of Robin, I made my way to him.

"Robin?"

He looked up and smiled, gesturing me to sit. It was unusual enough for him to call me, but to invite me to sit with him? It wasn't that Robin ignored me, but there were others who occupied his attention more than I.

"Have you eaten?" he asked.

Surprised, I shook my head. "No, in fact." Robin turned his head to say something to Little John, who got up and made his way to the table. I was curious as to why I rated such special treatment.

"How are the sick ones?" he asked.

"All but Jack of Nottingham are through the fever and doing well. If they don't catch pneumonia or relapse, we won't lose any of them."

"Good," said Robin, nodding sharply, seemingly pleased.

"Yes." I looked at his face, noticing faint worry lines. "Why did you summon me?" I asked, accepting the plate of stew Little John offered.

Robin smiled. "You always know when I am not asking you what I mean to. All right. What I have to say is this. Even though it is winter, I don't trust the sheriff to sit tight without looking for us. Not after the dent to his dignity at the fair."

I knew he referred to a foray I had not been a part of. The Harvest Fair captain had been slightly upset about the disappearance of a cartload of prisoners who had been up for hanging. Robin had liberated them, helping them flee to other parts of England.

"We're in a vulnerable position here. It's too close to Nottingham for comfort. We left this place once because it had been discovered, and we need to know what the sheriff is thinking. He was looking for us hard enough before the weather turned, and he may just guess we have retreated here."

"So you want me to go to Nottingham and find out," I said, nodding. I spooned up more stew to hide the rush of adrenaline surging through me.

"Right. No one there knows what you look like, so you should be able to go without suspicion." Robin was paving the way for me to prove myself to his men, and I liked the plan.

"Except from me." Mark stepped forward. I had seen him lurking nearby ever since my arrival in the cave. "Robin, you can't mean you trust this boy."

"But I do," he said mildly. "Don't you?"

Robin knew very well Mark did not trust me. I had been on

enough guard duty and robberies to earn Robin's trust, but he was in the minority, along with Will and Much. Many of the men still remembered Hugh and Gilbert . . . and Mark's accusations.

"No!" Mark said vehemently. "I don't know anything about this . . . this *child*."

"*I* know about him," said Robin, daring Mark to step out of line. Their gazes locked, Mark visibly struggling in a battle of wills. "I trust him."

Mark backed off, lowering his gaze, but he still listened.

"Now, for the rest of my plan. You will go to town in disguise, and someone will accompany you. Then," he said, looking pointedly at Mark, "those who don't trust you will feel better."

"What disguise?" This could be interesting.

"A woman," he said, smiling. "And your partner would be your husband. You are small enough to play a woman well."

I nearly choked on my stew. "Me? A woman?"

"Who better? Don't you think you'd fit the part well?"

"Well . . . ," I began, but couldn't think of anything more to say.

"And I'll go with him," said Mark, oblivious to the fact that Robin and I weren't paying attention to him.

I looked at Robin, his smile a challenge. I felt a slow grin spread across my face. "Yes. Who better?"

Robin looked at Mark. "What did you say?"

"I said I will go with him."

Robin turned to me. "Kay?"

I thought about it for a few moments, staring at Mark. He glared back fiercely. I had tried to stay away from him for five months. It was hard to avoid one person in such a small place, so I nodded, tired of running away from a conflict with him. "If you have no objections, Robin, I'll take him."

"After the storm breaks then. John, take him to get his disguise."

Robin stood in the mouth of the cave. I waved up at him as Mark and I moved into the forest, toward Nottingham.

I remembered what Will had said two days ago when I told him what I was going to do.

"Kay, you can't go off alone with Mark. He'll either get you caught or kill you!"

"Not until after we get the information. Hopefully I can prove myself to him before he does anything drastic."

"It's too dangerous. Tell Robin you want to take someone else."

I shook my head. "No. Will, I'm tired of hiding from him. I've got to take a stand."

"You can't do that! Once you've dressed yourself up, Mark will see. He'll know you're a woman."

"I know," I had said. "But it's the only way to get him to trust me. He knows I've been hiding something. If we pull this thing off, he'll at least know what I am and what I can do. Maybe knowledge will grow into trust."

"Kay, you expect too much from him."

"Maybe. And maybe I expect too much of myself, but he's coming with me."

Seeing he could not persuade me to take someone else, he gripped my hand. "Be careful."

Now, moving swiftly and silently through the bare winter trees, I hoped I was as good as I thought I was. A summer of practice in swordplay with Will had given me a fair amount of skill with the weapon, and my aim with the bow had improved. If I had to fight, I would be ready, but we could not let it come to that. Two outlaws on their own in a town full of soldiers would see dawn break from the hangman's gallows.

As much as I had skill with weapons, I knew I would need skill with words on this mission. Since finding myself in this time, I decided I'd found my true self. The social outcast I'd been in the twentieth century was gone. Now, when my wits were about me, I could talk my way out of almost any situation, and I counted on that to get us past the gate.

Over my regular clothes, I wore a long dress made of warm wool, and while running through the forest, I hitched the skirts up in my belt so my legs wouldn't get tangled in them. The scarf wrapped around my head was like what some women wore, but the sword buckled beneath my dress was not a lady's accessory. A special cut in the skirts would let me draw if I needed to, though I was not too worried about anyone seeing through my disguise.

To cover the ten miles between the caves and Nottingham, we traveled at a ground-eating trot through the winter-bare forest, slowing to a walk when we tired. We carried our bows and quivers, but we planned to stash them before entering the city.

"Take no chances," Robin had said. "Go into town near dark and go to Marian's father's house. Mark knows the way. If anyone asks, you're from Hertfordshire and are visiting your cousin. *Don't* mention Marian, she's not to be at risk. Make it a quick trip. Just get in, get the information, then get out. We'll watch for your signal through the night. Be careful. I don't want to lose either of you."

If we hurried, we'd make it to Nottingham before nightfall. We flew over the ground like ravens, while the sky, still dark, threatened another storm.

It was close to the fourth hour after noon when we stopped at the edge of the common. The walled city of Nottingham squatted like a toad in the field, its dependent village clinging to the outer wall on the far side of the city.

The stormy light turned the scene gray, giving the village and castle walls a haunted look and me the illusion of being back in my own time, a visitor to a long-abandoned ruin. When a guard stirred at his post and walked a few paces, a mere doll at this distance, I exhaled in relief.

"Right. We need the south gate," said Mark, and started to move off.

"Mark?" I grabbed him by the shoulder.

He turned, shaking off my hand. "What?"

"We've got to work together on this."

"I know," he snarled.

"I know you don't trust me, but you must have some faith in me." I tried to catch his eye, but he evaded.

"Look you, I have all I need to get me through this. I'll do whatever it takes to get the news back to Robin. You won't get in my way." He turned and moved through the trees, looking for the road to the south gate.

I watched after him for a moment, then ran to catch up. "Don't forget. We are husband and wife," I told him. He muttered an expletive and kept on walking.

Soon, we saw the road between the trees, and I pointed to a

place we could hide our bows and quivers. We cut some branches from the bushes and put our bows underneath the bracken. As an afterthought, I unbuckled my borrowed sword and put it under, as well. It wouldn't do for a woman, a "lady," to be caught with a sword.

Mark was already on the road, waiting impatiently, when I came out of the trees. We stepped out and made our way to the gate, past tall stalks of dead pasture grass that gave way to the field stubble of harvested grain. When I looped my arm through Mark's, he looked at me sharply.

"Husband and wife," I hissed. He nodded, angry. To my surprise, he composed his features before we reached the gate, turning into a cheery gentleman.

The gate, dimly lit by a hanging lantern, loomed in front of us. In the shadow of the wall, it was already dark as night.

"Halt!" called a guard, stepping up and eyeing us closely. He wore chain mail with a blue sleeveless tabard over the top of it, his hand obviously resting on his sword hilt. "Who might you be?"

Mark cleared his throat. "I'm Marshall Davidson, and this is my wife, Catherine."

The guard squinted from beneath his helmet, taking the measure of Mark, then moving on to me. His gaze lingered on my chest, which I had built up for that reason. "Where are you from? What's your business in Nottingham?" he asked, still looking at me.

"We're from Hertfordshire and have come to visit her cousin, who works in the clothiers," Mark answered.

"And your travel chests?" the guard asked, turning to Mark suspiciously. "Hertfordshire's quite a trip from here."

Mark swallowed audibly. I resisted the urge to kick him.

"It'll be along tomorrow," I said quickly, "if those terrible outlaws don't get a hold of it." To draw his attention away from what I was saying, I fluttered my free hand over my breasts in apparent dismay. "We just sent our escort back to that little village, whatever it was—dismal place—to see to it. I do hope it gets through all right." Wearing what I hoped was a suitably frightened look on my face, I glanced over my shoulder, ignoring Mark's tightening grip.

The guard looked at me and I smiled daintily. "We were stuck there in that . . . that hole in the wall for so long in that awful storm,

I couldn't stand it. I just couldn't bear to wait for our things. It will make it all right, won't it?" I asked anxiously.

"It should, milady," said the guard, relaxing. He smiled, as though to reassure me. "We haven't heard much from old Robin Hood this winter. Sheriff thinks he's holed up somewhere, waiting for the warmer weather."

"I certainly hope so," I said. "I have some valuables I would hate to lose. Is anything being done by you brave men to find out where the outlaws might be?"

Mark gave me a dangerous glance, which I ignored. I hoped the guard, if he saw it, thought my "husband" was angry with me for flirting so outrageously.

"We've got foresters on the lookout, but they've not seen cap nor boot of the knaves." The guard smiled, rocking back on his heels, looking pleased with his report.

"A pity." I pouted a little. "They should hang. All of them."

"I should say so, milady. It's getting late. You'd best be off to your cousin's."

"Thank you, sir." I made a small curtsey, then we passed through the gate.

"You watch what you say," Mark whispered angrily once we were out of earshot. His hand was rough on my elbow.

"I got us through the gate, didn't I?" I whispered, trying to hold back my anger. "Should I have left it to you to get us arrested? I got some information, too."

"Yes, you did, but he might have suspected us with all your talking." Mark glowered at me.

"Suspect a woman who says she wants to see Robin Hood and his men hanged? Mark, you're too paranoid." Smug at the confusion lighting his eyes, I turned back to the gate, saw the guard watching us, and waved daintily to him behind Mark's back. I saw him grin, elbowing his duty mate in the gut. "Which way to Marian's?"

Mark growled and strode off, making me pick up my skirts to keep up with him. Turning onto a wide street that led to the center of town, Mark slowed to a normal pace.

"Just remember that you are a woman," he said sharply.

"How could I forget?" I mumbled.

We walked arm in arm down the street, watching everyone.

Trying to act our parts, we chatted in amiable tones, but our topic was hardly marital in nature.

"When we get back," Mark said in a sugary voice, "I'm going to tell Uncle Harry you took unnecessary risks and put me in danger."

"If you don't keep your foot out of your mouth," I said, smiling sweetly at passersby, "we won't make it back to Uncle Harry alive." A covert glance behind us told me no soldiers followed.

Mark laughed heartily, though it rang hollow. "I'll make it back."

I turned adoring eyes to look at him. "When I get us out of here, you can tell Uncle Harry whatever you like. He likes me better. He'll believe me when I tell him you weren't any help at all."

Mark kept his mouth closed after that.

Ahead of us on the muddy street, lights flickered on. We soon passed the lightkeeper, shielding his torch against the fitfully blowing wind as he moved from lamp to lamp.

We approached a fine, large house with a blue and gold banner hanging above the door. The design on the banner, a leaping fish in a ring of red, declared the household's emblem. I pointed. "Marian's?"

"Aye."

At the door, Mark lifted the knocker and let it fall with a hollow boom. Before long, a servant answered.

"We've come to pay a visit to Lady Marian," I said.

The servant eyed us curiously. "May I ask who?"

"Tell the lady we are old friends," Mark said, using the code words Marian knew.

The servant ushered us in to wait in the foyer as he went to deliver the message. In a few moments, he came back. "Follow me. My lord and lady are dining. You will join them."

We walked down a hall and under an archway leading into the dining hall. Looking around the modest room, I saw the family eating fine meat and drinking wine from silver goblets. My mouth watered at the delicious smells and I swallowed, trying not to look as hungry as I felt. At the head of the table, a young woman sat next to a man well advanced in years.

We hovered in the doorway as the servant walked in. Before he reached her, Marian looked up and saw us, giving no outward indication of surprise. Excusing herself, she came around the table to us, gesturing to a room off to one side of the hall.

I got my first close look at the woman who held Robin's heart.

She was tall and thin with long, curly brown hair. Her features were petite—small mouth and small, sharp chin—but her expressive brown eyes were enormous. Other than freckles adorning her pale cheeks, her complexion was clear. She was a good-looking woman by any time's standards.

"See that we are not disturbed," she told a servant, then closed the door. When she turned to look at the two of us, I saw a flash of fear in her eyes. "Mark? What's wrong?" she asked softly.

"We've only come for news, milady," he said, looking uncomfortable.

"You should not have risked yourselves for news, Mark. But you are here." She let out a quick breath, allowing a small betrayal of her anxiety. "Sit then. Who is your friend?"

"His name is Kay," Mark answered, trying to dismiss the subject.

"He?"

"Yes." Mark waved his hand impatiently. "He disguised himself as a woman for this trip. He's new and Robin is testing him."

When Marian looked me over, eyes narrowed slightly, I smiled. She knew. She asked the question with her eyes. I shrugged, giving permission.

"Mark, do you mean you cannot tell Kay *is* a woman? This is no disguise. You see her as she really is."

Mark turned, looking at me sharply. He had been about to laugh, but a frown creased his brows instead. Then a look of shock replaced the frown, though it was quickly masked.

"Humph," he managed, embarrassed. "That explains about the rabbits then." He blushed, and Marian giggled.

About once a month, I'd go out hunting for rabbits. It was a habit that had half the camp bewildered. Rabbits had soft, very absorbent skins. Not as nifty as a maxi pad, but adequate for a woman's needs.

"Does Robin know?" he finally asked.

"Aye," I said. "And Much and Scarlet."

"You had me fooled, you did. But now I know . . . ." He scowled again. "I knew you were lying about something."

"I didn't lie!" I flared. I took a deep breath and struggled to calm myself. Mark got under my skin too easily. "I just neglected . . . failed to tell you."

"Oh? And what else have you *neglected* to tell us?" He leaned back in the chair, folding his arms across his chest.

I looked at him for a moment, biting back the urge to strike the attitude off his face. "I could tell you things about my life that would make your eyes pop out of your head, and you'd cross yourself and say I lied, though every stitch of what I'd tell you would be true. But this is neither the time nor the place for such talking." I looked from Mark to Marian, who had been watching me. "Milady, we've come to find out what the sheriff's been up to this winter. Does he know where we are? Do you have any news?"

Marian shook her head. "He has foresters looking for you, but they've no heart for it, not in the cold. I've heard a rumor someone has seen lights in the cliff caves where Robin once hid." She shrugged. "The sheriff will be sending men out once the rest of this storm has cleared off to see what he can find out." Marian saw the look on our faces and her eyes widened. "Robin's in danger. He *is* in the caves!" Her stricken gaze moved from my face to Mark's, where she received unwanted confirmation. "Oh no!"

"We'll be fine if we can get the signal up in time," Mark said, standing up. I stood, too.

"You're leaving in the dark?" Marian asked, also rising.

"We must warn Robin," I said. "We've sick ones, and they'll take time to move."

"All right then." She had already recovered her brisk manner. "Be careful leaving the city."

Marian showed us to the door, giving us each a kiss on the cheek for goodbye and good luck. I whispered into her ear that Robin sent his love. The smile on her face was enough to tell me she gave hers in return.

When her personal servant came back to report no soldiers on the street, we slipped out into the dark night.

CHAPTER

SEVEN

As we neared the gate, Mark outlined a plan. Before I could agree or disagree, he turned aside, as though to talk to someone. After hesitating, I walked on. It was a hasty plan, but I thought it would work.

Noticing my approach to the gate, the guard stepped forward. "Milady?" he asked. I cursed under my breath. I had hoped to get by without a scene. At least it was the same guard we encountered before.

"Sir," I said, still hoping for a clean exit. "My husband has told me to go to the inn in the village." I made to step past him.

The guard frowned. "Alone in the dark?"

My mind raced, trying to think of a plausible excuse before he wondered why I didn't just go the safer route through the city. I sighed heavily, affecting boredom. "He has gone to see about a horse and wants me to wait there. I will probably spend another lonely night."

"Allow us to accompany you, milady. There have been wolves howling as of late. I'd not want you to be attacked." I opened my mouth to protest, but he laid a hand on my arm. "I insist."

I didn't think I could handle two of them. If I had to have an escort . . . . "Would you . . . could *only you* accompany me?" I smiled as prettily as I knew how and fluttered my eyelashes, letting him know I was suggesting more than just an escort.

The guard caught on and doffed his helmet to me. He gave a rakish grin to his duty mate. "As you wish, milady." He made a low bow, then tossed his helmet to his mate and offered me his elbow. Taking it, I stepped out with him, leaving the city.

"Oh, thank you," I said as we walked into the darkness of the trail, away from the torchlight at the gate. "I don't like wolves."

"There's no need to be afraid, milady. They won't challenge two people. I'll protect you." He moved closer to me, putting his arm around my waist.

I smiled at him in the last of the torchlight, though I had tensed up. He was on my left, and my knife was strapped to the inside of my left leg.

When the torchlight had faded completely, I knew we couldn't be seen from the gate, and we both had our own reasons for wanting to be in the darkness.

As I contemplated how to reach my knife before he acted, I stumbled over a stone in the darkness and the idea came to me. "Oh dear," I said, leaning into him. "I think I've turned my ankle."

The guard looked back toward the gate. "There's little enough light here, but let me see if I can tell." We both bent down and I raised my skirt, as if to show my ankle, but my hand snaked under to grasp the hilt of my knife. "What's this?" the guard asked, amused, his hand on the fabric of my trousers.

I whipped out my knife, slid it under the chain mail at his neck, and buried it in his throat. Looking at me with his face upturned, he had presented a perfect target. He collapsed against me, a small sound of surprise coming from his lips, and I staggered beneath his sudden weight.

He hadn't even thought to be suspicious about my pants. I heaved his dead weight off me, letting him fall to the ground with a small clatter of armor.

I knelt and unbuckled his sword. *My kill*, I thought, *my sword*. I took the dagger I found in the opposite sheath, too, glad of the darkness so I didn't have to see my handiwork.

With a small sense of shock, I realized this had been my first kill and I'd done it without blinking, without even considering another course of action.

But there was no more time for thought. I picked up my skirts and ran across the field, making for the road to the forest.

Reaching the spot where our gear lay hidden, I uncovered the sack of supplies, along with my bow, arrows, and sword. I ditched the dress, buckled a sword on each side of my waist, and strapped my quiver on my back.

Working quickly, I removed an oil-soaked cloth from the sack and wrapped it around the tip of an arrow, then unscrewed the hilt of my survival knife. Adrenalin pumped through my body and my hands shook as I tried to pull out a single match, scattering several into the dark grass. The hilt of the knife was sticky, and I recognized it was blood. I turned and threw up, shaking violently with the realization of my actions.

Moments later, still shaking, I uncovered Mark's bow and carried everything to the edge of the woods. We would undoubtedly be in a hurry when he came, so I arranged his bow and quiver across my back, too. I was careful not to think about the dead man lying in the field back there. There wasn't time.

Mark should have been coming across the field by now, but no one moved in the darkness between me and the city.

"Come on, Mark . . . ." My gaze darted between the gate and the clouds threatening more sleet and rain. If the weather came any lower, they would not be able to see the signal from the cave.

I had no way to measure time, but waited as long as I felt I could for him to appear. He had said if it took him very long, it was because he'd been caught. And the weather wasn't going to wait.

Stepping a few paces onto the road, I lit the cloth on the arrow. It burned brightly as I nocked and shot it straight into the sky, crossing my fingers and hoping someone at the caves would see it.

The light went up, up, up, burning brilliantly. At the top of its arc, it dimmed, making a halo as it slipped into the low clouds, then completed its graceful arc back toward the earth. Panic seized me when I realized how small that light would look back at the cave, how easy it would be to miss.

A shout went up from the city and I turned, knowing the guards at the gate had seen it. I couldn't wait much longer.

Shouting, the soldiers came charging out with lanterns and swords at the same moment the arrow came down behind me, setting fire to grass the constant wind had sucked dry of moisture. That same wind blew toward the city and fanned the flames quickly . . . right at me. I dodged behind it into the woods, watching through the spreading fire as the soldiers approached.

Where was Mark? They were getting closer. I would have to go soon if I wanted to get out alive.

A prickling sensation at the back of my neck made me stand up straight. I turned around slowly, momentarily forgetting the advancing soldiers. I saw a light building, bright even in the light of the flames. My jaw dropped when I realized the shape it was taking.

The door had come back.

It reached out to me, invisible tendrils inviting me to come through, to save myself. I took a step forward, but the thunder of hooves made me spin around, searching for the source of the sound.

Then, through the flames, I saw a rider charging across the field and plunging through the line of soldiers, straight for me. By the flaring light of the fire, I saw who it was.

"That's Robin Hood!" someone shouted and loosed a crossbow bolt. It flew erratically, striking Mark just above the elbow of his left arm.

Forgetting about the door, I nocked an arrow and shot it straight into the man's heart, sending him tumbling into the grass.

The horse skidded to a stop, pitching Mark into the flames before it screamed in terror and raced off into the night, away from the danger spreading rapidly across the common.

Mark tried to climb to his feet and fell back, arms shielding his face. I dropped my bow and ran into the fire, dragging him out of harm's way. I didn't feel the heat scorching my hands and face until we were in the clear. Mark's clothes burned in several places, so I smothered the flames with my body, then hauled him to his feet, only delaying long enough to grab my bow.

We retreated to the edge of the woods, away from the heat. Mark batted at my leg, and I looked down to see my pants on fire. I dropped to the ground to smother the flames before they reached my skin. Then, despite my stinging fingers, I shot at the soldiers through the flames until they ran back to the castle, the roaring fire slowly chasing them. They shouted for water to control the blaze, more concerned with keeping the fire away from the city than with the two fugitives who were out of reach.

"Let's go," I said, helping Mark to his feet.

It began to rain. A hard, icy rain that blew into our faces. I knew the fire would soon be extinguished, but I wondered if anyone at the caves had seen our signal, or if the clouds had been too low.

We stopped to rest under the shelter of a dense grove of pine trees on a hillside far from the burning field. I tried to look at Mark's wound, but he pulled away.

"It has to be seen to, Mark," I said, exasperated. "You can't run the rest of the way with a crossbow bolt in your arm. You may have severed an artery. You could bleed to death!"

"Really?" he snarled. "I wouldn't be wounded if you hadn't set the whole common on fire. That was plain blundering stupidity."

"It wasn't my fault!" We didn't have time to argue, but I was unable to do anything else. "I waited for you as long as you said to wait, then I sent up the signal, *like you said*. The wind blew the arrow into the field. How could I stop that? Anyway, the fire was to our advantage. They won't pursue us until it's out. Now, shut up and let me work."

I moved to his left side and lifted his arm. He winced, but didn't say anything.

Drawing my knife, I cut away the sleeve of his shirt as gently as I could to look at the wound, leaning close in the dim light.

The bolt had gone in on the outer side of his arm, missing the bone, and out the front. It looked clean, all things considered. Careful not to jerk the bolt, I sliced the fletching off, making it possible to slide the bolt out without cutting in deeply.

I started talking to keep his mind off what I was doing. "Back home, we don't usually have to deal with wounds like this." I bent behind him and lit my last match to sterilize the knife. "People don't usually use bows and crossbows on other people. They have lots of other weapons." I tore off strips off my shirt for compress and bandages, preparing them for use. "Nasty weapons, too." Inserting the knife into the wound to spread the skin apart, I gently tugged on the bolt. "They can kill from a distance with only a small ball of lead, or blast entire cities in the blink of an eye."

I gave the bolt a good yank and slipped it out of the wound, letting it drop to the ground as Mark's arm spasmed, nearly jerking out of my grip. Blood flowed freely from the wound. I reached for the compress and applied direct pressure. It only bled a few moments before slowing, and I wrapped the bandage around it to keep up the pressure. A long strip torn from my ruined pants made a sling, which I slipped over his head.

"When my uncle let me live in the cabin, I learned to take care of myself. I was just learning to hunt and survive, so I hurt myself a lot." I didn't tell him I'd only read about this surgery. I'd never actually performed it before.

I gave his shoulder a little pat. "Move it as little as possible as we go, and have Hugh look at it and your burns when we get back."

Mark didn't move to get up. I sat back, absently wiping my bloody hands on my thighs.

"Do you miss it? Do you miss your home?"

The question surprised me. I thought for a moment, staring at the dark forest around me, but not really seeing it. "No, I don't. I don't think about it much. It's like a dream, like it wasn't ever real. There wasn't much for me to look forward to. I had no marketable training to get me back into town, no skills except hunting. And there were no people at the cabin . . . ." I smiled slightly. "I've grown to like company." I paused as I took time to really consider the last few months. "I don't think I ever want to go back."

"You're not from Italy, are you?"

I was so wrapped up in my thoughts, the question did not seem strange to me. "No, I'm not from Italy."

I pulled myself out of my reverie. "We'd best be going. We've still the long way around to go back. Have you rested enough?"

Mark nodded. We picked up our gear and started back to the caves. We couldn't afford to let the foresters track us, so we took the hardest route, walking most of our way up streams to lose the scent, just in case they came after us with hounds. The waterways were very cold, and we were both miserable by the time the sun came up and we could rest again. At least the weather had started clearing, warming the chill out of our bodies.

It was mid-morning when we finally got back.

"You two look like hell," Much said by way of greeting as he stood from where he'd been waiting. "We saw your signal, but we didn't leave until just before dawn," he told us as we caught our breath and snatched hurried bites of the bread he offered. We hadn't eaten since the day before, and then only a few travel biscuits on the run—and I had spewed those. We gulped greedily at the water he supplied. "We saw the sky lit with fire and knew they'd be busy. How'd that start anyway?"

"The signal arrow landed in a dry field and set fire to it. It was a good diversion for our escape. I wouldn't have made it out of there if it hadn't been for Kay. She saved my life," Mark said.

My mouth dropped open. Mark had just spoken nice of me for the first time. I could hardly believe my ears.

Much noticed he had called me "she" and looked at me sharply. I shrugged. "Marian told him."

"Ah." Much smiled. "She would know then. But we've got to get going. If we hurry, we can catch up before lunch. We're to cover their trail. The sheriff will never know where we have gone!"

WE CAUGHT up with everyone closer to sunset. Mark and I had been too tired to keep up the pace Much had set, and it was hard to look for any small signs the larger group may have left that would give away our retreat.

The new camp was in a wide clearing near a hill, a stream running nearby. The others had arrived only half an hour ahead of us and were still setting up when we passed the newly established perimeter. Men assembled the dismantled tables and benches, organized gear, and erected a shelter for the sick. Someone had started cooking, and my mouth began to water insistently.

Before we could rest, though, Mark and I went to Robin to report.

"Robin?" I said. He turned to us, smiling.

That quickly faded when he took in our condition. "Well?"

"It went well," said Mark. "We had a little trouble getting out, but I doubt anybody there really knew what was going on. They thought I was Robin Hood." He shrugged, then winced.

"You're wounded," Robin observed. "Give me a full report after

Hugh looks you over. Better yet, tell the whole story at dinner . . . if you think you'll feel up to it."

"It's worth telling," Mark said wearily, then walked off.

Too tired to comment, I turned away, looking for Will Scarlet. I found him propped up against a tree, waiting for the shelter to be finished.

"Hello." I sat down next to him. "How are you feeling?"

"Still tired, but otherwise well." He coughed some and sniffled.

"And that is the normal aftereffect of being sick," I told him. "You'll get your strength back soon. How are the others?"

"Same as me mostly."

"Jack?" He was the one I most worried about.

"He was pretty bad along the way. Hugh thought we were going to lose him, but he pulled through all right."

The journey had been a dangerous one for the sick, but we'd been lucky. The move could have undone everything accomplished in the caves, and some of them could have died. Now we had to be careful none caught pneumonia.

"Good. The rain stopped before you left, didn't it? It wouldn't have done to get you rained on. We'd have more than just you five lying sick. How was the trip here?"

"Hellish," he said, then grinned weakly. "Come on. Tell me."

"Tell you what?" It almost took too much energy to tease.

"Tell me how it went with Mark."

"Well, it started like usual, with him doubting every word I said. He didn't even notice how I looked in skirts until Marian pointed it out to him. He was . . . surprised. Marian told us the information we'd come for, and we started to leave. I went out first, while Mark tried to get us a horse to throw off the trail." I paused, then decided I would tell him about my first kill later. "I waited for a while. When I wasn't sure if he was going to come out, I sent up the signal. Unfortunately, the arrow landed in a field, catching the whole thing on fire, and the guards sounded the alarm.

"Mark came racing out on a horse, but he got shot in the arm. I was shooting away at guards like crazy and killed at least two of them. Wounded more." I hesitated again. I sounded so damn flip. "Mark's horse spooked at the fire and threw him, and I had to drag him out of the flames. We took off into the forest, while the guards were too busy with the fire to notice. Then I fixed up Mark's arm." I looked at my scorched hands, which had started to ache on the way back. They had done so much. They had killed . . . .

"You saved his life?"

"I guess you could say that. Mark does." I turned my hands, noticing the stained flesh, the yellowed nails.

"It worked out well then." Will didn't seem to notice my preoccupation, or he was trying to take my mind off it.

"I think so, yes."

He laughed loudly. "What I'd have given to see Mark's face when Marian told him you're a woman!"

I smiled. "It was a sight. He looked like someone had poured water down his shirt while he tried to act like he didn't notice. He told me I sure had him fooled."

"Are you going to tell everyone now?" Will pushed himself more upright against the tree.

"I don't have to." I gestured vaguely. "You've just shouted it out loud enough for a few people to hear. By now, all of them know."

"Really?" Scarlet asked, looking around.

"Really. See how they all look over here, pointing and whispering to each other? Some are even laughing, saying 'I told you so.' And now, Robert is going to tell Robin." I watched as he waited patiently, then spoke when Robin turned to him. Robin laughed kindly, then I heard his answer.

"Yes, I've known, Robert. I've known from the start. Kay didn't want me to tell anyone until she had a chance to prove herself among us. Like she did yesterday. Now, finish with your duties and our dinner will come all the sooner. Then you can hear the whole story."

Robin had spoken so all could hear. Slowly, everyone went back to work.

Will put a hand on my leg. I had been staring dismally into the trees. "You've never killed before, have you?" I shook my head miserably. "It's never easy to justify to your conscience, but it was either them or all of us."

"But maybe they had family. Children. What about them? Maybe he *would have* had children . . . ." I faltered to a stop. What if

I had just killed some distant ancestor of mine? Or of someone important?

"You did what you had to do," Will insisted, completely unaware of the new dilemma I faced. "It helps to tell."

I looked down at the tips of my dirty and scuffed boots and bit my lip, then slowly told him about the guard I had killed—murdered—in cold blood.

He was silent for a little while, then gave my knee a squeeze. "It's a brutal world, Kay, but you did right. You can't think any differently. You did right!"

But I wondered what I had really done.

MARK WAS AN ACCOMPLISHED STORYTELLER, sharing our mission with so much enthusiasm, the drama seemed much greater than I knew it had been. I would have been happy if he had told the whole story, but he stopped at the point where he tried to get a horse, then left the rest to me.

I blushed when he told about my flirting with the guard. Everyone laughed. They thought it terribly funny that a woman pretending to be a man would be dressed in skirts and flirting with guards.

I appreciated the humor. When I told my bit about luring the one guard out, I took refuge in entertainment and clowned it out, standing up to swish nonexistent skirts, smiling like a street whore. My antics received much applause and laughter, which made telling the next part easier. When I pantomimed grabbing my knife to make the fatal thrust, many of the men pounded their knife butts on the table, signaling their approval.

When I finished telling about the fire and sat down, I heard many comments. I was surprised that none of the men referred to me as a boy anymore. They might have known I was female all along. Perhaps it was as Will had told me that summer. Many of them had guessed, and the rest just hadn't thought about it. I supposed I had proven my point. They now accepted me since I had shown them I was reliable.

I was still worried about Mark and his buddies, though. He

couldn't have forgotten he didn't trust me, that he'd wanted me gone more than once. It worried me, but there was nothing to do except wait and see.

Like waiting to see if my killing spree had changed the future.

Long after the rest of them had gone to sleep, I sat up next to Will, watching him sleep. I missed our late-night talks, as well as his companionship, and was more than ready for him to be well again. I needed his calmness and reason to lean against. I needed him.

In a moment of tenderness I would have never allowed myself had he been awake, I reached out and touched a strand of his hair, moving it off his forehead. I wasn't sure why I didn't tell him I wanted to be more than just friends. I didn't know how to show my interest, didn't know where to start so he wouldn't turn me away. It would have to be his move, his idea.

I allowed my finger to caress down the side of his face, following the line of his jaw. Will smiled in his sleep and stirred. As I gazed at him, he opened his eyes.

"Kay?" he said in a hoarse whisper. "You should sleep."

"I know, but I can't. At least not for a while. I'm too keyed up." I wanted to try to explain my fears to him, but I didn't know how to start.

Will turned over onto his back and looked up at the roof of the shelter. "It's been a hard winter," he said, his eyes slowly closing as he returned to sleep.

It's just as well, I thought, and stood to find the one man who already knew half of my dilemma.

Robin was asleep not far from us, Little John and Will Stutely lying on either side of him.

I crept up and laid my hand on Robin's shoulder. He woke instantly, quickly and silently drawing his knife.

"It's Kay," I whispered, shifting a half step back to avoid the swing.

"What is it?" he whispered, sheathing his knife.

"I need to talk to you. Can we go somewhere?"

Robin reached down to touch John's shoulder. "John. I'm going with Kay. I won't be gone long."

Little John grunted sleepily, but I could see his eyes wide open, staring at me. I gestured for Robin to follow.

We walked a short distance from the camp, then he pulled me to a stop. "What is it?"

"You're the only one who knows where I come from, Robin." I paced away from him, then back, hugging my arms around myself. "To tell you the truth, I'm scared."

"About what?" Robin sat down on a fallen log, and I joined him.

"Robin, I killed some men yesterday. I'd say three at least. What do you think will happen?"

"Well, you're a true outlaw now—"

"That's not what I mean. What will happen to me?"

"I'm afraid I don't follow you."

I stood up again, pacing back and forth in front of him. How could I keep this simple so he would understand? "I'm from the *future*, Robin. What if one of the men I killed is an ancestor of mine? What if I'm never born because of what I've done?"

Robin was silent for a few moments. "You're still here," he said at last.

It was my turn to think about that. "Yes . . . ," I said. "I suppose I would disappear in time if I had. But, then again, it would have never happened and I'd still be here." I shook my head. "It's a vicious, confusing loop."

"I won't pretend to understand what you're talking about, but I can see you are concerned." Robin watched me pace in front of him. "I will say it again. You're still here."

I frowned. "It must work itself out. But what if I have to kill again?"

"If you stay with us, you will." There was no doubt or hesitation in his reply, his tone underscored with a hardness I didn't understand.

I didn't answer, and after a moment he sighed. "All right. What are your alternatives?"

I had already thought along those lines and didn't like the conclusions. I remembered the appearance of the door. "I could go back to my own time," I said quietly.

"Do you want to do that?"

"No! I would have gone already if that's what I wanted. I'd rather die here." I shivered, remembering the door had almost summoned me through on its own.

"You could go to the city. You might be able to stay alive and out of trouble there."

"And wind up the wife of some dirty old man, pregnant and barefoot until the day I die in childbed? No thanks."

"Then it sounds to me like you'll have to stay here."

"It feels so selfish, Robin. But it's what I want to do."

"Do what feels right." He stood to put his hand on my shoulder. "Take time to decide. Remember . . . . If you stay here, you are allowed to change your mind." He smiled wryly. "After all, you are a woman."

I smiled half-heartedly. "That's true."

"Do you feel better?"

"No," I said miserably.

"You'll work it out." Robin patted my shoulder. "I'm going back before John comes looking for me."

"I just don't know," I mumbled.

It was a long time before I came back to the shelter. When I did, I was so tired I fell asleep as soon as I hit the blanket.

CHAPTER
EIGHT

A few nights later, Robin beckoned to me after dinner. I followed as he led me into the trees, far enough away to ensure privacy.

Choosing a large boulder, he climbed up and perched himself on top of it. He didn't invite me to join him, so I stood there, looking up slightly to see him against snow-heavy clouds in the dark sky.

"Well?" he said at last. "Have you come to a decision?"

"About leaving?" Robin nodded. I straightened my shoulders, resisting the urge to pace. "Not until this very moment." I'd been thinking about it since we had spoken last.

"And?" Robin prompted.

"I'm staying."

"With no reservations?"

I knew he meant my worries about killing more people. "Does it matter?" I asked, unwilling to commit to that one. The doubts still troubled me, but my conscience spoke even louder.

"Of course it matters. Answer," Robin snapped, sounding like the earl's son he was.

I stubbornly refused to be pinned down. "I can't say at this point."

"Well, you had better, Kay. I need to be sure where my people stand. I want to know I can count on you."

I stiffened under his censure. "You'll ask me to leave if I say I cannot kill for you?" I asked flatly. "That leaves me little choice."

"No. You may stay, as you have chosen. But until I have your word you will do whatever is necessary in your service to me and the brotherhood, I cannot put the brotherhood's trust in you."

"That's—" I bit my tongue, thinking this through. I had been about to decry his words as unfair, but I realized they were the words of a leader concerned for the welfare of all his people. He could not, in good conscience, send a member out who was not willing to toe the line, to do whatever necessary.

I looked up at Robin's silhouette. "I see."

"And?"

I began pacing, feeling trapped. My mind raced along the tracks it had worn in the last few days until it suddenly clicked. I stopped pacing and stood, staring at Robin. It was all so clear now.

I had debated the morality of the issue, debated the future consequences of the actions I took in this past. But I had ignored the fact of the matter.

"Out there," I whispered, "when my life was in danger, I did not hesitate. When Mark was in danger, I did not pause. Self-preservation is a compelling master, isn't it?"

Robin didn't answer and I wasn't sure he heard me. I strode to the base of his rock to grasp his foot. I was waxing dramatic and I knew it, but this was a very dramatic revelation for me.

"My word is given, Robin. My conscience and existence are yours to command. Why did I think I could control my destiny? I am at the mercy of the fickle universe, as always."

"Eh?"

I laughed, giving Robin's foot a shake before letting go. I felt free of the burden I had carried since my arrival. I no longer cared about the future. I wasn't there. I was *here!*

"Count on me, Robin. I will not fail you."

SPRING WAS JUST STARTING to get warmer when things came to a head between Robin and Mark.

Mark and I had been observing a truce. Sure, he no longer

accused me of petty deceit, as he had all winter, but he gave no other indication as far as friendship went. He basically ignored me, which I found preferable to his persecution. But he ignored everybody, making me wonder if this was the calm before some storm.

It was a cold, sunny day when the storm finally hit. We had seen foresters too close for comfort, so Robin had ordered that no one except the watch leave camp for a few days, at least until we were sure they were gone.

Those days, hiding days, were the worst. We had to remain half-hidden the entire day—silent, listening for that special woodcock's call telling us someone was coming. Those days were tense. Worse, they were boring.

I was blending in with the scenery, doing nothing with the arrow in my hands, when I saw Mark stalk past me carrying his bow, his face an angry mask. I sat up, watching him. He wore a sword, too, as he headed out of the clearing.

Alexander of Grimsby appeared out of the foliage, holding up a hand to stop him. Frederick of York appeared, too. They exchanged words I couldn't hear, then Mark pushed Alexander. Frederick and Alexander both grabbed him before he could leave the clearing.

I got up silently to find Robin, located him in the improvised shelter, and beckoned for him to follow. We got back just in time to see Mark belt Alexander in the chin, knocking him to the ground. Frederick was already down, shaking his head.

"Mark!" Robin's voice was loud in the quiet. Mark turned slowly, his fists clenched. "What are you doing?"

"I'm going hunting," he said through gritted teeth.

"Mark—"

"I've had enough of you and your silly rules. I'll do as I please."

"You'll die at it then. There are foresters out there."

"Let them find me. I'll show them what a real yeoman can do! What an outlaw *should* do!" He lifted his bow and shook it. "Let them come! I'm no coward!"

"Who here is a coward?" Robin's tone was dangerous, his eyes lit with fire.

This is it, I thought.

"Anyone who sits here waiting for the foresters to come. I say we go out and find *them*!"

The clearing was perfectly silent. Mark and Robin locked stares, like they had so many times before. This time, Mark wasn't backing down. Both had a hand on the hilt of their sword. Mark had dropped his bow and quiver.

"Are you a coward, Robin Hood?" Mark whispered, venomous. Robin's knuckles whitened on his sword hilt, and I backed up a pace. "Are you a coward?!" Mark shouted.

Faster than the eye could follow, swords were out, just as a watcher gave a double warning.

Silence fell in the forest as the echoes of the warning faded in the air. Everyone present knew it meant a forester was near enough to hear Mark's shout.

"Stutely," Robin ground out. Will stepped forward. "Take some men. Stop that forester and anyone else he might be with. Stop them, then lose them." He hadn't taken his eyes off Mark. They stared at each other, like wolves with their hackles up.

Will pointed to seven men. They sped silently into the forest in the direction the warning had come from.

I stood back, watching as Mark stepped forward, determined to let nothing stop him.

He took another step, then they were fighting, hell-bent for steel on steel. Fast, hard, precise. It was hard to say who attacked whom.

They came to a deadlock, their swords crossed before their faces, legs braced, muscles straining.

"I'll put an end to this," Mark said through a fierce grimace, "when you're dead!"

"And if I win?" Robin asked curiously, as if it were merely a wrestling match or a game of dice.

"If you win," said Mark, straining harder. "*If* you win, I forfeit all."

"Done."

Quick as that, the deadlock broke and they started hacking again, harder than before. The stakes were set. Each had a lot to lose, but from the first moment, Mark never stood a chance. Robin beat him down with such intense force, it was all he could do to defend himself. Once again, Robin demonstrated his superior skill with weapons.

In the end, Mark lay on his back, disarmed, Robin's sword at his throat.

"Well?" Robin demanded.

Mark panted, breathless. "I forfeit." It was all he could manage.

"Swear that."

"I swear," Mark ground out.

"Good. From now on, you watch what you say and how you say it. You follow my rules, or by Saint Mary, I'll send you straight to Nottingham and we'll see how you fare with the foresters then." Robin whipped his sword away and sheathed it. "Don't forget. You brought this on yourself."

I saw the restraint he practiced in walking away. Mark had been a thorn in his side, and most of the outlaws would not have faulted Robin for killing him.

No one approached Mark where he lay catching his breath. No one wanted to associate themselves with what he had just done. After a long moment, he wiped at the blood on his cheek, a scratch compared to the wound that had cost him the fight. Cautiously, I advanced.

"Mark," I said softly and knelt next to him. "Your stomach . . . ." Blood slowly oozed from a long, shallow gash, precisely delivered so it wouldn't kill.

"I know," he whispered. "It hurts."

"I'll get Hugh."

LATER, after he was bandaged up, Mark asked me to stay when Hugh took his leave.

"Thank you for helping me." He gestured after Hugh's retreating form, then dropped his hand into his lap, shaking his head. "That was the single-most stupid thing I've ever done in my life. Robin was right. I brought it on myself."

"You did," I agreed, "but you would be a bigger fool if you didn't learn a lesson from it."

"I did," he said bitterly. "There's a reason Robin is our leader. He's the best, but I thought I could beat him." Mark rubbed his thumb against his fingers, and I knew he was remembering his initiation. "I swore an oath to him . . . two now. If I break this second one, I'll forfeit more than I did today."

LATE THAT NIGHT, Will Stutely and his seven men returned, dead tired, but successful. They had found and killed the foresters, three of them altogether, and "lost" them in another part of the forest. Even so, Robin ordered us to move once again.

Just as the spring rains started in earnest, we moved back to the spot we had camped in when I first joined. It was a good site, close to the river, with the cave and roads within a quarter day's walk, but not close enough to worry about accidental discovery. So far, it was still a secret.

I found England to be like Oregon. There were a half-dozen mini-seasons, and most included rain. Summer rain came and went in fits and storms. Then there was fall rain, which came out of the blue, then moved into the gray perpetual drizzle of late fall and winter. Spring rain ramped up into a proper deluge before one or two clear days signaled the beginning of summer, when the cycle started again.

I walked around in a bleary-eyed daze, unable to get much sleep. What sleep I got was uncomfortably cramped beneath a leather skin, crouched between the roots of an ancient oak. In the spring, the oak tree was an outlaw's greatest friend.

No one got much sleep in the spring. Even the hardest sleepers were miserable. No one wanted to lay in three inches of moldy-smelling mud or on soaked moss, so many men took refuge in the trees. Many men *fell out* of the trees, too, suffering sprained wrists, ankles, and one broken arm. We all missed the comparatively dry caves, but there was no hope of returning there.

The sheriff had put the pieces together and figured out why Robin Hood would come into the city, then light a signal when he left again. He had sent men to the caves, where they found signs of recent fires.

Word was now out, too, that there was a woman in Sherwood Forest. The sheriff had put the fear of his wrath into the women at the clothiers, trying to find out more about me.

Of course, there was nothing there for him to learn.

We spent most of the spring with colds and heavy heads from little sleep and general boredom. When Much came by and asked if I wanted to go hunting with him in the morning, I leapt at the chance. Anything was better than watching raindrops fall through the leaves.

During the night, the weather finally broke.

Much roused me about two hours before dawn. We got some food and ate quickly. No one else was up and moving.

"Anyone else coming?" I asked, shouldering my quiver.

"No. It's just the two of us." Much checked his arrows before clipping his quiver to his waist.

"Who's going to carry the beast back if we get one?" I asked. On all the other hunting trips I had been on, there had always been at least four of us to carry the deer.

"I will," he said, heading out from the camp.

"Whatever you say." I shook my head, figuring he was just expecting not to kill anything.

We trekked across the forest until the sun peeked up over a wonderfully cloudless horizon. Much spotted fresh sign, so we began to stalk what I gathered was a very large herd. I nocked an arrow to my bow, ready, and concentrated on being as quiet as I could. We moved very slowly, following the trail.

Much held up his hand for me to stop, pointing to our left. I saw some brown-red backs through the trees. Much tested the wind, signaling me to circle to the right of them to stay downwind.

Eventually, we positioned ourselves some thirty yards away from the herd grazing peacefully on the short spring grass in the tiny woodland meadow. Much gestured at me to take the first shot.

I picked out a good-sized buck and pointed him out to Much. He nodded in agreement.

Patiently, I watched for a clear shot. The beast moved from showing me its ass to quartering away, giving me a target. I loosed the arrow at its heart. True to my aim, it lodged in the buck's side. Much's arrow flew half a second later, striking it in the hind leg, which should have disabled it.

The buck bellowed and bolted for the shade across the meadow, and the rest of the herd scattered.

I readied for another shot, but the only target I had was its tail. I lowered my bow.

The buck reached the trees and disappeared. I was all set to run after it, but remembered myself as Much walked across the clearing to begin tracking. I followed so I wouldn't disturb any sign.

Much was an accomplished tracker. Half an hour later, we found the animal lying in a patch of sunlight, its legs collapsed beneath it. Much kicked it in the flank to make sure it was dead. The rack that beast carried could easily kill one or both of us.

Much stripped off his shirt and tossed it to me to keep it from getting bloody, then went to work gutting it, while I kept an arrow nocked and an eye open for foresters. Now was the time we were most vulnerable. We weren't on the move and were alone.

Using rocks and deadfall branches at its shoulders and hips, Much propped the animal on its back to expose the belly. I glanced down, noticing his handiwork, then trained my eyes on the forest again. I knew how to gut a deer.

A few minutes later, he was done, a steaming pile of offal beside the carcass betraying what had gone on here.

"Right," he said. "Let's get this beastie home before he spoils in his skin."

I nodded and put my arrow back into my quiver, looking around for a stout branch to use for a carrying sling.

Much didn't bother waiting. He lifted the carcass onto his bare shoulders and started back to camp. Astounded, I followed. That buck was one hundred fifty pounds if it was an ounce, yet he carried it with ease.

We had only been walking for about fifteen minutes before both Much and I stopped abruptly. A forester sat in a tree up ahead, looking to the far left of us. We stood still, watching.

Much quietly set his load down and picked up a stone. He motioned me to stay where I was while he crept up on the man. I watched, alert for danger. Drawing back his arm, Much hurled the stone, striking the man in the back of the head and knocking him out of the tree.

Another forester darted out from behind the tree and I ran after him.

Ten months of living in Sherwood had given me a lithe body. I could run like the wind. Faster if I didn't worry about noise. I caught up with the man and tackled him, sending us both crashing headlong to the ground.

I hauled him up to his knees, keeping his face away from mine. My knife was out and at his neck. "Tell anyone what you've seen, you're a dead man. Got it?"

He nodded, shaking with more than adrenaline. He was fast, but not fast enough, and he was scared. I thumped him hard on the back of the head with the hilt of my knife and let him fall, unconscious. We were far enough away from camp to leave him. There was sure to be a search of the area, and we would have to post extra guards, but I thought he would be out long enough for us to get away.

I ran back to where Much was picking up the deer. "I took care of the other one," I told him, resting my hands on my knees as I caught my breath.

"You didn't kill him, did you?"

"Nah, just put the fear of outlaws in him." I grinned.

Much laughed. "Good."

Half an hour later, we stopped by the river to rest and wash up. After putting the deer in the cool shade, we lazed in the spring sunshine we hadn't enjoyed in so long, taking a pleasant precaution to make sure we weren't followed.

It was near supper by the time we got back to the camp. Much sent me to fetch some rope from his pack while he deposited the deer beside a tree just outside the clearing. On my way, I saw Robin talking with a stranger in a corner of the clearing. Little John, Will Stutely and Will Scarlet were with him.

I returned to Much, casting another glance at the stranger before helping hang the deer. When we got it up, Much began to skin it.

I looked at the stranger again. He was in his late teens, dark and handsome. There was a look of sorrow about him that cast a shadow over his features, despite his agitation. He waved his arms around dramatically. Though I couldn't hear what he said, I could see Robin wasn't happy about it.

When Frederick of York walked up, I asked him who Robin was talking to.

"I don't know," he said, shrugging with mild curiosity. "Scarlet and Little John brought him in hours ago, the boy crying like a maid. Robin's been arguing with him, Little John, and Scarlet since he got here. By the look on his face, I don't think Robin likes whatever it is they have in mind."

Stephen of the Norfolk came up behind Frederick, his eyes bright with excitement. "That's Alan a Dale, the sweetest voice in England. Maybe he will stay and sing for us tonight." He abruptly turned to go. "Come on, Frederick. Let's get the table going. I can't wait for dinner!"

"Alan a Dale," I whispered, remembering an amusing story about him. "This should prove very interesting," I said aloud, crossing my arms and rocking back on my heels.

"What's that?" Much asked.

I turned to help him with the deer, but he was already done. The skin lay in a heap beneath the carcass, and Much was cleaning the last scraps from inside the body cavity. I helped him put the burlap cover over the carcass and hang it higher in the tree. It would cure there for a few days.

"I asked if I could have the skin," I lied. "I could use a new pair of boots." I didn't want to spoil this by having to explain it, and I certainly didn't want Much to ask any awkward questions I couldn't answer.

I noticed Malcolm, one of the widow's sons and our resident tanner, working over near Robin. Gathering up the deer hide, I wandered over to give it to him, then casually edged closer to hear what was going on. Some of the others obviously had the same idea because that corner of the clearing started getting suspiciously crowded with nonchalant men trying to listen in.

"Don't worry," I heard Robin say. "We'll stop the baron from stealing your sweetheart, then perhaps have a wedding of our own. Meantime, stay and sup with us. The wedding is three days from now, yes?" Alan a Dale nodded. "That's not much time." Robin frowned, scratching his beard. "We'll have to work out the details."

"We'll need a friar if we are to have a wedding," Stutely said. "I don't imagine the bishop will oblige us."

"I doubt the bishop will be in the mood," Robin agreed, "but I don't know of any friars who would do this for us, either."

I looked at Scarlet, smiling. He would speak up, then the plot would be set in motion.

"I know of a friar," said Scarlet, glancing at me. "One who would marry a couple such as Alan and his lady." Robin raised his eyebrow, and Will squirmed a little. I knew he had never told Robin of his contact in the outside world, a contact who might have proved useful before this day. Will looked down at his feet. "Some call him the Abbot of Fountain Abbey. It's not half a day from here."

Robin glared at Will for a moment, his jaw working in agitation. Then he stood, decisive. "Then tomorrow, we're off to Fountain Abbey."

Alan a Dale sang for us that evening, a love song designed to tug at the listeners' heart. Out of the corner of my eye, I watched Will until I saw him glance my way. Blushing, I looked back at Alan. When Will caught my eye later in the song and winked at me, I felt the blood rising to my cheeks again.

After the song faded wistfully into silence, Alan played folk songs everyone knew. The forest was soon full of men's rough voices, cavorting bodies, and the playing of a lute.

In the morning, Robin, Little John, Stutely, Scarlet, and I set off for Fountain Abbey. I had to see this unfold for two reasons— because it was amusing and because it was a test of the stories I had grown up with. It would be good to know how accurate I could expect to be.

When I had asked Robin if I could go, he reluctantly agreed. It was hard to convince him to take the risk of this rescue in the first place, and he didn't want to risk any extra men.

Scarlet led the way. Promising to stay out of trouble, I brought up the rear, walking carefully on moss, rocks, and tree roots. As the end of the column, it was my responsibility to watch for and erase any clues of our passage.

We were almost there when Robin called for a rest. We had joined a road a few miles back, and Will told us that around the next corner was a ford, the Abbey beyond that.

Robin looked at John and Stutely, catching both in a yawn.

"Why don't all of you wait here? I'll come back with the friar. I can see Little John is too tired to continue." He grinned at John.

"But Robin," began Scarlet, "you don't—"

"Wait here." Robin turned and walked on, turning the corner in the road.

I started to follow, but Scarlet grabbed me by the collar.

"Where do you think you're going?" he asked.

"I want to watch," I said, sounding like a child.

"Watch what?" Will pulled me off the road and into the tall grass, where the others already rested.

"Watch what happens, of course."

"Look, Kay, Robin told us to wait here, so here we wait."

"Look, Scarlet," I said, dislodging his hand from my collar. "You know this friar, and I know *of* him. What if Brother Tuck is not at his holy dwelling? Perhaps he's at this ford having a holy picnic. And knowing our master's dislike for getting himself wet, how much would you wager Robin Hood will learn an interesting lesson before the holy man is through?"

Will thought for a moment. "If Tuck is at the ford, what you say may happen. What are your odds?"

"Given Brother Tuck's eating habits and his love for nature, I think they're better than three to six in ten, depending on which side of the river Tuck is on. Shall we go see?"

Will grinned. "I lay odds you're wrong. Let's go see." He turned to Little John and Stutely. "Kay and I are going ahead."

Little John had already stretched out in the sunshine, and Stutely, sitting next to him, nodded. Both had eaten too well, stayed up too late, played too hard at the feast last night, and had complained about having to get up so early this morning. They weren't above making use of any excuse for a nap.

Scarlet and I crept up through the trees to the ford. We heard the commotion long before we saw it. I turned to Will with a smile. "Change your odds?"

CHAPTER

NINE

The river flowed cheerfully over the cobbles of the ford, and the sun shone on the small clearing where the road entered the water. The warm breeze toyed with the grass and the branches of the trees. On the near side of the river, a blanket with a half-eaten picnic lunch lay spread beneath a shivering willow. A raven in the distance called to her mate perched on a branch above the meal.

Two men, one clinging to the other's back, were mid-stream, crossing the ford—Robin Hood and a man in brown breeches, a green tunic belted around his ample middle.

Robin struggled to carry the very large man across the river, loudly swearing at the slippery stones in the water. From where Will and I watched, crouched amid the bushes just downstream from the ford, I choked, nearly laughing aloud.

"What's going on?" Will asked, trying to get a look at the other man's face.

"Well, I suspect that our Robin opened his mouth too far," I said. "Look over there. It appears this gentleman was eating his lunch beneath the willow tree. It does look like a lovely place to have a picnic. I would imagine Robin asked the gentleman to carry him across the river." The situation was by no means this clear, but I had a slight advantage.

"Then why is Robin carrying him back?" Will was perplexed,

though he smiled at the sight. The large man and his unlikely mount had almost reached the near bank.

"He's a big fellow. I'd wager he persuaded Robin to offer."

When the man clambered down off Robin's back, Will recognized the friar. "Tuck!" He turned to me. "How'd you know?" I shrugged, but Will insisted. "No. Tell me. How did you know Tuck would be at the ford?"

"I'll tell you later. Watch."

Robin managed to slip the friar's sword free from its sheath, liberating it as he let him down to the ground. Now he turned his own sword on Tuck. Words were spoken, though with Robin's back to us, we couldn't hear him over the babbling of the water. Tuck shrugged, holding out his hand. I was surprised to see Robin return his sword. Then Tuck turned his back to Robin, who clambered up. They began to cross the river once again.

Midway across, Tuck launched Robin off his back, throwing him into the water. The friar took out his own sword and smote Robin's buttocks with the flat of it as he struggled in the water.

His face flushed, Scarlet started to get up, but I held him back. "You know Tuck won't harm him."

We watched Robin try to regain his footing in the river, his arms flailing to ward off Tuck's blows. It was easy to see Tuck was playing with him, and it was such a comical sight, we were soon holding our sides, trying not to burst out laughing. We didn't want to embarrass Robin, but it was so rare to see him beaten, we couldn't help it.

After several moments, Robin regained his footing and began to fight back, but was still taking a beating.

Before too long, Tuck had knocked Robin into the water again. He came up sputtering and empty-handed, having dropped his sword.

"I'm afraid you have me at a disadvantage," I heard him say. He pushed his dripping hair from his eyes, watching Tuck carefully. "If you would give me leave to blow upon this horn at my waist, I would yield myself to your mercy."

Tuck nodded. I thought I saw a smile on his lips, but I wasn't sure at this distance. "Do what you will, and I will, as well."

Robin took up his hunting horn, tugging hard at the wet leather to free it from his belt. He shook the water from it, then blew.

Three soggy blasts sent spray into the air, and I nearly choked on a new fit of laughter.

Will started forward, but I held him back again. "Wait for Stutely and Little John," I said, biting back a laugh. "If Robin knows we have been watching—"

Just then, the Abbot of Fountain Abbey blew upon a wooden pipe that produced a shrill whistle.

We waited until Will Stutely and Little John came around the corner before we walked out of the trees. At the same moment, four very large wolfhounds leapt into sight on the opposite bank and splashed across the river to crouch in front of each of us, ready to attack. Will Stutely had his bow stretched taut, ready to loose at the dog before him.

"Beauty!" Scarlet said, kneeling to pet the dog in front of him. "How kind of you to come and greet us." Beauty wagged her tail. "But your master, it seems, has no such respect for *our* master. He has dunked him in the river!"

"Will Scarlet!" shouted Tuck, splashing across the stream past a shocked Robin to give Will a great bear hug.

Robin fished his sword out of the river and came up onto the bank.

Tuck turned to Robin. "If I had known you were Robin Hood, I wouldn't have done you such an ill turn, my son."

"Aye, but it was my own arrogance led you to it, friar. I beg your forgiveness." Robin removed his soggy cap with a bow.

Tuck gave a great shout of laughter. "You have it, Robin Hood. You have it."

Robin turned to Scarlet with a wry smile. "*This* is your Abbot?"

Will grinned. "Aye, Robin. He's sometimes called the Abbot of Fountain Abbey. More often, he's just called plain Tuck."

Tuck laughed, giving a short whistle. His great dogs backed off and came over to greet Will, tails swinging.

Will Stutely let his bow slack, a puzzled look on his face. He reacted swiftly to danger, but if the situation changed suddenly, like it did here, he had difficulty switching gears. He was a strong, loyal and vicious fighting man. He just couldn't catch on so quickly that the crisis was over.

Little John grinned. He could appreciate the humor in this situation. He knew well how Robin's quick temper could get him into trouble.

Robin began to explain why we had come to Fountain Abbey.

I took Scarlet aside a moment. "Didn't I tell you there would be something to see today?"

Will smiled. "Aye, but only Robin tells the story, right?"

"Aye," I agreed easily. "But he'll have some explaining to do to Little John and Will."

"As I recall, *you've* got some explaining to do to *me*." He fixed me with a stern glare.

"Later. We'll be too busy for a while, and the telling will take time."

Friar Tuck shouted in dismay and began lumbering toward his picnic, waving his massive arms. "My lunch! Lord bless all ravens! Shoo, you feathered scavengers!"

WITH NO LITTLE frustration on my part, I went on guard duty while plans were made for the rescue. I tried to find someone to take my shift, without success. Everyone wanted to be in camp to hear about this unusual event. I spent my hours in a tree wondering if I would get to go along.

Very early the next morning, twenty-five men in various disguises left camp and headed for Nottingham, where the wedding was to be held the next day.

Robin posted extra guards, including me. As much as I had wanted to go, I knew better than to protest his orders. At least I didn't have to cook. Anyone who wasn't on guard duty or with the raid was assigned to prepare a feast fit for heroes and King Richard himself.

The first day, things were normal. We didn't expect trouble until the next day, though we were ready for it.

Sitting in a tree waiting for something, anything, to happen, I thought about what I knew of this story, again wishing I could take part in it. Would it ever seem more than a story to me if I didn't participate in it?

The plan was for Robin and the others to attack while everyone was in the church. Then, using Tuck as the religious official, marry Alan to his lady right there. It seemed easy enough in theory, but I couldn't count all the things that could go wrong. Anything from not being able to get into the city to Ellen not wanting to marry Alan. How I wished I were there to see how it came out. Just because I knew the legend didn't mean it would really be the same.

Maybe I wasn't *meant* to go on this mission. I had decided not to care if history changed because of my presence here, but I still had to wonder if there wasn't a reason. Maybe it was my destiny to change history. But did I really believe in destiny? I never had. At least not in mine. How else could I explain the fact that I was here, though?

How could I find out why I was here when I sat in a tree while all the action went on elsewhere? All I could do was sit and wonder . . . and worry. I had a good idea how it would turn out, but it was impossible to really know. What if Robin and the others didn't make it back?

And what was I going to tell Will? I had to go and open my mouth to show that I knew something, to show off. How was I going to put him off when I had dropped a mystery right in his lap?

I hoped he would just forget the whole thing because if he asked, the story might just slip out, and somehow, that didn't seem like a very good thing.

After three days, which I spent in a tree with only short relief breaks, everything was ready back in camp. We had even brought women—"town girls," as Patrick called them—from Lincoln to help cook and entertain. The food was waiting for the fire and the women were getting antsy.

It was taking far too long. I started worrying the worst had happened when, finally, the first of the "wedding party" began coming back. We pieced together the story as small groups of men arrived and gave their report.

There had been a skirmish and pursuit, so they had split into several groups to make their way back to camp. Everyone made it, most injuries only minor scrapes and bruises, three with serious wounds. Not bad for tweaking the sheriff's nose in his own city.

Robin posted a double perimeter of guards on short shifts, but the rest of us were free to celebrate with the newlyweds.

The clearing was a merry sight. Charles of Watford had put up colorful wreaths of flowers, and the torches, though few, danced brightly. The trestle table was decked out with dozens of wildflowers. The town girls, gaily dressed in their best rags, wildflower garlands in their hair, whooped with excitement, grabbing the nearest outlaw for spontaneous turns of wild dancing.

Mouthwatering smells wafted on the air as the breads, venison, vegetables, and fish began cooking. Men laughed, dancing and jesting. Some of them wrestled, while Jonathan of Derby organized an archery match.

I joined in on the archery and did a bit of showing off. My accuracy had improved, so I seldom missed.

Eventually, though, I lost to Edward the Red when my shot flew wide in a fickle breeze. I surrendered to him, then sat next to Mark at the table. There was usually some room between him and the other men now.

"That was some fine shooting," he said.

"Thank you." I stretched my taut arm muscles in front of me.

"You've improved a lot since you came to us."

I chuckled. "I've done a lot of practicing. Scarlet and Much have helped."

We sat quietly for a while, watching Little John and Tuck wrestle. It was a fair match, but it looked like Tuck was winning.

"I'd like to hunt with you," Mark said, breaking the silence.

Surprised, I turned to look at him. He had been so different since spring. "You would? Why?"

Tuck gave a mighty groan and heaved Little John, head first, to the ground, flipping him onto his back and pinning him. John flailed but couldn't get up. Reginald O'Keefe, who was referee, called the match to Tuck.

"Because I want to," said Mark. "I mean, I feel like I should . . . I guess I'd like you to forgive me." He spoke the last in a rush, as though saying it faster would make it less awkward for him to admit. At any rate, his admission made *me* uncomfortable.

"Mark, there's nothing to forgive. You could have had me laughed out of Sherwood, but you didn't." A cup of ale appeared in front of me. Looking up, I thanked Henry of Stafford, whom I had bested in the archery match. I looked back at Mark. "When shall we hunt?"

"Soon," he said with a smile. "We'll hunt soon."

When the food was ready, everyone came to the table. Alan and Ellen sat side by side at the head of the table, Robin having surrendered his place to our guests of honor.

Before the women served the food, Robin lifted his cup. "To the bride and groom," he said. "May you live a long and happy life together!"

"So be it!" Little John shouted.

Everyone raised their voices to cheer, "So be it!"

LATER THAT NIGHT, Will and I sat the fire watch together, as had become our custom. After giving me a brief outline of the events at the wedding, he looked at me pointedly. "Is now the time to explain?"

I nodded. The moment I laid eyes on him when they returned, I knew he had not forgotten the promise I'd made. My heart sank when he voiced the question I had seen in his eyes all night.

"Good, because it's been driving me to distraction. How did you know what would happen down at the ford?"

"I read about it," I said casually, careful not to look at him. I didn't know what his reaction would be, but I couldn't make up a story about witches or angels or whatever.

"You . . . *read* about it?" he echoed, not willing to believe that. "Where? In the stars? Are you some kind of fortune teller?"

"Not exactly." I turned to look at him. "Let me tell you the whole story. I've only told Robin. Now I'm telling you, but it can't go any further. You'll understand when I tell you."

"What?" he asked impatiently.

"Will . . . ." I screwed up my courage. "I'm from the future. Your future." I winced, ready for an outburst.

"What?!" he exclaimed, not sure if he should be angry with me for playing him for a fool. His jaw worked, but he didn't say anything more.

"It's true," I said quickly. "Unbelievable, impossible, but true nonetheless. When I was a child, I read stories about Robin Hood. He was a legend. He was history. What happened with Friar Tuck at the ford was a story I read, so I knew how it would go." I paused. He shook his head, as though trying to deny it. I lifted a hand to gesture at the night surrounding us, wanting to make him believe, but not knowing how. "Sometimes this all seems like a dream to me, but no matter how often I pinch myself, I'm still here. I'm still living with my childhood heroes. I've even read about you, Will Scathelock."

Will looked at me keenly. "No one here but Robin and Mark know my real name. Christ . . . that's what you meant at Mid-Summer. I told you my name, and you said 'of course,' like you should have known. I never knew what you meant. But you're saying you know about all of it!"

"Not all, Will. Listen. In all the stories I read, there were no women with Robin Hood. And you know how you men exaggerate. The stories I read were blown way up, like all of you are superhuman. Something I think I know could turn out to be completely wrong."

Will wasn't listening. "Tell me what—"

"No, Will." I held up my hands, determined not to be the fortune teller. "You don't really want to know, do you?"

He thought a moment. "No, I guess I don't. Robin believes you?"

"Yes."

"Well, talk to me." He touched my shoulder hesitantly. "Make a believer out of me."

We talked late into the night about my world. My world that seemed less real now. It felt more like my childhood was the dream and this was the only reality.

I was surprised at how much I had to fight to remember.

I WENT hunting with Mark a few weeks later, but we had a luckless day of it. We didn't even see a deer, much less bring one down. We gave up at noon and spent the rest of the day sitting beside a small stream, talking.

I told him about my home—what it had been like, how I was raised. He talked about his own upbringing, his companionship with Will and how he had been outlawed.

"I've always been a troublemaker," he told me. "Always seeing how much I could get away with. I took it upon myself to bed one of the master's daughters . . . Will's sister. This was while Will was in Palestine. She was young, and she liked it at first. But then she started to think about marriage, and not to me. She had a fine young gentleman, a rich Norman's son, courting her. I had nothing to offer, but I wouldn't leave her alone. She told her father. Not the truth, I'm sure, but whatever she told him put him in a fine rage. I don't think she expected him to react the way he did, though. She wasn't a spiteful girl, just naïve.

"They took me in on false charges and sentenced me to hang, but I escaped. It wasn't the first time I'd been locked up, mostly for trivial things, so I knew how to get out. It was a game before, but this time I couldn't go back, so I went into the forest with some harebrained idea about making a living as a thief.

"About this time, Robin Hood was outlawed. I was making a bad job of thieving, so when I heard of this nobleman's son starting a gang of outlaws, I thought I'd join up." Mark paused thoughtfully.

"I've never been one to try for sainthood. I'm not a good person or a hero, but it feels good to do something to battle against the system I fought so hard . . . just in the wrong way. I fought against Robin, too, for a while. You were witness to that. I guess I thought he was doing it all wrong." Mark shook his head and laughed. "I was the one who was wrong, thinking I could shame Robin into doing it my way. But this life suits me." Mark gave me a wicked grin. "I make a good knave, don't you think?"

IT WAS A FRUITLESS HUNT, but both of us had been so caught up in telling our stories, it was getting dark by the time we passed the perimeter guards, eager for some food to fill our hungry bellies.

When we reached camp, everyone had already finished eating, so we snatched a bite and sat down with the rest.

It was then I noticed some people were gone. I couldn't see

Little John, Will Scarlet, or Alan a Dale. Ellen sat by herself at the head of the table, nibbling on some bread. That was strange, given the two lovebirds had rarely parted since the wedding. They were supposed to be leaving in two days to live with a cousin of Alan's down in Somerset.

Robin was nowhere to be seen, either.

When I saw Much serving wine, I grabbed his arm as he passed to ask what was going on.

"Robin's gone to London," he said, excited. "Geoffrey found a page wandering the road come from Queen Eleanor herself. She wants him, John, and Scarlet to shoot in the King's Royal Archery Tournament. Alan went, too." I let go of him and he continued. "Robin was looking for you before he left, but he couldn't wait—" Someone hollered at Much to bring around the wine, and he moved on.

Of course, I knew Robin had to go, but no matter how I searched my memories, I couldn't think of how that story turned out. Perhaps it was just as well I hadn't been there to advise him. I shivered with an eerie premonition.

"What's wrong?" asked Mark. My eyes had gone tunnel vision, and I couldn't see him.

"Nothing." I suppressed another shiver. "A gray goose just flew over my grave." I couldn't remember a thing about this, but I wasn't worried about Robin as much as I was the others. Robin lived. The stories went on. But I couldn't remember about Will. I couldn't remember, and there was nothing I could do.

"I AM YOUR HUMBLE SERVANT, *my Queen.*"

The voice echoed into stillness as I sat up, the rain on my face bringing me swiftly out of sleep. Frowning, I tried to catch hold of the dream, but it slipped from my thoughts. Only those last words stayed in my mind.

I stretched away the last clinging strands of sleep and looked around. It was very early in the morning—the sun was far from rising—and only the watch was awake. The rain misted down, muffling the familiar background into wet obscurity.

Robin, Will, and the others had been gone for two weeks. I had a feeling something wasn't right, but I couldn't put my finger on why or explain the feeling. I didn't understand how I could think I knew when my memory of this story still eluded me.

With a sense of dread, I was afraid I would have no explanation for a long while.

The night before, Mark noticed I was upset and had thought hunting this morning would take my mind off my worries. It was as good a diversion as any.

After stowing my gear against the rain, I went to wake Mark but stopped, my hand arrested above his shoulder. He looked different in sleep, lifeless, perhaps because I couldn't see his eyes. When they were open, his eyes were a telling blue—the mark of his Saxon heritage—which stood out vibrantly against his dark features. When they were closed, he appeared to be dead.

I shrugged off the spooky sense of premonition and shook him by the shoulder. He sighed a little in his sleep, then rolled over.

"Kay?" he muttered. "What is it?"

"Time to get up. We might as well get an early start." I felt a little guilty about waking him when he was sleeping so well, but the deed was done.

Mark nodded sleepily and got up, packing his things away against the rain. I went back to my blanket to buckle on my sword —the sword I had gained for myself when Mark and I had gone to Nottingham. I uncovered my bow and quiver of arrows, then met Mark at the cave.

"By the saints, Kay. You didn't tell me it was this early." He gave me a glare, along with some of the food he'd brought.

I shrugged slightly. "You would have been up soon with the rain anyway."

He yawned mightily. "I suppose. I sure couldn't get back to sleep now."

I told the man on fire watch we were leaving to go hunting. He nodded sleepily, so I told him to either stay awake or wake someone to relieve him.

We headed west. After about ten minutes of walking in the rain, the weather broke and a morning moon shone down between the clouds to light our way.

It wasn't long before we stumbled, quite by accident, upon a herd of sleeping deer. We were crosswind, so some of them began to stir as they scented us. I had an arrow nocked and signaled Mark as a fair-sized doe stood. She had no fawn, as far as I could see, so I shot. The arrow pierced her through the neck, Mark's crippled her, and my second shot in her heart finished her.

By this time, the herd was up, roused by the smell of blood and humans. They stampeded out of the clearing, the noise of their passage fading into silence. The doe tried to get to her feet as we approached, but couldn't. I slit her throat with my knife to end it.

I pulled out our arrows and inspected them for damage as Mark bent to begin gutting the doe. Standing up with two good arrows and the blade of the third, I looked up in surprise as the sun rose. I hadn't noticed the sky growing light. Except where the sun was, the sky was clouded blood red, as if in warning. My eyes were sun dazzled for a moment, and I reached down to grasp Mark's shoulder.

"Mark, I hear something."

He stood, listening. "I don't—"

"Shhh . . . ."

I heard the click of a trigger being pulled and the whiz of a crossbow bolt sailing through the air, and dove for the wet ground, pushing Mark with me. I grabbed my bow and slid an arrow from my quiver, the thrill of fear sending a burst of adrenaline charging through my system.

CHAPTER
TEN

I heard a crossbow being cocked and sat up, shooting an arrow off in that direction. A cry of pain answered it. A shadow moving in the woods caught my eye and I shot my next arrow at it. Another cry echoed through the forest.

"Where are they?" Mark asked. I felt him at my back, ready to shoot.

A crossbow bolt zinged past my ear and thudded into something soft. Mark grunted. I turned to see him drop his bow, clutching his neck. The barb of the bolt stuck out between his fingers, the fletching protruding out the other side. As I watched, horrified, a second bolt struck his chest and Mark went down. For a second, all I could do was watch as blood spurted from his wounds and his body twitched, eyes wide open, staring at the sky.

Another marksman released a bolt. I threw myself into the mud as it flew over my head.

Scrambling to my knees, I fired my own arrows at shadows in the trees. It seemed I could see them when it should have been impossible. There were some lucky strikes, verified by sounds of pain.

"How many?" I asked myself, searching the forest's edge. I couldn't see any more targets, and I was running low on arrows.

"Cowards!" I screamed, throwing down my bow and drawing my

sword. "Stop hiding and face me like men!" I turned in a slow circle, listening and watching for any movement. There had to be more.

A twig snapped behind me and I whirled to see a soldier wearing Nottingham colors holding a drawn sword.

"Are you the last?" I asked. The man didn't answer, so I raised my voice. "Well, you're all cowards. You send your comrade out to die while you hide like children?!"

"I am the last," the soldier said with the quiet dignity of youthful pride.

"Then you are a brave, foolish boy."

"Are you so sure of yourself that I am going to die?" he asked, haughty with that same pride.

I shrugged, moving away from Mark. I didn't know if he was still alive, but I had to be sure no one would give me trouble getting him back to camp.

"The sheriff won't be happy you've killed five of his soldiers. And you, just a filthy poacher."

That showed just how ignorant he was. What mere poacher carried a sword like mine? A sword identical to his.

"Come now," I chided. "Name-calling won't get you anywhere with me. What were you looking for out here if it wasn't poachers?" I drew a little closer to him as he moved toward me, raising his sword.

"We're looking for Robin Hood's men." He laughed harshly. "We intend for that outlaw to come 'home' and find all his men hanged. Then he will hang, too."

The fool, I thought. *His arrogance makes him a fool.*

I laughed. "I don't know much about Robin Hood, but you won't catch him so easily."

"Easily?" Our swords touched. A little chime of metal on metal sounded through the air. "We've got every man combing this forest. They won't escape us for long. Robin Hood will have no warning of what he's going to find."

"No warning from you," I scoffed, and took a swing at him.

His eyes widened as he blocked, finally catching on. "You're an outlaw, as well as a poacher!"

"Don't make it sound like an insult," I told him, laughing.

I made quick work of it. He was young and didn't know what he was doing. I finished him off, knowing if I didn't, he would sound the alarm. I made sure to grab his sword before I ran back to Mark.

He was unconscious when I got back to him, but still breathing. I searched for a pulse. It was weak, but it was there.

I stripped the feathers off the bolt in his neck and grasped the point end, sliding it out. Blood poured from the wound. Cursing, I ripped a piece of my shirt off and wrapped it around his neck, trying to staunch the blood flow. Minutes later, it slowed enough for me to let go and wrap another strip around it.

Fighting to control my shaking hands, I looked at his chest, my stomach roiling at the sight. It was a death wound for certain.

"Kay?" Mark croaked, and I realized he was conscious.

"Hush." I put a bloodied finger to his lips, unable to take my eyes from the wound. "It's got to come out, Mark."

His hand reached out and grasped my leg. "Do it," he whispered, his voice hollow and hoarse.

I gritted my teeth and slid my knife into the wound as far as I could in order to pry the skin apart. Then I yanked the bolt out, the barbs catching and tearing his skin.

Mark's scream burst from him and his grip on my leg tightened until I thought my circulation was permanently cut off. Then it slowly slacked as he passed out. I loosened the death grip I had on my knife, knowing I had to act quickly to save him.

Tearing off his shirt, I wrapped it around his chest as tightly as I could. It would have to do until I could get him back to Hugh.

I strapped my bow across my back, leaving my empty quiver, and stooped to pick Mark up.

A hiss of a projectile slicing through the air caught my attention. Before I could duck, a bolt struck my side, high up, coming in at an angle under my right arm. I stood up straight and clutched at the barb, crying out in pain. I knew I was in a vulnerable position, but I couldn't move. I'd never felt pain like that before.

I looked to see where the bolt had come from and saw a man collapse, an arrow in his chest. It was one I had shot before. The dying man had just enough left in him to shoot one more bolt.

Drawing in ragged breaths, I tried to ignore the pain as I knelt beside Mark. *What do I do?* I couldn't think. *Okay. Breathe, Kay. Close your eyes and think!*

I wouldn't be able to lift Mark with the thing sticking out of my side like it was. The bolt would catch on my arm, and I imagined moving it would slice up my insides. If it was in my lung and I pulled it out, the barbs could do even more damage. I needed to break it off, but not by using my ribs as a fulcrum. Could I get the leverage I needed to break it off cleanly using only one hand? I had to try, didn't I?

My skin prickled as I opened my eyes. There it was, just beyond Mark's supine body. The door was back, the rain-drenched pine trees calling to me at some subconscious level. The urge to stand up, to go through the door, was strong. I could get help, healing for my wounds, a miracle for Mark. We wouldn't have to die here. I started to climb to my feet, even as I shook my head.

"No! I won't go!" The compulsion grew stronger, the strength to resist draining with the blood from my wound. What had stopped it the last time?

Distraction.

Gritting my teeth, I reached with my left hand and wove my fingers around the shaft of the bolt. It was short and thick and took all the strength in my fingers to break it. Despite my efforts to hold it in place, I felt the hole tear open as it snapped. I fell forward across Mark's body, the sharp pain in my middle finger the only thing keeping me from passing out.

I closed my eyes, fighting back nausea. When I finally sat up, the door was gone. My breath exploded from my lips in profound relief.

Not this time, I thought.

Moving my arm to see if I had broken off enough of the bolt, I winced as the stub caught on my sleeve. It wasn't quite enough, but I lifted Mark into my arms anyway. I'd have preferred to sling him over my shoulder, but his wounds wouldn't have borne the stress. Knowing I had to start back before my own strength gave out, I half-bride-carried him, half-dragged him.

I was glad we hadn't gone far before we found the deer. I was strong, but Mark wasn't the lightest man in the Greenwood and I was losing a lot of blood. The only clear thought in the chaos of my mind was to get him to safety.

I was halfway back to the camp when Mark moaned. Quickly, I set him down as he opened his eyes to look at me.

"It's bad, Kay," he rasped.

"Yes," I agreed, forgetting to comfort him with lies. "But I'll get you back. You just hang in there."

He gave a fleeting smile before the pained look returned to his eyes. "I don't think—"

"Shhh . . . ." I didn't want to hear it. "We'll rest here until you're ready to go on."

He closed his eyes again and I winced at the pain in my side. I didn't want to tell him, didn't want him to tell me to go on without him. I was tempted to yank the bolt all the way out, but I would be no use to Mark if I passed out. I couldn't have tended it myself anyway, being under my arm like it was. I tried to breathe as smoothly as possible, taking comfort that I could. That meant my lungs were still whole.

I didn't know how long I sat there, fading in and out, but I finally realized Mark was unconscious again. I struggled to lift him, gasping at the renewed pain in my side.

They saw me before I ever got near the clearing. The perimeter guard gave a hoot, then shot out of his tree toward camp. I was still struggling along when two men came and took Mark away from me. My sight blurred with a red haze, so I couldn't see who they were.

"Kay?" someone beside me asked. I recognized Much's voice, fraught with concern. I felt myself swaying. "Are you all right?"

"Much, check my trail. I think I . . . was sloppy. Much . . . ." I reached out and grabbed at his shoulder, missing it. "I've been shot."

He caught me as I collapsed, snagging his arm on the shaft sticking out of my side. I cried out involuntarily as my awareness plunged into blackness.

When I woke, it was early morning, the sun just rising. I tried to sit up, but pain washed through me and I lay back, not at all surprised to hear myself groan.

Instantly, Much was at my side. He had a rumpled look to him, suggesting he had slept little, and his eyes were red. "How do you feel?" he asked.

"Like somebody shot me with a crossbow," I mumbled with pained sarcasm. I smiled a little to take the sting out of the words. "How long have I been out?"

"Just the night. I took care of you myself."

I nodded, giving him a fleeting smile of gratitude.

"What happened, Kay?"

"We were ambushed by the sheriff's men. Warn the others not to go out, not until Robin gets back. Old Nott's got men combing the forest for us. We've got to be extra careful. They know Robin's gone."

"It's already done. No one's left, except those who covered your trail and cleared the area." I knew he meant the bodies had been moved far away from camp. "We thought it would be best to stay quiet until we knew for sure what happened."

"Someone's got to go warn Robin. He'll be walking right into a trap." I winced as my agitated movement shot shards of pain through my side. "He must be warned."

"Don't worry, lass. When have you ever known Robin to be less than extra careful? He'll be all right. What we must do is sit tight. We can't let the sheriff find us now, can we?"

"No, we can't. How's Mark?"

Much frowned. "Not good, I'm afraid. Hugh's done all he can to ease his pain. It's just a matter of time."

"Take me to him," I said, struggling to sit up. Much started to protest, then changed his mind when he saw the determination on my face. He helped me stand and walk into the cave.

Ellen sat next to Mark, dabbing at his forehead with a damp cloth. Hugh slept, propped against the wall.

Mark was sweating, his dark hair plastered to his head. When he tossed a little, Ellen tried to hold him still to keep his wounds from bleeding again.

Much helped me sit at Mark's side, opposite Ellen, then he sat, too. I reached out and grasped Mark's hand, feeling how cold and clammy it was. Ellen looked up at me.

"You're a brave woman," she said in a fragile voice. "Mark was lucky to have you with him."

"Not lucky enough," I said, looking at him and remembering the feeling, the premonition, I had that morning. I would never ignore that feeling again. "He's dying."

Ellen nodded, looking scared, tired, and very close to tears. The white wedding dress she had worn since coming to camp was stained and torn. Now there was blood on the sleeves. She was young, maybe sixteen. How had I not seen it before?

Someone should give her something else to wear, I thought dully.

Hugh woke up and came to sit next to Ellen, then asked me how I was feeling. I showed him my finger, which he confirmed was broken. He set it and wrapped it with some cloth strips to bind it to a splint.

We sat in the cave for most of the morning, watching as Mark sweated his life away.

It was noon when he opened his eyes, a look of peace coming over him. He looked around at all of us, completely coherent. "Much," he said. "Ellen, Hugh." He nodded to each of them, then to me. "Kay."

His eyes closed slowly, the sweat on his face already beginning to dry. His hand, still in mine, went limp, and I couldn't find a pulse. Gently, I laid his hand on his chest, then placed his other on top of it. He looked like he was just sleeping.

The silence in the cave was tangible. No one moved or spoke for a long time. Mark lay there, hands folded across his chest, looking for all the world as though he would wake at any moment and yawn, giving us a smile.

"The wounds were too deep," Hugh said at last, as if it mattered. He wiped his nose with a grimy sleeve.

A void opened in my stomach and the bottom dropped out of my world. I looked at the tears streaming down Much's face, saw Ellen clinging to Hugh, her face buried against his shoulder.

Why can't I cry? I asked myself. I turned my face away from the others, ashamed.

Hugh stood and helped Ellen outside.

I looked up at the roof of the cave, trying to feel something besides the vacuum in my stomach, but there was nothing. Slowly, memories of Mark began to trickle into my mind. Swimming. Laughing. Fighting. The look on his face when Marian told him I was a woman. Charging across the common on a horse, his face lit up with firelight. Crossbow bolts piercing his body again and again and again. His last whisper, echoing in the damp cave. But the only emotions I felt were emptiness and the same slow-burning anger at death that I always felt.

I felt a hand on my shoulder and turned to look at Much. His face was red from crying, and he looked at my dry eyes with bewilderment. "Don't you feel it?" he asked, his words echoing the voice in my head. "Why don't you cry?"

"I don't know. I keep asking myself the same thing. It's just . . . I have always kept the hurting inside . . . . I don't . . . know how."

Much stared at me, knowing I wasn't some unfeeling brute who didn't deserve friends, yet he couldn't comprehend my words.

"It's like a wall inside me, built brick by brick every time my father hit me, every time someone I loved died, every time my trust was betrayed. I'm trying to tear it down, but I'm afraid, Much. What if I drown?"

Much pulled me into his embrace, his caring acceptance giving me strength. "I'm sorry, Kay." I put my arms around him and we sat there, holding each other. "Let go," he whispered, so softly I hardly heard him. "Let it go."

His strength warmed me. I felt . . . . It was hard to tell what I felt. It was like someone reaching inside me, soothing me, crumbling down my wall piece by piece. This catharsis was too much. The void in my stomach wrenched into a brief pain, and I sobbed. Real tears streamed down my face and drenched Much's shirt as I cried like I hadn't since childhood. Every tear I never shed . . . .

The tiny cave began filling with people, all crying, creating a special union in our tears. I was in a strange, wonderful place where I could sense their sorrow, their loss, their love for one another. I was a part of it, and it felt good.

Now I knew why we were together. We shared an intangible bond of love, joy, and sorrow. Somehow, I knew John, Will, and Robin knew of this loss, even across the miles separating us. Some grand gift of nature gave Robin Hood the ability to hold the brotherhood together in this mystical place. This Sharing.

Releasing my grief, both the old and the fresh, had brought me, with the help of my friends and Robin's gift, a content acceptance I had never felt in my life, and might never feel again.

WE BURIED Mark near the river, his grave marked with a stone bearing his name.

That night, I was still dazed from so much emotion surrounding me. It felt good to let out all the feelings pent up inside. I was able to accept the loss of Mark, of my father and mother, of people I knew were gone but hadn't really let myself think about. I felt like a load had been lifted from my heart and I would float away unburdened.

I slept like a babe, thoughts of the door the furthest thing from my mind. I didn't let myself wonder why it kept returning, why it insisted I walk through. I had resisted. That was enough.

NO ONE LEFT camp for days, and the watch perimeter was doubled. Everything was hidden away from sight. No benches, no tables, no formal meals, no fires. We weren't taking any more chances than we had to. No one hunted, so we had no fresh meat. We had to ration food until the time the soldiers left the Greenwood and we could hunt and trade again.

If we were careful during the winter, we were doubly so now. The night became an opportune time to reinforce Sherwood's reputation as haunted. We had "ghosts" in the trees, and when a search party came through, our ghouls scared the living hell out of them. We scattered the "hauntings" far apart, and always away from camp to avoid a great daylight search that would uncover us. After the first few days, there were no more hunting parties at night.

A week and a half after Mark was put to earth, Hugh let me take off my bandage. The wound was tender, but well on the way to healing. Only an angry red scar remained. Hugh told me the redness was from a bit of my shirt that had stuck in the wound and caused an infection. It had required re-opening and cleaning the wound. I was lucky the bolt had gone in at a shallow angle. Any deeper and it would have punctured my lung, and I'd be alongside Mark. The injury hadn't been bad, all things considered, but it was a wonder I made it back to camp.

Nights were dismal. There were no get-togethers before bed. No fires, no laughter, not much talking. I often sat watch or sat up by myself, leaning against a tree, watching the stars and worrying.

One night as I did just that, I heard a commotion. One voice was raised, cursing, then hushed. I jumped to my feet, drew my knife, then ran silently to where I had heard the voice.

In the moonlight, I saw five, maybe six men standing close together, whispering. I caught some of the words and recognized one of the voices.

"Scarlet." His name was on my lips in a silent explosion of relief. I sheathed my knife and moved toward the group.

When I reached them, they were already breaking up, melting into the shadows. I nabbed Will's sleeve. "Will!" I said, hugging him fiercely. Surprised, he hugged me back. "I was so worried about you—"

"Kay," was all he said, holding me tightly.

It felt good to be held like that. After a long moment, I stepped back, leaving my arms around his waist. "Did you all make it back? Is everyone all right?"

"Robin's not with us," he said quietly. "We separated early on to throw off the hunters. Thank God they didn't use hounds. He hasn't come back?"

"No, but he will. Come. You must be tired."

He allowed me to pull him back to the den I'd made for myself at the base of a hawthorn bush. He stretched out and I dropped a blanket over him. I sat down, just watching him, then I yawned.

"Come on, Kay," Will said gently, holding the blanket open for me. "It seems I'm not the only one who is tired."

I hesitated, then stretched out next to him. He put his strong arms around me while I snuggled into him. Sleep came easily in his comforting presence.

I WOKE JUST after the sun came up . . . alone. I almost thought last night had been a dream, but my arm was still warm where Will had lain against me. I sat up and stretched, then scratched vigorously at my head. I needed a good scrubbing.

Standing, I straightened my clothes as best I could and buckled on my sword—no one went unarmed these days—before going to get some food.

Will was there, munching on a piece of bread. "Did I wake you?"

"I don't know. I opened my eyes and you weren't there." I smiled, picking up my portion. He smiled back, making my heart skip a beat. Feeling my face heat from the thoughts coming unbidden into my mind, I looked down at my food and took a small bite of bread.

"I must have disturbed you when I got up then. I'm sorry."

I refused to look at him to see his expression. "No, it's okay. I would have been up soon anyway. I haven't slept much lately." I scratched my head again. "I need to wash," I said, looking in the general direction of the river. Anything in order to not look at his face. "Do you think I could sneak a trip to the river without foresters seeing?"

"Could be," Will said. "We didn't run into any yesterday. Perhaps if you went early enough . . . . But you shouldn't go alone."

"Is that an offer?" I asked, then bit my tongue and cursed myself for acting like a fool.

"Yes, well, I suppose it is."

I looked up to find Will grinning at me again.

THE SUN WAS SHINING by the time we got to the river. Far upstream from camp, we found a wonderful spot where the grassy bank sloped into the still, deep water and the riverbed was sandy.

I threw down my homespun towel and unbuckled my sword belt, then sat down to untie my deerskin boots. My old Danner boots had fallen to pieces in February.

"How did things go in Winchester?" I asked.

"Oh, it went fine—at first." He sat down on the grass next to me. "It took us the better part of a week to get there, then we feasted with Queen Eleanor. Alan played his harp, and we had an enjoyable time." He pulled up a stalk of grass and stuck it between his teeth.

"Is she pretty?"

"Eleanor? Yes, she is."

"I imagine you had a fine time flirting with her ladies-in-waiting," I teased.

"Nah." I quirked my eyebrow at him and he laughed, lifting his hands. "What do I want with pretty city girls? I've got no use for 'em."

Unaccountably, I blushed. "Go on," I said, trying to cover up my discomfort. "Tell me more."

"Well, when the archery tournament started, the queen had us stay disguised until the last round when she showed us off like we were her prized fighting cocks or something. Anyway, we all made it to the last round. Robin, of course, won the prize. Prince John got upset then. He had a lot of money on his archer. The queen made him promise to give us ten days to get away, but we were barely out of the shire when we heard all Prince John's men were after us. I guess he changed his mind. He was out for our heads. So we split up, Robin going one way, the rest of us going another. Robin took the more direct route, so I'm surprised he's not back yet. He must have run into trouble, though we didn't have any problems . . . ." He sighed. "I understand we lost someone while we were gone."

Though the subject change was abrupt, I knew exactly what he meant. I nodded, then finished taking off my boots. I had stopped as I listened to him. He didn't mention the Sharing. It wasn't something one talked about. "Mark and I were out hunting. We got ambushed by some of the sheriff's men."

"Mark?"

"Yes. He was hit twice with crossbow bolts—one in the neck and one in the chest. I had to carry him back to the camp." I took off my outer shirt. I wasn't sad about Mark anymore. It was easier to put it aside since I had let my grief out.

"Were you hurt?" he asked, concerned, noticing the dirty bandage around my middle finger for the first time.

"I took one in the side and had a bout of infection, but I'm all right now."

"Can I see?" he asked. I raised my undershirt to show him the still-pink scar. He touched it gingerly, and I tried not to wince. "Sweet Mother Mary, Kay. That's wicked."

"Don't ask me if it hurt," I said comically and waggled my finger at him. "Broke this breaking the bolt so I could carry Mark." I tilted my head toward the water. "Aren't you coming in?"

"I don't think so. I ought—"

"Come on," I said, stripping down to my undergarments. "You've been on the road for more than a week. You need to scrub as much as I do."

"Who's going to keep watch?" he asked in a last-ditch effort to stay dry.

"Who's going to bother a man and woman bathing in the river?" I countered. "If you don't take those clothes off, I'll pull you in with them on!"

"Oi, look who's getting cocky! You think you can take me just like that, eh?"

"Just like that!" I snapped my fingers.

That made him smile. He stood up and slowly, teasingly, took off his clothes, then he ran and dove into the water. I laughed and dove in after him.

When I came up, gasping from the cold, I couldn't find him. I knew he was playing games, so I stayed still, treading water. I pushed my hair back out of my eyes and waited for him to show. I heard little sounds, like he was coming up out of the water, but when I turned, no one was there. I felt small currents, but I couldn't see into the water from the angle I was in.

"Will?" I said, spinning in a circle. "Will?"

I felt a hand grasp my leg, and before I could do anything, I was jerked down. My nose filled with water, then I got a mouthful as I opened it to shout.

When I came up, I saw Will laughing as I choked and coughed.

"It's not funny!" I cuffed him on the shoulder and he laughed even harder. "Just you wait. Someday, when you're not paying attention . . . ." I let the sentence trail off, menacing, but he only smiled.

"I *always* pay attention," he said smugly.

"Well, I guess you don't have anything to worry about then, do you?"

"I guess I don't." He grinned.

On impulse, I grabbed his hand and kissed it. Then I swam to shore, grabbed his clothes, and threw them into the water.

"Oi!" he shouted, still playful. "That's a rotten thing to do."

"Your clothes are rotten, too." I grinned. "Be a help and wash them." I grabbed my own clothes and threw them in. Then I started to wash them with all the modern conveniences at hand. I scrubbed them together, swished them in the water, beat them on rocks, and watched an amazing amount of dirt float away. Will worked on his clothes with as much ferocity as me. When we were through, we spread them out on the grass to dry in the warm sunshine. They weren't exactly stain free, but they were clean.

Then we went to work on our bodies. I must have scrubbed off layers of skin, as well as dirt, with how hard I used the cloth and lump of oily soap. I dug the dirt from under my fingernails and scrubbed my hair until it squeaked, wishing for shampoo.

Nevertheless, I was clean again and it felt wonderful. Both Will and I were in great moods as we lay on the bank, waiting for our clothes to dry.

CHAPTER
ELEVEN

Back at camp, things were jumping like they hadn't been in weeks. I wondered what was up as Scarlet and I wandered in.

Much hurried over when he saw us.

"What's going on?" I asked.

"The soldiers are pulling out of Sherwood. One of the villagers got through with the news."

Robin had a spy network of servants, farmers, and villagers reaching farther than the length and breadth of Sherwood Forest. Only the king could draw on a more extensive source.

"Can he be trusted?" Will asked, shaking back his wet hair.

"Aye, he's one of our most reliable."

"If he's betrayed us, though, it would mean trouble." Will looked around at all the excited men.

"Go talk to him yourself. He's over there with Little John."

"Thanks, Much. I think I will." Will walked toward the man.

"That doesn't mean they've caught Robin, does it?" I asked, worried I had been wrong about Robin being okay.

"Nah," he said, dismissing the possibility.

"Are you sure?" He was acting strangely. I wondered what else had happened while I was absent.

"Positive." He smiled. "Robin came in just before you got back. He's in the cave with Stutely and Tuck. Tuck helped him get back."

I heaved a sigh of relief and hugged him. "Now, that's good news."

"Aye," said Much, releasing me. "And Robin's going to have a good story to tell us tonight!" His eyes were alight with anticipation.

THAT NIGHT, Robin told how, after he had split up with John, Will, and Alan, he had changed clothes with several unsuspecting people, including a bishop from Hereford. He had almost made it into Sherwood when a lone soldier, who turned out to be Sir Richard of Lea, confronted him. Sir Richard helped Robin get to Tuck by providing a disguise and himself as a visa. They had encountered a roadblock of the king's men, and Sir Richard was known to them as a man loyal to the crown.

I had never met Sir Richard, but I remembered him from the legends. Robin had saved the life of his son and lent him money to keep his estate, so Richard was in his debt. He was a good Saxon, a fair overlord, and had turned out to be an important ally.

Robin had stayed at Tuck's hermitage for a few days until the soldiers moved on, then he came straight back to the camp. He arrived only half an hour behind the messenger bearing good news.

The soldiers had given up. There were rumors Robin Hood had fled this part of the country, so successful had been our hiding.

The skirmish between Nottingham's colors and Mark and me had been attributed to twenty outlaws executing a wholesale slaughter of the soldiers. Then, according to the sheriff, being the cowards we were, we had fled the forest in fear of the greater search parties he sent out. Parties that never ventured far enough into the forest to come close to our camp.

A COUPLE WEEKS LATER, there was more trouble.

Alan had gone to his cousin's, taking Ellen with him, and things had settled down almost to normal.

Well, normal except for the fact Jerod Longfingers had taken over the group of men Mark had led before he died. Jerod was more hotheaded than Mark had ever been, and he wasn't nearly as smart.

After dinner, Jerod and his group of five were talking among themselves, arguing some point. The Gloucester brothers, Seward and Ambrose, stood beside him, while Eric O'Leary and Caleb the Welshman opposed them. Nathan of Ely stayed back, watching with his cool assassin's eyes.

Tempers flared between them. Ambrose got in Caleb's face, sticking his finger into the burly man's chest and speaking in a soft voice cold enough to freeze a waterfall. Seward was less controlled, pacing up to Eric and back, talking loud enough so people in the clearing could hear him, but not really understand him. Jerod was excited, too, dropping things in when Seward or Ambrose weren't speaking. Eric stood there, his face a mask of seething anger.

Everybody else mostly ignored them, but I watched from a place nearby. I noticed Robin watching, too.

Caleb was hot. He got right back in Ambrose's face, his voice getting louder. Ambrose was neither a small man nor quite sane. He was a killer, and that was about all he knew how to do. Caleb was pushing his luck. I stood just as Ambrose reached for his knife.

Robin was already there, Little John half a step behind him.

"What seems to be the problem?" Robin asked, his voice loud but calm.

Caleb's knife was half out, but he put it up when Robin spoke. Ambrose growled and spat angrily onto the ground, but he put his knife up, too, in deference to Robin's presence.

"Do it, Jerod!" Seward shoved Eric aside to step forward, and Eric jumped him from behind, knocking him down. Seward wasn't as big as his brother, so he couldn't get up from under the onslaught of Eric's blows.

Robin took one long step, grabbed Eric O'Leary by the collar and yanked him into the air, throwing him several feet away to land on his back.

Before Robin could say anything, Nathan stood up.

"Try it, Jerod, if you think you can."

Nathan was an average-sized man, but strong. He was cool, levelheaded, and smart. Ambrose was a killer, but Nathan was an assassin. He knew about people, what buttons to push to make them make mistakes. I'd heard about him, but this was the first time I'd seen him at work. Nathan was bad to the soul, but he only acted when he had something to gain. I wondered what it was this time.

"Robin," said Jerod, shaking with adrenalin, "I'm challenging you."

Everyone in the clearing stopped what they were doing and all eyes turned to Robin. The silence held until Robin laughed. "Challenging me? To what?"

"A fight." Jerod drew his knives, one in each hand. They were enough to daunt most men. Eleven-inch blades extended from antler handles, the tines left on in a doubled hook hilt to scratch or disarm an opponent. Jerod's skill with his chosen weapons was well known.

Robin stood still, refusing to draw. "Jerod—" he began.

"You're such a pig, Robin. Who here chose you to lead the brotherhood? Not I." Jerod turned his head and spat in disgust.

"So?" Robin was not impressed, though I could tell by his stance he was ready to fight if it came down to it.

"So Mark couldn't do it. He let you beat him, then fell for your little woman and let her get him killed."

I stiffened at the accusation, ready to draw on him myself. I should have expected these fools would think I had set Mark up. But Robin's next words stopped me.

"Oh, aye. Kay went through a lot of trouble to get Mark killed," he said, his voice so heavy with sarcasm, even the slowest wit would catch it. "Considering she was almost killed herself. I'm sure she shot herself and carried Mark all that way just for fun."

Jerod's face turned even redder as he took a step forward. "Mark should have killed you, but he failed. So I will. You're the only thing standing between me and leadership." His grin showed just how badly he had been misled by his so-called friends. Judging by the look on Nathan's face, I thought I knew who had pushed Jerod's buttons.

"Don't be a fool, Jerod. How many of my people—and make no mistake, they're mine—how many of them do you think will follow you after you murder me in cold blood?"

"Murder?! Cold blood?! This is a challenge, Robin! You have to accept or lose face."

"Lose face to a fool who knows nothing about leadership and even less about control?" asked Robin, his voice cutting into Jerod and shredding his resolve to ribbons.

"Coward," Jerod hissed, trying to provoke Robin, knowing a fight was his only way out without becoming the fool. He glanced at Seward and Ambrose for support, but they offered none.

"Coward, Jerod Longfingers?" Robin moved so swiftly, the motion was a blur. Jerod's knives flipped up into the air from precise blows by Robin's open hands. They stuck point down into the ground, Seward and Caleb jumping out of the way, as if the knives were adders. Robin held his own knife to Jerod's throat. "That's not the word for me."

"Then kill me!" Jerod cried out, near hysteria. "Or I'll kill you."

"When? In my sleep?" Robin asked, pressing the blade of his knife deeper into Jerod's throat. Blood welled around the blade and began to trickle down Jerod's neck. "There's a true coward for you, but that's the only time you'd have half a chance of killing me. And then you'd best not stay around. Better to try your luck with the sheriff."

Jerod lowered his head, fists doubled up, but he was not quite stupid enough to try anything. Robin stepped back. Jerod turned and stalked away into the forest.

We all knew he'd be back. I watched Nathan chuckling to himself until he saw me watching. *He* liked the outcome of this incident anyway.

Eric O'Leary was gone, and no one I asked had seen where he'd gone or when.

THAT FALL, Geoffrey and Adam came up with an idea, and Robin set them to work on it. Since we had lost the use of the caves to shelter in during the winter, the two men had designed a winter camp we would be able to use as long as it was undiscovered.

Robin had chosen a site in a shallow valley deep in the forest. He designated helpers for the two carpenters and they set to digging into the hillside. The dirt was reshaped to make a U of earth extending from the excavated hillside, which we would cover with a roof of trees and grass. The trees, a variety of small aspen that grew quickly, along with grasses and ferns we planted, would rest on a platform of shingled planks caulked with pitch. When done, the whole thing would look just like the side of a hill, but underneath would be a dry warren where all of us could sleep. Theoretically.

The work was slow going. Materials were hard to find, and we had to make our own planks and pegs for the platform. The digging turned into a nightmare with the arrival of fall and this year's constant rain. The earth turned to mud under the worker's shovels, and frequent slides kept the digging from progressing.

When we weren't working on that project, we hunted, picked sites for robberies, and set up blinds to use in emergencies. When we weren't doing those things, we were wet and bored.

Around mid-morning on one cold, rainy October day, Edward the Red and Matthew of Chester came running into camp.

"There's a carriage coming up the Lincoln road. It's nice, like a gentleman's," said Matthew.

"It's a noble carriage all right," Edward confirmed. "All shut tight against the rain. Must be a whole family in there."

"And their gold," added Matthew.

"They've got an escort of twelve, all armed, so the cargo must be important. There's not too many for a hardy lot like us."

Robin smiled at the two scouts. "Good work. We'll draw for the captain and get a team together." He took out the four drawing sticks—one for himself, Scarlet, Stutely, and Little John—and held them in his fist. There were few chances for a robbery in winter, and we didn't want to miss this one by not acting fast enough. "Let's get out there."

Scarlet got the short straw and Robin told him to choose up a team of fourteen. I thought that was a little too close in number for comfort, but I held my peace. Any arguments I made against Robin's virtuous fairness always fell on deaf ears. Besides, we had always handled ourselves well in a close match.

Will chose up his team, including me, and we made our way to one of the sites we had chosen just a week before.

We each found our places, two to a tree, and settled down to wait. The trees were winter-bare, so we all wore deer hide, brown leather, or unevenly dyed brown homespun to blend in the best.

Will and I shared a tree, my place a little higher than his since I was lighter and could climb onto smaller branches. The trees dripped rain, making the slippery bark uncomfortable to sit on. The waiting, never an easy thing for me, was made worse because it was impossible to tell by the sky what time it was or how long we had been sitting there.

"Curse this weather," I muttered.

Will spat over his shoulder. "I'd almost rather it snowed."

I agreed wholeheartedly. "I've forgotten what it feels like to be dry. I'll be glad when the shelter is done. I wish they would hurry."

"You know they can't. They can't work in this rain any more than we can sleep in it."

"I know, Will, but my skin looks like a prune. Nothing I own is dry."

We lapsed into silence. I was unwilling to voice any further complaint, and Will was unwilling to hear any.

My nose dripped snot until it ran along my upper lip. I finally gave a mighty sniffle, wishing for a dry cloth to blow it on. Shifting to ease a cramp, I slipped on the wet bark and caught myself painfully. I grumbled but stayed silent . . . until my stomach growled loud enough I was sure Will heard it.

"Are they never coming?"

"Mind yer mouth and listen," said Will, alert. I bit back my next complaint, straining my ears to hear over the falling rain.

There it was—the jingle of a harness and the steady thud of hooves on the roadway. Our mark was here at last.

Using an arrow, Will beat a brief tattoo on the tree trunk. Almost immediately, we heard it answered from five trees. A fleeting tremor of sound, like branches rattling in a small wind.

But someone hadn't answered . . . . There should have been one more reply.

"Will, who didn't answer?" I looked around, trying to see every-one. I could only see Patrick and Warren in a tree across the road from us.

"Too late," said Will.

The carriage lumbered into view. A large affair, finely made and closed up tightly against the rain. Will and I exchanged grins in anticipation of the riches inside.

The carriage passed us, right into our trap.

An arrow flickered across the road and into the trees. I cursed as I realized something was wrong on the far end of our gauntlet. The arrow had come from the ground and gone up. A warning.

"Will, did you—" I began in a whisper, but he didn't hear me. He made a high whistle, our signal to attack, as he leapt out of the tree, landing in a crouch and nocking an arrow to his bow.

Some of the others had seen the arrow and figured the attack would be called off, so when the signal was given, half our team was late in coming out of the trees. Two of them, Robert and John, never did.

The men escorting the carriage had also seen the arrow and formed a protective circle around it as I dropped out of the tree a heartbeat behind Will. Warren, Patrick, Henry, and Cedric were on the ground, as well. Our arrows downed some of them, but when they charged us, we had to draw our swords.

They weren't supposed to fight back. They should have given up! It seemed we had made a vast error. The escort was made up of soldiers for hire, not simple household guards. This was the kind of engagement we all trained for but tried our best to avoid.

Only two of the mercenaries were mounted, the rest on foot. And we were lucky it was so. The fight was an equal match, even without everyone there. Evan, Peter, and Walter joined the fight, and we started overpowering them.

I fought side by side with Will. Knife in one hand, sword in the other, bow across my back. I used the technique I had learned from him . . . dirty fighting. All the hours spent training narrowed down to this one event, and my mind locked into a cold, calculating place where my only focus was staying alive, by any means necessary.

During a scuffle with one man, my quiver upturned and all my precious arrows fell out to be trampled and broken in the mud. He nearly pinned me against his bulk, trying to immobilize me, but quickness was my best defense. I slipped away from his grasp, trying to find an opening.

I heard Will cursing and yelling as he kicked one man in the groin and followed up with a sword thrust into his back, then moved to the next man.

I engaged my opponent with my sword. While he blocked it, I slipped past his defense and drove my dagger under his sword arm, through the gap in his armor. I had been taught that most swordsmen did not expect such a blow, and my teacher was right. With a twist of my sword, I disarmed the shocked man, then kicked him in the head where he fell.

The next man didn't let me get close. It took far too long to disarm him and thrust my sword into his belly. By then, Will was ahead of me, nearly upon the carriage.

One of the horsemen turned his attention to me. I had my hands full, so I didn't see what happened next.

There was a creak of wet wood and an explosion of yelling. Will and Evan shouted wildly for retreat, and I risked a glance. The sides of the carriage had fallen open and more men scrambled out. Foresters dressed in light armor moved swiftly into the battle.

We had to get out of there. We were far outnumbered now.

I slipped in the mud as the horseman's blade whistled through the air where my neck used to be. Rolling away from the horse's hooves, I scrambled in the mud to gain my footing, slipped and rolled again, feeling my bow bending dangerously on my back. The horse turned in front of me as I got to my knees, the rider leaning down to take a swing with his sword.

Time slowed for an instant as I did something I would not have done in any other circumstance. I launched myself upward, reaching out with my dagger to slash the horse's foreleg, tearing open a gash up to his girth.

The horse screamed in pain. I screamed, too, hating myself for wounding a creature that was only doing what it had been trained to do. The horse reared up, throwing the rider, who was already off balance to make his cut at me.

Diving on top of him, I plunged the knife into his throat, his face a mask of horror in my vision.

Yanking the blade free, I stood and snatched up my sword.

"Kay!" Patrick shouted. "C'mon!"

Swinging my head around, I saw Will and Evan, four soldiers on them, trapped against the carriage.

"Will!" I started over to help him.

Mouth open in a wordless shout of fury, Will hacked at the soldiers, but more men joined against him.

"Kay! Look out!" Patrick shouted.

Without letting go of my dagger, I gripped my sword with both hands and turned to face the soldier running at me.

In an overhand stroke I didn't know I could execute so effectively, I cut clean through the man's blade and he went down, blood spurting from a wound in his forehead.

I almost took off Patrick's arm when he grabbed me. "Kay, move!" He dispatched an attacking soldier with a vicious blow to the head.

I saw Will go down amid the enemy.

"Will!"

But I ran away from him, four of the foresters coming after Patrick, Phillip, and me. With foresters in pursuit, we ran toward the blinds we had set up. Blinds we never intended to need or use.

Patrick tossed me his quiver as we ran. His bow had broken in the fight, and he was limping badly. "One," he counted, signaling he would use the first blind.

"Three," I said, clipping the quiver to my belt.

"Two," said Phillip.

The first blind was coming up. I glanced over my shoulder and saw the foresters following, though they weren't close enough to be a danger to our plan.

We crested a low hill and dropped down the other side, out of our pursuer's line of sight. Patrick dove to one side and into the waiting arms of a tree's roots, burying himself in the piled leaves.

The second blind came up quickly. After Phillip went to ground inside a rotted stump, I kept running for about one hundred feet, then turned, nocking an arrow to my bow.

The foresters, cresting the hill and seeing me ready to shoot, began to zig-zag. Banishing my fury so I could concentrate completely, I shot one of them as he crossed between two trees. Of the other three, two ran on and the third dropped to the ground to hide behind a rock. A second forester tumbled mid-stride, my arrow in his chest, and the other stopped behind a tree. I was ready to get off another shot, but I had no target. Of the two left, I could see neither.

I saw Phillip stealing up on one man, so I kept my eyes on the tree where my man was hidden. When Phillip dove on his, my man moved to attack him, just as I'd hoped. He was low to the ground, but I let fly my last arrow, which sank into his neck.

I drew my knife and ran to Phillip's aid. He was standing when I got there, and I looked him over.

"You all right?"

"Aye. Patrick was wounded."

"I saw." I retrieved two usable arrows from the bodies of the foresters, heedless that one man was still alive. My mind was back at the ambush, praying for Will. "Come on."

We went back to Patrick's tree and called to him, then helped him to his feet when he emerged from the cover of leaves.

"Can you make it back to camp?" I asked, swiftly using a strip of his pants to bind up the gash in his leg.

"I'll make it. What are you going to do?"

I stood up. "I've got to see if Evan and the others are all right. See if anyone's been captured and where they're being taken. See who's dead."

"I'm coming with you."

"No, Phillip," I told him. "Patrick will need your help to get back."

"I'm coming with you," he repeated. "My brothers are back there!"

I looked at Patrick.

"I said I'll make it. You two go, and see you don't get caught."

"All right. You be careful, too. Make sure you're not followed. Come on, Phillip."

Together, we jogged back to the scene of the ambush, keeping alert for more foresters . . . or our own people.

The mercenaries were still there, cleaning up the mess. We crept up on them as they loaded their dead and wounded into the carriage. Three of them hauled the carcass of a horse off the road.

Phillip and I edged closer. Will, Evan, Edward, Walter, and Peter were all tied up and unconscious, propped inside the carriage. A nasty wound on Will's head oozed blood.

"What'll I do with this one, eh?" one of the mercenaries called, kicking at a still form lying in the mud. "'E's dead."

"Leave 'im," came the answer. "An outlaw what doesn't get stretched deserves the wolf. Come on, you lot. Get that horse in the ditch and let's get out of here. Happen I don't want to be here after dark." The captain whipped the draft horses and started them pulling the carriage down the road.

I checked my quiver. Only two arrows. Not enough to start another fight to free Will and the others. But at least he was alive!

"What about the foresters?" one of them asked.

"What about them? If they're still alive, they'll find their way to Nottingham for their reward, I wager."

"Right," another agreed. "Let's get out of here. I don't fancy being here when they come back with help."

"Amen to that," agreed the captain.

The carriage rolled out of sight.

"It's Nottingham then," I said as Phillip and I made our way to the road, still watching for foresters. "Not that I really had any doubt."

"Aye. This reeks of His Excellency the High Worm Sheriff. Do you see anyone?"

"Not a soul. Look, I'll cover you." He blinked at me, so I clarified. "You step out and if anyone comes at you, I'll shoot. Right?"

"Right."

Phillip took the last few steps onto the road, heading for the lone body lying in the mud.

There was a flicker of movement in the trees across the road. I trained my sights on it, but I couldn't tell if it was a friend or foe.

I followed the movement until I got a clear look.

It was Matthew, and . . . . I shot.

The arrow cruised past Matthew's head to lodge in the body of the forester closing in on him.

Matthew spun to see the forester falling and finished him off with his knife. Then he turned to see me walking out onto the road, my last arrow nocked in my bow.

"It's Warren!" came Phillip's anguished cry.

I ran over to see Phillip cradling his brother in his arms. The body was covered in mud, the wound in his chest still seeping blood. His eyes were closed while the rain gently bathed his face.

I put my hand on Phillip's shoulder. "We'll take him back to camp, then we'll get Walter out of Nottingham." I nodded to Matthew, who came forward to help.

"No, I'll carry him. He's my brother."

THE FIRST PEOPLE I looked for when we got back to camp were Robert and John. They sat beneath a tree, Robert bending over John's legs.

"What the hell happened to you?!" I shouted, heading toward them. "The whole thing went to hell. We needed you. Warren's dead, and everybody's captured!" I was working myself into a mighty fit, then saw John's wrapped foot. "Oh." I slumped to the wet ground beside them.

Much and a few of the others gathered around to hear the news, and Robert addressed the crowd in general.

"He fell out of the damn tree right before the carriage came," he said. "I missed the warning, and by the time I sent the cease fire signal, it was too late. We ran into Cedric on the way back. He said it was a trap."

"You didn't see that?" I asked.

"No. I was helping John get back to camp."

"'Kay!" Robin walked toward me. "Where's Will?"

"Taken." The word dropped from my mouth like a stone into a canyon, bouncing off every other voice in camp with its gravity.

"Taken?" Robin echoed.

"And Edward, Peter, Evan, and Walter. Warren's dead."

Robin took a step back, appalled. "What happened?"

"Ambush. They were hiding in the carriage. It was a trap, and we didn't have enough men." I glared accusingly at Robin. "They demolished us. All we needed was a few more men."

"We've always been able to handle ourselves before," Robin said defensively.

"It only takes once," I snapped. I needed to vent my anger and frustration, and Robin was as good a target as any. I needed someone to blame. "I've always said—"

Robert broke in. "It was just bad luck. It wasn't anyone's fault. Bad luck and bad timing."

Robin was about to say something, but I stood up with a snap of energy. "They're being taken to Nottingham. I'm going with the rescue party."

"What rescue party?" Robin asked.

I stared at him in complete disbelief. Was he serious? "The group of *fighters* that's going to get Will and the others out of Nottingham."

"They'll be hung by morning, Kay. They're already dead." There was real pain in Robin's eyes, but also a firmness I didn't understand.

"No!" I grabbed him by the shoulders and gave him a little shake. "If you don't help, it will be me and Phillip by ourselves. I won't assume they're dead."

"Don't you get it, Kay?" Robin took my hands from his shoulders and gripped them tightly. "That's what they want. They want us to try to save them. It's another trap."

"Dammit, Robin! I don't care! Phillip lost one brother today. He won't sit by and lose another one. And I'm not going to sit by and lose Will, Peter, Evan, and Edward."

I stared at him for a moment. Robin didn't answer. "Jesus," I swore in disgust, grabbed my bow and John's quiver, and headed out of the clearing.

"Do you have a plan?" Robin called.

I kept walking. "I will have when I get there."

I heard someone following. From the corners of my eyes, I saw Phillip, Robert, and Much walking with me. I turned when I felt a hand on my shoulder.

"Kay, look at yourself," Robin said. "You're covered in filth, you need to sleep. If you walk into Nottingham looking like that, it won't be long before you join Will. Listen. Give it until morning. Then I'll have a plan."

I looked at Much, who waited for me to make a decision. I was grateful he was willing to defy Robin to help me, but I couldn't think of anything to say. Robin was right.

"Don't even think of leaving without me," I said in warning.

"Don't you think I like my life?" Robin's smile was grim, but I didn't regret forcing him to take action.

"But they'll hang them in the morning, won't they?" asked Phillip. He looked east, toward Nottingham.

"No, Phillip, I'm sure they won't. They want me to attempt to save them. They won't hang them before I do."

THE NIGHT WAS STILL and wet around me, and I wondered why I had woken. I didn't know the time, didn't know how long I had slept, but I knew we had to go. A feeling as compelling as a summons gripped me, and I gasped at the vision of a body swinging on a rope. I got up and made my way around camp, looking for Robin.

When I found him, I shook him awake.

"We've got to go," I whispered.

"What? Kay, I just got to sleep."

It wasn't that late then. "We have to go. Now. They're not going to wait. I know it. Everything feels wrong, and I saw someone hanging."

"You *saw* . . . ." Robin sat up, throwing back his wet blanket.

"Yes. We have to go."

"All right. I'll get the men together. Get yourself ready."

"Right."

Ten minutes later, a group of twenty outlaws headed toward Nottingham. I ran beside Robin.

"You have a plan then?" I asked.

"Aye. Listen . . . ."

TWELVE

Nottingham was silent as we ran along shadowed alleyways. We had entered town through the east gate after tricking the guard into opening it. The east gate was the smallest and the hardest to get to, and therefore the most vulnerable. We overpowered and tied up the four soldiers in the gatehouse, then left two men to defend our escape.

The sun was coming up, the gray sky beginning to grow light through the rain. As we passed homes, we heard people moving around inside, though no one moved out of doors, and we blessed the rain that kept shutters closed. In the center of town, the marketplace was deserted, but we could see they had strung the hangman's gallows with five new ropes.

Robin and I exchanged looks. "You were right," was all he said. Beyond him, Phillip looked at me, too. He knew I had insisted we leave during the night, and I could see he wondered how I had known.

I wasn't sure if it had been anxiety for Will or true presentiment, but Robin had been wrong. If we had waited, Will and the others would have died long before we could have arrived.

According to the plan, the men deployed themselves into hiding places around the marketplace. Robin and I hid under the hanging platform, flat against the wall of the building with straw pulled close around us.

It wasn't long before the town stirred, and as the bells in the tower pealed three times to summon the populace, people began to gather. Shortly after, the prisoners were led into the square. It was hard not to move when I saw them—still muddy and all with wounds left untreated.

"Wait for the signal," Robin cautioned in a muffled voice, reading my abortive movement correctly. "Little John will know when to do it." He looked up as the boots of the guards clomped across the platform. The prisoners' steps were soft, almost soundless. I would have looked holes through the platform if I could.

Someone started making a speech about the evils of outlawry— the Chief Forester, no doubt. We heard the stools creak as the prisoners were pushed up on them, the ropes slipped over their heads and tightened. There was a brief scuffle, heard over the speaker's voice, then a thud on the platform.

"Get up, scum," a guard jeered. "No more of your witless fussing. Die like a man."

We heard somebody get up and spit on the guard.

"Bravo," I whispered, then winced at the crack of the guard's blow. I knew even before I heard the string of curses that it had been Will.

Robin and I edged forward, each to separate sides of the platform.

The crowd milled about, jostling for a better view. Many held cloaks over their heads to keep off the rain. The speechmaker droned on about the justice of the high sheriff.

Then it came. The crowd in the far corner burst into shouts and curses. Several guards jumped from the platform and pushed through the crowd to the disturbance.

Robin and I scrambled out and hoisted ourselves up to find six guards had remained at their posts. All attention was focused on the corner and the shouting men. I reached around and cut one guard's throat. Before the man hit the platform, I cut the rope around Walter's neck. He jumped when he felt me touch him, but when the rope fell and I began to cut his hands free, he helped by stretching the bonds tightly. Once his hands were free, I shoved a knife at him and moved to Will, who was next in line.

Walter stabbed one of the guards, who still stood at the edge of the platform watching the crowd, and he cried out as he fell to the ground.

I cut the rope around Will's hands and gave him my sword. He slipped out of the noose as I moved to the next guard. They knew what was happening now, and the platform was a mass of struggling bodies. Someone shouted for reinforcements.

Looking around, I saw Edward hanging, but Robin had freed the rest. Men converged on the platform, outlaws and soldiers alike, while the townsfolk fled the vicinity. Frederick the Norman was up with us, his swords flashing like a steel hurricane. Moments before a soldier could run him through, I made a mad dash to reach Edward, ducked under his kicking feet, and came up directly beneath the soldier, cramming my knife into his thigh and throwing him off the platform. Frederick was nearby when I wrapped my arms around Edward's legs and lifted. One swipe of his sword parted the rope.

I crashed to the platform, Edward's dead weight on top of me. Unable to tell if he was still alive, I pushed him off and knelt to check his pulse. I thought I felt a faint heartbeat. I turned to shout at Frederick, only to see a soldier bearing down on me. Too late, I threw up my knife to defend against the unexpected blow.

He tried to run me through, but I twisted aside and the blade scraped across my midriff, opening the skin and cracking ribs. I rolled away from him as Frederick engaged the soldier. I put a hand on the wound. It was bleeding, but I couldn't feel much pain, only a slight drunkenness. I found myself in a pool of calm amid the battle and knelt beside Edward. Frederick caught my eye. He was a storm of action, his swords twin streaks of lightning as he fought the soldier who had wounded me. Awed at his skillful use of the weapons, I watched in amazement as he dispatched the soldier.

Then he knelt beside me, examining Edward. "He's alive. Are you badly hurt?"

"I don't know," I said. "Let's get him out of here."

Frederick handed me one of his swords and hoisted Edward over his shoulder. A soldier tried to stop us as we made our way off the platform, but I pushed him off the steps and ran over the top of him.

Robin and the others followed. The whole raid had taken only minutes, but we still had to make it out the gate before reinforcements came up from the castle, cutting off our escape.

I didn't know if everyone was with us, couldn't even remember who had come. Will ran beside me. Frederick carried Edward just in front of us, inside a wedge of outlaws.

Just before we got to the gate, a small group of soldiers came out of a side street, spreading out to block our way. It was undoubtedly a maneuver just to slow us down. They couldn't have hoped to stop us.

We outnumbered them two to one and rolled right over the top of them, desperation our best weapon. I got a kick in at one who had fallen to the ground beneath our feet, then we were outside, racing for the forest. There was pursuit, but it was unorganized, and we gained the trees without incident.

David, Gerald, and Reginald stopped just inside the tree line and turned to open fire on the pursuing soldiers, while the rest of us ran on, splitting up into several groups to throw off the trail.

Will and Much ran with me, following Frederick and Edward. I didn't get far before I stopped and doubled over, pressing my hands against my stomach. The adrenaline was gone, replaced by pain.

I had expected it ever since the soldier drew my blood, but when my skin prickled, I didn't have to look up to know the door was there.

"Go away," I whispered. The light grew against my closed eyes, all but forcing me to open them. My pain eased magically at the sight of the rectangular illumination, and euphoric tremors passed through me. Three steps. That was all it would take to go through. The world of my birth awaited with doctors to heal me, a roof to shelter me, regular meals, and a dry, comfortable bed. Three steps . . . two.

"Alone," I told myself, mustering up conviction. "I'll be alone."

One step. The radiance of the door bathed my face, the warmth gathering on my skin. An uninterrupted view of cloudless blue sky and sunshine reached through to caress me. It felt so good. Dryness, warmth. My eyes closed as I swayed forward.

Strong arms grasped my shoulders and I opened my eyes. There was a brief flash of the door before Will crashed through from the other side and the light withdrew. The immediate world came roaring in on me again.

"How . . . ? Didn't you see . . . ?" Pain lanced through me as I spoke, breath like fire in my lungs.

"C'mon, Kay. We've got to keep moving."

"I can't." I fell back to the ground, willing my heaving chest to ease. The motion killed me. "Oh, I can't."

"Kay?" Will's voice faded.

Unconsciousness didn't last long enough. I woke, balanced on a precarious contraption bobbing through the forest. Three belts strung between two stout branches formed a litter, and a shirt supported my head. I saw Much in front of me, shirtless, arms braced to bear my weight.

Closing my eyes against their jolting run, I grabbed hold of the sides of the litter to ease the feeling that I was going to bounce off at any second.

"Almost there, Kay." The sound of Will's voice was reassuring. I kept my eyes closed and tried to think of anything besides the predicament I was in.

The wound was a bad one. The energy I had spent after acquiring it hadn't made it any better. I was sure I had lost a lot of blood, and who knew what internal damage had been done.

I passed out again.

WHEN I WOKE AGAIN, true awareness was slow in reasserting itself. The darkness enveloping me resolved into the branches and leaves of a hawthorn bush, and sunlight chiseled its way through myriad holes in the makeshift roof above me.

Sunlight? Have I returned then? Am I even now in some thicket near my uncle's cabin, awaiting the strength to crawl to a doctor?

Sound intruded on my senses at last, and I realized I wasn't alone.

I lay under a lean-to shelter, Edward by my side. His breath came in strangled rasps, though I thought he was sleeping. My clothes were clammy, but my face and hands were dry. I could almost say I was comfortable.

My chest was bandaged tightly enough to keep me from moving easily when I tried to sit up. Lying still against the pain, I found it didn't feel too bad if I just lay there and breathed slowly.

"Edward?" I asked quietly.

"K . . . ay . . . ." It was a struggle for him to say my name.

"Shhh," I said. My throat ached just to hear him. I turned my head to look at him in the dim light. "Are we back at camp? Just nod."

He shook his head and gave a whimper of pain. "Tuck."

"We shouldn't be here!" Alarmed, I tried to sit up and gasped in pain. "They'll look here!"

Slowly, Edward put a hand on my leg. "Hidden." He took a deep breath, the air rattling horribly in his throat. "Will be . . . back soon."

I took Edward's hand and squeezed it. "It hurts you. I'm sorry."

"Not your . . . fault. You—" He broke into a fit of coughing and clutched my hand so tightly in an effort to stay quiet, I felt my fingers crunching together.

When his fit subsided, I gently took my hand from his and shook my fingers out.

"Sorry . . . ," he began.

"Hush. You'll cough again. That's got to hurt." I paused to listen, then added, "I don't know where we are, but we don't want to be heard."

There was a sound outside the shelter, then a footfall. I reached for my knife, glad to find it back in my sheath. I lay still, mustering the energy to sit up if I had to.

Edward sat up slowly, holding his head, a knife out and ready.

Branches rattled and a shaft of sunlight—undiluted sunshine!— pierced the gloom.

"Kay?"

I relaxed and put up my knife, sighing with relief. "Much. Who's with you?"

"Will. Are you both awake?"

"Aye. Open this place up and let me see the sun before it starts raining again." I heard Will chuckle. "Will, let me see you, dammit. I risked my skin to save yours. I want to make sure you're not in ribbons."

Will laughed, then the branches parted so I could see his face appear next to Much's. There was a bandage around his head, but he was smiling at me. "Am I whole enough for you?"

I snarled at him, annoyed at his cheeriness. "Can't see all of you, can I? Get me out of this dismal coop." I struggled to sit up once again, gritting my teeth against the pain. I glared at Will, whose mirth had changed to alarm.

"Lie down, Kay." He tried to push me back, but I grabbed his hand and held myself up. "You're split across the middle, woman. Lie down."

"Get me outside. I can't stand it in here anymore!" I fell back to the earthen floor as Will and Much opened the shelter. "How long has it been? Why the hell did you bring us to Tuck? So we could get him hanged, too?"

"That's enough, Kay," Will snapped. "Tuck was closest, and you and Edward needed his skills. You're lucky we did, too. He had to stitch you up. Nobody at camp could do that big a job."

"But the soldiers—"

"Won't come here. There are too many trails to follow, and Much went back to cover ours."

"Dammit. Everybody's been wrong lately. Do you trust that enough to risk Tuck's life? I can travel. We ought to go before they think to check here."

"She's right." Much looked across the small clearing to Tuck's hermitage. "They won't spare Tuck, even though he's a man of the cloth."

"Go," said Edward, nodding. He got up, and Much made room for him to move out of the shelter. "I . . . can . . . travel." He spoke slowly and clearly, but he had to put a hand on Much's shoulder to stay upright.

Much looked as though he would have preferred to stay and help me, but he and Edward started into the forest.

I grabbed hold of Will's arm, pulling myself into a sitting position. "Let's go," I said through clenched teeth. "Once I get up, I'll be all right."

Will helped me stand, worry in his eyes. "They'll be searching the forest, and we won't be able to move fast."

"I won't risk Tuck," I said firmly. I let go of Will to show him I could stand on my own. He watched me for a moment, then stooped to fix the shelter so it looked like a natural clump of bushes. When he turned back, he held out a hand to steady me.

"The sun feels wonderful," I remarked casually, "but it'll be going down soon. They'll quit searching when it gets dark." I turned to follow Edward and Much.

"Wait here a moment," Will said, and crossed the clearing to Tuck's dwelling.

I walked as far as the nearest tree and leaned against it, waiting. I couldn't see Much or Edward, and thought it was just as well we were traveling separately. No sense in all of us getting captured because one of us couldn't keep up.

Will strode back to me. I looked up at him, laboring to stand up straight. I saw the worry in his eyes, but he didn't say anything, just put his arm around me and helped me walk through the forest.

Silence followed us. We traveled a mile before it was broken. I sat down to rest, Will giving me his shoulder to lean against.

"I didn't think you would come." He reached up to brush a strand of hair away from my face. "Robin's never made a rescue before. Not like that."

"I was so surprised when he said there would be no rescue party. I was angry. I wanted to beat sense into him."

"How come you came then?" Will took his hand away. I missed the touch.

"Did you think I would give up on you?" I asked.

"No," he whispered.

"If Robin hadn't said he would come, it would have been just me, Robert, Phillip, and Much." I paused. "Something's been bothering me, Will. Did I do anything to make that robbery go wrong?"

"Someone's blaming you?" Will asked sharply.

"No. But what bothers me is if I did nothing to screw it up, you would have been captured no matter what—had I been there or not."

Will grasped my chin firmly, making me look at him. "It wasn't your fault."

"I know, but don't you see?" I couldn't keep excitement out of my voice. "It's the proof I've looked for since I came to this time. If I hadn't been there, you still would have been captured and I wouldn't have talked Robin into rescuing you. You would have died, but the stories from my time have you alive after Robin dies."

"They do?" There was a note of surprise in Will's voice.

"Yes. But now I'm confused. I had thought that my being here wouldn't have any effect, and even if it did, it wouldn't matter. But now it does. I don't know anymore . . . ."

The thought struck like lightning. "Will! I could save Robin."

That's why the door keeps coming back. It knows I can do it.

"What?" Will was having trouble following my thoughts, and I realized I shouldn't even be talking to him about it. It was something I would just have to do if I could.

"Never mind. I shouldn't confuse you with my babble. I'm ready to go." I started to get up to forestall any questions from him about things I was just beginning to try and work out.

As we walked, it got dark. Somewhere along the way, Will gathered me into his arms and carried me. I fell asleep to the jolting rhythm of his walk.

I woke once in the night, wondering where I was. It was dark . . . but warm. I heard Will's even breathing beside me, his arms wrapped around me. Comforted by that, I drowsed back into sleep.

In the morning, Will nudged me awake. I blinked against the daylight as he helped me sit up. The sunshine from yesterday was gone, the sky now a drab gray. "Ugh," I groaned. "More rain?"

"How do you feel?" he asked, putting his hand against my forehead to check for fever.

"I hurt." It was almost worse now than the day before. "Where are we?"

"I'm not exactly sure. I had to stop last night when I lost my bearings. I'll be able to figure it out once we get moving. Do you want to go back to Tuck? Your face feels awful hot."

"No. I'm fine. See?" I stood, leaning against him more than I wanted.

"Kay, what am I going to do if you catch the wound fever? What if that moldy bread mess he put on you doesn't work?"

"Moldy bread?" I echoed, wondering what he was talking about, then realized mold would be a primitive source of penicillin and a ward against bacteria. "Where did he get that notion?"

"I'd feel better if you'd go back to Tuck."

"Will, the soldiers will be sure to look there today. They know some of us were wounded. If they have any brains at all, they'll figure a forest priest may have sympathy for wounded outlaws. I like Tuck. I'd as soon not see him get into any trouble over me."

"You're a stubborn woman, Kay. I think you're wrong, and I've half a mind to carry you back to Tuck's. I won't, but you're walking by yourself today." He rubbed his arms woefully. "You get heavy after a while."

I grinned at him. "I didn't ask you to carry me."

A brief time later, as we sat beside a tiny stream so I could rest, I asked a question that had been on my mind.

"Will, when I stopped and you came back to me, did you see anything strange? Any lights?"

"No. You called out to me and I saw you weren't keeping up. Did *you* see lights?"

"Yes, but I must have been hallucinating."

I didn't remember calling to him, but I was glad I had. If he hadn't shattered the spell, I would no doubt be in a hospital right now. That, or dead on a mountain in Oregon.

"Are you all right?" Will put his hand to my forehead and I batted it away peevishly.

"I'm fine," I reassured him. "I just hate being an invalid."

AT DUSK, we finally got back to camp. I walked all the way, but we had to stop often. Twice we had to hide from foresters, but in both cases, they were hurrying back toward Nottingham.

The camp was just coming to life with the setting of the sun. Richard of Newcastle made a small fire, while Alfred of Ely uncovered the food cache for something to cook.

I looked around for Robin and saw him sitting beside Will Stutely, who knelt next to him, wrapping a cloth around his upper arm.

Scarlet and I walked over to him, and Will helped me sit.

"You were wounded?" I asked, feeling slightly foolish for stating the obvious. I didn't know what else to say.

"A scratch. You?" Robin had been watching Stutely work on

him, but he now turned to look at me. "Frederick said you'd been cut."

"It's nothing." I didn't want him to know how bad it was.

Will shook his head. "A little more than nothing, Robin. She was nearly cut in two. Tuck said she's lucky her ribs were only cracked."

Robin only grunted and I was glad he didn't make much of it. "We had a few other minor injuries, but nothing a little time won't cure. I heard that Much came in with Edward around noon. He's going to be all right?"

"He'll never sound the same, but he'll be all right," said Will, frowning slightly at Robin. "We saw foresters on our way here."

Robin nodded. "We had a couple close calls. Some of our people were out and had to hide. But no foresters came close to camp or the new winter site."

"Good," I said. "Robin, about yesterday. It was unfair of me to fault you . . . ."

Robin smiled as my voice trailed off. It was hard for me to say I was sorry, and he knew it. He put a hand on my knee. "Our next robbery, I will not worry so much about being fair."

"Why should we fight fair when the sheriff can pull aces out of his sleeves?" My odd turn of phrase barely even made him blink. I put my hand on his shoulder in gratitude. "Thank you, Robin, for helping."

He shrugged, then flexed his arm to test the bandage Stutely had tied for him. He put his hand on my arm as he rose. "It was a hard lesson for all of us. Let's hope we learned it, eh?" He lifted his brow. "We won't be able to pull off a rescue like that again."

I nodded, realizing he was right. They hadn't expected us to get there in time, hadn't expected Robin would take the risk when he hadn't in the past. They would not be caught unprepared again.

I watched him walk away, then saw Frederick the Norman coming into camp. "Will, help me up. I want to talk to Fred."

Frederick saw me coming and waited, his hand raised in greeting. I returned the gesture.

"You saved my life," I said. "I owe you."

He shook his head. "A life is given to us all. When one is saved, all are saved." His French accent was thick, but I understood him well enough.

"Then I thank you for being the one who was there. You are truly a master, and I would like very much to learn from you."

Frederick was a man of few words, so when he smiled at me, I knew I had amused him with my request.

"I will teach you, chère. You need the best of skills, and two swords are better than one, hmm?"

"Thank you," I said, trying to think of more to say, but failing. I hadn't really expected him to say yes, but I had to ask, having seen how he had used his weapons during the rescue. I envisioned myself whirling into a fight, blades flashing, no one able to stop me. Now Frederick would teach me.

I smiled as he walked away. Then he turned. "When you are healed."

It was a long time before I healed enough to begin my lessons with the Norman. But learn from him I did, and I soon began to wear two swords. I practiced until I became a master in my own right. Swordsmanship was my best area, with archery falling in right behind it. I learned plenty of tricks from Frederick, and we became good friends.

I began to forget I had lived anywhere other than Sherwood, had done anything else but hunt and thieve, had been anything but an outlaw.

We hunted, traded with the villagers, and held up wealthy travelers on the roads through Sherwood. We hid and moved constantly until it was rumored Robin Hood owned the entire forest.

More troubled and dissatisfied men joined our band. On a still summer night, two women did, as well.

CHAPTER
THIRTEEN

L ate one evening, after dinner was over and things were settling down for the night, Robin and I were sitting by the fire when I looked up to see two strangers approaching. I jumped to my feet half a second behind Robin. They weren't armed, so I didn't draw my knife, but I was ready as I took a closer look.

It was two women—one maybe sixteen, the other about twenty-five. They were dirty from travel and looked as though the trees had gotten the better of them at some point. They both had blonde hair that was cut short, as though by their own knives.

I looked behind them to see who had brought them in.

"Who are you?" Robin looked beyond them, just as I had. "Who brought you here?"

"We came ourselves," the younger woman said, her tone bold and proud. "Are you Robin Hood?"

Robin nodded and sized them up. "You came here on your own? You saw no one as you came in?" His voice was flat and I knew someone was in trouble for sleeping on duty.

"No one showed us. We found our own way." The young girl smiled smugly. "We saw your guard, but he didn't see us."

"He was awake?" Robin asked.

"Yes." The younger woman looked at the older woman, who wasn't smiling, and her face fell.

"Who are you?" Robin asked again. "Why are you here?"

"I'm Jenny, and this is my sister, Jana," the younger woman said. "We are here to join you."

Robin stared at them, then made a small signal with his hand. Behind the women, Edmond the Jew moved. I shifted my gaze back to them.

"You want to join us?" Robin echoed. "It is not an easy life, here in the forest."

Jenny stiffened. "You have women here, even one standing beside you. We—"

Jana whirled, grabbing Edmond's outstretched arm, twisting it behind him and bringing him to his knees. A knife materialized in her hand and she pressed it against his throat. Edmond was smart enough not to move.

Jana looked up at Robin, whose eyes widened in surprise. "We have been used badly enough, Robin Hood," Jana spoke for the first time, her voice hard and bitter. "We did not come here to be used again. Either you take us in, or we go."

"What will you do if I send you away?" Robin asked.

Jenny spoke up. "We'll go south, live on our own. That's where we were going, but it was my idea to stop here." Jenny was on her guard now, as well.

With a grunt of disgust directed at Robin, Jana let go of Edmond. He stood, backing away from the women. Some of the others snickered, and he turned to glare at them.

"Stay." Robin smiled at them. "At least for the night. We will talk tomorrow."

These women surprised me, especially Jana's anger. I didn't know what could have happened to make them come here on their own, but it must have been bad. Selfishly, I thought it would be good to have some female company at last.

As was his way, Robin considered the issue overnight, then spoke to them privately the next morning. When the three of them returned to the camp, the women stayed. Robin never told me why he allowed it, or if he had considered sending them away. He only told me they were good enough to stay. Just finding the camp in the first place and getting past an awake guard showed him they could be useful.

LATE THAT SUMMER, we robbed Prince John as he traveled to Nottingham. We knew he was coming and had planned our attack weeks in advance, this being the most daring of all our escapades so far.

Prince John traveled with an escort of a hundred men, so we knew we had to strike in the right place at exactly the right time. Granted, all the best soldiers were overseas fighting Saracens with their king, but these soldiers would have the numbers and fear of the prince's wrath to motivate them.

On the appointed day, every one of us hid along the road to watch the royal convoy pass. My heart pounded at the sight of all his men, knowing things could go wrong very easily. But we all had orders to retreat as soon as it looked like our plan was going awry. And we would know within moments if it was not going to work.

It was a hot, sultry summer day, and as the prince's carriage rolled into view, we saw it was open as much as possible to catch every breeze. Prince John sat there, looking so royal and important . . . and bored out of his skull.

Robin had chosen a heavily wooded section of the road to set our trap for two purposes. First and foremost was that if retreat was necessary, the trees would hide us and slow the heavily armored soldiers down. Second was that the trees would conceal us until precisely the perfect moment to attack.

When that moment came, it was Robin himself who led the charge, taking the guards around the carriage completely by surprise. Little John and Will Stutely beat back the few who had drawn swords, and Robin leapt into the carriage and put a knife to Prince John's throat. The rest of us slipped out of the trees, circling the party as best we could with our smaller numbers.

"Tell your men to lay down their arms or you die." Robin's voice carried to the soldiers around the carriage.

"You won't do it," Prince John said, backing up against his cushions. "I'm the prince, by God!"

"And I'm an outlaw." Robin wrapped his hand in the collar of John's princely robes and hauled him to the window of the carriage. "A bloodthirsty knave, as I recall you named me. Give the order!"

Prince John shrieked an order to surrender. Slowly, the surprised men dropped their weapons to the ground. The riders dismounted and handed the reins over to waiting outlaws.

Robin pushed the prince out of the carriage and into the hands of Little John and Will Stutely, then turned to see what treasures the prince traveled with.

The brightest gem of the entire affair came as a complete surprise. We were in the process of tying up the entire unit of guards and horsemen when Jana strode up, bold as you please, to where Little John and Will held the cursing Prince John. She stared him in the eye until he fell silent, then slowly and deliberately took the ring from his little finger, stowed it in her shirt, and moved to the next finger.

She proceeded to strip him of every gemstone and scrap of precious metal he wore, down to the gold buttons on his cloak, passing them into Jenny's eager hands.

When she was through, she drew her knife and held it under the prince's left eye. John's face was purple with outrage, but he held still.

"I would readily take more than I have," Jana said. "For Maria."

At the mention of the name, Prince John flinched, causing her knife to prick the flesh beneath his eye. A small jewel of blood formed. Robin stepped up and put a hand on her shoulder. She didn't look away, didn't waver, and I thought she would indeed take the man's eye, along with his jewels. But she let Robin draw her away.

She pointed her knife at the prince, and I was close enough to see it quivering with her rage. "Remember this, John, and let you think of it before you bed another unwilling woman." Jana's voice was thick with hatred, and she looked ready to take back the few steps she had withdrawn to finish the job she'd started.

At a signal from Robin, Prince John was tied to the nearest tree, then Little John and Will Stutely faded into the forest. Every soldier was bound hand and foot, their weapons left hanging in the highest tree. Whatever treasure they had carried vanished with the outlaws as everyone except Robin and Jana left the road. Jana stared at John, plainly despising him, while Robin coaxed her away. Finally, they turned and melted into the forest.

From my spot in the trees, I turned my back on the scene, leaving the furious prince screaming obscenities after us.

JENNY and I got along rather well . . . after the initial awkward beginning. She made good company as the nights lengthened through fall and into winter. At her request, I began to teach her the rudiments of swordplay, and she tried to show me a few ways to weave grass into baskets. I was an awful student. I could never keep the weave even enough, and my baskets were always lopsided and artistically dull.

Jenny was also quite good with wood carvings, often whittling away at a chunk of wood as we spoke. She gave me a carving of a wolf as big as my thumb, detailed to the row of teats on its belly.

"A she-wolf," she told me, "for the fiercest, most protective member of Robin's band."

I kept it in my belt pouch and often brought it out as I sat watch, wondering why she would say that of me when she hardly knew me.

Jana and I also struck up a friendship of sorts. She was not gregarious by nature, or by something that had happened in the past . . . . I was certain it was the latter. She spent most of her time with Jenny, always silent whenever I was there. The rest of her time was consumed with checking her snares. She was very good at trapping small animals. I invited myself along one day and we went around in silence, bringing back three squirrels and a rabbit.

After that, she often sought me out, gesturing for me to come with her. Without exception, I followed when she offered, but I never violated her solitude without an invitation. Being in her company was like waiting for a storm. She was almost serene, a wealth of patience and resources, but below the surface, I knew her anger simmered like a billowing thunderhead.

Every so often, she spoke. Always safe subjects, never delving into personal matters. When I went with her, I enjoyed the quiet company, something I hadn't had much of since I joined Robin's boisterous group.

It was Jenny who told me Jana wasn't really her sister, as they had always maintained, but that was all she ever said about their past. Whenever we talked, she always spoke about the present, never going back to a time before they came to the forest.

Fall was drawing to a close when Jana and I went out late one afternoon to check snares. We were nearly done when we heard a woman scream—a wounded sound abruptly cut off. I recognized Jenny's voice at once. Jana dropped the sack of rabbits she carried and ran in the direction the sound had come from. I followed close on her heels.

The last leaves clinging to the trees hid Jenny from us until we were nearly upon her. She was face down on the ground, wrestling against Seward, his hand clamped firmly across her mouth as he tried to pull down her trousers. Her shirt tore across her back as she kicked, struggling to get out from beneath him.

The scene burned into my mind an instant before Jana flew against Seward, knocking him off Jenny. She landed on top of him, pummeling him with her fists as he tried to defend himself and pull up his pants at the same time.

Jenny was on her feet, outrage clear on her face.

"Are you hurt?" I asked, futilely trying to fix her shirt where it fell off her shoulder, nearly exposing her breast.

"Not physically," she said, turning to see Jana battering Seward's face. "Jana, no!"

Jana drew her knife and pressed it into Seward's chest. He lay still, his hands up, while Jana straddled him, ready to plunge the blade into him. Jenny ran to her and put her hand on the knife handle. They stared at each other, Seward panting beneath them. All I could do was watch, horrified that any of this was happening.

Finally, Jana slapped Jenny's hand away with a growl and drew back her knife.

"Jana, no!"

Jana's blade was at his throat before Jenny caught her wrist. With Jana pressing down, Jenny couldn't pull her hand away without helping her slit Seward's throat. "Jana, let's talk about this—"

"What's there to talk about?" Jana growled, pressing her knife deeper into his throat. "He was *raping* you."

"We'll take it to Robin," Jenny said.

"No! He dies now!"

Jenny turned to me. "Kay, help me. Stop her."

"I'm not sure I should," I said, not moving from where I stood watching it all. I had never seen a rape before, and what I had just seen appalled me. It was one of my worst nightmares when I first came to the forest, but the dreams had gone after the first two years and only Alexander's drunken attempt. But this . . . . This act was exactly what I had feared.

Anger burned in my belly at the sight of Seward cowering under Jana's knife, knowing what he had tried to do. That was where men like him belonged. Under the knife of a woman who had been wronged in that way. I was not inclined to stop her.

"Kay, please," said Jenny, striving to catch my eye. I saw desperation in hers. "After Prince John, Robin made Jana swear she would never harm any of his men without first talking to him. She swore on her salvation."

I hesitated a moment longer. It didn't make sense to me that Jana would swear so heavily against something that so obviously disturbed her. Jenny was clearly more concerned than Jana, who might not have ever cared about her salvation. But Jenny was right. Robin was a fair man. He would dispense a fitting punishment.

I moved to Jana's side, putting a hand on her shoulder. She didn't stir, only stared at the blood welling in the depression her knife made in Seward's throat. His eyes were closed, his lips moving in what looked like prayer.

"Jana, come away from him," I said gently. "We'll do as Jenny wants and leave him to Robin."

She didn't move, so I tugged at her arm. She shook me off. I looked at Jenny, who made a lifting motion. "Jana," I said. "Come away."

Jenny gently pried the knife from her hand, while I crouched behind her and lifted. Jana went limp with resignation as I dragged her off Seward.

"Get up," Jenny told him, any trace of gentleness gone from her voice. "We're going to go see Robin."

I put my arm across Jana's shoulders and helped her back to camp as Jenny tied Seward's hands together. Feeling her totally passive under my guidance and seeing her blank face, I felt the anger returning threefold. Why did men have to do things like this?

"Jana," I said gently. "Robin will do right by Jenny. Trust in that."
She gave no response.

When we arrived back at camp, we caused quite a stir. A crowd quickly gathered around us as I helped Jana to a seat and Jenny pushed Seward to the ground in front of her. I looked up to see Andrew standing in front of me.

"Get Robin," I said flatly.

The crowd of men jostled to get close. Many of them questioned Seward about what had happened, making sarcastic comments that were quite close to the truth. He didn't respond. Some of them took in Jenny's torn clothes, Jana's sullen silence, and my tension, and realized what had happened. Their silence was worse than any jests.

I wished Robin would hurry.

Finally, he came through the crowd, his stony eyes surveying our small group as he came up beside me.

"What's this all about?" he asked. His gaze stopped on Jana. He'd seen the blood on Seward's throat.

I waited for someone else to speak, but no one did. Jenny looked at the ground, Seward at Jenny, and Jana at Robin.

I sighed, knowing this wasn't going to be easy. "Seward tried to rape Jenny," I said, not knowing how to soften the words. Not knowing if I should even try.

"She wanted it," Seward said, angrily looking up at me.

"Bull*shit*, Seward. When a woman screams like that and tries to get away, she doesn't want anything to do with you."

When Robin put a hand on my shoulder, I realized I had taken a threatening step forward.

"God, I'm going to be sick." I pushed my way through the crowd.

On the edge of the clearing, I threw up, the bile as bitter as my anger. Wiping my mouth, I leaned against a tree, listening to the argument raging in the clearing. I closed my eyes, tipping my head back until it thunked against the tree.

My stomach still roiled, threatening to empty further. The scene replayed again in my head. Seward poised above a struggling Jenny, pawing at her. The lust in his face as he tore her clothes. Desperation written in her eyes as her face pressed against the ground.

"Jesus," I said aloud, in the next instant hearing a familiar foot-step nearby. Without opening my eyes, I spoke. "Just go away, Will. I don't want to see anyone right now."

"I just wanted to be sure you're all right," he said, not coming any closer.

"I don't know." I scrubbed my face with my hands. "I'm sick and disgusted, and I'm not sure I want to see any men for at least a week." I pushed away from the tree.

"'Kay!"

I ignored his call and walked into the forest. I was afraid. Afraid to know what Robin's verdict would be, afraid he would side with Seward and none of us women would be safe. I thought I knew Robin better than that, but the fear still nagged at me.

I remained a coward, too. I didn't return to the clearing, spending a cold, uncomfortable night in a tree. I didn't sleep a wink with so many vile thoughts thrashing through my mind.

When I came back late the next day, the camp was preparing for the evening meal as though nothing had happened the day before. I watched from the trees for a while, looking for Jenny and Jana. They were nowhere to be found and I worried Robin had exiled them. I couldn't see Seward, either, which gave me a little hope that Robin had been fair.

Taking a deep breath, I stepped into the clearing, trying very hard to be casual. Most of the men didn't notice my return. Those who did lowered their heads, refusing to meet my eyes.

I walked to the fire to warm myself, my gaze restlessly roaming over the men gathered in groups. I saw Will at the same time he saw me and our gazes locked. He stood slowly, setting down the knife he was sharpening to come to my side.

"Are you all right?" he asked softly. He didn't touch me, keeping his distance, for which I was grateful.

From the corner of my eye, I saw Much hesitate in the act of approaching, then give way to Will's presence. I was even more thankful that my friends knew me so well.

I didn't answer his question. "What happened?"

"Jenny decided Seward's punishment."

"Which is?"

"He must wait on her and Jana, follow their every order, so long as Robin says he must. If he does not, he will be exiled."

"Ah." It didn't seem like enough to me. "Are they okay?"

"They're . . . fine. How are you?"

I sighed. "I'm okay, I guess. Mostly angry. If Jenny can get over it, I suppose I can, too." I looked up at Will and saw the concern in his eyes. "I'll be okay," I insisted. "But God help the man who tries that on me."

"He'd have to step over my dead body to get to you, Kay."

I tried on a smile, my face slow to oblige. "I'd step over his to bury you."

"That's supposed to comfort me?" Will asked, putting a hand on my shoulder in a compassionate gesture masked by the flippancy of his response.

My smile broadened into a grin, and I blessed him for knowing how to make me smile. "Of course. Do you think I would leave you to the crows?"

FOURTEEN

A light spring rain fell outside the shelter where I sat, tying up bags of silver. Robin planned to make one of his trips around to some of the outlying villages worse off than the others. He made regular visits to ensure the poorer folk kept up with their taxes, and I was helping him count money from our reserve to give out.

We hadn't filched much money lately, not since King Richard had been shipwrecked near Venice. Duke Leopold of Austria had captured him and was asking a substantial ransom for his safe return. Most of the money passing through Sherwood these days was on its way to Austria.

A man entered the shelter, giving Robin a half-salute. "A shipment of gold's going through tomorrow," said Oswald Eagle Eye. He was a Welshman who had joined two years earlier. His brother, Caleb, was in the group long before me.

Robin looked up, interested. Oswald was one of our best scouts. He wasn't called Eagle Eye for nothing. "What's it for?"

"The king's ransom."

"Then we'll leave it." Robin went back to his counting. "Richard may tax his people to death, but we won't be the cause of him remaining in the hands of his captors."

Oswald nodded and left the shelter. I sighed as I tied up another bag, then looked up to see Robin watching me.

"What?" he asked.

"I just hope the men don't get riled up." I set the bag down with the others.

"Oswald won't start anything."

"No, he wouldn't, but his brother might. Caleb's got one hard head, and since Jerod's death . . . ."

Jerod had been captured by the sheriff and hanged before we could even think about rescuing him, which had saved Robin any guilt he might have felt from refusing to go to his aid.

"They won't start anything," Robin said confidently.

"They're restless, Robin. We've made no raids in months." Years of associating with Robin made me comfortable enough to tell him what was on my mind. "I heard someone say you've gone soft."

Robin laughed. "That's why I'm taking all the pushy ones with me this time. Walking around Sherwood for a week or so ought to cool their heels a bit. It'll give them a chance to see their women, too. That's what most of them have been aching for in the first place."

We were quiet for a moment, the clinking of coins making small music in the shelter.

"I've always wondered," I said, a touch of anger returning, "why no one has ever approached me. I mean, what makes me so different from Jenny?" It was a thing that had puzzled me all winter.

Robin grinned. "Kay, you're forgetting Alexander."

"Alex was drunk."

"That didn't stop you from giving him a shave he'll never forget. The others haven't forgotten, either."

I chuckled. "No, I don't suppose they would."

I remembered the wide-eyed looks of respect I got for days after that incident. It was a rotten thing to do to a drunk man, but I couldn't help it. After I had knocked him out, the sight of his unkempt hair was too much. I had used a knife to give his hair and beard a trim. He'd come out of it looking marginally better, but my lack of barbering skills meant he had more than a little razor burn, not to mention a cold head until his hair had a chance to grow back.

But Robin hadn't answered my question. "Besides, his drunken groping was not the same as what Seward did to Jenny." I paused thoughtfully. "You know, that's the only time in four years I actually thought about going home."

"Why?" Robin's curiosity was sincere.

"It sickened me, Robin. I thought I knew these men, thought of them like brothers. When I saw Seward there, looking like he had every right to do what he did, I wanted to scratch his eyes out. I heard you all arguing and I thought, 'What I wouldn't give to be back in my uncle's cabin.' I even told Will to get lost."

Robin contemplated that. "We're not all lecherous bastards, Kay. But when there are no women around, even the most virtuous man's mind wanders. I've made it clear I won't tolerate any of that kind of behavior. Besides," he said and shook his finger at me, gently chiding, "you wouldn't have sent him off if you'd seen all the times Will has been in fights with others who talked about having a go at you."

"He fought for me?" The thought gave me a warm feeling, as well as a hint of anger that he was fighting my battles for me. *Having a go, indeed.*

"And I wouldn't be surprised," Robin continued, studiously counting coins without looking at me, "if the others thought of you as Will Scarlet's girl."

"Oh really?" I raised an eyebrow. "What has he been saying?" I was thinking I'd have an ear to box.

"He hasn't said anything, and that's just it. You can tell by the way you look at each other and the time you spend together. You mean, you two aren't passionate lovers?"

Seeing his smirk, I threw a bag of money at him, realizing he was teasing me. "Oh, get off!"

When I thought about it, though, it struck me that it was probably true. Will and I did almost everything together. We were very close. But we hadn't gone so far as to declare our feelings to each other, and we definitely hadn't made love.

Robin laughed as he finished up the counting, then cuffed me on the shoulder as he went out to call a meeting. "You two are of a kind, Kay. What you do is your own business, but *I* think you make a good pair." He winked at me.

I smiled as he walked out to call everyone to the front of the shelter. It wasn't until I finished bagging the coins and walked outside that I realized he had turned my mind away from that grim subject yet again.

". . . more than a week of traveling," Robin was saying as I joined the meeting. "I'm going to take seven men with me. Eric O'Leary, Will Stutely, Michael of York, Seward, Ambrose, Oswald, and Caleb." I thought that was a stark lineup of troublemakers, except for Oswald and Will. Oswald was a good kid. He and Will would help Robin keep everyone in line. "We'll leave at sunup tomorrow. Now, is supper ready?"

The table was surrounded with excited talk. People who wanted to go pestered the people going, giving messages for their women, parents, brothers . . . . People were generally cheerful for a change. Inactivity had made this spring particularly dull.

On the third day after they left, Will Scarlet woke me early in the morning. I remembered what he had told me the night before as we sat on fire watch, so I packed my things, buckled on my swords, daggers, and survival knife, then went with him to get some travel food.

We had just recently moved to yet another camp along the River Trent, and Will wanted to visit Tuck, now that he was only a day's journey away. From our winter camp, it would have taken three days just to get to the hermitage.

Will told the man on watch we'd be back the next evening, and we left camp.

When we arrived at sunset, Tuck was glad to see us, and the dogs leapt around happily. He brought us inside his little abode and fed us meat pies, fresh bread, and fine ale. He and Will chatted amiably while I stuffed my face. I had learned long ago to eat as much as I could as often as I could.

Contrary to the old legends, we didn't feast every night on fresh venison and wonderful fruits. More often than not, we had stale bread, hard cheese, and thin ale. After a big kill, we often had dried meat, but it wasn't easy to keep ourselves supplied well enough to feed fifty-four hungry outlaws.

After the meal was over and the dishes cleaned, I listened vaguely to their talk. My mind was on other things, like what Robin said about Will and me. Did the rest of the men really consider me his girl? I tried not to think about it, knowing I shouldn't try to guess how Will felt, but failed miserably.

I focused back on their conversation with a start. They had stopped talking about Gamwell Lodge and had mentioned the king's name.

"Richard's back?" I asked, cross with myself for not listening.

Will smiled. "Where have you been? Tuck just said he'd heard a rumor that the Lionheart was back from Austria. I told him the ransom can't possibly have gotten there already, so he must still be a prisoner."

"Uh, sorry. I wasn't paying attention. I had other things on my mind."

"What things, Kay?" Will asked, smiling.

Tuck got up and excused himself, mumbling something about firewood.

"Just something Robin said," I told him, looking down to find my hands twisting the end of my belt. I stilled them, a vague warmth in my cheeks telling me I was blushing.

Will put a finger under my chin, gently forcing me to look at him. "What did Robin say?" I shook my head, but the look in his eyes brooked no refusal.

"Did you know . . . ," I said with forced lightness, suppressing the shiver of delight his touch gave me. "Did you know some people think of me as your girl?"

"Some people?" he asked.

My eyes drifted closed, savoring his touch. "That's what Robin said."

We were silent, listening to Tuck moving around outside. I opened my eyes, finding Will so close, our noses almost touched. His brown eyes burned darkly with something I could not name. Forgetting every vow I had ever made to wait for his move, I reached up to caress his jaw.

"It wouldn't be such a bad idea," he whispered, moving even closer to me.

"What?" I asked breathlessly.

His lips brushed against mine as the door opened. I turned guiltily to see Tuck come in, and Will cursed under his breath. Tuck smiled, but the tips of his ears turned red.

"Sorry," he mumbled, dumping the firewood beside the hearth. "I'm going to turn in. You two might just want to stay in here to sleep. None of the other rooms have been warmed, and this old stone gets mighty cold on a spring night."

"Thank you, Brother Tuck," I said, standing up as he left.

Sleep was the last thing on my mind, but I took my blanket out of my pack and curled up on the rushes next to the fire, tense as a wound spring. Every nerve in my body burned with frustrated desire. It could still happen, this thing my body yearned for and my mind feared. I closed my eyes tightly, trying to shut out the vision of Will's bare body above me, doing things I had only glimpsed beneath the blankets of other outlaws when their women came to visit. I shivered, torn by the desire and confusion I felt.

Hovering in the back of my mind, too, was a vision of Seward's leering face, but I didn't want to let that image taint this evening. Will was nothing like Seward.

The lamp went out. My inner battle raged on as I listened to Will moving around. I studied the hearth, the stone blackened with age and smoke, the old iron arm stretching into the room, ready for a pot to hold over the mellow orange flames.

He came and sat next to me. "Kay?" he asked softly.

"Yes?" I answered. The indecision won. I faked a yawn and shifted to make myself more comfortable.

"It's not a bad idea."

In the firelight, I saw his hand as he moved to set it on my side. I touched it hesitantly, then held it. He sighed and whispered something that sounded like poetry.

"The end is always near, but we have all the time in the world. There's nothing that takes more time to learn than true love. Perhaps we have already learned it."

He leaned down to kiss me on the cheek, lingering to see my unintentional smile. Then he curled up around me, wrapping me in the cocoon of his arms—safe in the circle of his love.

Lying awake for a long time after Will fell asleep, I wondered at those words. They had to be his own because they struck so close to home.

EARLY THE NEXT MORNING, I woke before Tuck or Will. I watched Will sleeping for a few moments, thought about what he'd said, remembered his almost-kiss. The searing emotions from last night were gone, but their echo made my heart thud in my chest.

I tore my gaze away from him and got up quietly, stepping over the dogs as they raised their heads, tails thumping softly on the stone floor. Outside, the morning was fresh, and a sweet breeze blew across my face. I smelled rain and knew we would have a wet trip back.

Roaming around, I found the chicken coop and went inside. When I came out, I had eight eggs tucked into a fold of my shirt. Inspired, I went back into the kitchen to build a fire in the cooking hearth and hang the griddle on its hook. Then I found my way into Tuck's larder and hauled out a side of bacon. By the time I finished slicing up a loaf of bread, Tuck had come in and set up the table. Will came wandering in just as I set a tray of food on the table.

"Well, I'll be . . . ." He scratched his belly and yawned. "You two have been busy." He sat down at the table and began to spoon up some scrambled eggs.

"We have Kay to thank for this fine meal," said Tuck, sitting down.

Will raised an eyebrow as I sat, looking at me until I blushed. "She cooks," he remarked and raised a spoonful of eggs to his mouth. "I didn't know she had such wifely skills. I wonder—"

"Will Scarlet!" Tuck scolded with mock severity. "I must say grace. You may be heathens out there in your forest, but we pray at our meals here."

Will looked down, properly abashed, and set his spoon back on the table, but I saw him wink at me.

Tuck said the fastest matins in Latin I had ever heard, then laid into the bacon like a hurricane. The way they ate, I wished there had been more than eight eggs. I got my share and kept my hands far away from their flying utensils.

"This is good," said Will, wiping up the last crumbs on his plate with a slice of bread.

"I'm glad you liked it," I told them. "It's been a long time since I last cooked a proper breakfast. I wasn't sure I could still do it."

"You can," said Tuck, wiping his chin with a napkin. "And you do it very well, my daughter. It is very pleasant to eat a meal not of my own making."

"You're very welcome, Brother Tuck."

Will shook his head and muttered something I couldn't make out—something about the forest being no life—then stood and carried his dishes to the stone basin. "Tuck, if we're going to get back before nightfall, we'd best be leaving."

"By all means, Will. It's not safe to travel in the dark. Those forest thieves, you know." Tuck winked at me.

I smiled and began to clear away the dishes, but the friar told me he would take care of them since I had cooked. We were just to get ready to leave.

After we gathered our things, Tuck walked us to the gate of his hermitage, his dogs leaping and bounding alongside.

"Safe journey, Will Scarlet, and to you, Kay. Godspeed." He gave us both hugs, then watched us walk along the trail. I turned back once to wave, and he returned the gesture.

Several times during the trip back, Will started to say one thing, then said something else—like comment on the weather, which had started to sprinkle rain on us. Finally, heart in my mouth, I asked him what was on his mind.

"Kay . . . ." He inhaled deeply once, then twice. "I would ask you to be my wife," he blurted, then continued quickly. "I know my way of life isn't much to offer, but I can't see this ever changing. I love you. I have for years, but I always thought a man should at least be able to offer a woman a dry place to sleep when it rains!" He started to raise a hand to touch my face, then dropped it, turning away as he whispered, "I have nothing to offer you."

"Will," I said, wanting to touch him, hold him. *His wife!* He didn't know how happy that made me. "I wouldn't be here if I didn't enjoy our way of life. Who needs a dry place to sleep? Remember. I *chose* to be here. I choose to be with you." I took the hand he now offered to me.

"Marry me," he said simply.

I smiled. "I will."

The kiss he gave me then had nothing to do with friendship and everything to do with joyous love.

THREE DAYS LATER, Robin came back around mid-morning. The trip had gone well. The villagers were happy, and the troublemakers were satisfied, having had a little excitement on the trip. In keeping with his cheerful mood, he sent a hunting party out to bring in a couple deer for a feast.

On a whim, Robin also sent out a party to find a guest to attend our feast. It had been a long time since we had hosted a visitor at our humble table.

Little John chose up a team of five men who left with a light step to find a wealthy guest for our feast.

I was glad I had settled my turn at serving the night before so I wouldn't have anything to do for the feast but eat. My lot was to clean the plate with Alfred and Geoffrey afterward.

The sun shone warmly, and I stretched out in it to let the heat soak in. I heard people moving around in the clearing, and subconsciously tuned out the hubbub so I could only hear the soft strumming of a lute. Alan a Dale, who had come to visit, was stretching his fingers before the evening's songs. Before I could stop myself, I dozed off.

Some time later, I sat bolt upright, wide awake. It was twilight, and my spot of sunshine was long gone. I turned to see Much crouching next to me, an unusually thoughtful expression on his face. He held a feather, as though he meant to tickle me awake, but I didn't think he had touched me.

"Something wrong?" I asked, my voice gruff with sleep.

"I hear you've agreed to marry Scarlet." I nodded and saw a flash of hurt in his eyes before he covered it. "I never figured what you saw in him," he said with forced casualness. "Thought maybe you'd come around to me in time."

At a loss for words, I just said, "Oh."

Much had always been the greatest friend to me. I knew his feelings ran deep, but I hadn't suspected they ran *that* deep. He'd never let on, and I had always had my heart set on Will. Even if it were a good idea to try and explain, I didn't think I could have defined what drew me to Will, except maybe to say we were soul mates. I didn't think that was something Much wanted to hear. I opened my mouth to say something, maybe apologize, but he chuckled.

"It's just as well. Can't see me putting up with all your strange notions." It was a weak attempt at humor, and it only made me feel worse. His usual sly wit back in place, Much tapped my nose with the feather. "Our guest is come," he said, standing up from his crouch and deliberately putting his sober reflection behind him. "Tuck, too. Come see!"

Nonplussed by his chameleon act, I followed Much into the main clearing and immediately forgot about it upon seeing our guest. A burly man in a monk's habit stood talking with Tuck, the shadow of the heavy cowl he wore hiding his whole face, except his mouth. Even beside Tuck, who was large, the man was big. I was struck by the notion that I should know who he was.

I stretched, yawned, scratched my nose, and looked absently around for Will.

"Let's sit down," Much said, dragging me to a bench. My stomach growled in agreement, and I hastily took a seat. I caught sight of Will sitting in his rightful spot up the table with Stutely and Little John. I figured it was an important guest if Robin had his captains in their proper seats. Perhaps it was an abbot, or even a bishop.

Tuck sat beside our guest, looking a little disturbed. It was my guess he was pretending to be anonymous to us, and so we were to be to him.

When the meat arrived at the head of the table, the bishop—I had it in my mind that he was a bishop—blessed it, then took a lion's share and placed it on his plate. As the other courses made the rounds—bread, cheese, fruits, and vegetables brought back from Robin's mission to the villages—the bishop also blessed them, taking a huge share of each.

Talk and a great deal of laughter supplemented the meal. As it was on all such occasions, talk divided into two camps—that at the head of the table and that farther down. I sat too far down the table to listen in at the head, so I listened to the odd story from the lower end, like one of Edgar the Shepherd's tales about his life herding sheep near Derby. Edgar was known for his tall tales, which we often wound up listening to at the dinner table.

These "guesting feasts" were Robin's idea of soft revolution. He liked to get the nobility off their guard, out of their element. In the forest, he tried to show them we outlaws still had morals and manners and weren't as bad as some people said. He brought them in and treated them as equals. Showed them Robin Hood was generous, too.

Most of our guests were usually nervous, often frightened for their lives. Some enjoyed the fellowship in tempered good humor. But in all my years in the Greenwood, never did I see a guest react the way this bishop did. He seemed to be having a good time.

As the meal finished, I began to walk around, collecting dishes for the washing. With Geoffrey and Alfred helping, we hauled three large baskets down to the river.

We chatted as we worked, getting it done in time for us to go back to the clearing for the festivities. When we had guests, we always had games—wrestling, archery, quarterstaff, even some swordplay.

With Tuck visiting, I didn't want to loose any arrows. It was our tradition that any who missed in the first round got a good buffet on the head from Little John . . . or, when he was here, Tuck. I had had a little too much ale to guarantee accuracy tonight, and I wanted to keep my head whole.

I wouldn't wrestle this night, either. That was a skill I had never improved on, being too small to get the better of these ruffians. I decided to take up my quarterstaff. True, I was much better with swords, but staffs fought first. When I was through, I could sit back and watch the other events.

We drew straws for partners. As luck would have it, I landed a match with David of York, one of Robin's better fighters, and it was our turn first. It wasn't a pretty scene. I was lucky to walk out on my own two feet . . . admittedly with Much's help. I did knock David down once, but that was sheer speed taking him by surprise. After that, I fell like a leaf.

The bishop nodded and smiled at me as I limped off to clean myself up. He appeared to approve of my abilities, as though he knew I held up well under the circumstances. I found myself wishing I had chosen to fight with swords. Then he would have seen my best.

After the quarterstaffs came the archers. Stiffly, I sat down next to Will and got ready for a good show. We were always the best at archery. The finest longbowmen in all of England!

The target was a six-inch wreath of leaves propped up on some sticks. Man after man stood and shot three arrows through the wreath in quick succession. All precise, all accurate.

The first to miss was Arthur a Bland of Blyth. So far, Tuck had managed to play the part of an innocent guest, but now, as Arthur looked nervously at him, he stepped forward.

"My game is up." His smile was wicked for one who professed to be so holy. "Arthur, do you stand forward for your reward?"

Arthur swallowed hard and audibly, then nodded, bracing himself.

Tuck raised a fist and sent Arthur flying a full five feet, landing on his back.

"What's this?!" the bishop roared, standing. "Brother Tuck, are you familiar with these men?"

Tuck bowed his head. "Yes, I know them, Your Grace. I—"

He laughed. "It matters not. Continue with your games."

Robin was the last to step forward for the first round of shooting. Torches illuminated the targets in the clearing, but as Robin raised his bow, a breeze passed through and two torches went out as he shot. And missed.

In the sudden quiet came a hissing murmur—"Robin missed"— and Robin's own jaw dropped open. He looked at Tuck, who stepped toward him, a mischievous grin on his face.

"Wait!" said Robin. He quickly shot three arrows through the wreath with hardly a pause, then looked at Tuck. "The torch went out."

Tuck shook his head, raising his fist.

"Tuck," said Robin, holding up empty hands. His bow lay forgotten on the ground, and Alexander of Grimsby crept forward to pick it up. "I will take the blow from any but you."

"I will do it!" the bishop declared, standing up. Tuck looked about to protest, but backed off.

As I looked on, the bishop strode up to Robin. I suddenly remembered the tale of what happened this night and smacked myself on the forehead. *Of course!*

Robin sailed across the clearing. I thought perhaps he would have rather felt Tuck's fist.

"Robin Hood!" the man said as Robin stood, wiping blood from a cut lip. The man threw back the cowl he had worn all evening and I got a look at his face.

Robin gasped, dropping to his knees where he was. Everyone in the clearing, including me, followed his example. Tuck, standing with mouth agape, was the last to follow suit.

"Your Majesty, King Richard," Robin said, head bowed.

FIFTEEN

K ing Richard laughed heartily.

"Majesty, if I had but known—" Robin stumbled over his words. It was the first time I had seen him at a complete loss.

"Robin Hood," Richard said again, adopting the royal "we" as he continued. "You may rise in our presence. If you were any other man, you would hang, and all your men, too. You are extraordinary outlaws. You accost the rich travelers, but you don't take *all* their money. What you take always seems to make its way to some village or family having trouble meeting its taxes, while you live like paupers. We see your hollow cheeks that speak of not enough to eat. You kill the king's deer, but only enough so you can survive. Your people make up the best yeomen we've ever seen. And as king, we've seen many good men. You sit here at table and condemn the monarchy as being cruel and selfish, but in the same breath, you praise your king. And you did not know your king was with you."

"Your Majesty?" Robin asked. The whole clearing held its breath.

"We are generous, Robin Hood. Learn this lesson. Our barons and dukes have taken advantage of our generosity. They still tax the people for our ransom, though the money we needed was met long ago. This we have learned by traveling in disguise. We have come to set things straight. Learn that the king's generosity is taken away as easily as it is given. Tonight, we have seen you are not what our nobility had told us. Tonight, we will pardon you and all your people."

A collective gasp went around the clearing. A pardon! Somebody raised a cheer. Soon, we were all cheering our King Richard.

I found it strange, though I cheered right along with the rest. Robin Hood despised the monarchy and how it and the nobility abused the people of England. It seemed to me we were a group of thieves, vagabonds, and cutthroats cheering a supreme judge.

Then I figured it was loyalty. These thieves, vagabonds, and cutthroats were loyal to their king, but that didn't mean they didn't want to change the system. It was love of their country. To them, their king personified the country.

Richard held up his hands for quiet.

"We can see," he said in very royal tones, "you people are loyal to your king. Because of that loyalty, we will reward you handsomely. If you but ask, we will consider appointing you to your chosen position. Brother Tuck, please keep all this in mind to recall before the proper witnesses." Tuck nodded, still speechless. "Robin Hood?"

Robin stepped forward. "Majesty?"

"Ask, and you shall receive."

"Your Majesty," said Robin, something like hope glinting in his eyes. "I was raised an earl's son. For several years, I acted as Earl of Huntingdon before I was outlawed. If it please Your Majesty, it is but a small thing to ask."

"Aye, a very small thing. We appoint you Robert, Earl of Huntingdon, and give you back your land and estates." Robin knelt and kissed Richard's signet ring. "But there is one condition," Richard added, looking down at him.

"Your Majesty?" Robin looked up quickly, still holding the king's hand.

"Should we have need of you, Huntingdon, you will attend us at Winchester and in our army."

Robin smiled wryly. "As my king commands." He executed a formal bow before turning to go back to the table.

Next, Little John stepped forward, asking nothing and being given the sheriffship of Nottingham.

Will Stutely was made Robin's steward in Huntingdon.

Will Scarlet leaned over to me as Alan a Dale went forward to ask for his wife's lands back.

"How about it?" he asked, excited.

I looked at him blankly. "How about what?"

"I'm going to ask for Gamwell Lodge, Kay."

"And?" I smiled at his excitement.

"And I want you to be with me when I do."

I shrugged, still smiling. "All right."

He grinned, grabbing my hand to pull me forward as Much stepped away as steward to Little John at Nottingham.

"Your Majesty, King Richard," Will said as we knelt before him. Richard nodded. "I am Will Scathelock of Gamwell Lodge. My father was squire there before he was falsely accused of involvement in Prince John's rebellion. He was executed when I accidentally killed the new squire and fled. Majesty, if it please you, I would ask for what should be mine by birthright. And I would ask that this woman, Kay, be allowed to go with me."

Richard looked at me with raised eyebrows, then at Will. "We have heard of your story, Will Scathelock, and we recognize that your father had been falsely accused. We have heard a witness testify to our father that your accident was indeed an accident. Therefore, we recognize you as rightful heir to the lodgings at Gamwell." He looked back at me. "As for this woman, Kay . . . . We have an idea she will do as she pleases." He inclined his head ever so slightly to me.

I blushed. "That I will, Majesty. I do think it pleases me to stay with Will." I managed an embarrassed smile for both Richard and Will, who squeezed my hand.

"Thank you, Majesty," Will said. We both kissed his ring.

We stepped aside while others came forward. I tugged Will's sleeve, pulling him to the edge of the clearing. "Will."

"Oh, Kay!" He turned to me with an incredibly huge smile and picked me up to swing me around in a circle, then planted a firm kiss on my forehead as he set me down. "I'm going home!" He raised his hands high above his head and I grinned at his exuberance. He looked as though he would burst at any moment. "And you will come with me, won't you?" He brought his hands down to grasp my shoulders, the expression on his face full of hope, laced with a trace of doubt.

Still grinning, I nodded. "Of course, Will. I said I would marry you. I trust you still want that." I had to concentrate not to bite my lip as I waited for his answer.

"More than anything. This is so much more than I ever hoped for, Kay." Suddenly, he dropped to one knee. "Marry me, Kay. I'll give you the finest house to live in, ribbons for your hair, slippers for your feet—"

"Listen to you!" I laughed. "You'd think all I'd done out here was moan about the weather and my poor clothing. Being with you is all I need."

"Will you marry me, Kay?" Will took my hand and placed it on his heart. I felt it beating wildly.

I did bite my lip then. "Brother Tuck is right over there," I said and held my breath, terrified he would change his mind once he was back home at his lodge. I was no match for the exquisite ladies and pedigree beauties who were sure to find the returning squire attractive.

Will stopped to consider my proposal, still holding my hand to his heart. "Tempting," he said at last. "But now that I can, I want to give you a real church wedding, with a white dress, flowers, and the entire world as witness to our declaration of love."

"Ah, Will." I pulled him to his feet. "You're a terrible romantic."

"And what's wrong with that?" he asked, not sure if he should be hurt.

"Absolutely nothing," I assured him as we embraced.

DISPENSING positions to the rest of Robin's people took most of the rest of the night. Those who once held high positions were returned to them, but most had led a better life in the Greenwood. Those men either elected to serve Robin in Huntingdon or serve the king as soldiers or foresters in Sherwood.

Two people were not there for the pardoning. Jenny and Jana. They had been waiting for their second turn with the bow when Richard had shown himself, then they were gone. They left as silently as they had come. I never knew what had caused them to be outlaws, but they certainly did not wish a pardon.

The next morning, we traveled to Nottingham. There, King Richard the Lionheart would declare our pardoning and assign our positions before all the legal witnesses necessary.

I was excited. Not so much by the fact we were being pardoned —I think I would have preferred staying in the Greenwood—but that I had actually met King Richard, a character right out of my history books. It was almost as good as meeting Robin Hood for the first time.

Now, just by going to Nottingham with King Richard, we had finally defeated the sheriff without bloodshed, just as Robin had wanted it.

Nottingham Castle was absolutely unprepared for us. Someone from the gate had run ahead with the news of our coming, but he had mucked up the story so it had turned into Robin Hood coming to storm the place. Fortunately, the messenger arrived only moments ahead of the king, scarcely delivering his tale before Richard bellowed from the end of the hall.

"Sheriff! Is this how you greet your king?!"

We all laughed when we saw the old man nearly faint as he recognized Richard.

We filtered into the dusty hall, ranging ourselves along the wall, finding the open room uncomfortable to our sense of preservation. The light was poor, mostly candles guttering in the draft of stale, foul air oozing up from the recesses of the castle. Someone opened a shutter, letting sunlight in to make a bright square on the bracken-covered floor. More were opened, and soon, the hall was filled with early afternoon sunlight. A small breeze picked its way across the hall, clearing the fetid air as I opened the shutter near me.

This was my first time being close to the man who played such a notorious part in our lives. The man who had been my enemy, real and fantasized, in my childhood and my present. In my thoughts, I had created a monster embodying everything sinister. But this was only an old man. A very human old man.

The sheriff blinked and sputtered as Richard crossed the hall, stalking slowly toward him. Looming over him in a shaft of sunlight, Richard began to explain.

I think the sheriff *did* faint when Richard said he was to lose his post to an outlaw, and I almost felt sorry for him. Almost.

Most of the pardon was just politics, assembling the right people —including Prince John—to witness. We waited for them to arrive, waited for them to assemble, then said the right things at the right time. For all fifty-seven of us, it was a long and very boring two weeks. We were happy only for the feasting that came afterward. Annoyed by the pomp and fuss of the whole thing, I wished to be back in the forest, maybe fishing. I hated fishing, but I'd still rather be doing that than enduring this farce.

We stayed in Nottingham while all the details were sorted out, but Will and I readied to leave as soon as was politely possible to go "home" to Gamwell.

Out in the courtyard, we told Robin he should visit us once he settled in at Huntingdon. He smiled, giving us both hugs.

Little John, now Sheriff John Little of Nottingham, had some fair words and a bear hug for Will, then gave me an awkward kiss on the cheek. Will promised him we would visit.

Much gave me a lingering hug, unable to say anything other than "Visit" before giving me a kiss on the cheek. He shook hands briefly with Will, then briskly walked away.

Will Stutely stood aloof as he shook our hands. I knew he was uncomfortable in this place—I think we all were—but he had always held himself apart from the rest of us. He was Robin's right hand. Wherever Robin was, Will Stutely was always in the background, watching for trouble.

Alan shook hands with us and wished us well, while Ellen cried, hugged us, and told me we would have to visit once we settled in.

And on and on it went. Some of the friends were brothers who had congratulated me on my acceptance into Robin's band. Still others were newer members, but no less friends.

GAMWELL WAS ONLY an afternoon's ride from Nottingham, so we took our time. We rode our newly purchased horses through the peaceful green freshness of Sherwood Forest.

Will chattered happily about returning to his home. He couldn't wait. He was going to have his lands back.

Listening to him, I wondered if he was kidding himself about the way things were going to be. It had been seven years since he'd last set foot in Gamwell. He couldn't possibly think things had remained the same.

Then I remembered he had kept in touch with Tuck for those seven years to keep track of what had changed. Will knew what he was walking into, and I was happy he was getting what he had wanted for so long.

But this new future scared me. I was being thrust back into the kind of society I had never meshed with, having more strikes against me now that I had socialized with only outlaws for so long. And Will was delightedly telling everyone we would marry. That was the scary part.

The only married life I knew was Mom and Dad—always fighting, always hurting. Even though I knew better, I felt it would be the same way for me, too. I loved Will and would have readily married him while we were in the Greenwood. But I wondered if it could be the same living within four walls. My parents' problems had been from too much of each other with nowhere to go to get away. Whose freedom would be curtailed when I married the squire of Gamwell Lodge? I wouldn't be able to stand it if I wasn't allowed to get away when I needed to. I worried at my lip as we rode, knowing I had to push down my fears and embrace whatever time had in store for me.

We rounded a bend, finding Gamwell Lodge sprawled out before us, looking like a playhouse for a child. Will pulled his horse up and I stopped beside him, my mount nervously champing the bit and pawing at the ground. I pulled at the reins as she began to dance and we turned a circle. Horseback riding was something I had seldom enjoyed before my arrival in Sherwood, and I hadn't had any chance to practice. I clumsily brought the horse under control.

Will breathed in the air and sat up straighter in the saddle. "I'm going home," he said, his voice full of quiet wonder. Then he grinned at me and set off at a trot toward the main gate. I moved out after him.

THE GATE SWUNG WIDE open as we approached. A few people had turned out to cheer our arrival, and Will called to them by name. These were men and women who had stayed loyal to him even after his outlawry. These were the people who had supplied Tuck with the information that he passed on to Will.

We dismounted at the great hall of the lodge, handing the horses over to a stable boy, who led them away. Upon our entrance, the hall fell silent. It looked as though we had come in right in the middle of packing, and everyone stopped whatever they were doing to turn toward us.

I fidgeted, my feet more than willing to obey the signal to run away, but Will smiled. He marched right through the hall, and I trailed behind him, skittish as a horse in a thunderstorm. In an attempt to distract myself, I surveyed my surroundings, wondering what it would be like to live in these stark, stone walls.

Will turned to me and smiled, holding out his hand for me as we continued across the hall toward a man wearing a golden chain of office. When we stopped in front of him, Will made a short bow.

"My Lord Mowrey," Will said.

"*My* Lord Scathelock of Gamwell," said the other, bowing low.

A small frown crossed Will's brow, but his next words were unaffected sentiment. "My lord, I have heard you are a fair man. I have no quarrel with you, nor issue with your management of these estates these past five years. I regret it is you I am unseating and not some other, less deserving man." I knew he spoke about the man who killed his father. Will smiled. "I almost regret that I have been returned to my rightful position, but it is too happy an occasion for me to be back home after these long years." He looked earnestly at Mowrey, awaiting a reaction.

Mowrey nodded, a small smile tugging at his lips. "Well spoken, my lord. This is something of a surprise. You are not at all what I was expecting."

I nudged Will with my elbow and whispered into his ear. "I

didn't know you could speak so fair, love."

Will flashed me a grin, squeezing my hand, then he turned to Mowrey. "My lord, may I present to you my future bride, Kay."

Mowrey looked a little doubtful, glancing at my trousers, as though wondering whether Will were joking, but I smiled and made an awkward curtsey, knowing I looked like a clown.

"My lady," he said, bowing, but not quickly enough to hide his bemused smile. I thought that I liked this man and would like him as a friend. "Lord Scathelock, this is my wife, Margaret."

Will and Margaret exchanged courtesies, then all three turned to me. "Kay." Mowrey gestured to his wife. "My wife, Margaret. If you'll excuse us, ladies, we have much to discuss."

The two men walked off, and I found myself confronted by Mowrey's wife.

LADY MARGARET WAS YOUNG. Maybe twenty years younger than her lord. I guessed that put her somewhere around seventeen. I smiled uncomfortably.

She smiled back at me—all acid and starch. I didn't quite know what to say. She was a lady, while I had spent four years in the forest with fifty men, most of whom had very rough tongues and manners.

"My Lady Kay," she said, all honey and salt. I didn't miss the way her nose wrinkled as her gaze traveled down to my boots and back up to my leather jerkin. "I am Lady Margaret. Come. I will show you to our . . . your baths, then we will find you something . . . more fitting to wear." I didn't miss the reiteration of her name and title, and I also understood what she wasn't saying. I was a mess and wasn't dressed for the part of a lady.

Her spite was understandable. She was losing her position to me. Dressed as I was, I surely looked like some kind of barbarian woman, not a lady. It must burn her to lose out to someone who didn't even wear a dress.

"Thank you," I answered, matching her tone. I allowed myself to be led off, taking one more backward glance at Will, who was talking with Mowrey off to one side of the buzzing hall.

We went down a long, dim hall and entered a dark room through a thick wooden door. The smell of flowers and warm water drifted on the air.

"You have hot water?" I asked in anticipation as a maid lit a rack of candles with a taper. The room brightened.

"Yes," she said proudly, then added with a bit of a sneer, "I suppose they don't have that in the forest."

I chose to ignore her remark. It would take some getting used to, dealing with people who were indirect, selfish, and, well . . . hostile within their own small social pattern. We outlaws had been rude, grasping, and sometimes outright violent, but we were always open, direct, and honest about it. I would have to get used to social politics again.

"It must be quite a chore to fill it," I said diplomatically, gazing at the large tub, glistening water lapping gently at its sides. Then I caught the faint sulfur odor.

"Oh . . . . No, my lady. We have a warm spring. We tap the water in so we have no bothersome heating and adding new water constantly."

When she said tap, I looked around, almost expecting a faucet. Instead, I saw a miniature sluice gate that could be lifted to let water in. The tub, which was sunken, and its fragrant water beckoned to the part of me that longed to be truly clean.

"How nouvelle," I said, turning to Margaret with grudging appreciation at her cleverness. I should have known it hadn't been her innovation.

"Yes, isn't it? My husband thought it up for me since I so dearly love to bathe. Don't you?"

"Oh yes, Lady Margaret. And it's been such a long time since I last had a warm bath."

Margaret snapped her fingers and the maid stepped forward, reaching for the lacings of my shirt.

I brushed her hands away roughly, surprised by the movement. "I can undress myself," I said coldly.

"Lady Kay, that is for Maria to do. You are a lady now."

"I am accustomed to bathing myself," I told her, deciding to adopt her acid manner to see how much I could get away with. "Now, you are both excused." I turned away.

"My lady, it is hardly proper," protested Margaret. Then she scoffed. "Perhaps you would prefer one of the manservants to come in and bathe with you. It could be arranged, if you'd like."

My temper snapped. This sneaky little wench with her petty assumptions was too much. I whirled to face her and she shrank away, expecting a blow. Barely controlling my displeasure, I forced my fists open, refusing to begin my stay here with violence against a . . . a child. When she saw I wasn't going to strike her, she stood straight, chin thrust forward, daring me.

"Lady Margaret," I said through clenched teeth, "I am betrothed to the squire of the lodge. You would do well to remember that. You obviously have a low opinion of me, but I assure you, I do not whore around, as you have just suggested. Yes, I have lived four years in the company of Robin Hood's men, but not once did I couple with any of them. This includes my husband-to-be." I turned away from her in cold dismissal.

Over my shoulder, I said, "Another thing for you to keep in mind, lady. Having lived four years in the forest with men, I'm used to taking care of myself, and I have had little exercise for my patience." I looked away and made my voice chilly with command. "You are dismissed."

I waited until I heard the door shut. I turned to make sure no one was with me, then went to the door and bolted it. *The little wench*, I thought. *Everything sours in the sun.* It was a favorite saying in the shadows of the Greenwood.

Now I was in the sun, too.

I remembered the girls' school I had been sent to after my mother died. The calculating head games the clique girls played, exploiting and dominating the more vulnerable girls. It was a raw deal for everyone who wasn't in their little circle, including me. I didn't take their abuse long before I started fighting back. That hadn't gone over well, and I wound up getting expelled.

Living in this place was shaping up to be like that, but this time, I was in a position to stop it. I didn't like social politics, never had, and I wasn't looking forward to dealing with Lady Margaret. Despite her tender age, she embodied everything I despised in society. But I would deal with her in my own fashion. When the women's side of Gamwell was truly mine to manage, there would be no scheming, no conniving.

Shoving the distasteful, and perhaps unjustified, thoughts out of my mind, I undressed and slipped into the water, sighing with delight at the warmth. This was heaven.

I splashed around for a long time, scrubbing at my body and hair with soap I found in a basket on a shelf, and lounged in the sweet water until my feet and hands were wrinkled. Coming out into the cold, hostile world again did not appeal to me, but my mood improved with my pleasure. I thought perhaps I was letting my past color my perception of Margaret.

When I finally climbed from the water, I found a cloth to dry myself, then extracted a comb from the basket and began to work through my rat's nest. Once done, my hair hung all the way to my waist. It was so seldom clean and untangled at the same time, I hadn't noticed it had gotten so long. I almost braided it, as was my custom, but decided I would leave it down for a change. Wrapping the towel around my body, I gathered up my weapons and reached for my clothes, but then kicked the stinking mass into the corner. I could come back for them. Without thinking, I went to the door and unbolted it.

Someone scrambled to their feet as I swung the door open. A serving maid stood there, looking at me in surprise.

"Milady!" she gasped. "Where are your clothes?!"

I laughed. "I left them in the corner. They stink, and I am really clean for the first time in many years." I was in a good mood, and my comment made the maid smile.

"Well then," she said, a Northern burr to her words. "Where were you thinking of going . . . and you with no clothes?"

I stopped smiling, recalling the large hall with all its buzzing activity and pictured myself running across it wrapped only in a cloth. Margaret would love to see that. This was no place or time to forget about decency. "I don't know."

The maid looked up and down the hall, then gestured to me. "Come. We'll go up the servants' stair to a room where you can get a dress and change. There won't be anyone back here this time of day. Come quickly, lest you be seen."

I followed her up a staircase at the end of the dim corridor, along a passage on the upper floor, to a large room with a window overlooking the sunset.

The maid, whose name I learned was Andrea, shuffled through clothes in a wardrobe while I gazed out the window.

It was a rare sunset, gold, lavender, and pink, the trees burned to bronze. I sighed for the beauty of it. Our sunsets were usually plain red in the clouds, or the sun just disappeared. I told myself I would go south someday to see a lowland sunset. Christopher of Bristol once told me the marshes lit on fire when the sun set. He said a lowland sunset could tear your heart out—but he was a poet. I was of a mind to go and see for myself, now that it was a possibility.

"Milady?" Andrea asked. I turned. "Does this suit you?"

She held up a simple, light green dress with long sleeves and a modest collar, just to my taste—if I *had* to wear a dress. This woman could read me well.

"Try it on, milady, and I'll see what needs to be done."

Andrea dug up some decent undergarments. I dropped the towel and put on the first proper underwear I'd had in years, then slipped the dress over my head. Clicking her tongue against her teeth, she set to work pinning, letting out, and sewing. Soon, the dress fit like it had been made for me. She uncovered a mirror in the corner of the room so I could look.

Andrea nodded. "'Twill do for now."

I shook my head at her understatement. The woman was gifted at tailoring. I hoped she would stay for me. I could never do anything like that for myself.

"Andrea?"

"Yes, milady?" She looked up from inspecting the hem.

"I hate to say it, seeing as how this looks so good, but I feel naked in it without any breeches on. Do you think you could find me a pair to wear underneath my skirt?" The thin hose felt like I wore nothing at all.

She shook her head. "It's not proper, milady. Women should always . . . ." She trailed off, noticing how uncomfortable I looked, and smiled. "But you . . . . I'll find you some breeches. Give me a moment."

She slipped out the door and I heard her retreating down the hall. Moments later, she reappeared with a pair of earth-brown trousers draped over her arm.

"Old Alfred won't be missing them, and he's about your size. Here. Put them on."

They were a perfect fit. I tucked the legs into my boots, then turned for Andrea to inspect.

"Well, it doesn't spoil the dress any, and you *do* look a sight more comfortable." Andrea smiled.

"I *feel* more comfortable."

A bell rang from somewhere downstairs.

"Ah, that's dinner then. Come. I'll show you the way."

Andrea showed me to the dining hall, then went to the kitchen. I stood in the doorway for a few moments, unwilling to enter, watching the bustle. Then I squared my shoulders and walked to the head of the table to sit on Will's right.

Will looked up when I settled beside him, then did a double take, eyes wide. He leaned over to whisper, "You look good."

"Thank you," I whispered back. "I'm nervous."

"Don't be. Just be natural."

"But this isn't." I made a vague gesture at my dress, my surroundings. "Don't forget, I haven't been around this many people since I was fifteen." There were perhaps one hundred people in the room.

Will looked startled. "How old are you?"

I laughed at the notion he'd asked me to marry him but didn't even know my age. Funnier still, it took me a minute of adding in my head. "Twenty-three."

Will sat back. "You don't look a day over nineteen," he said, smiling. "And you're beautiful."

He waved for the servants to bring the food. They carried in trays and trays of it. I couldn't believe my eyes. I hadn't seen so much food, or such a variety, in many years.

My stomach felt unsettled, so while everyone else ate, I looked around the hall. Two lines of tables ran parallel to each other, making right angles with the high table. At the high table sat Mowrey, his wife, Will, and me. At the two lower tables sat some of the lodge's more important people, as well as the headman from the village proper. At the two lowest tables sat villagers and servants who had no duties at the time. Everyone had turned out to see the new squire.

CHAPTER

SIXTEEN

After the meal, a maid showed me to a room near where Andrea found my dress. It had the same view, as well as a big, soft bed. The chest at the foot of the bed was empty, so I dumped my pack, swords, knives, bow, and quiver inside, then looked around for something to pass the time while I waited for Will.

The room boasted a small shelf with a few volumes of leather-bound books. I perused the titles, mostly religious themes, until I spotted a worn copy of Homer's *Odyssey*. I flipped it open to make sure it was an English translation, then retreated to the window seat.

The hand-written pages were hard to read at first—I hadn't read anything in four years—but I was soon wading into the classic tale of a man called away to war.

I could only read a page or two at a time, and often found myself staring out the window into the darkness, listening to the unfamiliar nighttime sounds of the lodge. I must have read for about an hour before deciding I'd had enough of Homer for the evening. There was still no sign of Will.

It was too early to go to bed, and I shifted my position on the window seat, restless. Unable to sit still any longer, I walked to the chest and grabbed my knife, strapping it to my leg under my dress.

No one walked the corridors. In the silence, my deer hide boots scuffed softly against the stone, and the rustle of my skirts sounded loud as I walked downstairs to the dining hall.

I was surprised to find the room completely deserted, all the benches stacked against the walls and the fire banked for the night. I made my way to the cloaks hanging on the wall near the door and pulled one out to wear against the night's chill. It was large and dragged behind me, but I was only going out for a short while.

Outside, I breathed in the chilly air as I looked around at the unfamiliar surroundings. A light down at the end of the courtyard beckoned, and I made my way toward it.

Seeing the stable, I walked inside, past the slumbering guard, to look at the horses. They were poor beasts at best, except the two Will and I had ridden in on and one pregnant mare that looked promising. Clearly, the lodge had not prospered in recent years.

I shook my head. Will was going to have a lot of work to do to get Gamwell standing tall again.

As I left the stable, I shook the watch awake. He jumped, looking at me. "This is no time to sleep," I whispered. "It is the hour of thieves." I left the man staring at me as I walked into the darkness. Hearing him get up to check the horses, I shrugged. They would learn to trust me.

I was halfway back to the hall when the moon sailed clear of a cloud, lighting the courtyard. I looked up, seeing the stars gleaming in the sky beside the waxing moon, and closed my eyes, tipping my head up to the light.

I sighed. It wasn't the same. It would take a long time to adjust to living in a confined area again. I missed the trees, the sounds of the night animals, the forest . . . .

"Did you get lost?"

I dropped into a crouch, drawing my dagger and whirling toward the voice coming out of the shadows.

"Jesus, Will," I exclaimed softly. "Are you trying to get yourself killed? You of all people should know how jumpy I get."

"Well, if you're going to be so jumpy," he said with a laugh, "don't stand about in the middle of the courtyard, looking up at the sky."

"My eyes were closed," I said sheepishly, sheathing my dagger and straightening.

"Eyes closed . . . . That's worse. You should be flogged!"

"Only by your hands, milord," I said, winking at him.

Will held out his hand to me and I took it. "I went to your room, but you were gone."

"I couldn't possibly have gone to sleep."

He sighed. "I know what you mean. It's not very much like the Greenwood, is it?"

"Not in the least."

"We could be a lot worse off," he told me, leading me back to the hall. We walked slowly, enjoying the night air.

"Aye," I said. "But that won't stop me missing Sherwood and the times we had under the trees."

"No one is trying to stop you, Kay." He put his arm around my shoulders as we walked. I slipped my arm around his waist, finding this casual gesture immensely satisfying.

"Let's not forget, all right? This won't last forever."

"It'll last long enough."

I stopped, causing him to turn and look at me. "*Not* long enough, Will."

He frowned for a moment, looking into my eyes. I didn't try to hide the sadness stealing into me. "What do you know?"

"It won't last nearly long enough," I said around a lump in my throat, my voice sounding strangled to my own ears.

"Is it bad?" he asked. I was surprised. It was the first time he had ever asked me about the future.

I nodded, thinking I knew. "Not horrible, but bad."

Will lifted my bowed head with both his hands to search my gaze. "My love," he said gently. "We have now."

How could I tell him these days at the lodge were just a footnote in our story, that we would soon have more excitement with higher stakes than ever before.

I gave him a small smile and kissed his palm. "No wonder I love you."

"Come," he said, steering me back toward my room.

"What did you say to Mowrey?" I asked as we passed through the dining hall. They had been deep in conversation through most of dinner.

"I asked him to stay on for a couple months as my advisor. Told him I'd need his help with the people while I got to know them. It will give him some time to make more definite plans."

"I'm glad you did. I feel sorry for the old man. He got jumped out of a job without so much as a by-your-leave and no time to make any plans." At the door to my room, I invited him in. "Was he grateful?"

"Very."

"He seemed the sort. I like him. But I'm not so sure about his wife."

Will coughed a little, muffling a laugh.

"What?" I began to close the door, then decided to leave it open. Wouldn't do to have scandalous rumors flying about the lodge.

"She's one of the reasons Mowrey was so grateful. He said, 'My wife is used to the pleasant things in life. She's young. I'm afraid she won't take this change very well.'" Will mimicked Mowrey's voice comically.

I laughed. "She was needling me about my, ah, reputation. Making snide remarks."

Will sat down on the bed, and I sat next to him. "Oh really? What'd you do?"

"I told her to leave off or I'd do something violently barbaric." Will laughed. "She must think I'm an uncivilized whore."

"Why do you say that?"

"Think, Will. I've lived in the forest with fifty men for four years. What do you think a lady would assume?" I left my thoughts of Jenny and Jana unspoken.

"Ah," he said with a nod, reading the troubled look in my eyes.

Abruptly, he stood up and went around the bed to the pillow, lifting something. "I was forgetting. I brought this for you."

It was a midnight blue sleeping gown. The cloth shimmered in the candlelight as I got up and went around the bed to touch it.

I gasped. "Silk? This is silk?!" I pressed it to my face, sighing at its soft feel. "Thank you, Will."

He smiled, pleased at my excitement. "Try it on."

"Turn around," I said as I fumbled with the laces of my bodice. Without making sure he obeyed, I pulled the dress over my head and slipped out of my breeches.

Sliding the gown over my head, I sighed in ecstasy at the feeling of silk washing down my body and gave a little shiver of delight.

"It feels luscious," I told him. I didn't care that it was a little too big.

"Do you like it?" Will asked, turning to face me.

"Like it?! I love it! Thank you." I hugged him tightly, then gave him a kiss, which he returned eagerly.

"I love you," he whispered, then let me go. "I've got to go before more damage is done to your reputation." He winked at me and I smiled. Whispering a good night, I saw him to the door and closed it softly behind him.

When I turned down the thick quilts covering my bed, I found real sheets over a feather mattress, along with a fluffy feather pillow. I hadn't slept in a real bed in over four years, so I jumped in and pulled the covers up around me, sinking in with an exultant sigh. It was all I could do to put out the lamp and flood the room with darkness.

All the softness was heaven, but sleep evaded me.

I tossed and turned, every slight sound jerking me out of my slumber. They had let the dogs out into the courtyard and I jumped at their every bark and howl.

Finally, late into the night, I dozed off, only to jolt upright in bed, disoriented and feeling closed in by the walls around me. The echoes of the dream slipped from my mind, and I couldn't remember why I woke. I listened to the night around me but heard nothing. Even the hounds outside were quiet.

I disentangled my legs, smoothed the sheets, and tried to go back to sleep. I had nearly overcome the closed-in feeling to find sleep again when I heard a familiar bird call floating in through my window. Wrestling my way out of bed, I ran to the window casement and looked out. The courtyard was dark, the torches having long since burned out, but I repeated the call.

An owl hooted up at me and I frowned, wishing the moon were out. I thought I recognized the voice, though, so I searched for a candle, lit it, and made my way downstairs, a quilt pulled around me. Will joined me in the hall.

"Much?" he asked.

"I think so." Both of us wore frowns. At this time of night, it could only be unwelcome news.

Will walked to the door and cracked it open. Much slipped inside, blinking in the candlelight.

"What's wrong?" I asked anxiously.

Much smiled sheepishly. "I don't . . . . I'm not . . . ." He shrugged helplessly. "I couldn't sleep."

"Jesus!" Will exclaimed. We all winced at the way the sound echoed around the hall. He continued in a softer voice. "Is that all?"

"Sorry. Everybody's left Nottingham, and John has some woman in his bed. I just wanted some company."

"So you come and wake us up in the middle of the night?" Will asked, but the edge of his anger was gone.

"We all feel that way," I said. "I was having a devil of a time sleeping myself."

We stood together, huddled near the door like cornered wild things looking for a reason to fight or fly, until Will laughed. "Well, we may as well be comfortable in our misery. I'll get some ale if you two want to pull down a bench."

"Does Little John know you're gone?" I asked as Much and I set up a place to sit.

"Doubt it. I just left, didn't even think about telling anyone." He shrugged again. "I'm not used to the idea of having to answer to someone. It didn't occur to me until I was over halfway here that I could have taken a horse, or that my actions could be called desertion of duty."

"John won't hold it against you."

"I'm sure he won't, but I just wasn't thinking . . . ." He sighed. "This is going to take some getting used to."

"I know what you mean," Will said, returning with a pitcher and three mugs. "I woke more than once before your call, wondering where the hell I was. And I have lived here before. It all seems so strange."

Much sipped the ale appreciatively. "I'm glad I'm not the only one. I almost just stayed in the forest, rather than coming here."

"That wouldn't be any good. You'd be an outlaw against your friends." I realized how lucky I was to have Will, even though we couldn't sleep as close as we did in the forest. "Maybe you ought to just do like John and find yourself a willing woman."

"That'll have to do since the woman I want got herself engaged to someone else." He shifted his gaze from me to Will.

"Oh, Much," I said, hoping he wouldn't pursue it. It wasn't a smart thing to say in front of Will, joke or not. Much had always been my best friend, next to Will, and I didn't want bad air between the two.

But I needn't have worried. Much laughed. "You don't think I stand a chance with Marian, either, eh?"

We talked for about two hours, then Will offered Much his own horse to get him home, and I went up to bed. Talking about the open spaces made my room seem a little bigger. That, combined with the comfort of my bed, invited sleep immediately.

LATE IN THE MORNING, I woke to the sound of someone tapping at my door.

"What?" I said, instantly alert.

"Milady, it's Andrea. You've missed breakfast."

"Come in." I pushed back the covers and sat up. As the door opened, I rubbed at my eyes and swung my legs over the side of the bed. "Why didn't anyone wake me?"

"Milord Scathelock told us you were to sleep yourself out," Andrea said, coming around the bed. She set a lump of sky blue material down on the corner of the mattress. "But you'd told me to wake you early, so I settled on the medium."

"What's that?" I asked, nodding at the material.

"A dress, milady. Something I put together last night for you to wear today." She held up a simple but beautiful linen dress, and I was happy that Andrea really got the notion that I didn't want the kinds of fancy garments Margaret seemed to favor.

Andrea helped me into my new clothes, then we went down-stairs to find something to eat. I had Andrea accompany me, seeing to it she got some fresh fruit.

When I came out of the kitchen with a bread roll and a cup of goat's milk, I asked a servant where Will was and was told he was touring the lodgings.

As I ate, I wandered around the great hall, which had turned into a great workroom, and spoke to the various women there. I saw wool in several stages of being made into yarn, women embroidering in small clusters, women making clothing, weaving, quilting. I acquainted myself with them and watched. It was tedious, boring, arduous work. I was glad I was going to marry Will. A lady didn't have to work like that.

After I finished eating, I left my cup with a servant and went upstairs. On my way, I encountered Margaret.

"Good morning, Lady Margaret," I said courteously as I passed. She stopped, obliging me to stop as well, and I looked at her with a raised eyebrow. Her bright yellow dress was a gaudy affair—lace and jewels, a very low-cut neckline. I guessed the material was satin.

"Good morning, Lady Kay," she said brightly.

"You're wearing such a lovely dress," I told her, lying. "Did you make it yourself?"

"Oh, heavens no!" She laughed, tilting her head. "Andrea made it for me. She's a witch at making clothes . . . when you can get her to do anything. She's terribly lazy, but I don't know what I'd do without her to make my dresses."

"Witch, my lady?" I asked, cocking an eyebrow. I liked the turn of phrase, but it was a dangerous thing to say, even in jest.

"Oh, not a real witch, but you should see her work."

"I have," I said, looking up the stairs for a way to get away from this pointless conversation.

"Really?" Surprise colored her tone, but I thought I saw a trace of anger in the set of her mouth. "She's already made you a dress?"

"No, but she's fitted me to this." I gestured to my dress. "And also the one I wore last night."

"How sweet of her," Margaret said through clenched teeth, sounding more like she'd prefer to throttle Andrea. Then a blank look crossed her face, as though she wondered why she had stopped to talk to me. "Will you excuse me, Lady Kay? I really must run along. Will I see you at lunch?" I could tell she asked only out of courtesy.

"I don't think so," I said, turning to go. "I'm going riding."

"With Lord Scathelock?"

"No," I answered, bored with her questions. "By myself."

"Where?"

She was really trying my tolerance. "On the common," I said shortly.

"Alone?" Her voice squeaked up another octave.

"I told you. I can take care of myself." I left her standing on the step looking after me.

Someone had laundered and placed my old clothes in my room, so I changed into them and belted on my twin swords. I strapped my survival knife to my leg, then hid my daggers on specially designed loops inside the loose folds of my shirt. After a moment of consideration, I put my bow and quiver back into the chest.

Stepping into the hall, I saw a maid I knew as Hilda at the far end. When I called to her, she turned, dropping a curtsey when she recognized me.

"My lady?" she asked.

"I'm going riding," I said, feeling silly explaining myself, but knowing someone ought to be aware of my plans. Then I had an idea. "When I return, I want to review the household staff. Please tell them. I want this to be private, so please don't tell Lady Margaret. I'll try to be back the third hour after noon."

"Yes, my lady." She curtsied again.

At the stable, I got Sassy, my mare, out, while the stable boy looked on. She was clean, groomed, and fed. The boy, impressed with my swords and my recent outlawry, was more than happy to instruct me how to saddle and mount properly. If I was going out to practice my riding, those skills needed to be included, as well.

I retraced the route Will and I had taken through the little village to the gate, then I went out onto the common. I rode slowly, getting the feel for the mare and working out the aches I had earned from riding the day before.

Bright summer sunshine had already turned the day into a scorcher, and the sky was such a wonderful color of blue, I couldn't help but smile every time I looked up.

Sheep wandered across the meadow, cropping grass, followed by a herding boy. I remembered Edgar, who had chosen to serve in the king's army, and wondered if I would ever see him again.

Getting braver, I nudged the horse into a canter, bouncing awkwardly until I found a way to move with the natural motion of the horse. I even had her at a dead run for a little while, which was easier than a canter. I started recovering what little skill I had learned when I was much younger, sneaking away to my best friend's farm to play desperadoes and ride when we could.

IN THE HEAT OF MIDDAY, I stopped at a little cottage to look for something to drink. I tied Sassy under an apple tree near the door, and the mare dipped her head into the water trough on the other side of the short wooden fence.

It was a moment before anyone answered my knock, and I batted at the flies and midges swarming in the heat. When the door finally opened a crack, a woman peered out. I heard a child crying somewhere inside.

"Good morning, milady," I said, bowing. Being my first time approaching a stranger on my own, I wanted to use my best manners.

"Who might you be?" she asked grumpily, pushing dark hair away from her eyes.

I hesitated, then decided to use my new title. "Lady Kay."

Her eyes squinted at me, then widened. "A lady, are ya? Well, come in. It's a humble place, but yer welcome in anyhow."

I smiled. "Thank you."

As she opened the door farther, I saw she had a child on her hip, another hiding behind her skirts. A third stood in a makeshift crib by the fireplace, crying.

I stepped into the stuffy heat of the ragged hut and was immediately assaulted by the musty smell of the place. Wood smoke, decaying straw, and a pungent odor I couldn't readily name struck me first, then the smell of gruel cooking over the fire. Overall, it looked like a clean place, with none of the more noisome odors I knew from other places in the village. It was in much better shape on the inside than it looked on the outside.

"A lady, are ya?" she said again, clearing a place for me to sit while still balancing the child on her hip and managing not to trip over the other. "You don't look much like a lady. More like an outlaw. What're ya lady of?" She crossed the room to put the child into the crib, and the baby stopped crying.

I almost laughed at her lack of tact as I sat down. "I'm going to marry Will Scathelock, the new lord of Gamwell Lodge."

"Will Scarlet?" she asked, stirring the gruel. "He was an outlaw with Robin Hood, wasn't he?"

"Aye. So was I." I watched her taste the food and add some spices to it.

"Fancy that." She disappeared into the other room, then came back carrying some bowls. "How'd he come to be lord of Gamwell again?"

"You haven't heard the news?" I asked, watching the woman bustle about. She was in constant motion. I wondered if that was how she stayed so slim, even after three children.

"Nah. I haven't been no place fer a while. My cloth is 'bout ready for market. That's when I get t' gather news."

I recognized the smell then. It was dye. This woman made cloth and dyed it for sale. I thought it was strange she and her children wore tatters.

"Well, I'll tell you then. Robin Hood's been pardoned, as have all his people. Will's father held Gamwell before, so King Richard gave it back to him."

"Fancy that," she said again. "What 'bout Robin Hood then? And Little John and Will Stutely?" She was well informed about Robin Hood's people. I marveled at the serendipity that had brought me to this woman's house.

"Robin's got Huntingdon back, Richard gave John Nottingham, and Stutely is Robin's steward."

"So now yer all respectable—"

I heard a noise outside and craned my neck to look out the high window.

"That'll be Jamie come back from the sheep," the woman said without looking up.

"Your husband?"

"My son. Howard's been dead these past four months."

"I'm sorry," I said. "It must be hard for you." I glanced at the children.

"Ah, no. Jamie keeps the sheep, Ellie and me make the thread, and I weave and dye. Ellie's more than the wisp she looks. When Katie gets older, she'll help, as will Robert. Howard left us the sheep. We own 'em all. The rent on the land's not high. We're right well off. We just don't let folks know. It keeps the thieves and tax collectors off." She gave me a sidelong glance. "I would'na told you that if I thought you'd not keep it under yer tongue. Yer outlaw. You know 'bout secrets. Anyhow, most money goes to keep the sheep."

I nodded. The door banged opened and a child of no more than ten came in.

"Whose horse, mum?" he asked as he shut the door. Then he saw me and his eyes popped open wide. "An outlaw," he whispered.

"Hush, boy," said his mother. "This is no outlaw, though she was. She's to be lady at the lodge."

The boy bobbed his head obediently, but he couldn't control his curiosity. "Did you know Robin Hood?" he asked. "Did you ever kill anyone?"

"James Henry!" his mother scolded.

"It's all right, ma'am," I said.

"My name's Anne," she said, fixing her son with a stern glare before turning to the fire.

I nodded and looked at Jamie. "I was one of Robin's company, and yes, I have killed people, but only out of need or to protect. Killing is not something to do for sport or pleasure."

My lecture on principles didn't faze the boy. "Can I see your sword?"

I looked at Anne for permission. She shook her head, then changed her mind at the boy's hopeful expression and nodded. The older girl, Ellie, watched with wide eyes from the corner. I drew one of my swords to give him. It was too heavy for his young muscles and the tip fell to the dirt floor.

"Careful," said Anne, watching.

"Now then," I said, "that's no way to hold a blade, Jamie." Positioning his hands, I showed him the correct hold.

"Can you teach me to fight?" he asked, a light of excitement glowing in his eyes.

"James," his mother warned, and the light died. "Lady Kay, would you like t' stay fer lunch?"

"If I'm welcome." I gently took the sword from Jamie's small hands. "I would gladly share a meal with you."

"Yer most welcome," said Anne. She brought me a bowl of gruel and a spoon, then spooned up a bowl for Jamie, Ellie, and Katie, as well. It was a thin soup with some vegetables and a little rabbit meat. She fed Robert a kind of mush, taking a mouthful of soup for herself when the baby was busy dealing with what was in his mouth.

I watched the little family, smiling at the coziness of it all. The children were well behaved and quiet, though I suspected it was due to my presence. I saw Jamie kick Ellie once, and Ellie "accidentally" spilled her milk all over his shirt.

After the meal, I told Anne she should bring the family to the lodge to visit when she came to market. She didn't say anything, just shooed Jamie out to tend to the sheep. Ellie went out to the patch of garden to weed.

Anne sat down to card wool, Katie watching curiously.

"Anne?" I asked into the comfortable silence.

"Yes, milady?"

"Please, call me Kay. Would it be all right if I taught Jamie how to use a sword?"

"Why on earth would ya want t' do a thing like that?" she asked, not looking up from her wool.

"So he learns the proper way, learns respect for the weapon and what it can do. I'll teach him to use it as defense only. If he learns from someone else, which I think he would try to do anyway, he might not get proper training."

Anne considered it, then paused in her work. "It would be nice to have the boy to protect me when I'm gray. And I would'na want 'im to teach 'imself or learn from a thoughtless knave. Aye, I'm thinking it would be right if you teach 'im, but when 'e's a little older, eh?"

I smiled. "Yes, when he's older. I must go now, Anne. Will you come visit me at the lodge?"

She looked up. "When I go t' market," she said, nodding. "And yer welcome here whenever ya please."

Smiling, I got up and saw myself out.

It was hot, one of the hottest days so far that summer. I found Sassy beneath the tree where I'd left her and cinched up her saddle.

I waited a moment, then cinched it again. She had held her breath to keep it loose, but waiting made her let it out. I was pleased to have remembered that much from my old riding days.

Looking up at the sky, I saw it was about one o'clock. I had a little over an hour and a half to get back. I had ridden a long way before stopping, so I turned Sassy's head toward Gamwell and settled her into a canter.

CHAPTER
SEVENTEEN

B ack at the lodge, I washed up at the basin in my room, then changed back into the dress Andrea had brought me and walked downstairs. I found the staff lined up, waiting.

"Well," I said, "I'm more than a little nervous. I've never done this sort of thing before, so I hope you'll excuse any inadequacies. I think you all know who I am, but if you don't, I'm Kay, Will . . . Lord Scathelock's betrothed. Now, I'd like to ask each of you your names, what your duties cover, and if you intend to stay on here when Lady Margaret leaves."

"We have a choice?" one woman asked, surprised into speaking out of turn.

"Of course you have a choice. Remember that. All of you. That's why I asked that Lady Margaret not know about this meeting." I hesitated. I had forgotten that Andrea told me many of these were bondservants. "I may not be able to get you out of your debt of service, but I will treat you better than most, and I will let you make your own choice whenever possible. Now . . . ." I looked at a woman at the right end of the line. "Let's start with you, shall we? What's your name?"

There were thirty staff members for the main house. Twenty-two of them were female, eight were male. All but two of the men were leaving, along with seven women. Some of them were bondservants I said I would try to get out of service, some of them wanted to stay with Margaret. I didn't mind a smaller staff. It would be easier to keep in hand and be liked by. It would also be easier to remember their names and duties.

Andrea would stay, which made me happy. I thought she and I would be good friends, and she was already enjoying the boost in "rank" from being a favorite of mine.

After dismissing them, I got myself a cup of cool cider and sat down next to the cold hearth. The day was too warm for even a small flame to make starting the evening fire easier.

I cradled my cup in my hands and closed my eyes to think about my day. I felt I was doing okay so far, being someone who didn't know what she was doing. I had a lot to learn and discover about running a household and managing people. It was a far cry from anything I had ever experienced in my life.

The tinkle of jewelry and scuff of slippers on stone alerted me to someone's approach. Lady Margaret, no doubt. I kept my eyes closed, listening to her sit down on the bench across from me.

"Lady Kay?" Margaret asked, speaking softly.

Tempted to pretend I was sleeping, I opened my eyes instead. "Yes?" I asked politely.

"Oh, you're awake." She looked happy to find me so.

"Yes," I repeated, and had to work to keep my tone civil. "What can I do for you?"

"Just talk. I don't often get to talk to another lady, even if you are new at it."

I got a strange feeling she was only trying to dig up some dirt on me, or just get some information about me to prattle to other people. I sighed.

She talked, and I answered some of her questions, but I left most hanging in the air, with no answer to bring them down again. Flustered, she switched to domestic talk. So-and-so told her something, and so-and-so told her this, and so-and-so and so . . . . Having no ear for gossip, I got bored quickly.

"What do you do all day?" I asked when she paused for breath.

"Oh, whatever pleases me," she said, delighted I had taken some interest in her. "I sometimes bathe, or sleep, or eat. Sometimes I ride on the common with an escort."

I felt my eyes widen. "How do you stay so trim?" It was a wonder she wasn't a fat cow.

She leaned forward to whisper conspiratorially, "I know the church considers it a sin, but I wear a corset."

I couldn't help it, I laughed outright in her face.

"Don't you?" she asked, hurt. I kept forgetting she was only seventeen. "I thought surely, with your figure . . . ."

"No, my lady, I do not share that sin with you," I said, making an effort to stifle my laughter. "What you see is what I am. Lean, lithe . . . ." I leaned forward, enticing her closer, unable to resist the tease. "And deadly."

She leaned back, putting her hand to her mouth. "You . . . . You kill people?" Her voice rose to a squeak.

"I do on occasion," I said, leaning back and giving her a toothy grin. "But only if they *really* annoy me."

She stood and fled. When she turned to get one last look at me before she left the room, I laughed. I should have felt bad for terrorizing her, but I really didn't. She wouldn't bother me again anytime soon.

I drained my mug and went to look for Will.

He was in the stable, checking horses. He beckoned me over and I moved to stand beside him. We watched the stablemaster checking the gravid mare.

"My love," Will said cheerfully. "This is my last stop, then I'll be ready to come up." He frowned as the mare stamped her foot. "What's wrong?"

"She's nervous, milord," the man said over the mare's back.

"I can see that," Will snapped, leaning forward through the double-hung door. "Why?"

"I'm not sure," the man said. "She's near her time, but not that close. I think perhaps the foal is misplaced."

Will grunted, thinking. "Have a watch on her until she's foaled. There must be someone around to help her if it's breech. I don't want to lose either her or the foal. She's the best of our stock."

Will turned to me as the man muttered acknowledgment to his orders.

"What did you do today?" he asked, draping his arm across my shoulders.

"I went for a ride on the common." I leaned my head against him as we began walking.

"Did you?" he asked, interested.

"I talked to a woman who makes dyed cloth. She was very nice and fed me lunch."

"Is she part of Gamwell?"

"I'm not sure. It's close to the Nottinghamshire border, if not within it. But she told me she brings her goods to Gamwell for sale."

"Good," said Will, no doubt thinking of the trade market and good public relations.

"I reviewed the household staff," I told him.

To my surprise, he sighed as we entered the courtyard. "I'm sorry, Kay."

I looked up at him. "For what?"

"Living in Gamwell Lodge isn't going to be very exciting, I'm afraid."

"I wouldn't worry about that, Will. I've had quite enough excitement to last five years of content." Realizing my indiscretion, I put a hand to my mouth and looked up to see Will gaping at me.

"Five years?" he asked. "Only five years?"

I hadn't meant to spoil his happiness, however brief it would be. "I'm sorry, Will," I whispered, catching his hand and bringing it to my lips. "I'm so sorry."

He hadn't stopped walking. I could tell he was thinking hard. I guided him through the hall and up to his room, then sat him down on the bed and shook him.

"Will!"

He erupted back into himself with a small gasp. I tried to discern what was going through his head and saw a hungry, yearning look come over his face.

Startled, I moved to the open door, about to leave.

"Don't go," he whispered.

I shut the door and stood by it, unsure of what he wanted. When he only watched me, I took a step toward him, holding out my hands.

"There's so little time." I barely heard him as I crossed the room.

He took my hands, pulled me to him, and wrapped me tightly in his arms. I didn't know how long we stayed that way, just holding each other.

A knock at the door startled us both. "What?" Will rasped.

"Supper, milord," said a voice I recognized to be Norman, one of the manservants who was staying.

Norman bowed respectfully when Will opened the door, then said, "I called for your lady, Master Scathelock, but I couldn't find her."

Then he saw me and his eyes widened, but he didn't say a word. I imagined the thoughts running through his mind and knew this little indiscretion would be all over the lodge by morning unless someone did something.

"Norman?" Will glared at the man. "Whatever reputation my lady has is not confirmed. If I find it besmirched . . . ." He left the sentence hanging, and Norman nodded in comprehension.

"I'm not one to gossip, milord."

"Good," said Will. "See that you don't. You're a good man, Norman."

As we left Will's room to go down to supper, Will squeezed my hand. "Kay," he said, his voice thick with emotion. "I want to get married soon. The Summer Solstice is in six weeks. That would be a lucky day to marry, would it not?"

"Is that enough time to make plans? We have to send invitations—"

"Then you must start planning," he said brusquely, then turned to face me. "I don't want to waste any more of our time together being anything less than husband and wife. I love you, Kay. Five years will not be enough to satisfy me."

He let go of my hand and turned away, and as I watched him go, his shoulders slumped a little. I wanted to protest that our love wouldn't end when our five years were up, but there was no way to tell what would really happen.

All the stories I knew ended when Robin died.

I DROPPED the parchment onto the table and rested my head in my hands, uttering a low growl of frustration. "This is so mindbogglingly boring. I feel like I've been at it for months, not just a week. How many lists must we make?" I pushed the papers away and stood up to stretch.

Andrea looked at me with one eyebrow raised. "Well, you'll want everything perfect, won't you?"

"Andrea, I never dreamed planning a wedding would be so tedious. I figured I'd make a list of guests and the rest would just fall into place."

"Ha! You have to choose flowers, bridesmaids, matron of honor, the priest, the minstrels and songs for the celebration—"

"I know all that. You've told me too many times this week. But I don't care. Tomorrow, I'm taking a break and going riding. I've got to get exercise or I'll get too fat to fit into my dress. I trust your judgment, Andrea. I only want to be sure the invitations make it on time."

Will came to the door just as I was heading out. I slipped into his embrace, resting my head against his shoulder.

"I was coming to see if you wanted to take a break," he said, his voice rumbling comfortably in my ear.

"Desperately," I said.

We walked out together, heading for the roof of the lodge, leaving Andrea to continue with the plans.

"I haven't seen much of you lately," he said as we reached the top of the stairs. We strolled across the roof timbers to the far side and stood looking out over Sherwood Forest.

"I've been busy with details. Do you know how much work it is to plan a wedding?"

"Judging by the amount of time you've spent at it, I'd guess a lot."

"Everything is coming along. I've asked Tuck to be our priest, and he has agreed." I sighed and leaned against Will. He put his arm around my waist, and I took pleasure in the peace his embrace lent me. "I'm tired of making plans. I told Andrea I trusted her to make sure everything else comes out right. It's not fair to her, but she seems to be enjoying herself." I fell quiet, absently pulling on the lacings of Will's shirt.

"So," he said into my silence. "What else have you been doing?"

I pulled out of his grasp and walked to the edge of the roof, resting my hands against the rampart. "Not a whole lot. I feel so inadequate around the lodge. I don't know what I'm doing, or where to even start learning. The place seems to run on its own." I shrugged. "I feel pretty useless."

Will walked up to me, placing his hand on mine. "It will get easier, Kay. You'll see."

"I hope so. Right now, I feel like the best thing I can do is get out of the way."

I WOKE EARLY the next morning and dressed in my riding clothes, belting on my swords and knives, again leaving my bow behind. I twisted my hair into a braid that fell down my back. Downstairs, the kitchens were empty, except for the bakers. I had intended to break my fast with the household staff, but it was earlier than I realized. I grabbed half a loaf of fresh bread and a chunk of last night's boiled meat from the larder before making my way to the door. The guard saluted as I passed, and I asked him to please let Lord Scathelock know I'd be back in the afternoon.

At the stable, I saddled Sassy. Having made time to practice all week, I was much better at it now.

The sun peeked over the edge of the world as I rode out the gate. I circled the perimeter of the common, passing Jamie herding his sheep. He waved. I waved back, but didn't stop.

I explored my riding skills as much as the farmlands, switching up gaits to test my connection with the horse. Just before noon, I rode Sassy at a dead run into the forest.

The cool shade was a relief from the heat of the day and I slowed, breaking out the boiled meat to munch on while Sassy cooled down after her run.

As I went deeper into the trees, I got an uneasy feeling that someone was watching me. From the corner of my eye, I saw a shadow detach itself from a tree and scurry beneath the underbrush. Over the sound of Sassy's hooves, I heard branches moving.

Outlaws!

I had forgotten there were other bands besides Robin's roaming the Greenwood. Watching covertly as I rode, I counted. Four of them making for the bend in the road to surprise me.

Scorn replaced my initial surprise. They were stalking *me?* I wondered if they were as stupid as they were noisy. I kicked Sassy into a canter, rounding the bend ahead of my would-be attackers.

Scanning the trees above me, I dropped the reins and reached up, grabbing hold of a low, sturdy branch. I pulled myself up and waited.

I didn't have to wait very long.

As I suspected they might, my attackers had panicked when I started to run and broke out onto the road to chase me. One of them rounded the bend ahead of the others and I dropped on top of him, knocking him down. Wrapping one arm around his neck, I pulled him to his feet, my knife against his side to keep him from struggling.

"Hold still, or I make it hard for you to digest," I hissed.

The other three ran around the bend like idiots, skidding to a halt when they saw me.

I grinned and viciously thumped their brother on the back of the head. There was a dull thud as the hilt of my knife met his skull, and I let him fall when he slumped.

I put my knife away and drew my swords.

One of them had a longbow. He nocked it and drew. I hadn't counted on that, but a memory reminded me of something Frederick the Norman once told me.

The outlaw shot.

The forest became silent, save for the arrow whistling through the air. My eyes saw only the wickedly barbed broadhead as it spun straight at me.

Holding my ground, I twisted to the side at the last possible second and knocked the arrow out of the air with my sword.

For a moment, I watched it careen to the ground, then looked up. "Fair play," I said, my voice as casual as I could make it with the adrenaline rushing through me. I stepped forward, over their brother. "If you kill me, you do it hand to hand."

I could read the thoughts going through their minds, like water in a crystal glass. They were afraid of me.

"Well?" I made my question a demand for action.

One of the men stepped forward, sword drawn but held low.

"You've got a quick wit about you," he said, eyes searching my face keenly. He turned slightly to his companions, though his eyes never left mine. "I'd wager every silver penny I've got that this is one of Robin Hood's band."

One of the others had the temerity to laugh. "You haven't got many pennies, man."

"That's not the point," snapped the first. He turned his full attention back to me. I was still on my guard, not sure what to make of the situation. "*Are* you one of Robin Hood's outlaws?"

I straightened a little. "I was. Robin's gone to Winchester with the king."

"So we heard. Are you still outlawed?" the man asked. I shook my head. "What are you then?"

I declined to answer. "Do you intend to fight me or not?" I asked, giving in to impatience. "Do you intend to rob me or invite me to the king's next ball?"

"We could use you," the man murmured. His friends snapped their heads around to stare at him.

"Bran!" one man hissed. "You're mad! You don't know anything about—"

"I'm leader, ain't I?" Bran said sharply. "I'm not stupid. We haven't many men. We need anyone we can get."

I laughed. "You would take me into your band not knowing who I am?" The man was surely mad to even consider it. But as I thought about it, I realized there was opportunity here. These men could be security. They could provide a sanctuary in the forest when Will and I would need one most. I wondered if there was any hope for these outlaws—barring their leader's insanity. How much could they learn?

"You were one of Robin's, weren't ya?" Bran asked. "What's your name?"

"What's your friend's name?" I countered, pointing to the man at my feet, who was beginning to come around. I moved so he was between Bran and myself. "And those two? I already know *your* name, Master Bran." I grinned and bobbed my head in a mock bow.

Bran shrugged and pointed to the lad at my feet. "That's Geoffrey."

"Bran," one of the others warned.

He turned on the man. "We haven't got anything to lose."

"Just our lives," he quipped.

"Shut up, John." He turned to me. "The one with the mouth is John, and the other is Sydney. Now, what's your name?"

"Kay."

"Kay?" He tilted his head, as if trying to figure where he'd heard the name before.

I grinned. "Soon to be Lady of Gamwell."

Bran's jaw dropped. "A lady?"

"Aye, a lady," said Sydney, speaking for the first time. "If you'd a looked, you'd a seen it, my brothers."

John glared at him a moment, then turned his glare on me. He fingered his long bow, and I could almost feel his fingers itching.

Casually, I nudged the boy at my feet with the tip of one sword. He had been playing at sleeping, but I knew he was awake. He opened his eyes when he felt my sword at his neck. "Don't move," I told him, then looked at Bran. "I can help you, though I can't join you."

"What do you want in return?" John asked suspiciously.

"Nothing . . . yet," I said.

"And what's that supposed to mean?" He shifted his bow, as though ready to shoot me no matter what answer I made.

"Listen," I said, sheathing my left-hand sword. "We can't afford to stand in the middle of the road making threats. If you're serious, Bran, let's go someplace where we can talk."

I pulled Geoffrey to his feet and pushed him toward his brothers, then sheathed my other sword and whistled for Sassy. She had stopped down the road to crop the roadside grass.

"Why should we trust you?" asked Bran.

"I can't answer that. You suggested I join. Look to your own instinct." I grabbed Sassy's bridle as she trotted up. "But Robin trusts me. Has for five years."

Bran nodded, deep in thought. Then he nodded again and pointed into the forest. "That way."

WE MADE our way into the forest, I in the center of the group, Sydney last, leading Sassy. I had handed over the reins in a show of confidence that I wasn't afraid of them.

We didn't come to a camp, as I'd expected, but a small clearing. Bran gave the long, piercing whistle of a hawker, then bade me sit.

I remained standing with my back against a tree, showing him that while I did not fear them, I had no reason to trust them, either.

Bran shrugged and sat on a fallen log. Sydney tied Sassy to a bush and sat, too. Geoffrey was occupied with feeling his head, but John stood about six feet away from me, ready to draw his long knife if I moved out of line. We stared at each other, neither willing to break contact and admit weakness.

I was the first to look away when I heard a noise in the forest. *Two men approaching.*

"Your two friends are here," I said loudly. Bran looked up, surprised. "You should teach them better stealth," I added a moment later as they emerged into the clearing.

"What did you want us out here for, Bran?" one asked, not even looking around.

"Where's Peter?" Bran countered.

"He stayed at camp. He's got some rabbit cooked up and didn't want to leave it." He caught sight of Sassy, then me. "What's going on?"

Bran stood. "Eric, Milo, this is Kay. She's going to help us."

"She?" Eric asked, torn between curiosity and laughter. "What can a woman do to help us?"

Milo frowned under his heavy brows and spoke to me, his voice gruff and deep. "So, you're going to help us," he said. His tone put me on my guard. It struck me I'd seen the man before, but I couldn't put my finger on where. "Aye," he said, responding to the look on my face. "You remember me."

"I remember you, but not from where." My mind raced, trying to latch onto the glimmer of this man in my memory.

"Robin Hood's people are always so willing to help." He advanced a step toward me, hand on the hilt of his sword.

I kept my hands away from my weapons, unwilling to answer

this man's unspoken challenge. "I remember you!" I finally said. "You're the fellow whose son was killed by foresters."

"That's me," he agreed. "Robin Hood had come to help, but you were too late. My son died because Robin Hood was too late!"

"You don't seriously blame Robin!" A queasy sensation built in my stomach.

"I do," the man said icily.

"Then your lack of sense makes you a fool." Had he carried this silly grudge around all this time?

Before Bran could stop him, Milo drew his sword. "I challenge you," he sneered. "Since Robin Hood is not around to be killed, I will kill you."

"You are twice a fool then," I snapped, drawing one sword. Fair was fair. He had only one sword, which he did not hold well, and I had no intention of killing him.

Moving away from my tree, I stepped into the clearing, which quickly emptied of people. Bran and the others watched from the tree line as Milo followed me out into the open.

I schooled my temper, determined only to defend myself. If I killed him, any bargain I might strike with Bran was out of the question. Plus, they might gang up on me. I was strong and agile, but I knew I couldn't handle five at once.

"Milo, don't be a fool!" Bran shouted. "I've an idea about the way she fights!"

"So've I, Bran. I've seen her. Just you stay off." He lunged toward me. I blocked his attack and danced out of the way, aware of the thick grass and fallen branches that could trip me up if I wasn't careful.

"Milo," I said, containing my anger at the man's foolishness. The queasy feeling grew as I fended off another attack and slapped him on the back with the flat of my sword. His lunge had him overextended and my blow overbalanced him, though he recovered quickly. "Milo, don't make me kill you." He scowled, then attacked again. "We did our damnedest to get there on time. It was only Robin and me. They outnumbered us. We tried to stop them. Don't you remember?"

"I remember," Milo said, pushing another attack. He'd not been courteous about listening to my explanation. I had to dance about, avoiding his strikes while speaking. "I remember that *you*," he growled with a thrust of his sword, "didn't save the life of my son!"

He thrust again. In blocking it, my fear of the clearing floor was realized. I tripped and fell onto my back, but I rolled away and up. Milo's sword pierced the fern growth where my heart had recently been.

"Your son is dead, Milo!" I gasped out as I struck him hard on the back of his legs with the flat of my sword. "Nothing can change that!"

Milo faltered, and I took the moment to disarm him. He made a wild reach for my left-hand sword, still sheathed, and I turned aside like a matador, kicking his feet from beneath him as he passed.

He landed on his back with a thud, and the tip of my sword near his throat kept him from getting to his feet.

"Milo, I could kill you now." I put a small amount of pressure on his neck with my sword. "Be warned." I backed away a step, letting him get up. "If you wish to continue, I will not be so generous again."

He shook his head, slowly getting up without saying a word. I hoped he wouldn't be stupid enough to try taking me unaware.

"Right," I said, sheathing my sword after Milo had. I backed up another step so I could turn to Bran and still keep an eye on Milo. "Do you want my help or not?"

"What do you want in return?" John asked again, as though nothing had happened between this and the last time he'd asked.

"A promise," I said. "My help now for your help later. Don't worry. It won't be anything too dangerous or difficult for a gang of outlaws such as yourselves. You don't have to make your promise yet." I glanced up at the sun. It was later than I had thought, and my stomach clenched. "I'll return in a fortnight," I told them. "Here, in this spot. You have until then to decide if you want to strike a bargain with me."

When I grabbed Sassy's reins and started back to the road, none of the others made a move to stop me.

The incident with Milo's son had happened a long time ago, and at the time, it had stirred me up. It was sad for anyone to die at the hands of foresters, especially when the victim was innocent, as Milo's son had been. And it was no easy pill to swallow that we'd been too late. Time enough to see the boy tied up, some of the gang of foresters beating him while others held Milo down. Time enough to kill some of them before two came to the same idea and ran the boy through. But not time enough to save him.

Riding back to the lodge, feeling hollow and tired from fighting Milo, I checked the sun again. *How did it get to be so late?* Something besides the heat, my hunger, and fatigue worked at me, slowly and from the inside. I was still about a mile from the lodge when the countryside swam beneath me and I lurched in the saddle.

Clinging to Sassy's mane, I wondered what on earth possessed my body. My stomach heaved, as though turning itself inside out. I felt so nauseated that when another spasm struck me, I lost my grip on the saddle and fell. Blinding pain exploded as my head struck the ground. I opened my eyes to find Sassy nudging me, her large head looming over me where I lay.

"Go to the lodge," I gasped, in pain and not knowing why. Curled in a ball, I waved feebly at the horse, but she just stood there, gazing at me with placid eyes. Unable to understand what I was doing, she began cropping at the grass.

"Dumb horse," I moaned. I thrashed on the ground and Sassy danced away a few steps before stopping to watch me again. I couldn't figure out why I was unable to get up. It was too quick, and altogether unexpected.

CHAPTER

EIGHTEEN

Weak and drowsy, I woke in my own bed at the lodge. The pain was gone and I was able to think clearly about what happened . . . . How long ago?

What *had* happened? I had always enjoyed good health, there were no plagues roaming the country, I ate only what I chose with my own hands, I was cleaner now than I had been in seven years. What could have happened?

I tried to sit up, but the sharp pounding in my head told me it was an injudicious movement, and I fell back against my pillows. A sound made me turn slowly and look toward the window, where I saw Andrea in the chair, stirring awake. A glance at the sky outside told me it was early morning.

"Milady?" Andrea inquired, coming to sit on the edge of my bed. "Do you feel any pain?"

"Just a throbbing headache. What happened? How long have I been out?"

Andrea glanced out the window, much like I had. "Since Lord Scathelock found you, it's been two nights and a day. You've given us all a scare, milady. Mostly milord. It was as if he knew something was wrong. He was on his way to dinner when he asked after you. When he heard no one had seen you since morning, he ran out of the hall and for the stables.

"He told me that when he found you, bleeding in two places, he thought you'd been thrown by that fool horse that just stood next to you, like a bump on a log. I know something of healing, so they brought you to me. And look." She reached toward me and lifted a heavy amulet off my chest. "This is to ward off the evil in your stomach that made you sick."

I blinked, trying to figure out the correlation between an amulet and my physical condition, but it was too much to think through. "Andrea, what happened to me? I don't remember bleeding."

"You ate an evil spirit that made you ill, then I assume you fell off your horse."

"I remember falling. But I was bleeding?"

"Aye. On your head, here." She touched a bandaged spot on my forehead, which felt tender despite her gentle fingers. That must have been what knocked me out.

"You mean I got food poisoning?" I asked, finally catching on to what she was saying. "The boiled beef . . . . Did anyone else get sick?"

"Aye, most of us had a brisk bout with it. Yours was the worst because of the fall. But what we don't know is how you got this other wound." She drew back the covers and lifted my sleeping gown up my thigh, exposing a bandage. I looked down at it in amazement.

"How bad is it?" I asked. I must have gotten it fighting Milo, but I didn't remember him cutting me.

"Not bad. A scratch, really. Master Scathelock is all set to send out a hunting party to find whoever it was who hurt you."

"Has he?"

"No. What happened?"

I sighed in relief. "Um, I was riding in the forest and I went off the path. I guess a branch snagged me," I lied. I had to have a good story to tell Will in order to keep him from going after Bran.

"Is that your story?" Andrea laughed. "I'm sorry, milady, but I bandaged that wound. That's from a blade, or I'm a—"

"It's from a *branch*, Andrea," I said firmly. "At least as far as Will and everyone else is concerned. Did he get a good look at it?"

"No. It's small, but there was a lot of blood. Milady, if you don't mind me asking, what really happened out there?"

"I made some friends, Andrea. They're important. Never mind

my leg. I can't tell Will about it. Not yet. And you keep it under your tongue. Where do you think he is now?"

"I had Mary make him eat and get some sleep. He's been sitting up beside you and was dead tired. He kept getting in my way when I changed the poultices and gave you medicine. He said he wanted to make sure I was doing things right. As if he knows anything about healing."

"He knows more than you'd think, Andrea. How do you think we took care of ourselves in the forest?"

Andrea blushed and looked down, mumbling an apology.

My stomach growled and broke the embarrassed tension.

"Are you hungry?" she asked.

"Famished." I started to nod vigorously until the pain of that motion stopped me.

She hurried out of the room.

Uncomfortable, I shifted and tried to raise myself into a sitting position. It was then I realized just how weak I was. When I tried to move, my head began to ache. I lay back down, giving up until Andrea could help me.

She returned with a tray and helped me sit up. Glancing at the food, I got the impression all of it was healthful, meant to help me get my strength back. This woman certainly knew about natural medicine.

"It's all fresh," she said, mistaking my hesitation. "Master Scathelock had the warder go through everything in the kitchens."

"I'm sure it's fresh, Andrea. It all looks so good." I took a bite, then ate with a fervor, though not fast enough for my stomach. My hunger wasn't sated until I'd cleared the tray.

"How is Lady Margaret?" I asked as Andrea cleared the dishes, curious to know how she had been acting.

"That one . . . ." Andrea sniffed. "She's having a fit because she and Mowrey are to leave in two weeks' time."

I raised a brow. "This is news. Tell me."

"A day ago, a message came from some cousin or another of his up north. He's to go there for a position." Andrea snorted. "The sooner that woman goes, the better." She shot a quick glance at me, then bowed her head. "I meant no disrespect to you for letting her stay, milady, but she presumes entirely too much on the goodness of Master Scathelock and yourself."

I gave her a startled look. "What?"

"Oh, she flounces around the lodgings and orders everyone about, as if she's still the lady here. Frivolous things, like moving the furniture about and potting plants indoors. She even sent a man out to catch her a meadowlark so she could hear it sing. The creature, of course, couldn't be caught. She had a fit because of it, and the man wasted an entire day when he could have been working the fields. But Master Scathelock has told us to humor her in her last days here." Andrea paused, thoughtful. "You know, this started when you and Master Scathelock came here. It's as if she wants more attention than you, so she forces herself on everyone. When the master found you, she made a great show of fussing over you, like she knew what she was doing."

"Thank goodness I wasn't awake for that," I murmured.

Andrea made a sound of disgust. "I couldn't stand all her dithering, so I shooed her out, much to Master Scathelock's annoyance. But once I told him it was for your good, he stood behind me. Speaking of which, you ought to sleep some more. Sleep and the right foods will have you on your feet in no time at all." She bustled out of the room with the tray.

I chuckled at her industriousness, though it seemed that just from listening to her, I was too tired to move. I fell asleep thinking about going to the window to look out.

WHEN I WOKE AGAIN, it was late in the evening. Through shutters that were wide open to catch the slightest breeze, I heard voices drifting up from the dining hall. I was glad I had slept through the worst heat of the day.

Heaving myself out of bed, I staggered to the bureau mirror to look at the damage. I gently pulled off the bandage. My forehead was bruised nearly black, a scab where the skin had split open. I prodded it gingerly and winced. Definitely a minor concussion. It was a wonder I hadn't cracked my skull wide open.

My head throbbed steadily, but I tottered over to the window seat. The small effort left me panting as I looked out at the horizon where the colors of sunset were just fading.

In the courtyard beneath my window, I saw the light-bearer lighting torches so the supper guests could see their way home. I toyed with the idea of calling out and having him send Andrea up, but I tossed it aside. She needed to have some time to herself. I settled in to wait.

A short time later, Andrea came in. "Ah, you're feeling better then?"

"A little. I can't believe how much effort it takes to move around. I wore myself out just walking over here."

"Yes, well, the weakness will pass. Since you're up, I'll take care of your sheets."

Andrea bustled around, taking the old sheets off the bed and putting clean ones on while I watched from where I sat. Then she washed my face, carefully dabbing at the bruised cut on my forehead. I felt like a child as she helped me back to bed so she could change the dressing on my leg.

It was a small, shallow cut. I thought it might pass as damage from a branch.

"Andrea," I asked as she straightened the sheets around me. "Did you put something in my food this morning?"

"Milady?" She looked up at me.

"Something to make me sleep, I mean." Andrea hesitated. "I'm not angry. Just curious."

"I used a special herb my mother showed me. Sleep is best for you, milady. You should be able to get around easier tomorrow."

"Good. I can't stand inactivity. Is that my dinner you brought up?" I asked, pointing at the tray Andrea had put down when she came in.

"Oh, yes. I'd almost forgotten." She brought it to me. "Now, you eat it all," she commanded.

"Yes, Mother." I grinned. I knew this also had some special herb in it. "Before I get sleepy, did you tell Will about that nasty branch in the forest?"

"Aye, milady," she said. "He was doubtful. I'm sure he'll ask you more about it when he sees you're awake, but he hasn't sent anybody out to look for your attackers."

"Good. I'll explain it when I see him. When do you think he'll be in?"

"Not until tomorrow. You'll be sleeping soundly tonight."

I rolled my eyes. "How much did you put in here?"

"Enough." She smiled.

To pass the time until the herb took effect, Andrea gave me full reports on what had been going on in the lodge. I didn't doubt she told me everything, but I wondered how much of what she told me was lopsided toward her particular point of view.

Somewhere into her recital, I started to worry about being able to meet Bran and his people in a little over a week's time. I had no concern about getting my strength back, but since I had fallen on the common, I wondered if Will would give me a tough time about going out again. I had time to get fit enough to show him it would be all right when I did go.

Somewhere in my thoughts, I drifted off, Andrea still talking to me.

Despite what she said, I woke during the night. It was still and cool, the way nights get around four in the morning. I rose slowly to look out the window into the darkness. The moon had set and I only had starlight to see by, but I could make out the courtyard from the deeper shadows. I sat on the cushioned window seat, looking up at the stars, not really thinking of anything, my mind muzzy with sleep. Eventually, I put my head down on my arm and fell asleep while the night passed gently outside my window.

I woke, still sitting at the casement. Though it was early, it was already hot. A cool breeze came through the window, and I thought how nice it would be to go riding in the forest. Perhaps Andrea would let me go out today.

Then I heard again what must have woken me. The soft knock on the door brought me fully awake. I got up and opened the door.

"Anne!" I said in surprise, gesturing for her to come in.

She hesitated. "I was in town and heard you'd taken a fall," she said. "Are y' sure it's all right to come?"

"By all means, yes." I turned to the maid who waited patiently in the hallway. "Thank you, Meg. Please, bring up some drinks. Milk for me and . . . ." I looked at Anne.

"Mead is good," she said.

"Mead for my guest. At your convenience. Thank you." Meg curtsied, and I turned back into the room. "I just woke to your knock. I've been so lazy, but I guess that's all part of getting well. Sit down, please." I showed her to the window seat and sat down on the edge of the bed. "Where are the children?"

"They're with my sister in the village. I didna want to bother ya with 'em if you were ill. Jamie insisted I come to make sure you was all right, but I figured you'd be right soon."

"How are the little doves?" I asked.

"Healthy, but not so nearly doves. Jamie pestered me to let 'im drive, Ellie an' Katherine squabbled, and Robert cried all the way. 'E don't like t' travel much yet. 'E's still too young."

"Children." I smiled. "I can wait to have them, but to have a child of my own to love and teach . . . ." I trailed off, thoughtfully weighing the pros and cons.

Anne smiled, too. "They're something else, lady. I wouldna give mine up for all the king's gold, though I come close to throttling 'em at times. Am I presumptuous to ask, but are you and Master Scarlet to be married soon?"

I grinned like a schoolgirl. "We've a date set for the Summer Solstice."

"That's soon. In three weeks, is it? A big party? Or just a small ceremony?" she asked.

"As small as I can have it," I told her with a grimace. "I shudder to think of organizing a big party. But you and the children are invited."

"Ah, no. Not my brood. That'd be chaos!" Anne laughed.

Anne and I chatted for another hour, then she told me she had to get back to her children. I took her cup from her, wished her well in selling her cloth at market, and saw her to the door.

Directly after her departure, Andrea came in with my food. "I didn't want to disturb you with your guest, so I brought you breakfast and lunch together," she said, setting a tray laden with food on a table she'd set up for that purpose.

"Andrea! I can't eat all of this!" I exclaimed. "I've never eaten so much in an entire month, much less in one sitting."

"Milady—" she began in protest.

"I won't do it. Sit down and eat with me."

"Milady?"

"Yes, eat with me. I like your company, and if you don't help me eat it, it will just go to the dogs."

Andrea grinned, sitting down. "Aye, milady. I told the cooks you'd not eat so much." She winked. "But they didn't listen." We both knew Andrea was eating more now than she got in a week before my arrival. She had good reason to stay on my good side, but I knew she wasn't just buttering me up. She truly liked me for a mistress, as well as a friend.

Will came in as we finished up. Andrea looked up guiltily and started to gather the dishes, but he waved at her to finish eating while he sat down on the edge of the bed.

"Kay," he said, smiling gently. "How do you feel?"

"Much better, thanks to Andrea's care." I set down the bowl I had just taken the last spoonful from.

"Much came by, asking after you."

"I hope he came at a decent hour this time. Is he settling in all right?"

"Seems to be. I can never tell when he's serious. I'll send word that you're up so he can visit. You gave me a scare, Kay. When I saw you out there, I thought you were dead. I couldn't figure out what happened. Tell me."

I looked him in the eye. "I don't know for sure, but I think it was the food poisoning that made me fall off the horse. When I fell, I guess I hit my head and got knocked out. I don't remember anything but feeling ill and falling." I shrugged, looking down to fiddle with my spoon.

"What about your leg?"

"I was riding through the forest and got this idea to ride off the road. That horse has some wild ideas about avoiding trees. A branch gouged me before I got back on a trail."

Will sighed. "I thought someone had cut you. I was all set to send a party out to search the forest for outlaws. I hear there's a band of them out there."

I shook my head. "It was just me being clumsy. I'm still learning how to steer the damn beast."

That made Will laugh. He knew of my early troubles in getting Sassy to go where I wanted her to go. I rode much better now, but he had been too distracted with business to notice my improvement.

"All right, Kay. But learn how before you go off the road again. Right?"

"Okay, Will," I said, smiling.

"I'll leave you now and let you rest. You've been busy today. I don't want you to wear yourself out." He winked at me, then left, leaving the door open as it had been.

"Lady," said Andrea in a hushed voice, "you wouldn't have had me believe that, even if I didn't know the truth."

"But do you think he bought it?" I asked. Andrea gave a non-committal shrug. "I don't want to lie to him, Andrea, but I don't want him to hurt my new friends. I'll tell him as soon as I'm certain my new friends are going to work out."

I STIRRED awake just before dawn feeling strong enough to leave my room. I dressed in a soft pink dress, then went upstairs to the tower roof to watch the sunrise.

To my surprise, Will was already there.

He turned at my arrival, a delighted smile lighting his face when he saw me. I crossed over to him and slipped my arm around his waist.

"What are you doing up this early?" he asked, putting his arm around my shoulders.

"I might ask the same of you, milord." I grinned when he made a face at the use of his title coming from me. "I just got tired of sitting in my room. Andrea would flay me if she knew I was up here."

"I missed you, Kay," he said into my hair.

Together, we turned and watched as the first rays of light shot over the horizon. A thin, wispy mist clung to the trees of the forest, punctuated in places by the smoke of fires from cottages around the lodge.

I turned slightly to watch Will. The sun had risen, an orb dancing in the sky so bright, it could no longer be looked at directly.

"Your eyes are sun dazzled," I told him, caressing his jawline.

"Yes?" He laughed. "Well, you're a sunspot." He drew me to him, kissing me. I returned the kiss enthusiastically.

After a moment, he broke away with a laugh. "Are you sure you can wait until the solstice?"

"I don't know," I said seriously. "Maybe we should make it sooner."

Will sat on the rampart and took my hands. "What about all the lists you've made? All that work for nothing?"

"I don't care. Robin and the rest can come on the solstice and find us already married."

"You make that sound good, but it would hardly be the wedding I promised you." He pulled me onto his lap so he could hug me tightly.

"I don't need the frills. Just your ring on my finger and your body in my bed," I said boldly and planted a passionate kiss on his lips. I ran my hands up to his shoulders to hold him close.

When I pulled back from him, he reached out to me, but I wiggled out of his grasp.

"No. You'll just have to wait," I teased, grinning at him.

"Kay, you don't make it easy—"

"Neither do you!" I laughed, turning to run down the steps of the tower, followed closely by Will. Breathless, I arrived in the dining hall and collapsed in my chair, laughing. Will sat down seconds later.

He laughed. "I almost got you, sprite!"

The servants setting up the hall looked our way, surprised at the behavior of their master and mistress. They went back to work smiling, moving a little quicker.

CHAPTER
NINETEEN

I managed to get out of the lodge the day I had told Bran I would meet with him. Will was on some business in the village, and I succeeded in giving Andrea the slip long enough to change and gain the stable before she caught sight of me.

She was still worried about my health. Though I had ridden around the village many times, she still thought I was going to fall apart if she wasn't around.

"Milady!" she cried as I wheeled Sassy out of the courtyard. "Where are you going?"

"Riding!" I threw back over my shoulder, knowing I'd be in for a sound tongue-lashing when I returned. It wasn't that I let Andrea have her ways over mine. She knew who was lady. She just didn't curb her tongue, which was one of the things that had gotten her into trouble with Margaret.

She shouted something I couldn't hear over the drumming of the horse's hooves. I just laughed wildly at my freedom, passing through the gate at a full gallop.

I was adjusting to life in the lodge, but to one who had lived in the open, the walls choked and the bindings chafed in the summer. And by God, it was summer—glorious, even at its murkiest.

It was a cloudy day, raining off and on, but glorious nonetheless. I reveled in the sodden beauty after my long days of imposed inactivity.

Once in the forest, I slowed Sassy to a walk, not wishing to tire her after her own sojourn. The mud from the road made sucking noises as her hooves pushed in and pulled out. Big drops of water fell from the leaves of birch, oaks, alders, elms, and the many other trees thriving in Sherwood to make pockmarks in the road or splash on Sassy and me. Now and again, the sun broke through the clouds, cascading through the trees to fall onto the ground, much as the rain did.

It was beautiful and peaceful. It was Sherwood Forest, and for that moment, it was mine.

I was almost to the place where I would turn off the road to go to the clearing when I stopped, pulling back sharply on the reins. Looking up into the trees, I caught my breath, slipping a dagger from its shoulder sheath under my arm. Had I heard something moving up there?

There! I saw it. A foot, exposed from cover under the leaves. And there was an elbow.

A squall of rain swept through the forest, drenching me and the person in the trees, who had frozen when I stopped.

"Come down!" I called, and watched as a face appeared. It was Sydney. I laughed. "Where are the others?"

"Here now," he said in a muffled voice. "Move your horse up so I can get on back. I'm to take you down the road. We've changed the site. Milo thought you'd set a trap for us or something."

Sydney grunted as he slipped off the branch, caught himself a moment, then dropped out of the tree and onto Sassy's back behind me. The horse skittered forward a few paces, but I soothed her.

He chuckled. "I was trying to surprise you, but you saw me out. There's good ears on that head of yours."

"How do you think I lasted with Robin Hood? I had to keep on my toes or be sent to town, unworthy to keep my place." I urged Sassy forward. "Did you know I fought Robin Hood himself with staffs?"

"Didja now?"

"Aye."

"And how did you fare?"

"I got a sound beating. I was black and blue for days." Sydney laughed. "I'm much better at fighting now. That was over four years ago."

He became very serious. "Why did you want to help us?"

His blunt question took me by surprise. Taking a few moments to organize my thoughts, I held up my left hand with its silver engagement ring.

"You know I'm to marry Will Scathelock of Gamwell Lodge. He was one of Robin's men, too. King Richard has pardoned all of Robin Hood's people and given some of us positions of power. Positions holding a lot of sway with people who influence the king. Now, what do you think will happen when King Richard dies?"

"I dunno. Who says he's going to die?"

"I do. Listen. His Majesty went over to Palestine, and now France with his soldiers and his money, and spends them both fighting his wars. He takes foolish risks in battle. How long before he dies? When he does, John's going to take the crown, whether Richard names him heir or not. Prince John is not well-loved by Robin's people, nor does John have love for us. So what happens to Robin's people when John takes over?"

"Ah, I see your point. John will have you all executed as traitors —hunt you down and kill you."

"Right."

"And that will include you and your husband-to-be."

I nodded. "Can you now see why I will help you?"

"Aye. You want us to return the favor when John becomes king. You'll come running to the forest and we'll take the two of you in."

"Along with whoever else shows up."

"Hmmm. Stop here." When I did, Sydney slid off Sassy. He took the reins, leading the horse off the road into a clearing. "Wait here." He ran into the forest, then was gone. I didn't hear him after that. He had obviously been practicing his stealth.

I dismounted and gave Sassy her rein, letting her crop the grass. Every one of my senses on alert, I waited for an hour, listening for any sign of Sydney's return. Finally, I heard a rustle in the trees and half-drew my swords. Then I heard that piercing whistle of Bran's as seven men came through the forest to me. I assumed Sydney had told them my story, and I wondered what the verdict was.

Bran, Eric, Sydney, Peter, and Geoffrey stood before me, while

Milo and John sulked in the background. I could guess how the vote went.

"Kay."

"Bran."

"Sydney told us what you said."

"And?"

Bran scratched his beard. "It sounds reasonable." I smiled. "It's been decided if you help us, we will help you when you need it."

"Great," I said, and stepped forward to grasp his hand. We shook on it, like traders in the market.

"Listen. I'll come down the road on the first decent day each month. Anywhere between Lincoln and Gamwell, one of you can stop me. We'll talk, then I'll get you what you need. If I don't see you on that day, I'll ride in again every day until I see you." I was saying things off the top of my head. I had thought they would agree, but I hadn't planned on what I would say if they did. "If one of you is hurt or in danger, don't hesitate to come to me at the lodge for help. If you do come, speak only to Norman, a manservant at the hall, or Andrea, a maid. They're my most trusted. You'll have to find your own way past the gatehouse, though."

"But what if we're recognized?" asked Geoffrey.

I glanced at him. "You know people in Gamwell. You'll just have to be careful, won't you? I can't help you if you make careless mistakes. Do you know who Norman and Andrea are?"

Geoffrey nodded. "I've seen them. My sister and the maid are friends, and Norman was always at the tavern where I was apprenticed."

"Then you had better get good because you're the obvious one to go in an emergency. I've got to go now. I've been gone far too long as it is."

"Kay?" asked Peter, who I hadn't heard speak yet. I realized he was very young. He couldn't have been more than fourteen, and I wondered what he had done to be outlawed. "When Richard dies, how do we know who your people are? We can't just take everyone aside and ask them if they're looking for Robin Hood."

"Good point." The kid was smart. That was probably what had gotten him into trouble. "We need a code word, or some distinguishing clothing." I paused to think, stroking Sassy's nose.

"How about a colored band of cloth around each man's arm? Say, Lincoln green," suggested John. Despite his initial misgivings, he was starting to get into the spirit of the conspiracy. Milo still hung back.

"That's a clever idea, John," I said, smiling at him. "I'll spread the word. Lincoln green it is. And if I know of someone who is in trouble with the law, I'll see about sending them to you, if they're outlaw material."

I grabbed Sassy's reins and swung into the saddle. "A good day to you, my friends." I waved farewell before wheeling my horse to go back to the road.

It rained as I cantered toward Gamwell. Lightning flickered far away, and Sassy stretched into a full-blown gallop of her own accord when we had the lodge in sight. I didn't think I could have stopped her even if I wanted to.

I arrived, wet and dripping, and gave Sassy to the stable boy to rub down so she wouldn't catch a chill.

In the doorway, I stopped to shake off the rain and looked around the hall, crowded with people who had come in out of the weather. In a doorway across the hall, I saw Will speaking to a lady in fine clothes. I paused, frowning at their laughter. The lady giggled and curtsied, then skittered away in her fancy slippers. Will watched her walk away, a small smile on his lips. I scowled, anger flashing across my face to make it burn. I had planned to tell him about my outlaws today, but if he could have his secret meetings, so could I.

I stamped my feet to get the mud off my boots, and Will looked up as I walked in. He made to intercept me on my way to my room and caught up with me, matching his step to mine. "I was worried about you. Andrea said you gave her the slip." He followed me up the stairs.

"I wasn't aware I was on house arrest," I said, not slowing down. His possessiveness made me angry, especially after his flirting around. "I bumped my head, Will. I hardly need a twenty-four-hour watch. You of all people should know I can take care of myself."

"Kay, you were unconscious for nearly two days. I worry."

I blew out a breath, stopping at my door. "I'm sorry if I worried you, Will. I felt like riding today. Besides, Andrea told me I slept so long because she kept me sedated."

I tried to control my anger. I had never lost my temper with Will. A small voice of reason tried to tell me that I had no right to accuse him of playing around on me without confronting him about it. But another voice screamed of love and loyalty, and the flame of my anger burned hotter.

"I've been hurt worse and had only myself to take care of me," I said steadily. "What about when Mark died? What about the Ferris Castle bit, eh?" I opened the door to my room and went inside, not looking to see if Will followed. "You know I can take care of myself."

"Aye, but you didn't do yourself much good this last time," Will said from the door.

I turned around. "Will, you're right. Maybe I should lock myself —" I stopped, realizing I was blowing it way out of proportion. He didn't have a clue what I was really angry about. "I'm sorry. I shouldn't lose my temper over something like this. I'm used to my freedom, Will. Nobody hounded after me in the forest, so I'm feeling a little penned in."

Will's face turned red. "How do you think I feel, Kay? I haven't left this place since we got here. I haven't even been out on the common. I'm feeling the bit, too."

I hung my head, realizing how badly I had just acted. "I'm sorry Will." I walked to him and gave him a hug. "I just wasn't thinking." I hadn't forgotten the lady, but my temper had cooled in the face of his distress. It didn't seem like such a vital issue anymore. He could be so bloody reasonable that I couldn't stay mad at him for long.

Will hugged me back. I was glad he had kept his temper. "Why would you want to go riding on a day like this? You're soaked." He wiped a runnel of water dripping from my hair down my face.

"It wasn't raining the whole time. I just got caught in a downpour when I hit the home stretch. Do I have time for a quick bath before dinner?"

"Yes, I think so."

I unbuckled my sword belt and unstrapped my bow and quiver. I laid out the arrows carefully so they wouldn't bend while drying, then wiped down my bow. I didn't have to worry about the fiberglass warping from wetness, but it was a good habit. I gathered up a fresh dress and my bathing things.

Will stopped me before I left, putting his hand on my cheek. "Little Kay, I just worry about you. Why won't you take anyone with you when you go riding?"

"You never worried about me when we were in Sherwood, Will Scarlet," I said. I leaned into his hand since mine were too full to take his.

"You weren't my bride-to-be then. And you weren't to be the lady of Gamwell. I *did* worry then, but there's so much more now. As squire, I've got enemies out there—people who didn't want to see Mowrey go, as well as other nobility who don't like seeing a former outlaw and a Saxon in power. They might try to hurt me by hurting you."

"Oh, Will," I said, not knowing what to say.

"God knows you mean more to me than any title or land. I don't know what I would do if you were killed."

"I do," I said firmly. "You'd go on living. You wouldn't give up. But, Will, nothing's going to happen to me."

"Do you *know* that?" he asked, grasping my chin and forcing me to look at him. I had only said that to reassure him I could take care of myself, but I knew he referred to my being from the future.

"No." I shook my head slowly, then moved my chin from his hand, looking away from him. "I don't know what's in my future," I whispered. "But I'm careful, Will." I bent my head to kiss his hand. "I've got to bathe now if I'm to be ready for dinner."

I left him standing in the doorway, a look of helpless anguish on his face. I wished I could do something to ease that pain, but I couldn't think of anything. I couldn't predict the future or ease his fear. Ignorance wasn't any easier on me.

THE WEEK before the wedding was hectic. I almost missed Margaret's help with last-minute details. Almost. I knew she'd be good at something like that, but she was gone. As it was, between Andrea, Anne, and me, we got things settled. Guests, places for them to sleep, a priest, food . . . . The list was endless, but we got it done in time.

Guests started arriving at the gates the night before the cere-mony, and Will and I greeted them.

When Robin arrived, he gave Will a huge bear hug. Then he turned to me, picked me up, and whirled me in a circle, setting me down with a kiss square on the mouth before he turned to Will.

"I almost wish I'd be standing in your boots tomorrow," he said with a laugh, "but I've already got myself a wife."

"What! And you didn't invite us to the wedding?" I cried, thumping him on the arm.

"Didn't have time. King Richard saw me with my girl—you remember Marian—and he says, 'By God, Huntingdon, you should marry this lass!'" Robin's imitation of Richard was spot on. "So when both of us were willing, we called up a preacher right then and there and . . . ." He threw up his hands in surrender, "What do you know, I'm a married man!"

We chatted late into the evening, drinking judicious amounts of wine and reliving old times, as well as catching up on more recent happenings.

I went to bed very tired, happily thinking that this was the last night I had to sleep in this old stone room alone.

IN THE MORNING, Tuck arrived, as well as John, Much, and a handful of former outlaws who now made Nottingham their home. All the others had arrived the night before. I was far too excited to do anything but worry about how I looked and hope the ceremony would be perfect.

My white silk dress shimmered blue in the shadows. The bodice was over-layered with white lace, which came to a point just at my navel, and silk drawstrings closed the modest neckline, which came down just low enough to display the silver crucifix Friar Tuck had given me as an early gift. Lace covered the lower half of my arms, coming down over the backs of my hands, and the shoulders fluffed out loosely. A coronet of blue wild flowers cascaded down my back, ending with the length of my hair at the knees. The lace-bordered train trailed behind me for three yards, and Katie and Ellie held the tail of it as I descended the stairs to the great hall, hearing the *ooohs* and *aaahs* of the assembled guests.

The actual ceremony wasn't very memorable to me. I got tunnel vision. I could see only Friar Tuck, was only aware of Will at my side.

The voice calling the bans seemed loud in my ears. It echoed into silence as I held my breath, listening for anyone who might have protested our marriage. All I could hear was my blood roaring in my ears.

Somehow, I repeated my vows correctly, heard Will say his. Then the ring was slipped onto my finger "in the name of the Father, the Son, and the Holy Spirit." I remember marveling at the way the gold wedding band locked into place alongside the silver engagement ring. Then I kissed Will to a chorus of hoots from the former outlaws in attendance, and I nearly fainted with a feeling of vertigo. Yes, vertigo at the altar of a chapel.

The ceremony ended near four o'clock, the wedding feast beginning soon after. The hall was full of people celebrating. The music played and the wine flowed.

Will and I went from table to table, chatting and laughing, then we danced, ate more than our fill, and drank too much.

The festivities ended about one in the morning. Most everyone had either drunk themselves to sleep or just fell asleep where they sat. We had prepared sleeping accommodations for our guests, but the former outlaws didn't seem to care. The rest chatted in small groups, and somewhere, someone played a lute softly, lending an enchanted air to the evening.

And sometime around one, Will gathered me into his arms to take me upstairs. Soft light from a single candle guided him to the bed, and he set me down on the blankets gently.

Will's sensitive touch drove away any fears I might have harbored. My heart filled with such complete trust and love. The only thing on my mind was the way he made me feel at that moment.

I shivered with delight and anticipation as Will leaned over me and kissed my lips, my cheek, my throat. A gentle hand pulled the drawstrings of my bodice loose.

I reached around Will, caressed his back, and slipped his best tunic over his head. It fell to the floor. Moments later, my beautiful wedding dress was beside it.

SUNLIGHT SLANTING in through the east window woke me. I lay for a moment, smiling at the remembered pleasure of the night. I reached across the bed to touch Will, but he wasn't there.

A glance around the chamber confirmed I was alone. I hurriedly got up, washed with the cool water in the washbowl, and dressed. I ran down the hall and stairs, almost tripping over a sleeping body sprawled at the bottom.

So, some of the guests are still here.

I tried to rouse the man with my foot, but he was still too full of drink to move, so I let him be. My own head throbbed a bit, and my dry throat ached for some juice.

The hall was littered with snoring bodies. Even the smell of fresh bread from the kitchens didn't rouse them.

Will was seated at a table by the hearth, talking quietly with Robin and Tuck. He looked up when I came in, so I waved. On my way to the kitchen, I passed Much, curled up beneath a bench. I smiled and toed him on the knee. He groaned and rolled over, so I left him alone.

When I came out of the kitchen, I sat down next to Will.

". . . talking to one of the men back from the continent," Robin was saying. "He said Richard takes ungodly chances when he fights. He's already been wounded twice this year, yet he still insists on leading his men into the thick of battle. Now he has this silly quarrel with King Phillip of France. I tell you, he's not going to live much longer."

Will glanced at me, but I pointedly looked away. "Has he asked you to go with him yet?" Will asked Robin.

"As a matter of fact, he has. He's going back in August and wants me to head his archers."

"Are you going?" I asked. I already knew, but I almost hoped I could change his mind.

"Well, I have to, don't I? It was part of the agreement we made when he gave me Huntingdon."

"Have you been back home yet?" I asked, biting into some bread.

"I was there for nearly a week. Just long enough to be reinstated as earl." Robin sighed.

"And then you found someone to take over while you trotted off to Winchester with our liege Lionheart," I said crisply. When Robin looked at me sharply, I added, "Oh, I don't fault you. You don't have much of a choice."

"Aye," he said and sighed again. "I would have liked to stay, but Richard totes me about like I was extra baggage . . . or worse, a wild man from Sherwood he has tamed. But I love him, the old hound. It's almost a pity I do. Otherwise, I'd not put up with his . . . his treatment." Robin quaffed the remains of his juice and wiped his mouth on his sleeve. "I'm going back home after here."

We were silent for a moment. Then Tuck spoke up. "What about Prince John?"

Robin laughed. "What about him?"

"What do you think about him? What I mean is, when Richard dies, which won't be too long if what your man says is true, John is sure to take the crown."

"He's a devilish fiend, all right," answered Robin. "But what makes you so certain he'll get the throne? There's no love between Richard and his brother." When Robin glanced at me, I arched an eyebrow at him. He looked back at Tuck. "I think the people would not support him."

"That hardly matters, Robin. Richard has no heir, at least no legitimate ones. Prince John's already tried for the throne once. He's older and more devious now. If Richard dies without naming his successor, John will leap at the chance." Tuck nodded his great head, as if that was all that mattered. Indeed, it was. Tuck was a wise man to have come to the same conclusion I had, and he didn't have my obvious advantage.

"But," began Will, "if Richard dies without naming his successor, we may as well forget about Austria, France . . . or Palestine, for that matter. England will be dealing with civil war!"

"Exactly," said Tuck. "And that is just the tool John could use to get the nobility behind him."

"I'd never support him!" said Robin vehemently. "He's treacher-ous, greedy—"

"Which is precisely why you must be prepared for the worst when Richard dies," Tuck said, laying a hand on Robin's arm. "He has as little room in his heart for you as you have in yours for him. He knows you would not side with him, and he will condemn you as the whim of a foolish king."

I drew breath to introduce my idea of using Bran's outlaws, but just then, Little John stumbled in from outside. His clothes were all askew, his hair mussed, and his eyes still bleary with sleep. He steered his way over to us, grinning drowsily.

"Did she throw you out too early, John-o?" asked Will, who had seen him leave with a buxom blonde lass in the night.

"Aye," said John, but his eyes brightened with some thought. "Now there was a lass!" He chuckled as he sat down.

"Best be careful," said Tuck with a laugh, "else you get yourself illegitimate young sheriffs at your heel."

"Bah!" John clutched his side in laughter. "Can't you just see it?!"

Not many more people stayed asleep through his roar of laugh-ter, and our previous conversation was forgotten.

In August, Will and I went on a trip—a delayed honeymoon. I had forewarned Bran, telling him he would have to fend for himself while I was away. He laughed and said as if he hadn't been doing just that before I ever came around.

Will had a cousin in Glastonbury, and since we both had a desire to see the Summer Country, we made visiting an excuse to take a tour of the South. We were gone for a little over a month, and we stopped in at Nottingham before returning to Gamwell.

When we rode into the courtyard at Nottingham Castle, Little John was just coming out to greet us, Much hot on his heels. When he saw us, Much rushed past John and came straight to me to give me a hug.

"Kay!" he cried. "It's good to see you. How was your trip?" He didn't wait for an answer since he knew there'd be a tale-telling that night. "Will!" He gave him an equally enthusiastic welcome.

John was next to give me a hug, lifting me completely off the ground.

"John, you'll squeeze the life out of me. Put me down." I laughed, giving him a kiss as he set me on my feet. "It's good to see you both. It was a long road."

"Come inside and rest. Have you eaten?" asked John, not waiting for an answer before he continued. "No? Well then, have I got a feast for you."

CHAPTER

TWENTY

We sat in Nottingham Castle's formal garden in the fading twilight, lounging on the stone benches, quite stuffed from the evening's feasting. John had stretched out on the grass, gazing up at the stars. Much propped his feet on a bench, paring his fingernails with a knife, the prim garden behind him.

I thought they looked ridiculously out of place, but Will and I, leaning against each other on the same bench, didn't cut the picture of grand nobility ourselves.

"So, I take it Berkeley wasn't a pleasant place," said Much.

"Oh, it was perfectly nasty," I said, having just related our harsh stay there. We had been accosted on the street after sundown and thieves had tried to take our money. They had chosen the wrong victims. Will and I weren't about to give up without a fight. In the end, we bested them. "But that wasn't the worst place."

"Really?" asked John, his voice rising from the ground. We could hardly see him now because of the shadows.

"Really. There was Cardiff."

"Aye," agreed Will, nodding.

My voice was bitter with the memory as I spoke. "Cardiff was worse because it was beautiful on the outside. The people were fair to look at, the streets were clean, the houses in good repair, there was tasty food to eat. The dogs didn't even bark at people."

"Sounds nice. So what was wrong with it?" asked John.

"It was rotten at the heart," I said, almost able to hear again the sound of feet pounding down the cobbled street, the voices shouting. "Those fair people turned to hunters, the clean streets became a dangerous trap, the nice houses a last escape for a terrified quarry." I turned around on the bench and looked up at a sky full of stars—as full as I was with bitter anger at the memory of Cardiff.

"What happened?" asked Much. I couldn't see him, but it sounded like he had sat up or moved.

"There was a riot," answered Will. "They were after a witch, and Kay tried to stop them."

"Stop a riot? Kay, you're mad!" said Much, closer.

I didn't turn or say anything. I was remembering the jostling crowd, the sharp smell of fear. The group of men who turned on me as the girl momentarily slipped from their grasp.

"Was she hurt?" Much asked Will.

"She was knifed in the leg." I could tell Will was keeping him at a distance. I heard Much hiss in appreciation of my wound.

"It wasn't that," I said, not turning. "The knife was nothing. I don't even feel it. It was the fire . . . ." I trailed off. I hadn't gotten over it yet.

Will finished for me. "They burned the witch."

"Oh," said Much in relief. "Is that all?"

"Is that all?!" I repeated, turning on him. "She was no witch! Just a frightened girl! They burned her, damn it, and I couldn't stop them!" The horror of it was etched into my mind. I hadn't seen it, but I had smelled the smoke, the burning flesh, and my imagination did the rest for me. When I closed my eyes, I pictured the flames curling up, the girl's mouth open in a silent scream. The *girl!* I knew there was no such thing as a witch.

Will held me while I stared at Much, silhouetted in the lantern light from the hall.

"Which hurts worse?" John asked from the ground. "That they burned her, or that you couldn't stop them?"

"Which do you think?" I retorted angrily, surprised that it was still so close to my thoughts, still a tender subject. Then the fire of anger cooled. "I'm sorry. I shouldn't be angry at you two. It has nothing to do with you. It's just my own guilt at my shortcomings."

"Kay," said Much. "It seems to me you were lucky enough to get off with just a knife in the leg. I just don't give a rat's tail about some girl. *You're* the one I care about."

Much's words settled me more, and I realized I'd been acting like an ass. "I know. Thank you, Much."

I considered how he and Will would have felt if the door had taken me in Cardiff. It had been close . . . too close. Dodging it was what had gotten me wounded.

Just then, we heard someone approaching without a torch. John cursed loudly when the new arrival tripped over him, sprawling on the grass between the benches.

"Who's that?" John asked, irritated.

"It's Andrew, sir. I'm sorry, sir." The page picked himself up. "I'm to see if you wanted any lights out here, or if you were coming in soon, sir."

"God's breath, boy. Why didn't you bring a torch?" John loomed over the boy now, a shadow rooted in the darkness.

The boy appeared not to mind, though having John standing over you was not an easy experience. "Didn't think of it, sir. I didn't want to disturb you."

"Well, you certainly didn't do that, Andrew," said Much, reaching out to ruffle the boy's hair.

Andrew giggled. "No, sir." He pulled at his clothes, trying to straighten them.

John grunted, swallowing his laughter. "Go in and tell Mother Irene we'll be in shortly and she's to ready a guest room. The good one." With a swat on the shoulder, he sent the rascally boy back toward the hall. "That boy's lucky he's a page here. I don't think he'd get away with as much anywhere else."

I was surprised to see John smiling as he took a seat on a bench.

"Come, Kay. Tell us about Caerleon," Much said eagerly.

I smiled, willingly changing to this memory from the other. "Caerleon's is a ghost story," I said in a calculated whisper. "Listen while I tell you what I learned there." I paused, looking at each of my listeners—for effect, and for time to make up my story. I had the idea already, but I hadn't tried to organize it.

"If you come to see Caerleon, come in the night when the moon is out and shining brightly. Come with an open mind, so you can see what is before your eyes.

"At midnight, the towers shine golden in the moonlight. If you walk among them, you can hear the pennants snapping in the wind. And you'll find you're not alone. Caerleon is haunted by a host of gray souls crowding the streets. You can sense their waiting. Through the still air, you can hear the army approaching, the clatter of armor and jingle of harness. A cheer rises in the throats of the crowd. 'The king! Hail! The king is victorious! Arthur! Arthur! *Arthur!*' And you can see that wonderful man. He's shadowy gray, but brighter than the other wraiths. Then he turns—and looks at you. When the moon runs behind a cloud, the images vanish. The cheers become the moan of wood owls as they hunt for mice in deserted streets." I stopped, looking around at the others.

"Lovely, just lovely," said Much. "Where did you hear that story?"

"Nowhere," I answered. "I just now made it up."

"Ah, Kay, you're lying."

"Me? Lie?" I said innocently. "Occasionally, but not on this one, and never to my friends."

"She's good at that, you know." Will chuckled. "She has a tongue of silver in a tight spot. I think she could talk the moon out of the sky if given a chance."

"Aw, get off," I said indelicately. "You're a pretty liar."

"Well, then, you're simply pretty."

I snorted. "I've heard better than that."

"Enough," said John. "Save bedroom talk for the bedroom. As sweet as this night is, I think it's time we got off to sleep."

SUNLIGHT DAPPLED the forest floor as I rode out a couple days later. I turned off the main road and onto an ill-used game trail leading to the river. The water looked inviting. I thought about taking a swim, then denied myself the pleasure.

I turned upstream and followed the river to a clearing, then turned Sassy out on a tether and walked into the forest. I followed the river just inside the trees, then went deeper into the wood.

Using all my skills at stealth, I went to Bran's camp and watched their activities for a while. They were all occupied with one thing or another—Eric with sleeping—but I noticed they were all alert to what was going on around them. I think they felt me watching, and they were nervous.

I timed my entry to a moment where it would look like I had appeared out of thin air.

Geoffrey was the first to spy me as I stood three steps into the clearing, waiting to be discovered. "Kay!" he called. "What news?"

I smiled at his easy composure. "I just came to tell you I'm back, to say hello and see how you're doing." I crossed the clearing and sat down next to Peter. "I see you've been keeping busy."

"Aye," said John lightly. "Working at being good little outlaws."

"Practicing every day," agreed Bran with more gravity.

"Have you gotten any better?" I asked, looking at Eric, who still slept against a tree.

"Better," said Milo modestly. The dagger he'd held became a blur as he threw it toward me. I started to duck away, but it flew past me to stick into a tree, inches away from Eric's head.

Eric woke with a start and looked at the knife. "Milo," he growled.

"Milo," echoed Bran. "I've told you not to practice on people."

"How am I supposed to get better?" he asked, a lopsided grin on his face as he went to retrieve his knife.

"Kay!" said Eric, seeing me. "When did you get here?"

"Ha!" laughed Peter. "She's been here for a while, man. You sleep too much, you'll miss things."

"Hell," said Geoffrey. "She was standing here long enough before any of us noticed her. We *all* sleep too much."

"You're learning," I said. "That's all that matters. Hey!" I took my bow from my back and jumped to my feet. "Let's see what you can do with your bows." I chose a target and sent two of my arrows into it before anyone could say yea or nay. "Come on, ladies. Show me your skill!"

I stayed with them late into the afternoon, coaching and watching my team working out. I almost stayed longer, but I caught a glance at the sun.

"Will's going to have my hide!" I said, dropping the arrow

I'd been holding. I jumped to my feet and raced out of the clearing, gone seconds before any at our archery match knew it.

On my way back to the lodge, I reflected on how much happier I was during the time I spent in the forest. Most of my time at the lodge was onerous, educational, or tolerable at best, but not enjoyable. I wasn't any good at giving orders or organizing. The servants liked me, so they did as I asked, but things often went smoother when I let them take care of everything. I felt much more useful out here in the forest.

It was even worth the cross look Will gave me when I came in during supper. I settled into my chair beside him, still in my breeches and tunic, and kissed the frown on his brow. My good mood obviously infected him because he couldn't maintain his frown for long in the face of my good humor. I knew I ought to tell him about my outlaws, but it just hadn't felt right yet. Every time I had even a remote possibility, something came up to let me put it off.

IT WAS EARLY one fall morning when I heard Andrea come in, her skirts whispering as she knelt to stoke the fire. "Good morning, milady," she said.

I rolled over sleepily, aware of Will still slumbering beside me. "Good morning, Andrea." I sat up and ran my fingers through my hair, grimacing at the oily feel. It had been a week since I had washed it. I'd been too busy helping bring in the harvest, and the Harvest Celebration had been a two-day binge of every vice one cared to indulge in.

"Would you be wanting a bath this morning, milady?" asked Andrea, straightening. She moved to the windows and fastened the shutters on the window Will had opened during the night.

"Lovely," I muttered, never in my best mood in the morning anymore.

"Just a moment and I'll get your things." She finished at the window, then crossed to the closet.

"Really, Andrea. You'd think I could do it myself." I stood, bare feet on the cold stone floor, and stretched, groaning at the pleasant feeling.

"Then what would I do for a living?" Andrea asked, emerging from the closet with a basket.

"God knows."

She laughed. I smiled in return, starting to wake up out of my grumpy mood.

"You two," Will said from the bed, his voice muffled by the pillow, "are the loudest crows . . . ."

Andrea smiled and I grinned. We edged toward the door and Andrea opened it.

"Time to get up, Will!" I said loudly.

Andrea started to close the door behind us, but not quickly enough to keep back the pillow that sailed through, landing with a thump against the opposite wall. I opened the door only wide enough to take a blind shot to return the pillow. There was a thump and a chuckle, and I guessed I missed.

Once we were in the bathing room, I stripped, thinking Andrea would leave as she usually did. I frowned at my stomach, prodding at the extra flesh. I needed to get more exercise. I was getting fat.

I slipped into the water, which was just warm enough, and began to scrub at my body.

"Milady?" Andrea asked.

I looked up, surprised to see her still there. "Yes?"

"Beg pardon if I'm rude, but how long has it been since you've had your monthly cycle?"

I paused. That was a strange question. But stranger still was the fact I couldn't quite remember. I frowned, absently pulling on a strand of my hair. Then I looked at Andrea in surprise.

"Three months!" I looked at my stomach again, poking at it and putting my hands against it. It was firm, not like being fat at all. "Andrea?!"

"Milady?" Andrea began to smile.

"Are you thinking what I think you're thinking?"

"I think so, milady."

A shiver ran up and down my spine. I felt like screaming, but I knew no sound would come. "I'm pregnant," I whispered, unable to decide if I was happy or not. Motherhood was not something I had particularly looked forward to. I didn't much like kids. The thought of raising my own was rather overwhelming. There was one thing I did know, though. "Will's gonna be so happy!"

I finished bathing in a daze. Again and again, I counted the months and figured the child would be born sometime in April. I couldn't wait to tell Will.

Once dressed, I went to the great hall, unable to keep from smiling at the prospect of surprising my husband. He was sitting at the high table eating breakfast while looking over some papers. After fetching some fruit and bread for myself, I sat down next to him, moving the parchment out of the way as a blob of jam fell from his bread onto the table with a soft splat.

He looked up at me and smiled. "Good morning."

"Good morning," I returned brightly, biting into the rind of an orange so I could peel it.

"You're cheery this morning. What's going on?" he asked, seeing the smile I was trying to hide.

I spit out the peel and grinned. "I have news."

"Well, tell me. You look like you're about to burst with it." He leaned back from the table and looked at me expectantly.

I scooted over next to him and whispered into his ear. When I was done, I leaned back and grinned.

"A baby?" he asked, his voice a shaky whisper. He cleared his throat and tried again. "You're sure?"

"As sure as a woman can be."

He sat back in his chair. "This is great!" He laughed, the bemused look on his face describing his emotions—surprise, happiness, wondering . . . happiness.

His obvious joy eased my soul and put my half-formed misgivings to rest. It was good to see him so pleased. It could not be a terrible thing if it brought him so much pleasure.

We must have made quite a pair for the next few days. Will couldn't seem to get anything done. He would often seek me out during the day just to stand by me, smiling. I enjoyed the attention, so I couldn't stop smiling, either.

When the initial surprise wore off, I began to ponder the deeper ramifications of this pregnancy. As the child moved within me, growing toward completion and life, I wondered if I were changing some essential fabric of time, setting the course in motion that would culminate in my own creation sometime in the future.

Long ago, I had sworn that the future didn't matter to me anymore, but I couldn't help wondering . . . .

ON THE FIRST OF NOVEMBER, I went out riding as usual. The day had turned chilly, so I wrapped my fur cloak tightly around me. It looked like a storm would arrive by evening. I hoped Bran wouldn't make me ride all the way to Lincoln to see him.

The forest was quiet. A covering of wet leaves on the road made Sassy's hoofbeats next to silent. I noted the absence of singing birds and scurrying animals and thought perhaps the storm would hit sooner than evening.

I had not gone far when I heard a raven's call and a small rustle, then Peter dropped out of a tree and ran toward me.

"Peter!" I said, reining in. "What's wrong?" That he was waiting for me so close to the common spelled trouble.

"Milo isn't well. He's fallen sick, something bad. It won't bode well for him if he has to stay out when this storm hits."

"How long has he been ill?"

"Two days. He's fevered, coughs, and complains of a headache. Sydney's doing all he can for him, but he doesn't know much about it."

I made a decision. "I know a place I can take him not far from here. But we've got to hurry. Take me to camp."

Peter mounted up behind me and directed me off the road. We went deep into the forest, then left, plunging farther in. A few moments later, I saw the light of a fire and guided Sassy toward it.

Bran stood when he heard our approach. "Kay! I'm glad you're here. We've done all we can, but it's not enough."

I slid off Sassy and hurried to him. "I know a place we can take Milo. We've got to get a move on, or the storm will hit before we get there."

"Where is this place?" asked John.

"A widow's cottage just this side of the Nottinghamshire border.

She has some room to spare, I'm sure, and she's a good friend of mine. Come on. Help him up on Sassy."

We had to tie him to the saddle, but we finally got Milo to stay atop the horse, Sydney riding behind to steady him. I led Sassy, and Bran followed. I had directed the others to Robin's old winter shelter, where they could wait out the storm.

We didn't want to jostle Milo too much, so the going was slow, but we made it to Anne's before the storm really hit.

I beat loudly on the door and Jamie answered. He shouted with delight when he saw me, then stepped back, seeing the men.

"Jamie, where's your mother?"

"In the kitchen," he answered, staring at them.

"Go and tell her I need help."

Jamie gave a last wide-eyed stare at Bran, then ran off.

A cold gust of wind blew the door wide open, the first drops of rain flying into the house. Little Robert began to cry as Anne rushed out, wiping her hands on her apron.

"Kay?" She looked beyond me to the two men standing in her doorway, supporting the third.

"Anne, my friend is sick. Do you have somewhere for him to stay while the storm blows out?"

"Ellie, care for Robert."

Anne disappeared into the kitchen. When she came back, she carried a steaming cast-iron kettle in one hand, and a small bag tucked under her arm. She handed me the kettle and hurried outside, beckoning us to follow. Jamie shut the door behind us.

She led us to a door at the back of the house, barely noticeable thanks to the hawthorn bush growing beside it. I doubted I would have seen it on my own. Anne opened it and ushered us in. There were several steps going down into the earth, then the space opened into darkness. We all stood nervously until Anne struck a lantern.

"Put 'im there," she said, gesturing to a cot on the far wall.

I looked around while Sydney and Bran got Milo situated. I could see why she wouldn't want anyone to know about the door to this room.

Herbs hung to dry, making it look as though plants grew from the ceiling. The room was rich with the pleasant odor of spices and herbs. There were links of pork sausages and strips of mutton curing on meat hooks. I also saw deer hides heaped in a pile, which was quite illegal. I guessed this was where Anne's late husband had done his butchering and tanning. I hadn't realized he'd been a poacher.

"You," Anne said, pointing at Sydney, "go out to th' wood pile and bring some wood. We'll need a fire." Sydney obeyed. Bran was put to work gathering furs to put over Milo, and I went to the fireplace to hang the kettle on the hook, then got the hearth ready for the wood. From outside, I had only seen one chimney, so I assumed this one must let into the main chimney inside the house.

Anne was bent over Milo, gauging his illness, when I looked back.

"How is he?" I asked.

"As well as can be expected, Kay. You did th' right thing, bringing 'im to me."

"What is it?"

"He has the measles." She showed me where the rash was just starting on his cheeks.

Moving swiftly and confidently, she mixed some herbs into a pan of hot water from the kettle. With each ingredient she put in, she recited its name. "Boneset, feverfew, and ginger to ease th' fever. Chamomile to cure th' headache."

After allowing the potent blend to steep for a few minutes, she put a cloth over a cup and strained the liquid. Then she bent over Milo again, lifting his head to help him drink. Once satisfied he'd had enough, she settled him back on the pillow. But she wasn't done yet. She reached up and brought down a dried bundle of rosemary and one of lavender, which she stuffed into a linen sack and crushed until the air was fragrant with the mixed scent. Muttering what sounded like an incantation, she tore off a strip of his tunic and used it to tie the bag closed, then put it under his pillow. Milo had been moaning about his aching head, but when she did this, he sighed and lay still.

I smiled down at Anne, both impressed and amused at her remedy. The ingredients of the herbal tea I recognized from my uncle's book of natural remedies, but the aromatic pillow was new to me, and I wasn't sure the incantation would produce any effect whatsoever. I looked at Bran, who had watched the entire procedure. Unsure of what his reaction to Anne's "medicine" would be, I didn't look away.

Bran stared back, then slowly closed his eyes. I understood. As far as he was concerned, he hadn't seen anything. He might have decried Anne as a witch, but instead, he accepted that her method would help cure his friend.

The door at the top of the stairs flew open and Sydney came down with another armload of wood, breaking our little spell. But Anne's larger spell held.

"Measles?" I asked, as if nothing had happened. "That's contagious. You had better be careful then. You don't want you or the children coming down with it."

"Aye," she said, nodding. "I'll keep him isolated down here until the rash has been gone for at least a week." It was then I realized she was ahead of her time in recognizing the cause of a contagion and how to prevent it from spreading.

I nodded. "Listen, I've got to get back to the lodge before the worst of this storm hits. Will would be expecting me by now. I'll come back after it's blown off. You'll be all right?"

"If these men are friends of yours, I'll be fine. Go then, before ya have to stay, too."

I gave her a farewell peck on the cheek, said goodbye to Bran and Sydney, and wished Milo well. Then I climbed the steep stairway to the door. A good push sent it crashing against the house with the wind, and I fought to get it shut again.

Sassy, tied beneath a bare elm tree, whinnied when she saw me, her eyes rolling with fear. I ran to her, my hair whipping in the tempest, tangling with her mane. With frozen fingers, I fumbled to untie her, then vaulted into the saddle, still agile in my fourth month of pregnancy. Setting off at a gallop, I crouched low over Sassy's neck, no need to urge her on. I just held on and prayed I wouldn't meet Will coming out to look for me.

By the time I got home, the sky was dark as night, though it was still early afternoon. Clouds roiled and twisted, and the wind drew its sharp claws across the land. Sleet came and went, driving into the skin like lances. The cold was intense.

I hoped John and the others got to shelter in time.

"God, I'm glad you're back all right," said Will when I sat down next to the fire. "I don't know why you insist on riding out on the first of every month. You could have caught your death of a cold. You ought to take better care of yourself. There's more than just you now."

I laughed. "You're as bad as Andrea." I tapped him lightly on the chin. "I know how much you want this child, my dear. I wouldn't do anything to harm it. You should know that." I snuggled up against him to get warm. "The storm caught me by surprise, that's all."

Before I knew it, I was asleep, my cheek against his shoulder. It had been a wild and taxing trip back from Anne's.

I woke to the smell of broth and looked around the hall. I couldn't have been asleep long, but it was time for dinner and Will had ordered me some warm beef broth, thick enough to be a stew. It smelled delicious. I took the bowl with a warm smile of thanks for the boy who brought it. There was a hard roll on the plate beside it and I dipped it into the broth to soften it.

Once I finished eating, I snuggled closer to Will, hearing the wind howling outside. "I'm glad we don't have to be out in this," I whispered to myself.

Will must have heard me because he held me closer.

TWENTY-ONE

I t was a long storm, lasting five days before it exhausted itself into a soft breeze and a steady drizzle. The sixth day dawned bright, though cold. The east wind pushed the scattered clouds before it, their shadows racing patterns across the fields.

I slipped out just after breakfast, saying I had to check up on Anne to see how she had weathered the storm. I needed to get out, too. Five days was a long time to be shut up. I felt a need to stretch my wings.

All along the road, I saw the results of the storm. The common was flooded in some places. In other places, toppled trees had torn up the ground, scattering debris. In one flooded spot, I saw a dead cow, bloated and lying half in and half out of the water. I made a mental note to find out whose it was and help them with the price of a new one.

A flock of sheep—Anne's, judging by the mark on the ear—wandered across the fields. I took note of their position so I could tell Jamie.

The boy was just heading out to look for them when I rode up.

"Hey there, Jamie!" I called. "I saw those sheep of yours just off Langley's mill. They were going east."

"Thank you, Lady Kay!" he shouted, his face brightening. I could tell he had been dreading a long search. He took off toward the mill at a loping run and was soon out of sight.

The cabin's door was wide open, no doubt to let in fresh air after being closed up for so long during the storm. Inside, Ellie was feeding Robert soup and Sydney was helping Anne wash dishes at the fireside. I watched them and smiled. Those two seemed to be getting along well.

"Well, how is everyone after that dreadful storm?" I asked by way of hello.

"Kay!" cried Anne. "'Tis good to see you." She got up from the buckets by the fireplace to give me a hug. "Milo's come along quite well. 'E gets better every day, and the rash is already fading. A few more days and we'll be able to let him out of the cellar." I saw a hatch in the floor had been opened and walked over to look down into the space where Milo lay on a bed, looking up at me. I felt sorry for his isolation, but he seemed at peace with it.

"Sydney's been a fine help, too." Anne awarded Sydney with a smile. To my surprise, he blushed.

"Where's Bran? Didn't he stay?" I asked.

"He left right when the storm gave out yesterday," said Sydney. "He wanted to check on the others."

"I hope they're all right," I said, worried. "If they couldn't find the shelter, it would have been a hellish six days."

"They'll have found it all right, Kay," said Sydney, drying the last of the dishes. "Peter's a great one for finding places, and I think perhaps John's been there. He once said he'd hidden from foresters in a large cave."

"Then they will have found the supplies we'd stashed there, too. That's good luck. How are you feeling, Milo?" I called down to him.

"I'd be a lot worse if not for you." A faint smile touched his lips as he looked up at me.

"Me?" I asked, surprised.

"You . . . . Thank you. I just wanted to say that."

I smiled at him. There wasn't a need to say anything.

"Rider!" Katie screamed in excitement as she burst through the doorway. "A rider, Mama!" She was bewildered at the response her call prompted.

I hurried to look out the window and saw Will riding down the road toward the house.

I turned around, about to tell Sydney to hide, but all I saw was his head disappearing down the trap hole.

Anne dropped the door and placed the rug over it to cover the cut boards.

I went outside just as Will dismounted and tied his gelding beside Sassy.

"Hi!" I said, going to him and giving him a kiss.

"You left so quickly, I didn't have a chance to offer to go with you. If you'd waited ten minutes, I'd have ridden out with you. I wanted to see if there was anything I could help with."

"I'm sorry. I should have asked if you wanted to come. Anne's property was hardly damaged." I pointed to a grove of tall birch trees. "Those trees must have helped a lot. I reckon they were in the path of the wind to take the brunt of it, but they aren't close enough to fall on the house—and they attracted the lightning. See?"

Several of the birches were down or leaning perilously, looking as though the slightest breeze would cause them to sway past their limit and send them crashing to the ground. One of the trees had drawn of bolt of lightning and all that remained was a charred trunk reaching blackened fingers into the sky.

"Oi, that one must have made quite a pop when it went," said Will. "Somebody had a good head about a place to build. Anne! How are you?"

"Me an' mine are fine, Master Scathelock. 'Tis kind of you and milady to come out to check on us."

"Well, we do what we can for our people." Will smiled at her.

"And I'm one that's grateful for it, milord."

"Will?" I asked. "Did you see that cow on the way? We should find out whose it is and help them get a new one."

"I saw, and had the same idea. I think it was the Smith's. I'll send Mallory out when we get back. He'll find out and give them compensation. I'll have him check with all the folks out here." Will looked around Anne's property. "But now, let's get that pen put up so young Jamie has a place to put the sheep tonight. Anne, you be sure to let us know if any of them turn up missing."

"Aye, milord." Anne smiled.

We struggled briefly to mend the broken section of the pen, then said goodbye to Anne and went to the next house to see what help we could offer. There was a lot of damage as we made our way back to the lodge. People were glad for our help, though surprised to see their squire and his lady rolling up their sleeves to help rebuild.

I enjoyed the workout, though Will wouldn't let me do anything strenuous until I pointed out a woman who was twice as pregnant as I, slopping in water past her knees to help repair earthworks destroyed in the storm. Half their field had been flooded.

Will went to help her as I continued filling the burlap sacks with mud and hauled them to the men in the water. I did take care to lift carefully and only take one at a time.

When Will and I finally got home, it was well after dark. We were filthy, tired, hungry, and satisfied with a good day's work. And we both got a sound tongue-lashing from Andrea as she shooed us into the baths.

A WEEK LATER, we journeyed to Nottingham to attend the fair celebrating the start of winter. I had other things to see to, though.

Will and I planned to stay two days and a night. Norman, Andrea, and a few other servants came along. The uncharitable would say we brought them to look successful and rich, but we enjoyed their company and wanted to give them a chance to get out and have some fun.

The town buzzed with activity as we came in just before noon. We rode straight up to the main hall and Sheriff John Little came out to greet us. Much was only two steps behind him.

"Little John!" I shouted, infected by the fervor of the festival and feeling like a child. I slid out of the saddle and ran to hug him. Will followed, as eager as I to greet our friends.

John laughed. "I thought you two were nobles, and you riding in with a whole bloody train of servants!" he said, hugging Will.

"Aww, John. They're just here to have fun!"

"That's more than any of mine will have today." John waved a pair of boys to see to our baggage. "There's too much to do. But I'll let yours stay in the servants' quarters while they're here."

"More than yours will get," I repeated, teasing. "John, won't you let them have any fun?"

"Bugger off, Kay, my darling. They're servants!" John tipped his head up, affecting a haughty nobleman. His grin spoiled the effect.

Much snorted. "He's promised them their own festival if they work hard," he said. "And they've the evenings for the market, with bonus silver in their pockets."

"You heartless slave driver." I laughed.

"That's me." John hiked up his trousers, looking ornery until his grin again split his face. "Come on then. I've a feast you wouldn't believe for supper, but let's have a little lunch now." He patted his stomach, which audibly growled.

As Much held out his arm for me, I laughed at John's antics.

John looked at me sidewise. "Speaking of feasting," he said slyly. "It doesn't appear that you've been sparing the cooks at Gamwell."

My jaw dropped at his comic audacity. "You beast!" I said when I found my tongue to make a comeback. I smoothed my dress over my round belly. "I'll have you know it has taken me many months of indiscriminate snacking to achieve this belly. Of course I didn't spare the cooks."

Little John's eyes went wide when he saw the true shape of my belly. He looked at Will with a grin. "Well, you didn't waste any time at that now, did you?" I laughed at John's tactless surprise. "I guess congratulations are in order?" He shook Will's hand, giving him a bawdy wink.

I snorted. "As though I have nothing to do with it," I said, putting my hands on my hips. John laughed, turning to give me a great hug. Much hugged me, as well, before we continued to the hall.

Much and I walked arm in arm. "I'll take you around the fair after lunch," he said. "John's got some things to talk to Will about, so I'm to escort you. How does that sound?"

"I'll enjoy your company, Much. I trust you'll show me the best wares."

"What do I know of buying things in the marketplace?" he exclaimed. "Do you think I've already succumbed to the fripperies of nobility?"

I laughed. "Your very fine dagger gives you away, Much. Unless you hid it in a tree in the forest, you purchased it here."

He harrumphed, but the gleam in his eyes suggested I'd caught him out.

Because of the feasting later on, we ate a light lunch of salted fish and a selection of cheeses on flatbread. After we were through, Much showed me around.

In the surprisingly warm day, we perused the marketplace stalls, stopping to watch wrestlers grapple or jugglers perform on makeshift stages. I had never seen very much of Nottingham—all my previous visits had been on missions, not tours—so Much took me up to the parapets of the castle walls to point out many of the sights he would show me later. Then we took a few turns on the dance square and drank some fine wine imported from France.

Much and I sat in the grandstand to watch the archery contest, sipping wine and talking. I was working on turning the conversation a certain way when Much brought up the very end I was trying to achieve.

We had been talking about whether Nottingham's guards should be trained with crossbow or longbow when he said, "John thinks King Richard's going to get himself killed." He drank the rest of his wine and held out his cup to the passing serving woman. She stopped to fill it for him, then moved on. "It bothers me. He's working for the king, but he talks about him dying."

"He's not the only one to think so," I said, overcoming my surprise at the subject change. "Robin, Tuck, Will, and I think the same."

"Really?" He seemed surprised. "I told John he was talking treason and ought to be careful."

"We all ought to, Much," I said. "Little John is worried about who gets the throne when Richard dies."

Much snorted. "That would be Prince John. The man's a cheat. It won't matter who Richard names." I nodded in agreement. "I don't like him. And he doesn't like us. You saw him at the pardoning, looking like he'd swallowed the Channel. He's never liked us since we robbed him and Jana took all his jewels. He lost a lot of money there. And Robin killed his man—the bounty hunter,

Gisborne. Did you hear him when he left the pardoning? He said, 'If I were king, I'd hang them all.'" Much grunted in disgust.

"Much," I said, deciding he was the right man for what I had in mind. "You know it's going to be dangerous when John becomes king. Dangerous for anyone who was with Robin Hood."

"Aye, I know. But there isn't a damn thing we can do about it while Richard is alive," he said, quaffing his expensive wine like it was home-brewed mead. "Here there! Bring more wine," he called. To me, he continued. "We'll be sitting ducks when he's dead."

The woman came back with the wine jug and filled Much's cup. She offered me more, but I declined.

When the woman was out of earshot, I leaned toward Much. "But there *is* something we can do, Much."

"What? What do you mean?" When he saw the intent look on my face, his eyes lit up. "You've got a plan?"

I nodded. "A good one." I told him all about Bran's men and the plan I had.

When I finished, Much looked thoughtful. "They'll take us in? What good will that do? We can just go back by ourselves."

I sighed. "We can't 'just go back,' Much. Think about it. Here's all of us who can, coming back from all over the place. How are we going to find each other? Any food stashes we had will more than likely be gone. What if he dies in the winter? Where will we get our food? We'll be outlaws again, so we won't just be able to go in and buy from the local village. What if my group of outlaws weren't on our side? What if they attacked us as we returned, on our own and vulnerable? What if they decided to turn us in for reward or a pardon? With their help, we'll have a place to go, supplies, and help posting watches for the rest of our group."

Much looked up, catching on to the significance. "Oh, I see!"

"Yes," I said, sitting back. "But I need your help."

"How can I help? It sounds like you've got it under control."

I smiled. "Mostly, but I need help now. You see, with the baby coming in April, there will be a time I won't be able to go out. I need you to meet with them for me until I can go out again."

"But why won't Will go? Doesn't he approve?" Much looked around, as if expecting Will to show up and hear us.

I sighed. "He's a busy man. I haven't told him yet. And you mustn't tell anyone, either. Not until I say to spread the word."

"Why not?" Much looked surprised. He wasn't a conspirator at heart and tended to talk if you didn't tell him to keep it quiet.

"Because we cannot risk loose tongues," I said firmly. "Prince John must not find out what I am doing."

"But how will we know when to spread the word? We can't just guess when Richard will die."

"Trust me. I'll know."

Much shook his head, not understanding.

I set my cup down. "Come on. I want to look around the marketplace."

WE SPENT the rest of the day weaving in and around booths, looking at wares. I bought some fine material for Anne so she could make herself a dress from linen she hadn't produced with her own efforts. I bought myself some, as well, with a notion of asking Andrea to make something special for me.

After we left the marketplace, Much showed me to some of the bigger attractions of Nottingham, taking us beyond the milling crowds of the fair.

We walked outside after visiting an old abandoned chapel to find long shadows stretching across the street. "Uh-oh, look how late it's getting. We'll miss the feasting!"

"Race you!" I said, picking up my skirts.

"It's hardly proper," Much said, close on my heels nonetheless.

I was just beginning to tire when we rounded a corner and almost ran into some folk who were headed in the same direction. We stopped to catch our breath and make a more dignified approach to the main hall.

"Oh, Much," I said, gasping for breath. "I'd forgotten how fun it is to run for the sake of running. But . . . ," I put both hands over my heaving belly, "that's likely to be the last run I'll have for a while."

"Are you all right, Kay?" he asked, concern lacing his voice. He touched my arm to make me look at him. He wasn't even breathing hard.

"I'm fine, just more winded than anyone has a right to be." I finally got my breathing under control. "But I still beat you," I said, grinning. "Shall we go on?" I held out my arm.

"Certainly, milady, fastest of the heavy-footed runners."

I tweaked his cheek and hooked my arm around his as we continued at a more sedate pace.

It wasn't long before a tide of people heading the same way carried us along to the main hall for the feast.

We got inside moments before the food was served. I sat at Will's left, Much sitting down at Little John's right. The inner courtyards where John had opened the feast for the public were packed, the hall crowded with merry-makers.

I began to tell Will about the things I had seen, but stopped in surprise, watching the servants bringing in the food.

"Will, is that what I think it is?"

Two trays holding huge portions of venison were brought forward to John's high table.

"John!" Will exclaimed. "Are you mad?" It was a hanging offense to hunt the king's deer. Even the sheriff couldn't get away with it.

"Not mad, friend. Not at all," said John, spearing a steak and dropping it onto his plate. He laughed at the look on Will's face . . . and probably on my own. "King Richard needs money for his war. His solution is to sell the forest. I bought some of the land nearby, and the deer go with it. I limit the hunt to once a month and only three deer, but it's better than no venison at all."

It made sense to me. "You're sure?" I asked, knife poised above a cut of ribs.

"Positive," he said, shoving a piece of meat into his mouth and chewing loudly. He licked his knife for extra juices. I didn't need any more persuading.

Will looked at John, at me, then over at Much, who was eating as well. "It's been a long time since I've eaten venison," he said, looking at the platter of steaming meat.

"What're you waiting for?" I asked, my mouth full. "It's heavenly."

"Well . . . ." Will looked around at all of us. "I guess we'll all hang together." He speared a steak and began to eat. The taste was added incentive, and Will ate eagerly.

John wiped his mouth on his sleeve. "Can you just see it? Richard would have to hang the entire shire of Nottingham if he changes his mind." He laughed.

When we were through eating, I sat back and sighed, content. I felt like belching, but I was a lady. It wouldn't be proper. I whispered this to Will, who grinned, leaning over to kiss me.

"You know," said John after a while. "I've heard from a very reliable source that the king plans to sell more of his forest and deer. Do you think you'll buy some around Gamwell?"

Will scratched his head. "Gamwell's come along very well since I've taken over, but it'll be a while yet before I can afford such a luxury." He laughed. "Imagine. Buying Sherwood! We *used* to own it!" His laughter had a trace of acid in it, and I studied him over the rim of my cup as I drank. John and Much laughed, too, but it was a short, brittle sound.

The next day, Will and I spent the morning touring the stalls in the fair, then ate the noon meal and took our leave.

As I kissed Much on the cheek, I whispered, "Come riding with me the first of the month. Wear a band of Lincoln green on your arm." He smiled as we departed.

When we rode out, Will urged his mount over to me and we slowed, letting our escort pull ahead. "What did you say to Much?" he asked casually.

I was instantly alert, though I tried not to show it. "I asked him to come riding with me on the first of the month."

"Why? You usually go alone."

"I know, but you've been after me to take someone, and Much is my friend." Will made a strange sound in his throat, almost like he was holding back a comment. "You're not jealous, are you?" I asked, teasing, but half-thinking he might be.

"Should I be?" he asked, not looking at me.

"Of course not!" I reined my horse to a stop. "Will! You know I love you more than I love life. But I also love Much and the rest. Would you have me give that up? We're like family. You love them, too, don't you?"

Will turned around to come back to me and urged his horse close to mine. He grabbed Sassy's saddle blanket and leaned over to me. "Yes, I do," he whispered, his horse dancing beneath him. "I'm sorry. I want you to know——" His horse broke out of control momentarily, and Will pulled him around to the other side of me. "You are everything to me," he finished.

I reached for his hand and held it as we rode. I opened my mouth several times to tell him about my outlaws, but I didn't want to spoil the quiet moment.

I JUST FEEL FAT," I told Andrea as we walked the corridors toward the stairs. "I have never been this big in my life."

"Lady, you're still small for five months of pregnancy. You don't have any trouble getting around yet. Count yourself lucky."

"You mean it gets worse than this?" I groaned, putting a hand on my belly.

"You know it does. But it will be worth it."

"It had better be, Andrea."

I stopped on the landing, looking out over the great hall. Will was already at the table, speaking to Lady Nancy, the daughter of a visiting lord. I leaned against the railing, about to call out to him, when he reached out and caught her hand, bringing it to his lips. Her laughter was bright, ringing across the room. He leaned close to whisper in her ear.

I turned away, unable to watch him flirting so outrageously. My hands shook as I clenched them into fists. "Tell my lord I have no appetite tonight," I said to Andrea. I heard her follow me as I ran up the stairs to my room. I didn't bother shutting the door before flinging myself onto my bed.

"Milady?" she asked, closing the door.

I didn't answer. How could I tell her how hurt I felt by such a betrayal?

"What's wrong?"

"You saw him," I muttered. "Right there in front of everyone." I got up and moved to the window. "I know I'm a cow right now, but I'm carrying his child!"

"Milady?"

"Look at me! I'm fat enough for two women. I hate it! I don't want this baby. What am I going to do with a baby, Andrea?" I slumped into the window seat. "Will won't even look at me anymore."

"Don't be silly, milady. Of course Master Scathelock looks at you. He loves you. Everybody can see that."

"But I'm so fat and ugly. I don't blame him for flirting with that woman."

"Shhh." Andrea came to me and gave me a hug. "This is an emotional time for you."

"But I saw him—"

"Hush. He was only being an attentive host. Will you come down to supper?"

"I'm not hungry."

Andrea retreated to the door. "I'll tell him you're not feeling well."

"No, tell him . . . . Just tell him I'm not coming down."

My anger dulled to a lingering resentment as I thought about my baby and what it meant to me. Loss of my freedom . . . . How could I go wherever I chose when I had to lug a baby around with me? And what about the way Will had been acting lately? What if I lost him? Where would I go? Who would care for me when I held another man's child in my arms?

I was still sitting in the window seat, head resting on my arms, when Will came in. He paused in the doorway, but I didn't turn around.

"You're not coming down, ever?" he asked lightly.

"No," I mumbled moodily into my sleeves. I just wished he would go away.

"I missed you at supper."

"Lady Nancy kept you company, didn't she?"

He obviously didn't catch the sour note in my voice as he entered the room. "Yes. She was quite charming." He waited for my response, but when I gave none, he cleared his throat. "Andrea said you were upset." He sat beside me, resting his hand on my knee.

Curse her, I thought. *She wasn't supposed to tell him.* That was the only reason he was here and not with Nancy. I let my anger simmer while I refused to answer.

Will's pause stretched into silence as he waited for a response. Finally, he fumbled on. "Is it because of the baby?"

"You could say that," I grumbled.

"Don't you want it?"

I buried my face in my arms, determined not to cry. How could he be so dense about the cause, yet still get the reason right?

"Kay, what's wrong? Please, talk to me." He stroked my shoulders, leaning close.

Finally, I looked up at him. "I want the baby, Will. I want it gone. I'm tired of being fat, tired of the restrictions on my freedom, tired of—"

"You're not fat, Kay. You're pregnant. You're carrying my baby, and I love you."

I sighed, knowing I was never going to be able to address the larger problem, or explain my convoluted feelings. "It's just getting to me, Will. Andrea says a lot of women get extra emotional about now. I'm just feeling weird. I suppose I *do* want the baby. I'm just tired."

Will smiled and took my hand, pulling me into his arms. I hugged him tightly, loving him so much and hurting that he would wander away from me. He stroked my hair and rocked me gently until I took comfort in his presence.

TWENTY-TWO

November thirtieth, Much arrived, ready to ride with me the next day. We had a special dinner in his honor, and Will and I stayed up late talking with him.

Andrea came in at dawn to wake me. Will stirred as well, but pulled a pillow over his head after recognizing her. I got up and dressed quietly, buckling on my swords and knives. After letting my belt out another notch, I put my hand on my swollen belly, thinking about the life growing there. Sometimes I was able to forget I was going to be a mother. It was at times like this I wished it was over with. Extra weight, extra restrictions on my movements. I had always gone where I wanted when I wanted. That freedom would be gone once the baby came.

I left for breakfast feeling quite grouchy, but when Much met me halfway down the stairs, my mood began to improve. Who could stay a grump when your companion always had a ready smile?

The sun came up, promising a clear, albeit frigid, day. The morning shadows grew short as the day lived up to its potential.

"Like old times," said Much with a grin as we reached the forest. "We should make a day of it."

I laughed. "A bit cold for swimming." Unaccountably nervous for him, I double-checked Much's left arm, making sure he wore his Lincoln green. "And we didn't bring lunch."

"Well, a morning of it then." We laughed as we rode into the forest.

Halfway to Lincoln, I heard a call. I'd known someone was in the underbrush, following us, but I'd ignored him. He was just making sure.

When I heard the call, I pulled up short. "This is it, Much," I said. "And it's about time." Much nodded. I knew he'd known about our "shadow," too.

"Who's that?" Peter asked, with no greeting. He didn't come out, but I recognized his young voice.

"Much," he said, gesturing to the green band around his arm.

Peter didn't answer, obviously waiting for me.

"You've heard of Much the Miller's Son. He was one of Robin's," I tried to assure him. "I brought him to meet Bran."

Peter came out a little, but stayed in the shadows. "The clearing by the river. You know the one." Then he disappeared. We couldn't hear his retreat.

"I guess he doesn't trust me," said Much.

"He will. He's young and smart enough not to make any decisions on his own. But he'll trust you. They all will. We've got to backtrack a little to the river."

Fifteen minutes later, we were in a small clearing at the Trent. Off to one side of the clearing, under a drooping willow, a rock was propped up. The name chipped into it had filled with moss.

Much smiled when he recognized where we were. "A lot of memories here," he whispered, more to himself than me.

We dismounted. While we waited, I squatted in front of the stone and traced Mark's name with my fingers. Recalling the day he died no longer saddened me, just brought fond memories of our brief friendship.

It was a few minutes before Bran appeared.

"Kay," he said by way a greeting. "Who's this?"

"This is Much," I told him. "He's going to take my place."

"What for?" asked Bran. He hadn't come very far into the clearing, and though he didn't look behind him, I knew there were others.

"I won't be able to come out again for a while," I said, putting a hand on my belly for emphasis. My pregnancy was beginning to be quite obvious.

"Ahh-mmm," Bran mumbled, his ears turning a bit pink. "So," he said, trying to come to a point without saying the obvious, "Much here is going to check up on us while you're, ah, detained?"

An almost imperceptible twitch of Bran's fingers brought Peter and John out into the clearing to stand behind him.

I nodded to them, but spoke to Bran. "That's right. He's a good man. I'd trust him with my life. Have more than once, in fact. I love him like my brother. We were with Robin Hood together and he was my first friend."

John commented, "I know he's who he says he is. I've seen him in Nottingham." At this, Bran relaxed visibly.

"Much," I said, "this is John. Over there is Peter, and this is Bran, their leader. I assume Sydney is with Anne, given how much they enjoy each other's company, but I don't know where the others are." I leveled my gaze on Bran. "Can you learn to trust Much as you trust me?"

He thought for a moment, then turned to Peter. "What do you think?"

"He's got the look of a fair man. Besides, he's a friend of Kay's," Peter said, shrugging a shoulder slightly.

Bran hesitated a moment longer, then offered his hand to Much. He reached out and took it, shaking firmly.

"It's well met then," said Bran, smiling. "A friend of Kay's . . . ."

Much smiled back. "I know the way of the meeting, but we'll have to change it to the Nottingham road. Do you need anything?"

"Perhaps some arrows," Bran said. "Milo makes the best, but he's still recovering. Some fresh bread and cheese would be nice, as well as some ale."

"Ah, ale . . . You really get to missing that, don't you?" Much laughed. "We would always raid the ale trains of Lord Pickerney. He was dim enough to pay first, instead of on delivery. I don't believe he ever caught on."

Peter laughed as Bran smiled, while John looked thoughtful. Bran requested a few more items. Much shook his hand again, then mounted his horse.

When I began to mount, I experienced my first real difficulty. I strained a little before Peter, who'd been watching, helped me up. It seemed I had organized my takeover just in time.

"I'll bring the goods here on my way home tomorrow. Oh, and don't let anyone catch you robbing Lord Pickerney's ale train." Much winked at John.

"Yes," I said. "Do stay out of trouble." I gave Much a stern glance as we turned to ride away.

On the way back, we stopped at Anne's to check on Milo and Sydney. Nobody was outside keeping watch, so I almost gave Milo a heart attack by walking in the front door without knocking.

"Oh, Kay!" he said, clutching his heart dramatically. "You did give me a fright. I thought I was going to hang for sure when that door opened."

"And well you should have with no one keeping watch. Where are the children?" I asked, looking around. When Much came in behind me, Milo looked at him warily.

"They're in Gamwell, visiting her sister. Who's this?"

"Milo, this is Much. He's going to be my replacement while I can't ride. It looks like you've been busy." I pointed to the arrows stacked at his side.

"Oh, aye. Got boring, sitting here with idle hands. I figured Bran could use some of these."

"We just came from talking to him," said Much. "He was indeed asking after some arrows. He'll be just as glad to see you've been keeping busy."

I left Milo and Much talking and went to find Anne and Sydney.

They were together in the kitchen. I smiled when I saw how love had grown between them. They made a good pair.

When I cleared my throat, the lovebirds spun to face me. "Anne? I've someone I want you and Sydney to meet."

Anne blushed, but Sydney grinned at being caught in a kiss. I grinned back, motioning them into the other room.

"I didna hear you come in," said Anne, dissembling. She gave a slight smile. "We're not being too careful, eh?" She followed Sydney into the other room.

"Anne, Sydney, I'd like you to meet Much. He's going to act as courier between Bran and me while I'm unavailable."

Much shook hands with Sydney, then bent to kiss Anne's hand.

He could be such a charmer, but when he saw Sydney bristle, he made a short bow to him, stepping back from Anne.

We talked for a while, letting them get familiar with each other until it was time to leave.

"Well, Much will be dropping off supplies for Bran tomorrow. If you have any dealings with me, you'll need to see Much. I'm not going to be doing much riding by next month. You take care of yourself, Milo. All of you. No troubles, okay?"

"No troubles," agreed Sydney, looking at Anne.

Much and I mounted and rode back toward the lodge, walking the horses and enjoying the day.

"Not a bad lot," said Much. "I think we can trust them to do the job right. Perhaps when they trust me more I can spend some time with them and check on their training."

"That would be wise. I'd have done it, but I think they'd have resented a woman telling them what to do. All I can do is show them up, give them incentive to improve. I did tell them they had better practice stealth, though. They've improved since I first ran into them."

"Yes. The fellow earlier was very quiet, though he's young yet, easy to teach."

I smiled proudly. "They've all learned well."

By TORCHLIGHT early the next morning, we packed up the things for Bran, then Much mounted. I reached up to take his hand.

"Remember. This same time every month, and come see me after every visit. I'll get the supplies ready for them. You can't ask it of Nottingham when the sheriff doesn't know about this project. Don't involve Anne unless it's absolutely necessary, either. Goodbye, Much, and Godspeed."

"Farewell, Kay." He bent to press his lips against my hand. Then, his packs full of supplies, he smiled before digging his heels into his horse's flanks. Norman closed the courtyard gate behind him.

Turning around to go inside, I stopped short. Will stood there, staring at me. "Good morning, my love," I said, my voice not quite sounding normal. I hesitated, then started toward him.

He put up a hand and I stopped. "What . . . ," he said slowly, and I winced at his tone of voice. "What is going on here, Kay?"

I pulled the door shut on the courtyard.

"What's going on?" Will asked again.

I swallowed in a throat gone dry, trying to keep my eyes steady on his. "Much was leaving," I said, evading his real question.

"With enough food to feed a family for a fortnight? Where is he going? Where has everything that has disappeared this summer gone?" Will took two strides forward and grabbed my hand, squeezing as he stared into my eyes.

"Will, stop it. You're hurting me!" Using all my strength, I wrenched my hand away from him, but dropped my eyes from his gaze. "Let's go somewhere we can talk. I can see I've got some explaining to do."

"Some?!" Will exclaimed.

"Some," I said softly.

We went to a small room off the main hall. It was a room Will used as a conference chamber and private office. We each pulled out cushioned wooden chairs and sat down.

Will glared at me for a few moments, then looked up at the window glowing with dawn's light. I couldn't see his face well enough to read the emotion there, but I knew he was angry. Very angry. He didn't speak, just continued to look up.

I sighed, not looking forward to this explanation. I could see my mistake in not telling him in the first place. My reasons for with-holding the information seemed petty to me now. Yes, he had hurt me. Now I had hurt him. And he didn't know the half of it yet. I sighed again, not surprised at the quivering of my breath.

"I'd have had to tell you eventually. I know it should have been sooner, but—" Seeing he was about to interrupt, I held up a hand. "Listen, please. Do you remember the day I got sick?" I didn't wait for his confirmation. "When I was riding through the forest, I noticed some men following me in the cover of the trees. Just like we used to when we would rob some wealthy fop. But these were much noisier about it. Worse than me when I first came to Sherwood." I paused, but Will made no comment or movement at this small attempt at humor.

I cleared my throat and went on. "I surprised them before they could ambush me. You remember the wound I said was from a branch? It was a blade." I bowed my head, but continued before he could say anything. "I lied to you. But I made a deal with them. I agreed to help them out when they need it. In return, when the time comes, they will take us into Sherwood and keep us from harm." I sat back, spreading my hands to show I was finished.

After a moment's silence, Will stood up, crossed to the door as though he would leave without saying anything, then came back to stand behind me. "We can protect ourselves!" he said emphatically, leaning against the back of my chair.

"I should hope so," I said before he could continue.

"Then what the hell have you been doing?" he asked, exasperated.

"What about the rest of us, Will? I'm not working only for ourselves, or the three of us, Little John, and Much. I'm working for *all* of us. What happens when Prince John is hounding Robin's outlaws across England? Men who are weary of fighting. Men who have just come back from Richard's war. Sherwood Forest is big, Will. We all know that. How on earth are we to find each other without help? Chances are, even knowing it's coming, we will be taken by surprise when John sets things in motion. We may have to fight our way out of here. Won't it be nice to have a place to go? Won't it be nice not to have to worry about food or shelter, or even other outlaws who have found Sherwood Forest a kindly place for criminals? They are good men, Will. They will be a welcome security in the time of the wolf ahead of us."

Will was silent for a long time. I wondered if he even heard the things I said.

"The things that have disappeared have been going to these outlaws? These men in the forest?" Will asked at last. I nodded. "Clever. So, you were banking I wouldn't notice and this plan of yours would make everything all right whenever you got around to telling me." He paused. I winced at the derision in his voice. "Do you have so little respect for me, so little faith that I would back you up in a thing like this?!" Will came around to the front of my chair, squatting down to be on my level. "Kay, I can't believe you don't trust me."

"I *do* trust you, Will," I said, reaching out to touch his cheek. He stood up, away from my gesture, and moved around behind me again. I turned in my chair to watch him pace back and forth. "Will—"

"Answer me this. Why'd you keep it from me?"

"You were all set to send men out to find my outlaws. I couldn't let them get hurt."

"You couldn't trust me to think about this rationally? Jesus, Kay!" Will threw his hands up in disgust.

"I was going to tell you, but . . . ." I stopped. Could I tell him the real reason?

"But what? Give me one good reason and I'll forget this whole mess. Just one good reason."

I bowed my head. It was hardly a good reason. I couldn't tell him, but I was unwilling to lie to him anymore. I gasped as he grabbed my chin, forcing me to look at him. His eyes were blazing wells of fury, and I winced under his glare.

"One reason."

I couldn't think of any half-truths, either. I started to open my mouth when he strode away from me in disgust.

I panicked. "You were flirting with her, and I was angry," I yelped. "I know it's not—"

Will spun to look at me, incredulous. "Flirting with who?"

"Lady Nancy," I muttered, ashamed.

"Her? She's a child. You were jealous, Kay?" Will slammed his chair into another one, sending them both crashing to the floor. *"Jealous!"* he roared. "You deliberately kept this from me because you were jealous?!"

I opened my mouth to apologize, to say something, but Will turned away from me, his shoulders shaking with unspent fury.

"Kay, I can't talk to you now. I'm angry, and I'm hurt."

I leaned back, pushed myself to my feet, and walked to the door. "Will," I said, my hand on the handle. I had to try to salvage this situation. "I have no excuse save bad judgment for not telling you. What I'm doing is for the good of the brotherhood and I will continue with my plan. Think about it. And if you can, forgive me." I looked at him, willing him to turn and see me. He stood with his back to me, looking up at the window where sunlight streamed through to strike the wall high above my head. I opened the door and walked out. As I closed it behind me, I whispered, "Forgive me."

Tears threatening to break free, I turned and ran blindly to the stables. Throwing open Sassy's stall door, I belatedly remembered she'd been put out to pasture last night to be serviced by a visiting stud. Momentarily set back, I dropped to the straw and sat with my head in my hands.

In all my plans and actions, never had I thought Will would react like he had. I really blew this one, all because of my stupid pride. I had thought I was above things like pride.

The snuffling of the horse in the next stall finally penetrated my awareness. I turned, finding a black snout pressed to the knothole behind me. I peered through and the horse snorted gently. In spite of myself, I smiled.

"Midnight," I said. "Would you like to give me a ride?"

I DIDN'T COME BACK until early the next morning. I had spent the day riding through the forest and the night shivering in an abandoned shepherd's shack. I would have liked to have come back with everything worked out in my head, ready for whatever would happen. That was not the case. I was just as messed up as before.

Two things had brought me back. Midnight needed proper food, and so did I.

It was still dark when I rode through the gates into the courtyard. After the guard admitted me without question, I rode to the stables.

I took a few soothing moments to take Midnight's saddle off, feed her, and rub her down before reluctantly heading for the hall. In the kitchen, I pretended not to notice the curious looks of bakers who were just starting their day as I scrounged up some day-old bread to quell my rumbling stomach.

The bread was dry and tasteless in my mouth as I trudged up the steps. I almost turned to go to our room. I knew Will would be there—perhaps sleepless, perhaps not. Instead, I kept climbing the stairs to the roof. The eastern sky was just beginning to brighten as I opened the door.

The quiet beauty of the sunrise did nothing to alleviate the sense of loss I felt. If nothing else, it accentuated it. I feared I had alienated Will beyond reparation. I didn't know how to begin to say I was sorry. And if he didn't listen, what good would sorry do? What would I do if he never forgave me? A hollowness in my chest where my heart used to be threatened to swallow my soul.

I sat down on the edge of the roof, watching the courtyard below beginning to stir to life. Against my will, the scene blurred as tears filled my eyes and crawled down my cheeks.

When I heard a footfall behind me, I didn't turn around. I was ashamed to let anyone see me cry.

"Lady?" It was Andrea. "I seen you from the yard. Have you been up here all along? Should I get Master Scathelock?"

I shook my head mutely, fearing my voice would betray my tears.

Andrea came closer and touched my shoulder. "Are you all right? The master and I have been worried."

I nodded and cleared my throat. "I'm fine," I tried to say, but my voice sounded hatefully fragile. I tried again. "I just needed some time to myself. That's all."

"Are you sure, lady?" Andrea asked, moving her arm around my shoulders as she bent down to look at my lowered face. Again, I nodded. "Would you like me to sit with you for a while?"

I started to shake my head, but the answer came of its own accord. "Yes, please stay." I turned to her and she folded me in her arms, rocking me gently as I cried into her shoulder.

After a while, my tears ran out and I simply sat, letting her rock me as I thought of all the things I should have done or said. I finally sat up, surprised to notice it was nearly mid-morning.

I wiped my eyes, avoiding Andrea's questioning gaze. I looked out over the forest. "I've been lying to him, Andrea, and he found out."

"About those outlaws?" she gasped. "Lady, was he angry?"

"Very," I said, sniffling. "But not for the reasons I thought he would be. What am I going to do if he never forgives me?" It was a plaintive question and I looked down at my hands, ashamed of sounding so weak.

"He'll forgive you, lady. He loves you, and you love him." Andrea sounded so sure, but I still wasn't.

"But I betrayed that love and our trust in each other. I didn't think he would back me up, didn't trust him to stand behind me. Worse, I accused him of unfaithfulness. What was I thinking?"

When Andrea didn't say anything, I glanced at her. She seemed to be thinking. "You need to talk with him, Kay," she said, using my name with a familiarity that would have shocked any other lady. "You need to work it out between the two of you."

"But that's just it, Andrea. He won't talk to me. I tried, but he told me he was too angry."

Andrea smiled. "Then it's simple. You need only wait until he's not angry."

"Simple?" I echoed. "I've seen Will dwell on his anger for days. I think I would go crazy before he comes to me. But I'm afraid to go to him."

"Afraid of what?"

"Afraid he won't forgive me, maybe send me away."

"No."

Both Andrea and I turned to the doorway, startled. Will stood there, looking at me with an unreadable expression. Andrea scrambled up and hurried away, looking at her feet as she passed Will.

Frozen, I stared at him. My heart throbbed twice in my chest, either with fear or anticipation, then went back to normal as a painful thrill went from my stomach to my throat. I bit my lip, then whispered, "Will?"

He crossed the roof and sat down next to me to look out over the forest, much as I had done. Then he looked at me, tentatively taking my hands. "You're back," he said quietly. "I was worried."

"Will," I cried softly, not moving for fear he would remember his anger and turn his back on me again. "I know it's not much, but I *am* sorry. If I could take it all back, I would. If I could do it again—"

Will put his fingers against my lips and I fell silent, searching his eyes for answers. "I know, Kay. I heard the things you said to Andrea. I was so angry with you. You lied to me. I wonder how long you would have gone on lying if I hadn't awakened early that morning. That's what hurts the most. That it would have gone on and on. It hurts that you went to Much before you thought to come to me. But your jealousy wounds me even deeper. I would never bed another woman, Kay. I thought you knew that. It hurts to think you were afraid to tell me—of your plans and your worries. Were you afraid of my anger . . . or rejection? I don't understand your reasoning in any of this, but I'm going to let it go, Kay."

My jaw dropped slightly and I squeezed his hand. "Will? I . . . I don't know what to say."

"Just answer one question." I looked into his eyes again and saw a passion burning in them. "When would you have told me?"

"I don't know," I said truthfully. "Perhaps next summer. I hadn't thought about it." I looked down. "It seemed to make sense, Will, until you found out. Then everything went all to hell." I frowned, trying to keep more tears at bay. "I didn't know what I was going to do. I thought I had lost you."

He gave a small smile. "You didn't lose me, Kay. I don't think anything but death could take me away from you."

A chill went down my spine at his words and I reached out to him, hugging him fiercely. "Not even that," I whispered. "Never that." I couldn't stand the thought that he would die and leave me alone.

Will laughed, leaning away from me a little. "Not so tight, love. You'll squeeze the stuffing out of me."

I laughed a little, too, but the sound had a slightly hysterical edge to it, so I clamped it off and loosened my hug. "It's just that I love you so much."

TWENTY-THREE

T he child came in April. It was so early on the sixteenth that it might have actually been on the fifteenth. I went into hard labor immediately after dinner on the fourteenth.

How could I describe the feeling? It was like I was pinned to the ground under an onslaught of ocean waves. I couldn't breathe properly, and the pressure came and went like the waves, starting in my belly and spreading through my entire body. The pain was intense, like someone twisting my spinal cord. There were times during the nearly thirty hours of labor when I would have considered it a mercy to fall out the window and end it all on the flagstones of the courtyard.

Andrea stayed by my side through the long, long hours of labor. I was scarcely aware of her, unaware of calling out Will's name.

Afterward, Will told me it had taken both Norman and Russell, the stable hand, to keep him out of the room the first time I'd screamed. It wasn't until later I thought about how often women here died in childbed, and I counted my lucky stars things went so well.

Andrea washed the babe in lukewarm water, then wrapped the squealing thing in a soft cloth and laid it on my belly. "It's a boy," she said.

I closed my eyes. A boy. Another contraction, softer this time, assailed my body. I involuntarily clutched my baby boy. He screeched for a moment, then settled in to suckle. His tiny warmth was like a fire in my heart. I could have cried out in joy at the love I felt for this little human.

"I witness this child's birth—alive, healthy, and male," said Andrea. "What do you name him?" It was common practice at birthing to ask for a name. Will and I had talked about it, but I was so very tired, I almost forgot the name we had chosen.

"Paul," I whispered. With the child still suckling, I fell asleep.

When Will came to visit the next day, his face lit up when he held his son. "You named him Paul?" he asked. I nodded. "He's such a strong boy, yes?" He cooed at the child, then looked at me and grinned. "I think I'm going to like being a father."

MOTHERHOOD DID NOT COME EASILY to me. Diapers and I didn't agree. I often desperately wished for some Huggies. I was supposed to be bonding with my child, but I didn't understand any of his cries. After six straight nights of no sleep, Will and I agreed we would hire a nanny. I didn't get along with the first two women we tried, but the third was indeed the charm.

With the nanny chosen, I settled down to the business of learning how to care for my son. *My son!* The love I felt for him burned like a fierce fire in my heart every time I looked at this fragile being. But I was afraid to pick him up, afraid to do more than caress this defenseless babe.

Sybil, our nanny, assured me I would get over the fear. But even after I grew accustomed to holding him in my arms, as well as my heart, apprehension remained. I didn't understand or remember what it was to be a child. There were so many mistakes that could be . . . would be made.

A year rolled by, with the growing child to mark its passage. I spent my time helping take care of Paul and trying to get myself back into shape. He grew quickly. By one year, he had most of his baby teeth and was walking well.

I rode around the common quite a lot the first months to keep my seat on a horse in good practice. I went to see Anne and showed

Jamie a trick or two with a bow. Sydney visited Anne often and was teaching the boy how to wield a sword, but he was no hand with a bow, so I taught him.

Much came every month to get supplies for Bran. By April first of Paul's first year, I was ready, and had time, to ride out to meet my outlaws again.

Riding out in the spring morning, the scent of fresh air made me happy to be going into the forest again. It had been a long time since I ventured into the deep woods, and I reveled in the peaceful beauty of it.

There was a small sound I pricked my ears to, then John jumped into the road from atop a small bank.

"John!" I said, swinging my leg over and hopping out of the saddle in one swift movement. "Good to see you!"

"Kay!" He grabbed hold of Midnight's halter to keep the spooked horse from running off. "Your man Much might have said something," he scolded. "I wasn't expecting you. You look well." John grinned and hugged me. "How is the child?"

"Growing like a weed. He has his father's face . . . and my eyes, I'm told. He's an angel."

"He'll be a devil soon enough, I'll wager," John said. I laughed. "I'll have to see him sometime before that."

"Yes," I said proudly. "Perhaps I'll bring him with me tomorrow."

"Hmm." John stroked Midnight's nose and crooned a little. Then he grinned at me. "We need aught but some flour, and perhaps some salt."

"That's all? You must be doing well at providing everything else then."

John gave me a devilish grin. "Well, knowing about Lord Pickerney's ale train helps."

I laughed. "He *is* quite the fool, isn't he?"

"Aye. But we don't push it. We let more of them go by than we stop, so they never know when or where we'll strike."

"Good. No sense in taking extra risks." I looked at him, appraising the difference a year and five months had made in the man. "You look well. I'd say you've put on some weight."

John slapped his belly. "Oh, aye. I'm amazed how much more

game we get when we don't make noise and scare them off before we ever see them."

I laughed. "I was amazed, too. I always thought the forest was just empty of any animals bigger than a squirrel. Okay. Flour and salt? You shall have it then. Now, do we ride together while you tell me what's been going on?"

"What? Hasn't Much been keeping you up on us?" he laughed, gesturing for me to mount up.

"Well, yes, but I want to hear it from you."

John mounted behind me. As we rode, he told me of the happenings while I had been busy with Paul.

Much had been teaching them the tricks of living in the forest and all the skills an outlaw needed to sneak up on people. The only one having problems was Milo. He said he was just too old to learn new things. John said he wasn't the same after his illness. Everyone else was getting along fine.

Much also tested their skills with the sword, bow, staff, and knife. I was given to understand they had all improved.

I hadn't been told any of this by Much. I guessed it was to have been a surprise.

"I'll have to come out and practice with you folks. I've gotten some time in the practice yard, but not nearly enough. The men at the lodge all worry about hurting me. Even Will. No matter how badly I beat them, they still think I'm fragile." I grinned. "The fools. They wouldn't have to worry about hurting me if they'd let me practice as I should."

John laughed. "I agree. You're welcome in Sherwood any time."

"Don't I know it," I said, turning my head to wink at him.

THE NEXT MORNING, when I rode up to the agreed meeting place in the forest with my saddle bags full of the requested flour and salt, I found myself surrounded by grinning outlaws. Peter was the first to reach me, lifting Paul from my arms and swinging him around. I slid out of the saddle to greet the rest of them, slapping each on the back, giving and receiving bear hugs. It was a happy reunion. It almost felt like coming home.

Paul laughed, waving his arms and tugging on beards as he was passed around from man to man. He felt entirely at home with Bran and his men, for which I was glad. I decided I would bring the boy with me more often so he would grow to love the forest as Will and I did.

Everyone but Geoffrey had come to welcome me back. He had to stay at the camp to keep an eye on things. I was surprised at the amount of affection the men displayed for me, but I was just as glad to see them. I welcomed their hugs and greetings.

When Paul began to fuss, Peter grimaced anxiously and handed him back to me in a hurry. I laughed and found a fallen tree to sit upon so I could bounce him on my knee. The others ranged themselves around me.

"So, tell me!" I said, looking at all of them. "I want to hear what you've been up to while I was unable to come."

They began to tell tales, wildly exaggerated and very humorous. I laughed until the stitches plagued my sides. When Milo brought out some dried deer meat to eat, I fed Paul some mush I'd brought along. He fell asleep while Bran told a more serious story.

"Yesterday when I was out hunting," he said, "I ran across a group of foresters. They were hard at work, holding up the trees with their backs and scaring the animals with all their talking." Bran smiled at his humor. "Since they didn't see me, I stayed hidden and listened. It never hurts to know if they're planning something. One of the fellows was going on about how Sheriff John is being put upon by the prince to have the forest cleaned out. That means us." He made a motion of a noose being slipped about his neck and tightened.

"Little John wouldn't hunt outlaws," I said, standing up to pace. Paul stirred in my arms, so I passed him off to John. "He's been an outlaw himself, remember?"

"Nah," agreed Bran. "He won't hunt us himself, though he's under pressure. Prince John is threatening his sheriffship if he doesn't obey. But your Little John is holding out. Now I heard Prince John's ordered the king's foresters to do it. They're under royal orders, and the sheriff can hardly refuse a hanging if they bring him an outlaw."

"Are there any other outlaws in Sherwood?"

"Aye, there's a band by Lincoln. We've had a couple run-ins with them. They're a rowdy lot. They carry off women, slaughter live-stock, murder—"

"Damn!" I said hotly, slapping my fist into my open palm. "The fools! They'll ruin all of it! I've got to speak to Little John and tell him the plan."

"Is that wise?" Bran asked.

"I have to. He'll know what to do about it, and he'll keep it under his belt. There's precious few as trustworthy as Little John."

"I've got to go to Nottingham," I told Will before dinner that night.

"Why's that?" he asked, putting his arm around me as we walked toward the dining hall.

"There's trouble brewing in the forest. A band of outlaws over in Lincolnshire are doing the cooking, and Prince John's breathing down on Nottingham to hang them all. I've got to tell Little John to keep the foresters away from our group or we could have problems."

"How so?"

I looked at him sidelong, wondering why he couldn't see the problem. "If the foresters bring one of Bran's to Nottingham, Little John will have to hang him. Prince John would have his head if he found out otherwise."

"Won't Much be able to say something?"

"Maybe, but I told him this was a very big secret and he must not tell anyone. Not for a while yet. He might not say anything."

"Even to save a life? I think you underestimate Much," said Will. We stopped outside the door. "Prince John can't force Little John to hang anybody. He's been holding trials for his prisoners, hasn't he? He'll know, with Much to tell him, to let the boys off with a warning."

I sighed, not feeling like making any decisions right now. "Maybe I'm overreacting."

"Look, I know I'm right. Don't worry about it. Much will help. I'm sure he's already aware of the trouble and is watching for it."

"I hope you're right," I said, taking the arm he offered. Together, we entered the dining hall.

NEWS of the war in France occasionally came through on its way to York or Edinburgh in Scotland. King Richard was pushing the enemy back, or he was defeated in such-and-such place. Places I had never heard of. It got old. The same stories of bravery and loss, just different names. I stopped coming out to listen to the messengers after a while. If there was any news of Robin, Will would tell me.

Paul grew more every day, as children his age do. By three, he was a regular yeoman, or that was what his father told him anyway. Will loved his son. He made him a toy bow and arrows long before the boy could hope to pull it, much less do anything but wave it around. He made a wooden sword, as well, and gave Paul his own pony. He learned to ride, but still preferred to ride in front of his mama or papa on the big horses.

Will, my sweet Will Scarlet, could often be found telling stories to a sleepy Paul or singing lullabies in a voice better suited to bawdy ale songs. The two of them were a pair, and I thought we made a fine family.

IT WAS the start of the new year before we had our first bitter cold snap, the weather proving very mild that winter. The moon, which had raised her swollen belly over the horizon before dark, was near setting when I heard a soft tapping at the door. I sat up, instantly awake. Will rolled onto his back and mumbled something, but I caressed his cheek and told him to go back to sleep.

Shivering in the chill of the room, I got up and pulled a robe around myself just as a second tapping sounded at the door. I opened it to find Andrea huddled in her robe. She frowned, looking like she'd rather be in bed with her current lover.

"There's a man below who wants to see you, milady. Norman said something about a sign," Andrea whispered, "and that it's important. I was minded to let you sleep."

I grinned. "And you, too, eh? Go down and tell him I'll be right there. Then get yourself back into bed with Simon."

Andrea's eyes opened a bit wider and she glanced at Will. "Milady . . . . He's not a . . . a . . . ?" She couldn't bring herself to say the word for what she was asking.

"Not likely, Andrea." I chuckled at her suggestion, then put a finger to my lips with a wink. "More likely he's one of my outlaws. Now go and do as I say. Simon will be getting cold."

As Andrea departed, I went to the chest at the foot of the bed and got my hunting clothes out. I dressed quickly, strapping on my swords and knives. Then I left the room and went downstairs, silent in my forest boots.

I found Geoffrey waiting. I paused at the foot of the stairs, then hurried to where he stood by the door. Norman leaned against the wall, half-asleep, only one eye on his guest. Geoffrey seemed nervous, looking around the hall, ready to bolt out the door at the drop of a hat.

"What's wrong, Geoffrey?"

"It's Milo and Peter, Kay. They've been taken to Nottingham, and Much is away."

I cursed. "What's the charge?"

"We were stealing chickens." I gave him an incredulous stare. "Kay, it's a fair."

"Oh crap." The reprimand I was ready to deliver would serve no purpose now. I put my hand on my forehead, trying to think. "Little John will have no choice then."

Geoffrey nodded. "They're to be hanged at mid-morning."

I looked up, ready with a plan. "All right." I turned to Norman, who straightened. "Listen, Norman. Wake Milord Scathelock and tell him I have gone to Nottingham. Say that two have been taken and Much is away. I'm doing what I can. Got it?"

Norman faithfully repeated the message, then I sent him out to saddle my horse.

Geoffrey and I stood in the archway to the courtyard. "Meet me outside the gate. I didn't see how you got in and I don't want to know, but leave the same way. Meet me down the road. I don't want anyone else to see you."

Geoffrey nodded. As I watched, he appeared to melt into the

shadows. I nodded in satisfaction. Even with my knowing eyes, his exit had been hard to follow.

I went to the stable and arrived just as Norman led Midnight, my preferred horse, out. My old Sassy was too busy being queen of the breeding herd to serve as my steed anymore. Midnight snorted a cloud of vapor as I took the reins and leapt into the saddle, leaving behind a bewildered watch as I galloped out the main gate of the lodge.

A sharp whistle reached me over the sound of Midnight's hooves and I pulled her to a stop. Geoffrey came out of the shadows and leapt up behind me, panting from his run. I kicked the horse's flanks and she surged forward.

When the sun rose, we were better than halfway to Nottingham. I slowed Midnight's pace, then stopped, letting Geoffrey off. I told him to wait there for my return.

I continued alone, whipping Midnight up to make it before mid-morning.

Astride a sweaty, foam-flecked mare, I arrived in Nottingham, scattering crowds all the way up to the gallows, marginally avoiding pedestrians and other riders.

"Sheriff!" I shouted when I saw Little John leading Milo and Peter out of the prison room. He turned as I called.

"Kay! I haven't seen you in a long time. Is it the fair that brings you to Nottingham?"

"No, sir," I said breathlessly, Midnight dancing beneath me. "Not pleasure, but business."

I saw Peter give Milo a look that said *I told you so* and guessed Milo had been the pessimist.

"Ah, business." John frowned. "Much as I hate to wait, we can discuss that at lunch. I have a hanging to see to." John's frown deepened. I could see he wasn't pleased with the idea.

"My business concerns these two." I pointed at Milo and Peter, who looked like they had spent an uncomfortable night in a damp cell. I had hoped to see John in private, but seeing that a scene was unavoidable, I fabricated a quick story. "They cannot be hanged here today."

"What?" John asked, his eyebrows shooting up his forehead in surprise.

"They must be brought to justice in Gamwell." That statement brought a look of surprise from Milo and Peter. "They are two servants from Gamwell. They stole some weapons from Will's . . . Milord Scathelock's armory and ran off. Milord fell off his horse in the chase and twisted his ankle, elsewise he would be here right now."

Little John gave me a queer look, but motioned his guards to put the men back into the prison room.

"You and I will talk," he said, waving a servant forward to take my horse.

I dismounted and gave Midnight a pat on the muzzle. "Walk her, then rub her down well, boy," I whispered into the servant's ear. "See that she gets water and some oats, and I'll see that you get another of these for the fair." I pressed a shilling into his hand and ruffled his hair. The boy's eyes lit up as he took the reins.

TWENTY-FOUR

J ohn took me to the inner garden where we had often talked before. We sat down on a bench in the shade of an apple tree.

"You never were a good liar, Kay," Little John began, leaning back and crossing his arms in front of his chest. "Will Scarlet fell off his horse?" He raised a brow.

I laughed as my face grew hot. "I must admit, it was one of my worst lies. I guess I'm out of practice."

"At least you have the presence to blush. Do you want to tell me the truth now?"

I scratched the back of my head, smiling. "I suppose I ought to. This is what it is. Much would have told you, if he had been here. Those men you captured . . . . They're part of a plan of mine."

John groaned. "Not a plan? What have you been up to, Kay?"

"Providing for the future, John. You know what will happen when Richard the Lionheart dies, don't you?"

"Aye," John said with such a look of distaste, I knew he had a good idea.

"Then you know we must go back to the forest."

He nodded.

"The two men you captured, and more like them, are outlaws after our own fashion. I don't know what the deal was with the chickens, but they, just like we did, rob the rich to survive. They keep it small to keep the foresters off their backs, and I help them when they need it."

"You're helping outlaws?" John asked, sitting up. "Those wild ruffians who have no care for anyone besides themselves? Kay, how could you?"

"No, John. Listen. There are two groups in Sherwood. One of them is near Lincoln. My band has had run-ins with them. They are the ones who cause all the trouble. My band is near Gamwell, and they believe in the same principles we do. I have been guiding them for years now, preparing for the time when Prince John becomes king. When that happens, these men will be in the forest, ready with supplies and a place to stay, ready to help us gather everyone together. When we go back, the forest will still be our friend."

"And it's not now?" John asked, frowning.

"Not to some. Think, John. It's been four years. You and I have stayed close to the forest, and so have the others who accepted service as foresters. But what about those who have been overseas all this time? And those who have been south, in the king's service? Four years is a long time, John. Long enough to forget. Things change."

John nodded. "It's a good plan, Kay. Friends in the forest will be welcome, to be sure. Better than those ruffians near . . . . Where did you say they were based? Lincoln? Yes, friends will be a help."

"Then you'll let them go?" I asked. "If I don't get them back, I'll have enemies on my hands where I used to have friends. And we will need their help soon."

Little John quirked his eyebrow at me but didn't comment on my grave words. "I'll let you take your 'servants' back." He sighed.

I got up and hugged him. "You won't regret it, Sheriff."

"I hope not." He stood, towering a full two heads above me. "I don't want this to come back and haunt me, so take care your records show discipline," he said gruffly. Then he smiled. "Will you be staying for the fair then?"

"Oh, I think so. It's not the time to be moving prisoners. Besides, I have a feeling Will may be along soon. I must be near to warn him about his 'twisted foot.'" I grinned rakishly and put my arm in John's as we walked back out to the fair. "And you must tell him to be careful with horses. They can be such wild creatures."

John laughed as I took my arm away. Dressed as I was, I didn't want to give John a reputation as a lover of boys, though I was sure any single woman in the town would testify against that.

In Nottingham, there were two of me. One was Lady Kay, who wore dresses and danced in the square at fairs. The other was plain Kay, a messenger who practiced fighting with the men and occasionally drank enough ale to put the sheriff's steward under the table.

We went through the front hall and out to the steps of the main courtyard, where we stood for a moment, looking over the crowds for a horseman.

"He shouldn't be much longer. I told Norman to wake him after saddling up Midnight." Just then, two riders entered the street from the direction of the main gate. "There they are." I skipped down the steps.

I nodded at Will and Norman as they stopped, then grasped the reins of Will's horse and held it steady. "How is your foot, Milord Scathelock?" I asked him and winked, hoping he would get the message.

"What?" he asked, narrowing his eyes.

"Your foot, milord. It was a bad fall. But not to worry. The sheriff has captured the villains, and I have delayed the hanging. They will go home with us to be punished."

Will nodded. "Good. Get your horse, Kay. We will ride soon."

I smiled. "Milord, the sheriff has invited us to stay for lunch." I liked playing the part of Kay the messenger, trying—as any page would—to talk my lord into staying for free eats.

"How kind of him," Will said, glancing at the sun to guess the time. He looked down at me and smiled. Then he dismounted, affecting a limp, as I told a lingering servant to take his and Norman's horses.

"Don't forget to keep it up," I whispered as I walked beside him up to the castle. I didn't take his arm as we walked. It would seem strange to those who thought I was just a favored page at Gamwell Lodge. It wasn't a masquerade that fooled many, but I kept it up because those people who *were* fooled would make the most fuss about a lady dressed in breeches and scampering about with fighting men and servants.

Will sat at the high table with Little John, and I sat farther down next to Norman, in a position befitting a servant.

I ate and drank my fill, but my thoughts were with Milo and Peter when I stuffed a hard roll into one boot, cheese into the other.

Sitting back and belching loud and long, I decided I liked being Kay more than Lady Kay. Except for the fact that Lady Kay could reach out and hold Will's hand when he came to speak to her.

"Come," he said, leaning over the back of my chair. "We must go take care of business."

We accompanied Little John to the prison room. It wasn't a classic dungeon. No skulls hanging about or instruments of torture, no poor victims chained to the wall. Rather, it was simply a deep pit with a mesh of bars across the top and a ladder nearby to let prisoners up.

At Little John's request, the guard lifted the grating, and I peered down into the semi-darkness. A square of light lit a patch of straw-covered dirt, but I could only see the feet of the prisoners below.

"Peter and Milo of Gamwell Lodge," Will called into the pit. "Do you choose to go back to Gamwell and accept your punishment, or do you wish to stay in Nottingham and be hanged?"

A face I knew moved into the square of light. Milo. He looked up, saw me, and nodded. "I'll go to Gamwell."

Peter stepped forward. "Me, too."

The ladder was lowered and Milo climbed up first. It was a rickety old thing, allowing only one man up at a time. When he reached the top, Peter stepped up onto the first rung.

Before he could go any farther, another prisoner pushed him aside and rushed up the ladder. Will and I drew our swords in an instant. The guards were slower.

The prisoner reached the top, ducked away from Will, and ran for the door. The guards, taken by surprise, almost let him go by without moving. The boy was quick, but I moved quicker, barring his way with my body, swords at the ready.

The boy dodged to one side, then tried to go between my legs, but I clamped down on his neck with a horseman's grip, stopping him, though he squirmed to get free.

At last, a guard moved, yanking the boy to his feet. By that time, Peter was up and being held, along with Milo, by guards with drawn swords. The grate over the pit was already down. At least *someone* had been thinking. Will or Little John, no doubt.

I sheathed my swords and approached the would-be escape artist. I tried on my best icy smile.

"Do you want so badly to go to Gamwell to get the same as these two?" I gestured to Milo and Peter. "Perhaps you are tired of Nottingham and want to try your luck with me?" I imagined my voice was steel and saw the boy and the guard holding him wince. Will and Little John might have known I liked the boy, but no one else. He was quick and strong, with more than a little courage.

The boy, he couldn't have been more than nineteen, looked straight at me, his eyes shining steadily, burning like a fire. He shook, but I thought it was from adrenaline rather than fear. He didn't say anything.

I turned to John. "Milord, what did this boy do?"

"He's a marketplace thief, pickpocket, and a housebreaker. He *is* going to rot for his crimes." John gave me a look, warning me against saying more.

I turned back to the boy. "A thief deserves to rot," I said, stepping aside so the guards could throw him back into the pit. I suppressed a shudder at what I had said. I knew people really did rot in those dungeons.

The metal grate clanged down into its locks after the boy, and I stared at Little John, who stared back at me.

As our group walked across the crowded courtyard, I moved closer to speak into John's ear.

"I want that boy, John."

"You can't have him, Kay," John said, not looking at me.

"Why not?"

"He's wild. No one could control him. He'd be back in someone else's marketplace the minute you turned your back on him."

"Who says I'd turn my back on him? John, you know me. I'm no slackard. And if you know me, you as good as know my boys. These two you caught are the least of them. Milo's the oldest, Peter's the youngest. Your men never saw Geoffrey, who was with them. They won't let the boy out of their sight. They'll keep him tied to a tree if they have to, but I want him on our side."

"Why, for Christ's sake? Kay, he's a street thief, not a forest outlaw. They're as different as night and day. Who says he can or even *wants* to change?"

"Who says he can't? Hell, John, who are you to say which man should rot for his sins?" I stopped walking, putting my hands on my hips.

John turned, indignant. "I'm Sheriff of Nottingham—" he began.

"You were an outlaw before you were ever sheriff, Little John. And a better outlaw you made." I saw a spark of anger light in his eyes, so I softened my approach. "You're a good man, Sheriff John Little, but I'm sure you remember what it's like to sit at the bottom of a hole like that. You spent your own time in Nott's very own cell, didn't you?"

John nodded, the anger dying away as quickly as it came.

"What if Robin hadn't thought to include you in his escape? From your own admission, he could have made his escape easier if he'd gone alone instead of freeing all the prisoners. Remember when you got out? The feeling you had? Remember how you chose to serve Robin to your last breath? Remember, John, and give me the thief."

Little John sighed, a sound of long sufferance. "Very well. Take him. But if that boy gets loose and goes wild, I'll skin you alive. When do you want him?"

I grinned. "Tonight," I said. We moved to catch up with the others. "I'll be outside the gate to the city when the watch changes at ten. Tie him up and bring him out. I'll take care of it from there."

"I'll see to it myself. There'll be no trouble if I let on that he's to be killed. My guards may think me cruel, but after his stunt this day, they may think it warranted."

We reached the place where my horse waited. Will and the others were already mounted, Peter behind Milo on the same mare.

"Good," I said. "Tonight then."

I mounted Midnight and rode out after the others, turning once to wave at Little John. The two guards had stayed behind. It was just Will, Norman, myself, and my two outlaws.

When we entered the forest, Will sent Norman ahead. He knew what was going on, but Will didn't want him to witness the release of the prisoners. If anyone asked, he was to say he thought we killed them in the forest.

Around midway between Nottingham and Gamwell, Bran and Geoffrey jumped out onto the road from the sheltering trees. They spared a quick glance at Will, but they knew who he was.

"Thank God," Bran said, taking hold of Milo's reins. "I was afraid Kay wouldn't get there in time."

"She did," said Milo, giving me a look I couldn't quite interpret. Was he referring to the incident with his son, contrasting this to the other outcome? Was he finally letting my old failure rest?

"And it was a good thing," said Peter. "I didn't fancy swinging." They dismounted and Bran hugged them both.

"Don't do anything so stupid again," he admonished. "We've got to be careful."

"Aye, especially when I bring you your new man, Bran," I said.

"What?" asked Will, who had been watching everything.

"What?" Bran echoed.

"I'm going back to Nottingham tonight. John is going to let me take that boy, the thief. Bran, I'm going to leave it up to you and your men to watch him and make him see that living in the forest is better than working the towns, but also show him he can't survive by himself."

"Why?" asked Bran, practical as ever. I could see he wasn't looking forward to taking on a green boy.

"Why not?" I countered. "He's young. He's got the right instincts. He's still trainable. We might be able to use him later. I'd hate to see someone so young rotting in a hole for the rest of his short life."

Bran shrugged, but I knew he was thinking.

"I'll teach him," said Peter. "I talked to him while we were down there. He's got lots of ideas."

"Good," I said. "What's his name?"

"He said people call him Thomas the Thief."

I smiled. "Thanks, Peter. Bran?"

"It could be worth our while," he said thoughtfully. "It never hurts to have someone who knows his way around the towns."

"It *will* be worth it, Bran. Bring yourself and Peter to the stream crossing about a half-mile back . . . . You know the one I mean?" He nodded. "Good. Be there at midnight and wait for me."

I turned back toward Nottingham, beckoning Will to follow. Before we had gone ten feet, Bran and the others had disappeared into the trees. I stopped and turned to Will.

"What's the deal with this boy, Kay? Why bother?" Will shook his head. "I don't understand."

"I like him, Will. And I don't think anybody should rot in a prison cell like that. He's just a kid, a marketplace thief. It's not like he went on a killing spree or beat up old ladies. Besides, he's got potential." I winked. "He got past you."

Will grunted and gave a nod. "True. I just don't understand what gets into you sometimes. You pull ideas out of the air, and somehow make people see your point. I'm always surprised by things you do."

I smiled. "I'll take that as a compliment, dear."

Will shook his head, but he smiled. "Go get the boy, Kay. Do you want me to come, too?"

"No, I'll be fine. You're needed at the lodge, I'm sure."

"Aye, no doubt. And I'll go out and get some practice to sharpen my *failing* reflexes."

I laughed and leaned over to kiss him. "You're just getting old," I teased.

"And you're still a baby. Now, get out of here."

DARKNESS SETTLED as I stopped outside the city. The moon wasn't up yet, so there was no light. I saw lanterns at the gate, but I stayed back from their illumination.

I dismounted and hobbled Midnight, then moved a few yards closer to wait. In the quiet darkness, kneeling in the cold grass, I dozed off.

A distant sound jolted me into awareness, and I looked up as the lanterns beside the gate moved, then disappeared.

John was coming.

I stayed low and alert, and heard the steady clip-clop of a horse being led toward me. It came closer and the horse nickered, sensing Midnight. Midnight whickered softly in return.

"Kay?" John whispered.

"Here, John," I said, standing up beside his horse.

By the faint starlight, I could dimly make out John's giant outline and that of a horse, the deformed shadow of Thomas tied across its back like a dead man.

"Just as you said, Sheriff," I said. "I thank you for allowing me the privilege. I'll take care of him."

"Good," said John. "Then I won't have to. It'll be painless?"

"I can't guarantee that, but it'll be as neat as possible."

"Good. I will see you when you visit next. Keep the nag. We don't need her here." John disappeared into the night.

Thomas spoke for the first time. "What do you want with me?" His voice quivered once, betraying his fear.

I didn't answer him as I unhobbled Midnight.

"Where are you taking me?" No waver then, just anger, hostility, curiosity.

I mounted, taking hold of the mare's lead rope and moving off toward the forest.

We traveled in silence for about ten minutes, then Thomas spoke again.

"I'm . . . having trouble breathing," he said, trying to sound brave and unafraid. I heard the strain in his voice, the wheeze that meant a lack of oxygen from being folded across the saddle for so long.

Still not speaking, I reined Midnight up and dismounted. I moved over to the boy's head and lifted it by the hair to consider his face. "Don't do anything stupid," I said, then dropped his head. I reached down and cut the rope holding his hands and feet together. The boy must have been hurting because he slid off the horse and collapsed to the ground opposite me.

Not knowing if he were going to try something, I dodged beneath the mare's belly and put my knife to his neck.

Thomas choked back a cry, trying to distance himself from the knife. "I'm not going anywhere. I can't feel my legs."

I backed off a little and helped him sit up.

"Wait until the feeling returns," I said, grinning. "Then you'll wish for the numb."

There was a small silence, then he asked, "Are you going to kill me?" He was just a frightened young man.

I sat back and looked at him. "Do you know who I am?"

"Look," he said, "if I offended you somehow today, I'm sorry. I'm just trying to survive."

I nodded. Thomas turned his head to the right. "There's no place for you to go, bound as you are," I told him. "Who am I?"

"Your name is Kay," he said, still looking over his shoulder.

I nodded. "Go on."

He turned and looked at me. "You . . . dress as a man, but you are a woman. You keep company with Lord Scathelock of Gamwell —" He stopped, but I motioned him to continue. "I'm thinking you are his lady."

I smiled. "You're a bright boy. And what do you know of the lady of Gamwell?"

Thomas paused before answering. Even in the darkness, I saw the gleam in his eye. "I have heard she is a kind and just woman. And merciful."

I laughed softly. "A sweet tongue, as well. Do they really say such things about me?"

"The woman who spoke of you said so," the boy said eagerly. Then he slumped again. "But she also said others say you are a mysterious woman. That you . . . ." His voice trailed off.

"No, go on. I want to hear what others think of me."

"Well, they say you disappear from the lodge and reappear hours later, sometimes with game, sometimes leaving with something and coming back empty-handed. Once, someone saw you come back with a bandage on your hand."

I smiled then, remembering John's little trick that had cost me a few drops of blood. Thomas saw my smile and started to edge away, but I moved my knife blade up a fraction and he stopped. He went on with his narrative as though nothing had happened.

"One other swears he saw you go to a house on the common where ten men came out to greet you. But nobody believes him."

"It wasn't nearly ten," I said slowly, thinking we had to be more careful. "But that's true enough. Most of what you've told me is accurate. Do people do more than talk?" I asked. The boy shook his head. "Good. Well, boy, if I untie your feet, will you run off?"

Thomas shook his head, eyes wide. It looked as if he wanted to ask a question, but held back. "If I did, I couldn't go very far. You move quickly," he said, then added, "for a noble."

"Aye." I ignored his last remark. "And you can be sure I know this forest better than you, even in the dark. It would be best if you stayed with me."

"That depends on what your answer to my question is," he said, determined not to show his fear again.

Before I answered, he gasped in pain. I laughed. "Your legs have come back to life then?" He made no further sound, but I was sure he was very uncomfortable. "If you behave, Thomas the Thief, you have nothing to worry about from me," I said, cutting the bonds around his feet. "Mount," I told him. With help from me, Thomas obeyed, then I mounted, again taking the mare's lead rope.

As I urged the horses forward, Thomas asked, "But what do you—"

"Shhh," I hushed him. "You'll know more later. For now, be silent. These woods have more in them than just you and me. It's not safe at night."

We moved on in silence, the only sound the shuffle of our horses' hooves in the dirt. The moon rose as we rode, bathing the world around us with her cold light.

Just after we crossed the stream an hour later, Bran and all his men leapt out of the scrub and surrounded us, standing silently. Peter and Sydney moved to grasp the horses' halters.

Thomas' nag danced, smelling strange men and her rider's fear. Midnight stood very still in the heart of men she knew. Thomas turned wild eyes on me, unaware that he was the only one moving. "Milady! Loose my bonds so I can fight for myself."

"There's no need for fighting, Thomas. This is your future."

"Have some pity, milady. If my destiny is here, let me meet it armed!"

I laughed, not unkindly, and he realized he was the only one making any fuss. I leaned toward him. "I said *future*, not destiny. Look who holds your horse."

Thomas looked down and saw Peter holding the nag's halter,

smiling at him. He stopped struggling, and I cut the rope binding his wrists.

"Thomas, these are my friends. In matters such as these, they answer to me. I have said you have nothing to worry about from me."

"But what—"

"Listen to me closely," I said, cutting him off. "These men are your future. You will stay with them, live and learn the way of the forest, the way free men live."

"What if I don't want to stay with them?" Thomas asked, eyes on me.

"Then you may go," I said, and Thomas began to dismount. "But you'll go back to the marketplace and they'll catch you. And, by God, you'll hang . . . or worse. If you stay, you'll have my protection as long as I can give it. You've seen how I take care of my own." I pointed to Milo and Peter.

Thomas looked around, shifting back into the saddle. "Why are you doing this for me?"

I smiled. "I believe everyone should have a chance at doing things right." I leaned down to shake Bran's hand. "Good luck. Take care of him and see that he doesn't misbehave. If he does, you take care of it however you must. Keep the mare. Perhaps Anne can use her." I sat straight in my saddle. "See you." I whirled Midnight on her haunches and galloped into the night.

CHAPTER
TWENTY-FIVE

When I walked in around four in the morning, I found Will asleep in the dining hall and woke him with a kiss.

"It's not fair," he said when he opened his eyes and saw me.

"What's not fair?" I stood beside him and stretched, my bones cracking.

"You get to romp about the forest in the middle of the night, while I have to stay here." He stood up to kiss me and we headed upstairs.

"You have to keep care of the lodge," I said. "That's a heavy responsibility. Plus, you have to maintain a good reputation, while mine doesn't matter as much." We walked into our room. "Did you know, my husband, I am something of a mystery to people? I get the impression they think I'm some kind of wood elf. They tell stories of my disappearing for days in the forest, or going out and visiting men who can disappear in the blink of an eye. It's true, but they make it sound magical." I stretched out under the covers, weary to the bone, and yawned. "I think it's rather funny."

Will sat on the bedside and gave me a stern look. "You shouldn't, you know. What others think of you *is* important when you're the squire's wife."

"It never mattered in the forest," I said rebelliously.

"It matters here."

"It shouldn't. Besides, it's not much longer that we'll be here."

"I wish you wouldn't keep reminding me," said Will, blowing out the candle.

"But you can't forget, Will. Remember, our survival depends on it."

"None of the brotherhood forget anything, my dear." He kissed me. I returned the kiss as he eased into bed beside me.

"Where's Paul?" I asked, glancing at the open door leading to the boy's room.

"With Sybil." Will kicked at the covers. Andrea always made the bed into a stretcher and Will couldn't stand it. "I had her take him when I left."

"Good," I murmured. I was tired. If I'd been standing, I could have fallen asleep on my feet. I felt Will's lips brush mine, an invitation. I managed to whisper an apology before falling fast asleep.

IT WAS mid-morning before I got out of bed. Around nine o'clock, Will had come in to wake me, and I apologized the best way I knew how for falling asleep on him, taking advantage of Paul's absence to make sweet love to my husband.

Afterward, I took a bath, then slipped into a clean dress. It was lunch by the time I made my appearance downstairs.

When I got to the dining hall, Paul broke away from Sybil and came running. I caught him and swung him around, planting a kiss on his forehead.

"Paul," I said, hugging him tightly. He took the restriction for only a moment, then squirmed to look at my face.

"Mama! Guess what!"

"What's that, my boy?"

"Ganny had a baby!"

"Really?" I was mildly surprised. Ganny was a mare in our stables. She had been carrying for a while, but we hadn't expected the foal so soon.

I carried Paul back to the table while he told me what had happened while I was gone the day before. He told me all about a small person's world—friends and animals, grown-ups hurrying by looking very important, telling the children to stay out of the way. From a child's perspective, it was a very hectic, busy day.

Paul spoke very well for a child of just three years and four months. He was a strapping boy, too. He had his own real dagger that he wore proudly at his side. It looked more like a sword on his small body, but he never drew it except in "practice." He and his father had mock battles with wooden swords in which Paul was always the victor.

As Paul grew, I took more interest in his care. I often took him with me when I went riding. He loved the stables, spending as much time there as anywhere else in the lodge, and I encouraged him. He was my boy, my son. I loved him like nothing else in the world. The love I had for Will wasn't the same as the love I knew for the tiny being from my own flesh. Every time I looked at him, I reaffirmed a vow that I would never lose him. The feeling of such love flowing through me often made me giddy.

I hugged him tightly before I set him down to go sit with Sybil for lunch. Then I smiled at Will and gave him a kiss before I sat down.

"AND HOW IS OUR THIEF?" I asked.

"He left us once," said Bran. "I thought for sure he was gone for good. We woke up one morning and he was nowhere to be found, but the next morning, we woke up and he was back. He's quiet. Got past our guard. Anyway, he brought some belongings back with him. He must've had a drop somewhere in town. He's got all kinds of things. Some knives he knows how to use, but mostly money and jewels. He's working out fine. Doesn't talk much, just soaks everything up. He's a quick learner."

"Good. I'll want to talk to him next month, if he's still around. So have him go with Geoffrey, but don't tell him what's on, okay?"

"All right, Kay. I'll see you tomorrow for the supplies then." Bran leapt up the small bank he had so recently descended.

"At Cold Creek Crossing," I said.

"At Cold Creek Crossing," he repeated, then he was gone. I

followed his movements for a few moments, then I heard only the cry of a woodcock.

I wheeled Midnight, heading for the open common and the warmth of the spring sunshine.

THE AIR SHIMMERED, even in the forest. I wiped the sweat from my brow with my forearm and flipped my braided hair over my shoulder. It had to be at least ninety degrees in the shade on this hot June afternoon.

As I rode through the humid forest, I thought how time was running down. We'd had word last month that King Richard had been wounded yet again. Not badly, but it only served to show how reckless he was in battle. The time of the wolf was getting close. It wouldn't be long . . . .

I was riding out to meet Geoffrey and Thomas. This would be the first time I'd see the thief since I left him with Bran's people five months earlier.

The forest was sweltering. I could have been breathing water, the way the air caught in my throat. I thought I could smell a thunderstorm on the way. Rain would be welcome. We had such little rain this season and the crops were barely coming along.

I had brought my bow with me, hoping to get a rabbit for Anne. It was still my trusty compound bow, though I'd had immense trouble trying to fit a new string for it a few years back.

Some wood pigeons flew upward with their shrill cries. I halted Midnight with my knees and drew back my bow.

I shot and brought one down, armed again before Geoffrey jumped out of a tree onto the road. I didn't aim at him. Instead, I aimed at Thomas hiding behind a bush at the foot of a tree. He looked out and saw me, eyes wide at the arrow trained on him. I laughed, relieving the tension on my bowstring.

"Thomas, come out!" I called. "Geoffrey, would you go fetch the bird I shot down. It's over there." I made a vague gesture in the general direction of the fallen bird, wanting to speak to Thomas alone. Geoffrey nodded, and I knew he understood. He was a quiet one, and still waters ran deep.

I dismounted, hanging my bow off my saddle, then wrapped the reins around a bush before walking up to Thomas.

"That was sloppy, scaring up those birds," I told him, pulling a pair of biscuits out of my belt pouch before sitting down on a fallen log.

"I've never had to worry about ground birds before," he said. "At least not ones that fly."

"You'll learn." I offered him one of cook's tasty treats and motioned for him to sit.

He accepted the offering and sat down on one of the fallen logs. "What are you doing here? I was told we were going to do a robbery, but then we see you."

"No one's told you then?"

"Told me what?"

I popped a bite of biscuit into my mouth before answering, making him wait. "It's best I tell you. Getting the story straight from the source, you see. I've told you these men do as I say in some matters, yes?"

"Yes."

"Well, what I say in some matters is as good as coming from Robin Hood."

"Robin Hood? But he's—"

"In France, fighting King Phillip? Yes. But the day is coming when he will return to Sherwood. Bran and his people, and now you, are merely . . . keeping the home fire lit, as it were. When Robin Hood comes back, and he will, you and Bran's people will all become Robin Hood's men." I wasn't sure if that would excite the boy or not, but his reaction showed me he was impressed.

Thomas' eyes sparkled. "Robin Hood . . . . It wasn't so long ago I wanted to join up with him. But by the time I was old enough, he was working for King Richard." The gleam faded from his eyes. He turned, spat, then looked at me. "Robin Hood working for King Richard, and Little John the Sheriff of Nottingham."

I shook my head, chiding his harsh judgment. "Do you know why Robin is in King Richard's service?" I selected another morsel of biscuit.

"Because he isn't the hero I thought he was?"

"No." I smiled in spite of myself. "It's because he is loyal to

Richard, and despite his faults, he loves his king. I don't quite understand Robin's motives myself, but love is one of them. And it was for the love of Robin we took the positions Richard offered us."

"But I don't understand. After all nobility has done to him, he kneels and does their bidding like a hound." Again, Thomas turned and spat into the bushes. "Has he forgotten the wrongs done in the name of royalty?" He made a sweeping gesture, as if to encompass the entire world.

I grabbed hold of Thomas' arm, his biscuit falling to the ground. "No one ever forgets, Thomas. *Ever.* I'm sure the memories burn in Robin's mind, even as they burn in mine. Such a fire could never be put out in so short a time. But Robin is forgiving. That takes more strength than holding any grudge."

"But how could he desert us?" Thomas asked, seizing my hand. I heard the emotion in the boy's throat. I loosened my grip on his arm and took his hand in mine.

"Don't you ever get tired, Thomas? You're young yet, but have you been tired?" Thomas nodded. "Have you ever been so tired, you just want to sit down and cry? Tired in here, in your heart." I put my hand over my heart to emphasize. "So tired, you can't believe in anything anymore?" Thomas shook his head. "I have. I know how Robin must have felt four years ago. He needed a rest. We all did. You can't be a legend all the time, boy." I paused to let that sink in, thinking to myself how true those words were. "But we'll be back, and just as strong as ever. You'll see." I squeezed his hand and he smiled a little.

"Meanwhile, we have people in positions of power who know what it's like to be hungry and poor, who are sympathetic to the common people's needs. Thomas, all of us are doing what we can, while we can."

We were silent for a moment, then Thomas asked, "Do you know when Robin will come back?"

I nodded. "Soon."

Geoffrey came up, dropped the wood pigeon at my feet, and sat down beside us.

"Here's the important thing, Thomas. If you ever see anyone coming through the forest with a Lincoln green band on his left arm, take him to Bran. If he travels with someone who doesn't wear a band, let them go. The green means they are Robin's men. The terms of the arrangement with you people are just that. I help you now, you help us later. Can you agree to that, Thomas?"

"I think so," he said. The glint came back to his eye with a strike of lightning. "Robin Hood is coming back to Sherwood," he said, satisfied with that fact.

Thunder rumbled not too far away.

"That he is," I said. "And you'd best know the art of living out here. Otherwise, he may throw you out on your ear!" I tweaked Thomas' nose, and we laughed as the rain began to fall.

THE NIGHT before riding out to meet my outlaws for our August visit, my mind was in turmoil and I couldn't sleep. I climbed out of bed and went to the window. A breeze blew in, stirring the curtains, bringing with it the smell of earth and grain ready for the harvest.

I sighed, thinking about all the things that had happened since my arrival in this time. Now I was actively taking steps to keep history from coming out the way I knew it. Was that why I had come? Or was that why the door kept returning to take me back? Because I could change things?

A hand caressed my shoulder and I startled, turning to see Will standing there. "There's a storm brewing," he said, shifting around until he sat behind me on the window seat.

"Aye," I whispered. "It will hit in winter when we don't want it to."

Will put his head on my shoulder, his warm breath seeming to soak into me. "I meant outside. The air is alive with static. Can you smell the rain?"

I nodded, leaning into him for support.

"What's wrong?" he asked.

"Just thinking."

"About what?"

"Things," I sighed, reaching up to touch his chin. He grasped my hand and kissed it. "I think about how I came to be in twelfth-century England. It's like everything in my childhood built me up for this life. Kay, the loner. Kay, the one who practiced archery while the others practiced flutes. Kay, the one who dreamed. Kay, the one who lived alone in the mountains . . . . The why is easy. It all comes down to how. How did the door come to be there?"

And why does it keep coming back?

"When the door opened, something inside me knew what it was and pushed me through." I stopped speaking for a moment when I felt Will's arms around me. It felt good. I couldn't understand why I was so lucky to be the one touching Will's life, and having him touch mine.

"You don't want to go back, do you?" Will asked into my silence, lifting his head.

"No. This is my home." Will nestled his head back onto my shoulder. "I don't want to go back."

"You'll never leave me, will you?" His voice was muffled, like a dream slipping away. I reached my arms back and held him tightly.

"We are together now. It would kill me to leave you and Paul," I said with conviction. I would die if the door took me back. I wouldn't want to go on living.

Will planted a kiss on my lips just as the first bolt of lightning jumped out of the sky. I jumped a little myself. I hadn't expected lightning. Will chuckled softly, then got up and walked back to bed.

"Let's try to sleep," he said.

"I'm not tired. I'll go down and get some warm milk." I shuffled out of the room and paused in the doorway. Instead of going down, I turned and went up the hall—up the stairs to the roof.

Just as I stepped out onto the lookout, the first warm drops of rain began to fall. A south wind picked up and thunder roared. I leaned against the ramparts, letting the rain drive into my face. I was drenched in minutes.

The wind whistled in the stone gutters. Every once in a while, it sounded as if it were calling my name. I shivered, but not from the wet or cold. Feeling eyes on me, I turned. Will stood in the doorway, wearing only a light pair of breeches, just as drenched as me. He crossed the rooftop and put his arms around me, holding me closely.

"Will!" I cried over the noise of the storm. "What if our plan doesn't work?" I had sent Much out to start spreading the word about Bran and Lincoln green. Word had been running all summer.

"Don't look for answers like that, Kay. Just go day by day. How can tomorrow matter when we have today?"

"I don't know what's going to happen, Will. I'm scared. I knew before, but I've forgotten. I only know the plan has to work in order to save as many of us as possible." I clung to Will tightly, desperately. "Will Scarlet!" I wailed. "I don't remember who dies!"

"Shhh . . . . Easy, Kay. It's all right. Hush. Listen to me. I've never known who will live and who will die. We'll find out in time—"

"Too soon," I whispered.

". . . and when we find out is the time to be sad. You said yourself. We are together now. Not even time can keep us apart."

I hugged him tightly, not wanting to let go. "You make me strong, Will."

Will gave me a quick squeeze. "Let's go," he said, and gently guided me inside.

THREE DAYS LATER, I was in the practice yard, riding maneuvers with Midnight. Will was in Lincoln on business, and Paul was attending his first classes to begin his education. With nothing better to do, I had gone out to get some exercise.

I rode a simple practice maneuver around obstacles in the yard. It was a demanding skill, requiring a lot of concentration. Just what I needed to distract me from thoughts of the future.

I came around a turn and saw someone, covered in dust from the road, standing in the gate to the yard. I rode a little closer, trying to figure out who it was.

CHAPTER
TWENTY-SIX

"Much!" I rode up to him, dismounting to give him a hug. Midnight nudged him and snorted, either saying hello or berating him for interrupting our practice. "When did you get back?"

"I've just come up from London. I haven't even been home yet."

"How did things go? How many did you find?"

"I found twenty-some myself. They said they would spread the news. I was lucky. I caught Robin at Huntingdon."

"You did? What did he say?"

"He wanted to know whose plan it was. When I told him it was yours, he asked how long we had. I told him I didn't know. Do *you* know how long we have, Kay?"

I evaded his question. "Things are going to start moving fast soon. I just hope we're prepared."

Much stroked Midnight's nose thoughtfully. "It's scary, Kay. I wish I knew what was going to happen."

I grasped his shoulder firmly, as much for my comfort as his. "Me too, Much. Me, too." I took hold of Midnight's reins and we walked toward the stable. "Will won't be back today. Will you stay and sup with me?"

He grinned. "I was hoping you'd ask."

I smiled. "You can wash up, then you must tell me who you spoke to."

Much and I stayed up late into the night. He told me of those men who were known to be dead.

The widow's sons, all three of them, died in France fighting Richard's war. Robert of Lincoln and Richard Donaldson, too. Patrick of the Scots died of old age, as did Geoffrey of Warwick. Jack of Nottingham died of dysentery, John Ainsley was killed in a brawl in Blackpool, Caleb the Welshman was stabbed in the back in a dark alley in London. Seward of Gloucester, Ambrose's brother, died in a hunting accident some said was no accident, though no one was charged with murder. Alfred of Ely had disappeared and everyone assumed he was dead.

"He was always a strange one anyway," was Much's comment.

Twelve had died in the last four and a half years. Who knew how many more would not return when John became king.

It was a sad total. More than we had lost in the forest during the years before the pardon. But I was working for the living. The dead were beyond any need of refuge.

Much also told me about those he knew were alive—those who had accepted the news of my plan and those who had turned a deaf ear.

WILL CAME BACK mid-morning the next day to find Much and I asleep in the conference room, the hall bustling outside our closed door. He woke us and sat with us as we ate breakfast. Brooding over the news Much had told me and my inability to take any action had curbed my appetite. I fidgeted, feeling like I was forgetting something. Something important.

Matthew came in to remind me I was supposed to run an errand before noon. Glad for the distraction, I told him to have my horse saddled and went to clean up while Will and Much talked.

My errand was to deliver some stock chickens to a landholder and his wife. A fox had broken into their coop. Half their chickens had run off, so they were in sore need of more laying hens. I took Paul, just to have him with me for a while. He was big enough to ride his pony, but I settled him in front of me and wrapped my arms around him. He didn't understand why, but seemed to understand my need to have him near me.

When we got back, it was time for lunch. Much ate with us, then left for Nottingham. A cold feeling settled in the pit of my stomach and didn't go away until dinner and five cups of ale were inside me. By then, I was well on my way to being roaring drunk.

THE NEWS SPREAD like wildfire across England. Travelers coming to stay the night in inns told it as they stood in the doorway, scarcely out of their boots. Richard the Lionheart was dead—an arrow in the throat that took two days to kill him. He had declared Prince John heir to the throne of England.

For us, the news came from one of our own people wearing a band of Lincoln green on his left arm. He told us Robin would come home to England as soon as possible, and on his orders, the brotherhood was to follow my plan.

Prince John hadn't made any open move against Robin, but then again, he hadn't been crowned yet. After the coronation, we needed to be on our toes. The man was as bloodthirsty as a leech and as treacherous as a viper. He wouldn't just sit idle and watch us waltz back to Sherwood.

As soon as the man gave us the news, I sent him on to Nottingham with a bowl of hot soup in his belly, then I personally rode into Sherwood to warn Bran.

It was quiet in the forest, as usual in late fall. Then a body slipped out of a tree, spooking my fiery little Kathleen. The deep red thoroughbred had replaced Midnight after the horse had dropped a foal only a fortnight ago. Kathleen reared up and almost threw me. I held on with my knees as I drew my sword. It was a moment before I recognized John.

"Kay!" he said. "What are you doing here?" He caught Kathleen's bridle and tried to soothe her. She rolled her eyes but started to calm when I relaxed. "Is something wrong?"

"Plenty. John, take me to camp. I have to speak to all of you."

John nodded and led the mare off the trail. I dismounted as he tied her to a tree, then followed him through the bare birch and oak.

We soon came upon the camp. The others, going about different tasks, looked up as we came in.

"Kay? What news?" asked Bran, setting down the arrow he was making.

"I do have news." I nodded, glancing around to see they were all there . . . except one. "Where's Thomas?"

"Here, Kay," he said from behind me. "I was in a tree and saw you come in. I thought I'd come and greet you."

"Hello all around," I said and gave him a half-smile. "Okay, listen up. This is it. Richard the Lionheart is dead. Prince John is to be crowned in three weeks' time. The brotherhood is beginning to come to Sherwood. Are you ready to live up to your end of the bargain?"

All but Sydney nodded right away. I could tell his heart just wasn't in it.

"Sydney," I said thoughtfully. "How did you become an outlaw?"

"Taxes. I couldn't pay them and they drove me off my land."

"What shire?"

"Nottinghamshire. Why?"

I smiled. "I happen to be a good friend of the present sheriff. How would you like to have a clean slate so you can marry Anne?"

Sydney blushed. "I'd like that very much, Kay. We're in love."

"As anyone could see, Sydney. True love deserves more than a life in the forest, man." The irony of my words did not escape me. After all, it was all Will had offered me in the beginning. But Anne had many children, while I had been an outlaw, too. "I'll speak to the sheriff before he leaves office." I clapped him on the shoulder.

"Now then, the rest of you . . . . Watch *every* road. Most of us will be coming from the south, but some will come from the north. Watch every day and be extra careful. Things are going to get hot from here on out. I've got to get back. Sydney, I'll let you know."

FOUR DAYS LATER, the few things we were taking into Sherwood were packed away. Will had appointed a fair and capable man,

Mallory Donaldson, as the new squire. He was a well-liked man. The lodge's residents were for his takeover for as long as King John would let him.

Will instructed the people to act as though they were glad John was king and he was gone, saying it was for their own good. Who knew if King John would take vengeance on the people who had lived with one of Robin's outlaws.

Paul, who was only four and a half, was confused but excited. He rode his pony and gave orders to the other children of the lodge. He kept one hand on the hilt of his dagger, as though it were a sword and with it he would protect the entire lodge from the bad king.

I loaded all our belongings onto a pack pony, mostly warm clothing, our best weapons, and food, while Will and Mallory spent the last moments behind closed doors.

I was a bundle of nerves. I paced back and forth, waiting for our departure, wanting to take one last bath to relax, but knowing there wasn't enough time.

I thought about finding Andrea to say a final goodbye to my friend, but I didn't think I could endure another round of mutual tears and meaningless consolations. She had spent double the usual time brushing out my hair, while we laughed and cried over memories of our nearly six-year friendship. By the time she finished braiding the long tresses, we had lapsed into silence. Then she hugged me and fled the room without saying farewell.

We ate at noon, then left, setting off like a family on vacation. I wondered how many others would bring back families.

How many others wouldn't even come? Many of them had told Much their names were so obscure in connection with Robin Hood, they were sure they had been forgotten.

I hoped all would come. The Prince was a man bent on vengeance. There was no way John would forget anyone connected in any way with Robin Hood. I was sure there was a book somewhere with all our names written down—all who had been pardoned —and next to each was written "Outlaw: Robin Hood."

The woods were quiet. Hardly a breath of wind stirred the bare branches of the trees. The horses, which had started out prancing, now shuffled along, snorting clouds of vapor into the chilly air. They were nervous, spooking at the slightest sound. And honestly, so did I. I kept adjusting the green band on my arm.

Paul was sleepy. All the activity of the morning had worn him out. I hoisted him into the saddle with me and he quickly fell asleep in my arms. The pony trotted alongside Kathleen.

We were well into the forest when I heard a noise just before a man slid down a bank beside us to grab Will's horse's reins.

"Well, bless my soul. If it isn't Will Scarlet," said the man, grinning.

"Gilbert!" cried Will, dismounting. They gave each other great bear hugs. "How have you been? Where have you been?"

"I'm well. I was up north, almost to Scotland in a little no-name village, when I got wind of this plan of Kay's. I thought she was cracked." He smiled at me and nodded, then continued. "Life up there was getting dull, so I started back down south. I was just past York when I got the news off a Humber trading ship that Richard was dead. That's when I traded my walking stick for a horse. I got here yesterday. Your man, Sydney, was just leaving and they needed a man for the watch, so I offered to take a post."

"How many have come so far, Gilbert?" I asked as Paul stirred awake.

"A few. When I left this morning, there were five of the old group."

We dismounted, unloaded our belongings, and sent the horses back toward Gamwell, knowing Mallory would find them. We shouldered all our goods and headed in the direction Gilbert Whitehand pointed us to get to the camp.

When we arrived, Little John, Much, Edmond the Jew, Albert, and Stephen of Lancaster were there—all the men who had been living in Nottingham.

Everyone greeted us with hugs. Paul was delighted to see his friends, but I didn't think he knew what was going on yet, or how long we would be staying in the forest.

After things had settled down a bit, I took him aside and tried to explain again.

"Do you remember how long we're going to be staying here, Paul?" I asked him.

"Real long," he said. "Because Prince John is coming to get us. Why, Mama?"

"Because the king is dead, and Prince John will soon be king. He doesn't like us, dear. You do remember what I told you about Prince John, don't you?" Paul nodded. "He would kill us if we stayed at home, so we have left. This is our home now. More men will be coming soon, and we will be a big family."

"And Robin Hood will come, too?" he asked, anxious to see the hero of the stories his mama and papa had told him.

"And Robin Hood, too." I ruffled his hair.

"That's all right then." Paul smiled.

THE WEEKS FOLLOWING our arrival in Sherwood were tense. Little John, our acting leader until Robin's return, decided that only the watchers could go out each day. The rest of us were to stay at camp and prepare. But after the first few days, there wasn't much *to* prepare.

We could hunt, but only when we absolutely had to. We went out in large groups so if there was trouble, we could handle it. So far, the watchers in the trees hadn't seen any soldiers or foresters.

The waiting was awful. We began guessing who would come next as we watched the woods for anyone's approach. Little John didn't want any locals to know we were gathering. It was going to be a surprise for King John that we were already together when he made his move.

Soon, all the brotherhood who had stayed near Sherwood were gathered. It was a while before anyone showed up from farther abroad.

In the first two weeks, Reginald O'Keefe, Christopher of Bristol, Stephen of the Norfolk, Ambrose, Henry of Stafford, Cedric the Smith, and David of Doncaster arrived. Tuck joined us in the forest after some soldiers had casually stopped in at the abbey to chat. It was another full week before anyone else arrived.

The time for the coronation had passed, and though we heard no official news, the watchers began to notice soldiers walking the roads of Sherwood and foresters walking the less-traveled ways.

I woke up from a nap, the crackle of the evening fire telling me it was night. Something warm at my left side shifted position. Paul. He was asleep. Feeling someone holding my right hand, I turned my head. Will. His touch had awakened me.

"Shhh, don't talk," he whispered. "Evan of Chester is here. He just came in. Listen and you will hear why no one else has come."

Evan began to speak. I heard him clearly above the popping of the fire.

"When I got the news about King Richard," he said in a soft voice, "I wasn't sure what to do. I knew the plan and all, but I wasn't sure Prince John wasn't going to keep the pardon. I couldn't decide whether I should go. I mean, I was set up good. I had a tavern in Northampton, lots of customers, plenty of women. I didn't want to leave, not if John had a change of heart. So I waited, willing to chance it and stay put. Not too long after that, Hugh of Lancaster came to me, his wife and two children with him." Evan paused.

"He told me he'd been attacked by bandits in his own home, his baby daughter killed in her crib, most of his belongings taken. He was sure it was Prince John's doing and that we had to go to Sherwood.

"I knew I'd waited long enough. I threw some things into a sack and left my tavern." When he took a sip of ale, I saw his hands shaking.

"But what happened to Hugh?" asked David of Doncaster.

Evan shook his head, setting his cup down before he spilled it. "We all left together, the two of us and his wife and boys. We were trying to be careful, not to attract attention, but once we were out of Northampton, barely out of the shire, we were attacked. They got Hugh's wife first. Chopped her down as she ran screaming after a man who had her boy." Evan hung his head, unable to go on.

"Who were they?" asked Edmond.

"Soldiers," Evan said, then spat over his shoulder. "Oh, they were dressed like beggars or outlaws, but they were soldiers. Filthy, damnable soldiers. Hugh and I tried to fight them, but we were outnumbered. They just kept coming. We'd take one down and another would step into his place. When I saw Hugh go down, I had to run."

When he fell silent, I felt the magic of the Sharing begin. I opened my heart to it, feeling the tears sliding down my cheeks as they hadn't done in years.

The bastards! Killing women and children!

WE HEARD many more such stories as the weeks went on. Evan's was by no means the last, or the worst. As the weather got colder, the stories got worse. Starvation, frostbite, even hypothermia from falling into the river. The dead included Edward the Red, Andrew of Lancaster, Peter of Stavely, Alexander of Grimsby.

The death toll mounted. But so did our numbers!

Oswald Eagle Eye, Eric O'Leary, Richard of Newcastle-under-Lyme, Kenneth of Richmond, Phillip and Walter, the two remaining brothers from Dover, Adam of Lincoln, Gerald of Bristol, Michael of York, Edgar the Shepherd . . . . All of them had returned to Sherwood, including three wives and two with small children. We numbered thirty-eight, excluding the children.

Alan a Dale and Ellen, along with their two children, had relocated to Ireland to escape the hunt, and we heard no further word from them. None of us who had married could blame them for leaving. They had never been part of the brotherhood in the first place, though their names would be on the list of those pardoned by King Richard.

All of us were anxious for Robin's return. The waiting was a tangible thing. Little John worked like a demon to give us things to do. He was always around making sure there were no problems, but the waiting touched us all.

I would find myself in the midst of some chore and would stop to stare off into the woods—always south—straining to catch some sound, some sense of the coming. There was none.

I saw others doing the same thing.

One day, I was seated on the fringe of the clearing, just inside the trees. I was trying to carve a small toy for Paul, a horse, but it wasn't coming out well. I had no talent for carving, though Jenny had tried to teach me. I just needed something to keep myself busy.

I sat perfectly still, my knife arrested in the middle of a stroke. My eyes focused on nothing halfway between myself and the nearest object. The branch of the bare tree had no definition in my eyes.

My thoughts rested on an image of running feet. I could almost see them before me. I strained my imagination, as if I could force my mind to achieve some kind of prescience and figure out whose feet they were and where they were running.

A small hand on my forearm startled me, bringing me back to the present. Paul looked at me, a perplexed knit to his tiny brow. I smiled at him in apology and ruffled his hair.

"You didn't answer when I called you," he said, frowning.

"I'm sorry, darling. I've been thinking."

"You musta been thinking real hard, Mama. Why?"

"Robin hasn't returned yet and we've had no word. I'm worried."

"Is everybody worried, Mama? They're all thinking hard."

"Yes. We're all very worried."

"Then I will worry, too." Paul stared off into the trees.

"Oh, Paul!" I laughed and hugged him. His small arms snaked around my neck.

"Mama, when are we going home?"

I didn't answer him right away. He had asked that question a lot in the last few weeks. He was too young for living in the forest. I thought maybe I should send him to live with Andrea, or Anne. Just the thought broke my heart.

"Mama, look!" Paul said, alarmed.

I turned around and stood in one swift motion, drawing my swords. A strange man stood just three trees away. He made no move as Paul backed up.

"Go get Bran," I told the boy and he ran off, quick as a hare.

TWENTY-SEVEN

W e stared at each other, this stranger and I, the forest oddly still around us.

It was a moment before the man spoke. "Is every stranger greeted so grandly in Sherwood?" he asked. Turned away from me, only the right side of his body was visible.

"If the stranger gives no sign," I said carefully, "he is greeted as an enemy."

"Even though he may be a friend?"

There was something familiar about this man, but I wasn't sure who he was. "A friend would know better."

The man turned slightly and I caught a glimpse of green on his left arm.

"Who are you?" I asked.

He turned toward me, and I did indeed see a band of green about his arm.

"I am the friend who knows the sign. And once I was a tanner who met a fellow on the road in Sherwood—"

"Arthur!" I cried, just as Bran and Peter came up. "Arthur a Bland of Blythe!" He looked older and far more careworn than I remembered. I sheathed my swords and ran to him, giving him a hug. He hugged me in return.

"You're a welcome sight, Kay. Was that your boy? He's the spitting image of Will. Who's this?" He gestured to Bran and Peter.

"New men. These are two of them who made it possible for us all to return to Sherwood."

"If that's so," said Arthur, "then I'm thinking I owe you both thanks." He shook hands with the two of them.

"Come on," said Peter. "Let's go back to the others. Paul will have stirred them all up by now."

"Yes, he will," I agreed. "And you've got a story to tell us, Arthur!"

"Aye, do I."

BEFORE ARTHUR HAD TURNED UP, Paul had found me to call me to dinner. Back at the clearing, we sat down to it, eating what food there was while it was still hot, as Arthur began his story.

"When the Lionheart died, Robin was near him, one of the first to hear the news. He gathered us together—what was left of us fighting in France. I was with him when we left the country. We landed at Dover and started back. Everything was fine, no problems. We traveled openly and by day. King John wasn't crowned yet and hadn't organized the hunt. I think Richard's death was as much a surprise to him as it was to all of us. As the fifteen of us traveled, we began hearing things—little things that made us keep off the beaten track and travel by night.

"One night, our man Henry of Norwich went into a town for supplies and never came back. That dawn, we spotted his body hanging on a tree at the main gate.

"William of Chester and Jonathan of Derby were shot. A lone arrow out of nowhere for each. We had no time to bury them.

"By the time we reached Huntingdon, we were being chased outright by the king's soldiers. On Robin's orders, we split up. We were to get out here on our own, without leading the soldiers to your camp."

"King John's determined this time, isn't he?" asked Much.

"I guess so," someone answered. The rest were silent, each of us enveloped in our own thoughts.

"Why does he hate us?" Much continued. No one answered, thinking it was a rhetorical question. "I'm serious. I want to know. I mean, we've tweaked his nose a few times, but is that justification enough for this brutal hunt? All we've done is be ourselves. Be what the law made us."

"I think that's it, Much. We're ourselves," said Will. "We stand up for everything he tries to knock down. We're opposites. Two sides of . . . of a torch. We are the light, shining into the darkness, straining to be free of the bonds holding us back. The branch that holds the flame is John."

"But the flame could burn out," said Much.

"Aye, or the flame could eat up the branch, destroying it."

"Then the flame would go out for sure."

"There is a price, Much. There's always a price."

WE WERE HELPLESSLY CUT off from the rest of the world in between arrivals of more men. Even then, the brothers who came were none the wiser, having been on the run and unable to stop in any town for updates.

We were desperate for news of the outside world. Robin hadn't returned yet. We needed to know if he was dead or alive. Thomas was selected to go to Nottingham, on his claim that he knew all the ways to get into and out of the city unobserved. He was gone for three nights. Just as we started to fear the worst had happened, he came back, cold and wet in the middle of a sleet storm.

He told us there were a lot of rumors in Nottingham. But most of it concerned us, not King John. Robin Hood was back. He was dead in France. He was a prisoner in King John's tower. There were hundreds of men gathering in the forest. There was no one in the forest. We had all sailed for Ireland or fled into Scotland. What little was said about King John was that he had sworn to hang us all. We could believe that.

Thomas had stayed for two days to make sure he heard everything, then he came back, dodging soldiers and foresters the whole way.

ONE BY ONE, they arrived.

Charles of Watford, Matthew of Chester, Nathan of Ely, Oliver the Smith, Evan the Younger, Fredrick of York, David of York, Eric of Chester. Sometimes two or three came in a day, but never together.

All had found their way through the forest—some traveled the road in disguise, some were hunted and rescued by groups we had in the trees.

When Robin showed up, relief spread like rain in a parched field. Will Stutely came last of all.

Robin Hood was a changed man. The laugh lines at the corners of his eyes were gone. Only wrinkles remained. Streaks of silver ran through his golden beard and in his cropped hair. New scars adorned his hands and face. His aura, his presence was still there, but there was so little kindness left.

Tears filled my eyes when I looked at him. All I saw was sadness. I'd heard Marian had died giving birth to their daughter—stillborn —early on, and it had broken Robin's heart. Those five years had not been kind to Robin Hood.

So many people had died . . . .

When I looked at Robin before, I thought of a warm spring day with growing things and lovers, the kind of blue sky you only see in spring. Bright green trees, gentle breezes playing and tossing leaves, a proud eagle floating gracefully in the arms of the wind. That had been Robin Hood.

Now all I saw was a rain-drenched forest. Majestic with age, slowly soaking up the fall rain as it spattered against the tree trunks, the small creatures getting ready for winter.

I watched him that night, eating cold stirabout by the fire, and a tear slid down my cheek. It was just the middle of October.

ROBIN ORGANIZED US. We were forty-three.

Some of us made new arrows and bows, others went in trading parties for new arrowheads, swords, and knives. Some were sent hunting, still others were set to repairing old weapons and chain mail.

"It looks like we're preparing for a full-scale war," I commented to Robin one day as he passed by my spot just outside the clearing. I was fletching arrows by myself. Paul was off somewhere with Will.

He stopped and turned to look at me. "We are, Kay. It's not like before. We can't go back to the good old days. They're gone. We must fight for our existence now. King John has declared war on us in his own way. And I am answering the challenge in *my* own way. He wants us dead, and he's got the power of the crown behind him now."

"But what about the people?"

"What people?" Robin asked flatly.

I stared at him in disbelief. "The people of Britain. The people we're supposed to help. What about them?" Was he forgetting what made Robin Hood? Without the people, he was just another outlaw.

"I'm not forgetting them. This is survival, Kay."

"Don't you see what you've done, Robin? Don't you see? It's not the people's fight any more. It's yours." I stood. "It's your own private war against King John, a war just for you. You've forgotten what makes you special."

Robin gave me an ice-cold stare. "Are you saying I don't care?"

"Do you? You're going to get all of us killed. Where will the people be then? Where will they be without Robin Hood? No legend. No nothing."

Robin slammed me up against a tree so quickly, I didn't even see it coming. He stood, hands wrapped around my shirt collar, and held me there, on my tiptoes, staring into my face. Breathless, I stared back.

"Robin Hood does not forget the people," he grated out, fire smoldering in his eyes.

"You're doing it right now. You go to fight John this way—" I breathed. He slammed me into the tree again, taking away my breath to continue.

"John has *got* to be dealt with." Robin let me go. I sank to my knees, trying to catch my breath.

"Let the people do it," I whispered, remembering something.

"John has to be dealt with! And I am going to do it. Times have changed, Kay. This is my fight."

"Damn it, Robin!" I looked up at him as I regained my feet.

"Who's going to keep the legend alive? When you die, who's going to help the people?"

Robin said nothing, just turned and walked away from me.

I cursed under my breath. He was leaving the clearing unarmed. I grabbed my bow and quiver and followed, catching up with him at the river.

"Robin," I said, but he didn't look at me. "You're killing yourself, you know. Martyring yourself won't . . . ." I trailed off, seeing a different angle.

"Won't it?" Robin turned around. "Do you see now?"

"I do. You're doing it on purpose! How can King John fight a full-fledged legend, one who died fighting for the people? You're not destroying the legend. You're making sure it goes on."

"Exactly. And do you know how I know it will work?"

I thought for a moment, then my eyes went wide. "Because of me. You know because I came back eight centuries to see you. Because I knew of a legend named Robin Hood." I put a hand up to my mouth. "Oh, Robin . . . ." A tear slipped down my cheek. "What about you?"

AFTER LEAVING Robin alone in the forest with one of my swords, I walked back to camp with a heavy heart. The idea that I could still somehow change his mind consumed me. Between that distraction and being careful to walk quietly, I didn't notice Eric O'Leary and Michael of York until I was almost on top of them. I stopped, half-hidden by bushes.

Eric was talking.

". . . do I care about what happens to him?" Eric said angrily, pacing back and forth. His movement was what had attracted my attention.

Michael shook his head. "I don't know, Eric. He's—"

"I was trying to help him," Eric said, rounding on Michael. "And he threw me off like a hound. There's no reason I shouldn't—" He broke off when he saw me watching him.

He stared back at me until I moved away, still feeling his eyes on me. I wondered who he was talking about. It could have been anyone, but I knew him to be just that—a talker. I went back into my own thoughts as I reached my arrows and got back to the work of fletching them.

ROBIN WASN'T BACK MORE than a week before we started going on raids, scouting for the soldiers who looked for us. We'd learned they were harassing villagers on the edge of the forest, trying to goad us into responding. Robin planned to give them what they wanted, although he had no intention of losing.

I didn't go on most of the raids. Someone had to stay with Paul since the other women with children had been sent on. Robin could not tolerate the small children running about the camp. They were a liability. He had arranged for the women to go to Ireland, and their husbands had gone with them.

He had tried to convince me to go as well, but I refused. Paul was well-behaved and there was no way I was leaving Will. Since there was no way Will would leave Robin, we stayed.

I taught Paul to defend himself. The best defense for him was to be able to run and know the surrounding territory like he knew the lodge at Gamwell. So we played games of hide-and-seek, flying on silent feet through the forest around the camp until he knew the area well. He was deft at hiding so quietly, even I had a tough time finding him. Often, I would have to call for him to come out. It was all a big game to him. I had to impress on him that he mustn't giggle. But at night, when we went to sleep, he would curl up against me on the hard ground and ask when we were going back home.

Maggie, Cedric the Smith's fiery little wife, was the only other woman allowed to stay. Her husband had taught her how to use a knife for things other than chopping vegetables, and she was quite handy at throwing them, even at moving targets. Maggie had no children, though she dearly wanted one, so when I did go out with Will or another group, she took care of Paul.

After the first skirmish with soldiers, in the defense of a village accused of harboring outlaws, three men were wounded. They were men who had settled down in the last five years, men who were out of practice. After the second raid, Christopher of Bristol was taken prisoner and hanged at Nottingham that very day. Two others had been wounded. The well-oiled machine of Robin Hood's outlaws had been left out in the rain and had rusted with disuse.

Little John and I were having a bite to eat together when Robin walked by with Will Stutely. Used to his own command for five years, John now hailed Robin as an equal.

"John," Robin said, stopping to acknowledge him. Will Stutely stood next to him. He had grown even closer to Robin during their years in Richard's army, and he now acted as his personal bodyguard. The two were inseparable. Stutely bristled now, like a hound ready to slip his collar and attack. He and Little John had never gotten along well.

"Robin. Two more men were hurt today." This was news to me. I stood as John did.

"Really?" asked Robin, frowning. "How did this happen?"

"They were following some soldiers and made noise, had to start the fight before they were ready. They barely escaped with their lives!"

"I—" Robin began.

"They *made noise*, Robin! That would have never happened before."

Robin shrugged slightly, more like a shiver than a dismissal. "The men are out of practice."

"Precisely my point. We're moving far too swiftly. We need more time to prepare. We're not silent, not honed. Not like we used to be."

Stutely bristled more, his hand sliding toward the knife on his belt. I watched him, ready to strike if he actually had the gall to draw on Little John.

"They will learn again. In the meantime—"

"In the meantime, we're losing too many men!" John broke in. "We have to slow down. Practice. If we don't, we won't have any sound men left to fight this little war of yours."

"We don't have time. It's too late." Robin shook his head. "We can't stop now. Not now."

"Don't be a fool, Robin! We're losing more men to wounds than we can afford—"

Will Stutely drew, beginning to lunge at John. Springing forward, I grabbed his arm at the wrist and kicked his legs out from beneath him. He landed on his back with a grunt, and I threw myself on top of him, slamming his wrist into the ground repeatedly until he dropped his knife. I grabbed it, my knee on his chest, his own knife keeping him still.

Neither John nor Robin had moved.

"Now, here is one who has not grown soft," said John. "But I see we have been apart too long. *We* have been wounded, as well." Little John looked at me. "Thank you, Kay." He turned and walked away.

I got up and offered my hand to Will, but he didn't take it. He scrambled to his feet and held out his hand, a silent demand for his knife. I returned it to him, hilt first.

He took it and waved the point at me. "Think you could have done that if you hadn't surprised me?" he hissed, his eyes dark with anger.

I smiled sadly, neither baiting nor mocking him. He had once been a likeable man. "Probably not," I answered. "But one surprise is all it takes." I started to follow John.

Robin caught my glance as I turned and I paused, searching his eyes. There was a kind of despair there, a wild look of uncertainty. I reached out and took his hand, knowing he needed reassurance. "We're still yours, Robin." I traced the scars on his thumb, then traced my own. "We're blood."

Then I followed John.

OUR BATTLE WENT on into December. We engaged in short, fierce skirmishes with the king's soldiers, lightning attacks because we could not afford to engage them for long. We fought far away from villages whenever we could, having learned to our horror that when we defended a village, more soldiers came and burned it to the ground, slaying every man, woman, and child.

We killed many, leaving a bloodbath for the surviving soldiers to sort out. We lost some men, but we brought them back for burial near the camp. We didn't want King John to have any idea how many of us there were, or how many had died.

The weather turned colder as the season progressed. We had to abandon any thoughts of returning to the old winter shelter. The thing had collapsed a year before and was not fit for use.

On the second day of December, a brutal storm raged through the forest. All activity ceased as we crowded into makeshift shelters and tried to hold out until the weather broke.

I woke one morning to a stillness so complete as to be disorienting. The storm had passed. I quietly got up, covering Paul so he would not miss my warmth, and went outside the small lean-to we had used to keep out of the weather. The storm had left a downy blanket of snow over the forest, magical in its freshness. It was still snowing heavily, the early morning silence wrapped tightly around the clearing as I moved toward the supply shed to get something to eat.

As I passed Michael of York at the watch fire, I nudged him to make sure he was awake. He fell over, exposing his blood-stained coat. The snow did not melt as it hit his face. He was quite dead.

I ran to the nearest lean-to and woke the sleeper inside. "Oswald, spread the alarm! The watch is dead!" Then I ran to the little cave where Robin slept.

"Robin! Robin! Wake up!" I knelt beside him. "Someone's killed the watch!"

He didn't respond, and for a sick moment I thought he was dead, too. But he stirred and opened a groggy eye.

"Kay," he whispered, and moved his right arm a little. I looked and saw a puncture mark at the wrist, on the blood vessel. The surrounding skin was an angry red, like . . . .

"Poison . . . ," I said. "Oh, Robin."

TWENTY-EIGHT

Little John and Will Stutely both woke at the same instant and were beside me in moments, talking over one another.

"Poison?"

"How?"

"What happened?"

I told them how I had found the man on watch dead, and how I had come to tell Robin and found him like this.

"It had to have been an inside job," said Little John. "No one else could have gotten close enough to a guard to kill him without making a sound."

Stutely glared at me, but Robin cut him off from making an accusation. "Not Kay," he groaned. "Eric . . . ." Then he passed out.

"Which Eric?" I asked. There were three. Eric of Chester, Eric O'Leary, or Bran's man Eric.

My question was answered as Much ran in. "Eric O'Leary is run off. Cedric the Smith saw him, but he didn't think anything of it. What's wrong with Robin?!" he asked, catching sight of Robin's supine form.

"Poison," said Will Stutely, venom in his voice.

"Where are we going to go for help?" asked John, at a complete loss.

No one answered. We all just looked at Robin.

"Kirklees Priory," I said at last, biting my lip in misery as all doors but one closed on Robin's fate. "They'll know what to do."

I had thought it all out, thought I could change the future and save Robin's life. I should have known it wouldn't work. I was living proof that it couldn't work.

"Aye," agreed Much. "I think he's got a cousin or something who's taken vows there."

"But that's in Yorkshire, almost twenty leagues from here!" exclaimed John.

"We can't take him anywhere closer. Soldiers will find him. If this was planned, they'll be watching. It has to be Kirklees." Much backing up my statement was a bitter affirmation of what I remembered about Robin's final days.

"I'll meet you there," growled Stutely. He ran out of the cave, stopping only to grab his knives and sword. I could guess where he was going and almost felt sorry for Eric O'Leary when Will caught up with him. Almost.

"Let's pray we can get him there in time," said John, covering Robin with his blanket. "Kay, can you get a cart and horse?"

"Aye."

"Get it and bring it to the Lincoln-York crossroads. We'll meet you there."

I went out of the cave and thought for a moment. Then I woke Will and Paul. I told Will what had happened and what I was doing as I pulled a warm coat and cloak over Paul's sleepy form. He would help with the disguise I had planned.

We arrived at Anne's without incident a little before noon.

"Come inside. Quickly!" said Sydney, ushering me into the house and looking outside to see if I was followed before shutting the door. "It's not safe for you to be here."

"I know," I said, setting Paul next to the fire and opening his coat to the warmth.

"What's happened? Has Will been . . . ?" asked Anne, fear showing in her wide eyes.

"Will's fine. It's Robin. I need a cart and a mule. The rattier the better." I opened my cloak to the warmth. It had been quite a trek through the snow. I had to carry Paul most of the way, and it was near freezing with the little wind that had picked up.

"Robin?" asked Sydney.

"He's been poisoned. We have to take him to Kirklees Priory."

"Can't you bring him here?" asked Anne, reappearing with the baby, William, in her arms. The child had been a big reason Sydney wanted to marry Anne.

"Like Sydney said, it's too dangerous. The soldiers would find him here. They know you and I are friends. This was an inside job, but I'm sure the king had something to do with it. I can't put you at any more risk than you already are just by my being here."

Sydney looked out the window, trying to see if anything was going on outside. "You can have the cart and the old mule. We were going to chop him up this spring anyway. Nothing's moving out there. You'd best leave while it's still quiet." He went out to see to the cart.

"Anne, I'll need some cloaks, some bundles of cloth, and some burlap bags. And furs, if you have any. We'll need to cover him to hide him from soldiers and keep him warm." I began to pull a skirt I had brought along over my trousers. "I hate to put you out, but I'll make it up to you."

"Don't fret. Everything I have is yours, Kay." Anne set about gathering the things I had requested. I wrapped my head in a scarf and looked at Paul huddled by the fire. I could see he was afraid, but there wasn't time to comfort him.

Sydney came in to say everything was ready. I bundled up Paul again while Sydney loaded the cart. I climbed into the driver's seat and Anne handed Paul up to me.

"Would you like me to go, too?" Sydney asked, putting a hand on my knee.

"Honestly, yes, I would. But you stay here. Anne and little William need you more than I."

"Well then, take care," he said and slapped the old mule on the rump. The rickety cart lurched forward. I drove down the Lincoln road, looking back once just before we were out of sight.

We saw no one until we reached the crossroads. Then Little John came out from behind a row of bushes, waved to me, and disappeared again. He and my Will came back out, bearing Robin.

They loaded him onto the cart, covering him with the bundles of cloth and burlap sacks. I started the mule moving again as Little

John sat on the back of the cart and Will, tense and worried, joined me on the driving bench. He took the reins from me after giving me a quick hug and kiss.

I had explained to Paul what was happening, that he had to be ready to run if I told him to. He watched his father, curious and still a little frightened, but schooled well enough to know not to break the intense silence.

We rode in that silence, no words spoken between any of us. Robin slept. The poison was a slow one—agonizingly slow. The cart rattled along all night, and the only being we passed was a trader on his way to Nottingham.

The next morning, we passed a small group of soldiers patrolling the road. We played it as well as we could, making sure Robin was completely covered up. Unfortunately, Little John gave us away. His frame could hardly be mistaken by anyone who had spent any of the last five years near Nottingham.

Fortunately, it was a small company of seven who were surprised to see us riding in the open. Will had brought my bow. I shot two of them before their cry of recognition died in the frigid air. The others were dispatched with an economy of blows by Will and John. The last one, who had turned to ride back with the news, I shot in the back. He fell to the ground, landing on his back with his face upturned—an accusation as we passed. Little John rounded up the horses and tied them to a tree so their presence, minus riders, would not arouse suspicion from anyone until, hopefully, it was too late.

We rode on, leaving the massacre in the snow to puzzle whomever came along.

Late that evening, we reached Kirklees Priory. Little John beat on the timbers, calling for the doorkeeper to let us in. An elderly nun opened the door, shushing us. It was time for the evening prayers.

Will calmly explained that if she did not fetch the healer and let us in, he would burn the place down around the woman's ears. She blustered at the threat, but when she saw Little John lifting Robin out of the cart, she let us in, leading John and Will to a room where they set Robin down. When their healer came in, the woman shooed us out, reaching for her jar of leeches.

After a while, another person pounded on the door. Moments later, Will Stutely walked in, coming to keep vigil beside us outside Robin's door. When the healer left, the men went into the room and locked the door. My husband told me to go with the nuns and get some food for Paul and myself.

I wasn't hungry, but I went for my son's sake.

After eating, I tucked Paul into one of the guest beds. Once he was asleep, I went and sat outside Robin's door, keeping my own solitary vigil for the night and most of the next day. The healer came and went several times and I heard voices, but I couldn't understand what was being said. Perhaps I didn't want to.

As the sun went down on the second day, I heard sobbing from inside the room. Paul was sitting in my lap when the door burst open and Will Stutely came storming out and down the stairs, his tear-stained face twisted in anguish. I heard him as he ran out into the garden courtyard, then out the gates to the forest.

Little John came out next and began to descend the stairs. He seemed to collapse in upon himself, dropping onto the third step down, crying.

Will came out last. I went to him and held him as he cried onto my shoulder. Paul, who knew enough by now to know what was happening, hugged our legs, sharing our grief in his own small way.

"He's dead?" I asked, my voice tight. I looked past Will into the room, seeing the still form on the bed. A bow lay on the bed beside him, a quiver of arrows spilled out onto the floor. Tears filled my eyes and tracked down my cheeks. The man on the bed was so pale, so lifeless . . . . So unlike Robin.

John was speaking. It took me a moment to hear him. ". . . to bury him where the arrow falls. He'll face the rising sun, and his resting place should be kept green, like the forest he loved so much. He asked only that his weary bones not be disturbed."

We cried, but there seemed to be no easing the pain of this death. Such a man!

It didn't feel like we had attended the birth of a legend.

We were still crying when Will Stutely came back.

"I found it," he said, his voice soft. He choked on a sob. "It didn't go far."

THE NEXT DAY, we buried Robin Hood. The arrow had landed in a small meadow not far from the abbey. We laid him six feet under, his head turned to the east, and marked his grave with a stone.

The night before, Little John had carved these words:

> *Here underneath this little stone*
> *lies Robert, Earl of Huntingdon*
> *Never an archer as he so good*
> *And people called him Robin Hood*
> *Such people as he and his men*
> *will England never see again*
> *Died December 5, 1199*

LOOKING BACK ON THE LEGENDS, it is said that after Robin Hood died, King John left his men alone. I know this to be untrue.

John hounded us all through the winter, and we were constantly on the move. We functioned at night and hid from soldiers during the day.

We spread the news that Robin was dead, killed by treachery and the king's decree. The killing of their hero outraged the common people. It started a fire that eventually burned King John out.

The people resisted the high taxes, protesting to barons who increasingly listened to their problems. The barons began rebelling against King John's demand for overseas service to continue the war with King Phillip, who continued attacking King John, as well. They tired of his ways of insuring personal loyalties by intimidation. Tired of increased taxes, which the lower class could not pay.

At Runnymede on June 15, 1215, sixteen years after the death of Robin Hood, King John signed the Magna Carta under duress. The charter gave the English people civil and political liberties never before known in England and started the long road to a democratic society.

But for all of us, King John was a powerful figure. He commanded legions of soldiers to put against us. With Robin dead, it was easier for him. The fight went right out of the brotherhood, as if Sherwood itself had given up.

Will, Paul, and I continued to live in the forest, struggling to keep the shreds of the brotherhood together. It wasn't easy.

Will Stutely left us at Kirklees and didn't come back to Sherwood. We never heard what became of him. Little John left, too. Perhaps going back to his sheep in Chestershire, perhaps up north to Scotland. Much went with him, but not without pleading for me to leave Will and come with him. It broke my heart to tell him no, even though he claimed he knew I'd turn him down. The loss of my dear friend saddened me.

The brotherhood seemed to dissolve slowly into the forest. We never knew if they were killed by soldiers or if they just left. Each day, there were more and more gone. Soon, only Bran and his people remained.

Eight men, a woman, and a child left to keep the legend alive, but there didn't seem to be much point in doing that anymore. We couldn't rob anyone. There were too many soldiers about, and everyone knew Robin was dead. It was hard to stay alive, harder still to find a reason to continue in the forest.

The outside world became a thing of the past for us. We didn't dare contact anyone who was a friend or lived close to a city. Any news we got was weeks, sometimes months old. And that news was indifferent enough.

Eric O'Leary had been made a hero by King John, martyred in service of his king and country. However, the common folk viewed him as the traitor he was and were glad he was dead. It was a hard lump to swallow that I hadn't figured out Eric O'Leary's role in the legends. All the signs had been there, even to the point of hearing him talking about it. I just hadn't put the pieces together. If I had only figured it out, I could have saved Robin's life . . . .

So much for my gift of future knowledge.

King John's wolf hunt across England didn't make him any more popular. He looked for any and all outlaws to justify his actions to the people, but he couldn't disguise the fact it was Sherwood's outlaws who were hunted the hardest. We were often just one step ahead of the hunters.

It was worse when they used the hounds. We got very good at silencing them before they got too close. A lone arrow for each hound, and soon, they either decided they couldn't afford the cost of the hunt—a good hound was worth more than four soldiers—or the breeders stopped supplying them with the animals.

Paul grew into his seventh year in the forest, hardened by the constant running, grown up too quickly in a hostile world. He was tough and would make a fine man . . . if he lived that long.

FINALLY, there was an end. For three years, we had been hunted, though there were fewer encounters each month. There came a day when we had seen no soldiers for an entire month. We finally felt we could move about with more freedom, felt that the nightmare was over.

Paul, Will, and I went hunting one day. Paul was just old enough to pull his first real bow well enough to make the fatal blow. We congratulated him on a fine kill, and he glowed with the pride of a young hunter.

While we prepared it for the trip back to the camp, Will stopped in the middle of showing Paul the knack of gutting the deer. I noticed his attentive stance when he looked up, so I looked, too.

We were too close to the road. Just as I reached for my pack, twelve soldiers stepped out, surrounding us with crossbows leveled.

"So poaching is a family affair now?" said one.

"But we have more than poachers," another said, grinning. He was an officer, and I thought he looked familiar. "The man there is Will Scarlet, one of the late Robin Hood's men."

"Ho! Ho!" crowed the first. "What a catch! I didn't think there were any cowardly outlaws left around here. King John will be pleased to see his head hanging on his gates with the others."

"Aye," said the officer. "And a handsome reward for us, no doubt. As for the other two, the woman is fair—"

"Paul, no!"

Paul let the arrow fly, ignoring Will's call. Along with the soldiers, I hadn't been watching my son. The arrow caught the officer in the throat and the man fell, choking on his own blood.

I dove on my bow and rolled, coming up to shoot. Two men fell to my arrows before Will and I had to draw our swords.

"Run, Paul!" I screamed. I caught a glimpse of him running at a soldier, his dagger up and ready to strike. The soldier's sword—

"*No!*"

Paul fell, disappearing from view. I didn't feel the crossbow bolt ripping into my left shoulder.

They killed my son!

I fought like I never had before. A red haze blurred my vision, but I hacked and swung at anything that moved.

Someone came up behind me and carved a strip out of my left shoulder as I turned to engage him. I let out an incredible scream of pain as the stroke cut the bolt sticking out of my skin in half.

"Kay! Get out of here, Kay!"

I dimly realized I was being overpowered, was losing the fight. Somehow, I fought off my attackers enough to run.

A few yards away, I turned around and saw Will surrounded by four soldiers. He was going down.

"*Will!!*" I screamed before primal instinct took over and I had to run.

I was just in front of my pursuers, but I knew the territory better and they were weighted down with armor. I ran as fast as I could, carrying my pack, along with my bow and quiver, at my side, my swords in my other hand. I could hear the men coming clumsily after me.

I might have lost them, but I'll never know. Running in a wide circle, I made my way back to the clearing where I had left Will and Paul. I thought I heard Paul's voice raised in fright, calling for me, and I ran faster.

Realizing I was too close to the road, I turned sharply to avoid running out onto it. Like a nightmare of *déjà vu*, I caught a glimpse of a tree with an old scar on it just before a flash of light hit me right between the eyes. I fell flat on my face, dropping everything.

I sat up, disoriented. It was just before dawn and everything smelled wrong—different. It smelled like . . . fall. I rubbed at my eyes. The trees . . . . They were firs. No more birch or alders. No more oak. I turned.

"No!" I howled as the door closed on Sherwood. I scrambled forward on my hands and knees, but it was too late. It was gone . . . closed forever.

I climbed to my feet and kept going, right through the spot where the door had been. I didn't care where I was going. I couldn't stop moving or I would fall down and never get up. I didn't want to live—Paul and Will were dead—but I didn't really want to die, either. So I walked.

A shout made me realize there was someone nearby. "Are you crazy or something?"

I turned toward the voice. The man had a strange accent.

"Are you crazy?" he shouted again. I whimpered, realizing his accent was American. "Running around in deerskin during hunting season? I almost shot you! Oh, hell!" The last was a yell of shock as I stumbled. "Larry, get over here. Somebody's hurt."

CHAPTER
TWENTY-NINE

I woke up on a hospital gurney, staring at the walls racing by, hearing running feet. Though my head reeled savagely, one thought broke clear of the chaos in my mind. I was back in the world I thought I'd left behind.

Tears welled in my eyes, spilling down my face to leave a pool of wetness on the pillow.

"She's awake!" one of the paramedics said, noticing my tears.

God, I didn't want to be wherever I was. I wanted to be home in Sherwood, to die with my family, my friends—the people I had loved for the thirteen years I had spent there.

I didn't feel my wounds. I wanted to go home. I couldn't remember this world. I didn't want to remember that my family was dead . . . .

The cart rolled into a curtained-off space in a large room and a man's face appeared before me. "Miss, I don't know if you know where you are or what's happened to you . . . ." I nodded, but he ignored me. "You've been in an accident up in the mountains. You were attacked by a wild animal and you've been unconscious—" He paused, wondering at my silent laughter.

He went on, but I paid no attention to him. He was an idiot. An animal, indeed. A stab of pain reminded me of my wounds.

"We'll have you under a stronger pain killer in a moment," the man concluded.

Pain killer? Like a catalyst, the word triggered the flood of memories. I tried to shut them away again, as if denying them would make them null. I didn't want them, but the tide caught me. Overcome, I remembered my buried past.

Noises and sight faded, then I was aware as someone put a mask over my mouth and told me to breathe deeply. My head lolled uncontrollably, but I was still conscious of things going on around me.

The rustle of bedclothes reached my ears. "Jesus!" the doctor gasped. "I thought you said this was an animal attack."

"Shhh . . . . She can hear you," the voice cautioned.

"What a mess!" the doctor continued, his voice braying in my ears. "No animal did this. That's from a knife of some kind, or . . . or a sword. And that . . . . Lord, have mercy. That's part of an arrow sticking out of that mess there. Where in the hell has she been?"

The world went dark and the doctor's voice faded away.

It wasn't hell, I tried to tell them as I slid into oblivion. *I want to go back.*

MORNING SUNLIGHT STREAMED into the dark room as the nurse pulled back the heavy curtains. I hadn't been aware I was awake until I heard her enter.

"Oh, you're back with us!" she said cheerfully, then walked out into the hall. She returned with a tray she set up on my bed table. There was oatmeal, orange juice, and a cup full of pills. "It's breakfast time! I'm going to feed you. You're not to move your shoulder."

"I'm not hungry." I turned away.

"Come now. How can you get well and go home to Paul and Will if you don't eat?"

I stared at her, eyes wide. "What did you say?"

"I said, how can you get well and go home to Paul and Will if—"

"They're dead!" I snapped before I could stop myself. I fought back the tears, the pain at saying those awful words. "I saw Paul go down. I'm afraid Will's dead, too. I ran away. He needed me, and I ran away." I closed my eyes and momentarily gave in to the grief that failure brought. "How did you know about them?" I opened my eyes to look at the startled nurse.

"The night nurse said you were asking for them. Naturally, I assumed—"

"Paul was my son, and Will was my husband." She looked so distraught at her mistake, I took some pity on her. "I'll eat it myself," I said, reaching for the spoon.

"Oh, you mustn't. The doctor said I should feed you."

"My left shoulder was wounded, not my right. I'll manage," I said shortly and shoveled the spoon into the food.

She yielded. "All right, but I'll stay here and make sure you don't need anything. Someone will be in to check your vitals when you're done."

"Fine," I said around a mouthful of oatmeal. I didn't feel hungry, but my body knew better. I hardly tasted the food, which was probably for the best.

When I finished, another nurse arrived and took my pulse and blood pressure, made notes, then fiddled with the machines beside my bed. When she handed me the cup of pills, I dutifully took them all, hoping something in there would knock me out until kingdom come.

"Go away," I said after I finished the orange juice.

"I'm supposed to check your bandage," the nurse said, reaching for my covers.

"Come back when I'm out again. I want to be alone!" I threw the spoon across the room, wincing at the pull in my shoulder. It bounced out the door and between the legs of the man standing in the doorway.

"It's all right, Kelly," said the doctor. "I'll see to her bandages. Will you excuse us, please?"

"Yes, Dr. Simpson." She picked up my breakfast tray and left, a relieved look on her face. I heard the tray clatter on the cart outside the door.

The doctor sat down in the chair beside the bed.

I blinked. In a flash, I saw Will coming to sit on the edge of my bed, leaning down to kiss me. I gasped and looked with dazed eyes at the place where Will should be.

"Young lady," the doctor said, as though beginning a lengthy conversation.

It was then I realized I *was* young, that hardly any time had passed while I was away. I was the same me, except for my memories—sweet memories—and my scars. I wondered if I had grown older at all in Sherwood.

"You present a mystery to many people," the doctor went on. "What were you doing up in the mountains all alone?"

I turned away from him. "Why should I answer your questions now? I've just had surgery."

"My dear, that was three days ago."

Three days? I mouthed the words, then looked at him. "But I just woke up."

"We kept you sedated. The police have some questions. They say you resemble a young woman who lived in the mountains and disappeared about six months ago."

Six months, I thought. *Six months to live a lifetime.*

"They want to know who you are. If I don't get you to talk, they will come to discuss this with you."

"And I'm not supposed to want that, right?"

"I would be kinder than they would, I think. The Sweet Home Police aren't known for their . . . tact."

Sweet Home. I wasn't in one of the larger hospitals down in the Willamette Valley, then. I considered that a blessing—even if the police had a reputation for being closed-minded. My uncle's cabin wasn't out of reach from the tiny country town nestled in the foothills of the Cascades.

"All right. If you must know, I live up in the mountains by myself. I may be the woman they thought had disappeared—I haven't been down in a long time. It's my uncle's cabin. If he reported me gone, I must have been on an outing and missed him."

"I see," the doctor said. He motioned toward my shoulder. "How did you get those wounds?"

I was silent for a moment.

"They're pretty nasty," he continued. "Who did it to you?"

"I've had worse," I said coolly, ignoring his question. I sucked in a deep breath, glad when I realized the pain meds were starting to kick in.

"Oh really?" He cocked his eyebrow, clearly not believing me.

I pulled back the sheets and showed him where a crossbow bolt had lodged into my right side. The long line from the makeshift surgery Much and Hugh had performed accompanied that scar, the edges jagged from the stitching, the scar still raised and puffy.

The doctor leaned forward to get a closer look.

"That wound is eleven years old. Do you know what caused it?" I asked.

"It looks like someone . . . ." His voice trailed off as he stared at me.

"Stitched me up?" I finished for him. "Someone who has no college degree or practice as an intern? My friend did that. He saved my life. The wound had been infected."

"With what? Gangrene?" The doctor seemed truly interested.

"Part of my shirt got stuck in the wound." I pulled the sheets over me again.

"Really?" Again, the cocked eyebrow.

"You don't believe me? Why don't you go out and get shot with a crossbow bolt, have your neighbor stitch it up for you, and see what it looks like."

"Did your friend hunt with a crossbow?"

I laughed scornfully. "Only soldiers use crossbows. My friends and I only use . . . used longbows."

"So who gave you that wound?" Simpson asked, indicating my shoulder and sitting back in the chair.

"Soldiers."

"In the Cascades?"

"No," I sighed. "Sherwood . . . . England. They caught us poaching and tried to kill us. They—" I stopped, realizing what I had said. The man had gotten me to talk. I wondered if he was a psychiatrist.

"I thought you had a peculiar accent. How did you get from Sherwood to the Cascades?"

"Skip it. You wouldn't believe me," I muttered, looking away from him.

"All right," Out of the corner of my eye, I saw him writing something on my chart. Still writing, he asked me another question. "Who is Paul?"

"My son." My vision blurred as my eyes filled with tears. "My beautiful seven-year-old son." I turned my head to find the doctor staring at me.

"You have a seven-year-old son?"

"Had. I think they killed him."

"Who?"

"The soldiers."

"I see."

I could see he was beginning to think I was a nutcase.

"And Will . . . . Was he killed by the soldiers, too?"

"I don't know. He told me to run and I did. I almost didn't get away. Then the door appeared . . . ." I didn't care what I said anymore. I closed my eyes, trying not to cry. Not in front of this doctor.

"Will was your husband?"

"Yes."

"How long were you married?"

"Eight years," I said, eyes still closed.

"And you were in England, right?" Without thinking, I nodded. "Who was king?" I didn't even think it was a strange question.

"Richard, then John the Second," I said, then bit my lip as I focused back on the doctor.

"I see." He didn't bother to write any more on my chart.

"I'm sure you do. Do I have to answer any more questions, Doctor?"

"No. I think I've heard all I need to know." He got up to leave.

"Doc." He stopped in the doorway to look at me. "I'm not crazy."

He gave me a small smile. "Of course not." I expected condescension, but instead his smile seemed to suggest a kind of *knowing*. He closed the door behind him before I could ask if he'd heard a similar story before.

AFTER TWO WEEKS, I was sick of questions and everybody treating me like I was insane. Doctor Simpson never came back, though when the police didn't ask about soldiers I realized he hadn't shared the details I'd let slip. I stopped trying to explain. I just kept telling them I wanted to go back, but they didn't understand. "Back where?" they always asked. I couldn't answer because I didn't even know how to get there.

I couldn't stay any longer. One night, I broke the lock on the cabinet in my room, grabbed my clothes and knives, and slipped out. It wasn't hard to get out of the small country hospital. Then I hitched a ride on the main road.

The guy who picked me up asked if I had heard about the crazy girl they had found in the woods. He said the cops figured she'd escaped from some psycho rapist up in the mountains, but she'd gone insane trying to get back home. He told me they figured they'd never know what really happened because she was a real nut.

He dropped me off at the tiny gas station at Mountain House and I walked into the forest from the road, making my way the six miles up to my old cabin. The pine forest seemed alien, unfriendly. I missed the English breeze in the oaks.

Inside the cabin, I lit a lamp. I could tell Uncle James had been there since I'd been gone. The place was a mess. I rooted around in the pantry and found a can of pork and beans to heat on the gas stove. After eating, I curled up on the small bed and fell asleep. I dreamed myself into Will's arms, listening to Paul's boyish laughter.

IN THE MORNING, I hiked into the forest.

I had to try to get back to Sherwood. It was still so real, the anguish so poignant, I had to shut the memories inside or I would give up. I couldn't give up on my family, my home.

I would find my gear and find a way back.

Wandering around in the woods, I managed to cover a lot of territory. I had no idea where I'd been found, so it was slow going. I wasn't fully recovered from my injuries, and I had to stop often to rest.

Once, I startled a herd of deer. As they bounded into the woods, I longed for my bow to bring one down. My fingers twitched, but I sighed as they disappeared.

It was well after noon before I found my open pack, its contents scattered. Some raccoon had probably investigated it. The food was gone, but I found everything else. I collected it all and bundled it into the pack, strapped on my swords and quiver, and picked up my bow.

The memories came flooding back when I felt the familiar curve of the weapon in my hand. Dropping to my knees, I wept for everything that had been taken from me by a casual flick of the fickle universe's wrist.

I didn't know how long I stayed there, but when I finally climbed to my feet, my knees protested audibly. I could do nothing but look for the way back, and I had a good idea where to start. Determined not to waste any more time feeling sorry for myself, I headed up to the bald knoll where my adventure had started.

It was nearly dark when I reached my destination. Exhausted from all the energy, emotional and physical, I had expended that day, I collapsed to the ground near the old stump. As the stars came out one by one, I pulled my blanket out of my pack. Lying there under the stars, I could almost believe I was still in Sherwood. Almost. The constellations were in the wrong place in the heavens.

I finally fell into a fitful sleep, my pack close at hand. If the door should return, I was ready to leap through it.

Morning came, and a small wind picked up. I huddled under my blanket, only moving away long enough to find some late blackberries to eat. I waited, a thrill of anticipation coming and going as the slow minutes passed.

It will come back. The door will be there. It has to be.

Clouds began to blow in sometime after noon, a mighty storm working up. I rocked beneath my blanket, humming the lullaby Will used to sing to Paul, while the wind whipped my hair and cold drops of rain stung my cheeks.

"It'll come. It'll come." My litany wasn't working. When lightning struck the neighboring hilltop, I leapt to my feet and screamed out in frustration.

Lightning struck again, on my knoll this time, raising my hair up straight off my scalp and sending a tingling sensation up my legs. I grabbed my pack and ran down the slope, cursing the whole way. Once below the tree line, I turned and shook my fist at the sky.

I screamed in wordless rage, then slumped to the ground, tears slipping down my cheeks. "I can't get back to you!" I wailed. I covered my eyes, felt hot tears filling my hands. I had thought to somehow go back to the moments before the ambush, stop them from killing Paul and Will. I thought I could save them. The torture of knowing I couldn't was more than I could bear.

I felt so alone in this world where I was born and raised. A world I'd rather have forgotten.

"Kay." I looked up, startled. No one was there. *"Kay, my love. No matter what happens, I love you, and love has no ending."*

I remembered Will saying that. I remembered holding him and saying, *"We'll always have dreams, if nothing else."* I mouthed the words from my memory. It had been our last night in Gamwell.

Now dreams were all I had.

I had watched them butcher so many of the people I loved. Paul and Will, Mark, Frederick, Christopher . . . . The list went on. I remembered them all. I still carried Robin's arrow—the one that marked his gravesite. I had taken it when the others couldn't.

I had taken nothing with me to Sherwood. Coming back, I had only the arrow, memories, sadness, and wounds. Memory made me a little richer. The sadness would stay for a long time. My physical wounds would fade into thin white scars, but my soul would still bleed.

I conjured a vision of Will wrestling with Paul. That playful game taught our son how to survive.

Suddenly, my memory altered and Will stood, taking Paul's hand. They looked straight at me.

"Never forget us, Mama," Paul said in his sweet voice.

"Yes, Kay. Never forget. Your world is for you now, and you must go on. Life is now, and now is the only thing that matters. Remember us. We will be waiting for you."

"I love you, Mama." Paul blew me a kiss before the vision vanished.

My heart nearly jumped out of my throat. They had never said anything like that to me. It was no memory. This message had crossed time's barrier to reach me.

I knew Will was right.

Life was now, and now was the only thing that mattered.

Slowly, I turned and walked through the wind and rain to the cabin.

I lit a lantern against the gathering darkness and set it on the old wooden desk, one of the few items of furniture in the cabin. Numb, I stripped off my drenched clothes and slipped on one of my old wool shirts. I sat down on the bed, my mind refusing to function.

"Life is now," I murmured at last. I felt the truth of that statement in my heart. But I had to put this behind me somehow. I couldn't just walk away with only a memory that would fade with time.

I picked up a pen from the desk and pulled a sheet of paper in front of me.

Hiking high up on my mountain, I wrote, *the melting snow slushed beneath my feet and the sky arced like a dome of crystal blue above my head. I stopped often to inhale deeply, savoring the crisp air of the brisk day.*

Spring had erupted in full glory, and it was a perfect day to be outside.

EPILOGUE

William looked up guiltily as the door of the cabin opened. He hadn't meant to stay so long. The drenched figure in the doorway wasn't who he'd expected. He stood quickly.

"Do you live here?" he asked. "I . . . I didn't mean to—"

Steel-gray eyes flickered to the desk where the manuscript lay, the last page exposed. Rage like fire lashed from her eyes, and William took an unconscious step back.

"I'm sorry. We got caught in the storm and came in to get out of the—" He took another step back as a knife materialized in the woman's hand.

"You've got no right." The woman's voice was low with rage, her British accent as thick as his own. He hadn't heard the like since he'd awakened. When she stepped forward, William backed up, his heel striking the wall. He held his hands up, palms out.

"It was there. The story . . . . It seemed familiar somehow. I just . . . . I had to read it. I'm sorry . . . ." His voice trailed off as he caught her expression. She had frozen while he spoke. His mind raced back, remembering the word that had stopped her.

Familiar.

So was she, in fact. Without seeing it, he knew her hair would fall the length of her back. He could almost feel the silky tresses running through his hands like water. He felt as though he knew every curve of her slight body. And those eyes . . . . He had once gazed into those eyes.

"Kay?" The name slipped comfortably from his lips. It made him wonder—not for the first time—what had happened in the time before the accident. Before he'd woken in a strange, sterile room having no memories of anything other than a blinding white light and pain. The doctors told him he'd been in a car accident, was found wandering along a mountain road carrying his son. Clothes and skin had been shredded with multiple wounds, the scars of which he still bore on his face and body.

"Who are you?" she whispered.

"I—"

Before he could continue, the woman swiftly sidestepped to the wall by the door. Her sudden motion startled William.

"Father!" The boy shot through the door without seeing her. "I saw deer. A whole herd of 'em."

William knelt and grabbed the boy's hand, pulling him against his chest. "Paul!" he said, instinctively putting his body between the woman and the boy. He looked up when her knife clattered to the wooden floor.

She stared at his son, eyes wide, her hands over her mouth. Surprised, William watched her drop to her knees.

"Oh god." Her words were strangled. She held her arms out wide, as though to encircle the whole room. "Paul?"

Paul never hesitated. He ran into her arms. They clung tightly to each other for a few moments before the woman looked up at William.

"Can you be true?" she asked, gently setting Paul back from her. "Both of you?" For a moment, William thought he saw unshed tears shining in her wondering eyes. Once again, he was caught by the familiarity of those eyes, blue now that her anger was gone.

Paul stood still, studying her with uncanny perception for an eight-year-old.

"I'm William Wilson." He took three long strides forward and put his hands on his son's shoulders. "This is my son, Paul. We got caught in the storm."

"So you said." The woman stood, her movements graceful and sure, like a cat. "I'm Kay."

"I know you." Paul took her hand and she looked down at him. "You've been in my dreams ever since I woke up after the accident."

"Accident?"

"Six months ago. Neither of us remembered anything from before."

She stared at Paul a few moments more, then moved swiftly around them to the desk. Will followed her with his gaze. She stood with her back to him, looking down at the final page of the manuscript. "Has it only been six months?" she murmured. Her shoulders began shaking ever so slightly.

"I know you too, don't I?" William asked, coming to stand beside her. That sense of searching, of needing to find some place, something, or someone was gone now. The force that had driven him to walk into the mountains with his son was finally at rest.

Gingerly, he put his hand on her shoulder, wondering at her tears—wondering at his own.

Slowly, Kay turned the page over, placing it neatly on the pile.

LEAVING SHERWOOD

A FICKLE UNIVERSE COMPANION

CHAPTER

ONE

Light rain woke Will Scarlet from sleep at dawn, reminding him once again of everything his family had lost in the three years since Robin Hood was murdered. His wife, Kay, snuggled closer to him in the hollow between two roots where they'd made their bed, but he knew she'd be up soon. Neither of them could sleep when it rained. Not so their son, Paul. That boy could sleep through a deluge.

Before they'd been blessed with King Richard's pardon, rain had just been a fact of life under the Green-wood, but the five years they'd spent in Gamwell Lodge had spoiled Will more than he cared to admit.

He tightened his arm around Kay and pressed a kiss to her forehead. She mumbled in response and snaked her arm around his middle.

I'm so sorry, he thought, not for the first time. They should all be back inside four walls, comfortable, warm, and dry. They should be safe. Not that it was his fault they had been hunted across Sherwood Forest until they were little more than ghosts of the free folk they'd been. No, that fault belonged to John, the bloody king who'd inherited the crown from Richard the Lionheart. John, who was set upon destroying anyone who had seen him humiliated by Robin Hood.

And he'd nearly succeeded. All Robin's men were either dead or fled, and only Will and his family remained of the band of outlaws who had made history under the great oaks of Sherwood.

He knew they'd made history because his wife, Kay, had come through time from the future to live with them, to love him, and to try to save Robin's life. She hadn't managed to change Robin's fate, but the life she'd carved out for herself had changed Will for the better. He couldn't imagine life without her and the son they'd created together. Even if it was currently living out in the rain, with no roof and no shelter but each other's arms.

Kay was moving over him now, her touch more intimate. After eight years of marriage, she always seemed to know when his thoughts had taken a dark path, and she could always bring him light in the best way possible. Their lovemaking was slow and sweet, until he forgot about the rain, forgot about the loss . . . forgot about everything except the strong, beautiful, capable woman in his arms.

Afterwards, as she lay sprawled across him, kissing his neck gently, his thoughts gathered into what they would do for the day. As always, Kay was ahead of him.

"We're nearly out of dried venison. Shall we hunt?"

Will grunted, thinking. It had been a month since they'd had any run-ins with soldiers. The odds of them being able to hunt, cure, and dry a whole deer's meat without having to leave it behind were better than ever before, but still he hesitated. They had to eat, so delaying wasn't really an option, but something about the day felt off.

He put it down to the rain, and kissed Kay's forehead again. "Better wake the boy. I think he's old enough now to try for his first kill."

At seven years old, Paul was everything Will could have hoped for in a son. Strong, smart, and lively. He knew how to stay silently hidden, could run fast as a woodland hare, and was already as good a marksman as his mother. He supposed some of it was paternal pride, but Will thought Paul could grow into the best yeoman Sherwood Forest had ever seen—bar none. Better even than Robin Hood.

But the boy was sleepy, now, protesting his mother's attempt to rouse him. It wasn't until the words "hunt" and "your turn" penetrated his resistance that he jumped up quick as a squirrel, immediately ready for the day.

Will chuckled and ruffled the boy's hair before he stooped to uncover their bows from the deer hide they used to protect the precious weapons from the weather. There was little enough food to break their fast. A hunk of dried venison, a handful of oats, uncooked and thick to choke down, a couple blackberries each that hadn't yet turned moldy, and water from the brook nearby.

What he wouldn't have given for a flagon of ale and the cold stirabout they'd been able to manage even on the poorest of days when Robin was still alive. But he grinned at Paul's enthusiasm, and as the sun burned off the clouds and the rain stopped, he felt hopeful about the day's prospects.

Few words were required to indicate the direction they needed to go. Kay had seen sign of a large herd the day before, off to the southwest, and Will knew that would be the best direction to start. They traveled silently through the alders, birch, and oak trees, Kay in front, Paul in the middle, and Will bringing up the rear of their little column. One line, to hide their numbers should anyone find their path and track them—though Will was proud that he did not need to cover any marks. His wife and son left less trace than a summer breeze passing through the leaves around them.

An hour later, Kay slowed and held up her hand, fingers spread wide to indicate prey, not danger. Head down, studying sign, she pointed to their left, then stood aside to let Paul lead. They'd taught their son how to track well, and fifteen minutes later they could see the brown backs of at least a dozen deer through the trees, grazing on the tender leaves of grass growing in a sunlit clearing, blissfully unaware that death was stalking them.

Paul made a hand gesture to indicate his target and Kay nodded. The two-point buck never stood a chance. First one arrow pierced his heart, then a second arrow so close after the first that Will had to check and see whether Kay had shot, too. But Paul had made the kill on his own.

"Well done," Will said, letting his pride show in his voice. Kay hugged the boy as the rest of the herd scattered, smelling blood and —too late—humans.

"We'll eat well tonight!" Paul said as they moved forward to claim his kill.

It was something Will himself would have said, and he could feel his heart near to bursting with love and pride. He moved into the clearing after them and began test Paul on what to do in order to prep the deer for transport. They'd need to gut it, then wrap it in burlap to keep the flies off. Once they'd found a camp where they could safely spend several days, they would cure, butcher, and dry the meat. And they would eat well of fresh meat, too. Will could almost taste the fire-roasted haunch of venison.

Kay kept watch while he guided his son through the process of gutting the animal, but a slight sound made him look up. Her head snapped around in the same instant as he heard another noise, the sound of a crossbow being cocked. With a start, he realized where they were . . . mere steps from the main road between Nottingham and Lincoln.

Before he could do more than put a hand on Paul's shoulder, twelve soldiers stepped out, surrounding them with crossbows leveled.

"So now poaching is a family affair," said one of the soldiers.

"But we have more than poachers," said another, grinning. Will recognized an officer who had come to Gamwell several times in service to Lord Crandall of Lincoln. "The man there is Will Scarlet, one of the late Robin Hood's men."

"Ho! Ho!" crowed the first. "What a catch! I didn't think there were any cowardly outlaws left around here. King John will be pleased to see this head hanging on his gates with the others."

"Aye," said the officer. "And a handsome reward for us, no doubt. As for the other two, the woman is fair—"

"Paul, no!" Paul let the arrow fly, ignoring Will's call. No one had been watching his son, though he realized too late he should have. The arrow caught the officer full in the throat and the man fell, choking on his own blood.

Kay dove on her bow and rolled, coming up to shoot. Two men fell to her arrows before she and Will had to draw their swords.

"Run, Paul!" Kay screamed.

But Paul was running at a soldier, his dagger up and ready to strike. The soldier's sword cleaved the air where Paul's head had been, but the boy ducked and rolled across the ground, coming up to stab at the soldier's leg. The blade skidded off chain mail, ineffective.

"No!!!" Kay cried out. Will looked to see her anguished face, and a crossbow bolt ripping into her left shoulder in the next second.

Will was torn. He stood between his wife and his son, and both were in mortal danger.

A soldier approached and Will hacked at him, dispatching him with an economy of blows. He looked up just in time to see a soldier come up behind Kay and carve a strip out of her left shoulder as she turned to engage him. She let out an incredible scream of pain as the stroke ripped the bolt that was already there in half.

"Kay! Get out of here, Kay!" Will shouted, two soldiers advancing on him. When he engaged them, two more came from behind, and he had to focus or be overcome by their sheer numbers. He had mobility in his favor over men weighed down by chain mail and bulky shields better suited to a battlefield than a focused attack. But the sight of his son also being surrounded distracted him enough that the men closed in, and two swords pierced him—one in the arm, one in the side.

He heard Kay scream his name and caught a glimpse of her running from the clearing.

Good, he thought, *I'll catch up with her later*. But Paul was in real trouble. Two soldiers lifted his slight frame off the ground, hanging on despite the boy's wild thrashing.

With a mighty roar, Will threw off the soldiers bearing in on him, though not without cost. He felt the bite of at least two more blows, a slice across his chest that shredded his shirt and exposed muscle and bone, and a thrust from behind that glanced off his collarbone and nicked his ear as he dodged aside. The blade continued across his cheek to his brow, blinding his left eye with his own blood.

Shouting in wordless fury, Will spun in a circle, mowing down three soldiers like so much wheat at the harvest. Then he ran to his son and thrust his sword so hard at one soldier's breastplate that it pierced it and stuck, the man's dead weight pulling it out of Will's hand as he fell to the ground. The other soldier dropped Paul in favor of fleeing to protect himself, and Will scooped the boy up and began to run, knowing there was no way he could fight off all the soldiers.

Pain lanced through him as another blade thrust through his back, the point passing all the way through to pierce his son's side, too.

Then a blinding white light enveloped him, and he knew no more.

CHAPTER

TWO

I t was a long time before Will became truly aware again.

There were moments, vignettes, jumbled together in his mind. Blinding bright light. Falling through space. *Pain*. Shock of icy water. Struggling to the shore of a lake. Carrying his son. *Pain*. More lights. Voices. White sterile halls. Questions with no answers. *Pain*.

When he became aware that some semblance of order had returned to his world, he had no idea how much time had passed. He didn't know where he was, and dimly realized he didn't know *who* he was. The past was a yawning blackness hovering on the edge of his awareness, and only two things shone like lights: he had a son named Paul, and Paul had a mother . . . . He couldn't remember her name, only that he loved her very much.

After awareness came an intrusion of soft sounds. Faint humming and birdsong . . . if the bird sang only one note, over and over. *Cheep, cheep, cheep*. Something rattled off in the distance, and voices murmured; some of the words were English, but spoken with an accent he couldn't place.

He opened his eyes, and nothing he saw made sense. Shadows crowded the dimly lit room; tall, thin things—not men—with tiny blinking lights that were not flames. The bed he lay on was soft, with fine, crisp sheets. The frame was metal, bright as any sword, smooth and round. Light shone from under the door, and it didn't flicker like firelight. The floor was shiny, not wood or stone or dirt.

All these images were sorted and cataloged in his mind, and he had a feeling it should mean something. They didn't make sense; there were no images to compare to. He could name things like floor and light and fire, bed and sword, metal and wood. He knew words like soft and smooth and shiny, even knew what they meant, but they were like words written in the sparks of a campfire, significance gone in moments.

He lifted his hand to touch the bed frame and was surprised to find something attached to it. Closer inspection revealed some kind of hollow string that flexed when he lifted it, only to discover that it disappeared under his skin! Horrified, he clawed at it, pulling out what looked like a big sewing needle, blood glistening on the end of it.

The bird started singing faster—*bip bip bip bip bip*—then the door burst open and a woman entered the room. Bright light blinded him and he cried out, throwing his free hand over his eyes.

"Easy does it," the woman said, but Will pulled away from her reaching hands. She managed to grasp one arm, then cried, "Orderly!"

A large, burly man entered the room and swiftly moved to the other side of the bed, grabbed his arm and held him down.

"Calm down, sir!" the woman said. "We're not going to hurt you!"

Eyes adjusting to the brightness, Will's gaze flicked from the woman to the man, then back to the woman. He didn't see any sign of aggression from either of them, saw only kindness in their eyes. Kindness and . . . pity. Everything in him shouted that he should run, shouted of danger, but he forced the tension from his body, to lull these strangers into releasing him.

Then confusion came back. He knew the opposite of strangers was friends, but he couldn't think of anyone who might be a friend. The only other soul he knew for certain was . . . .

"Paul," he croaked, his voice so rusty with disuse the word was nearly unintelligible. "My son."

"He's here," the woman said. "In the next room. Sleeping."

At those words, he tried to rise, but again the man she'd named "Orderly" held him down.

"You can't get out of bed yet, sir. We have monitors on you. You'll rip them off."

He didn't know what a monitor was, but thought of the needle in the back of his hand. "Remove them," he demanded, but the woman shook her head.

"If you promise to stay put, I'll bring the doctor, and he can decide. Please," she added, when his muscles tensed of their own accord.

It was that word, please, that stilled him. Something, an instinct more than a memory, told him dangerous people didn't say please.

He jerked his head in a nod and saw an answering relief in her eyes. "Thank you. I'll be right back, I promise."

There was that word again. Promise. Another word he didn't think dangerous people used. When she left the room, he turned his gaze upon Orderly. Despite the man's bulk, he had a kind smile for Will.

"We're excited you're awake, man. You and your son are the longest running mystery Deschutes County General Hospital has ever encountered. We have a betting pool as to what your story is."

Orderly's words were foreign. *Deschutes? Hospital? Betting pool?* And the woman's word, *doctor*. Why did he only understand part of the words spoken to him? If it was a different language, would he understand any of it? His confusion must have shown in his eyes, because Orderly patted his hand. "Never you mind, man. It will just be good to call you by your name instead of John Doe."

My name? he thought. Again, that blackness yawned in his memory, and he became conscious of his hand balling up the fabric of the bedsheets as he tried to remember something. Anything. This other name Orderly called him, John Doe, didn't feel right, but what name did?

Again, Orderly patted his hand, and didn't say anything more.

Moments later the woman walked back into the room, accompanied by a man in a white tunic, holding a thin board of some kind in his hand.

"Hello," the new man said. "I'm Doctor Baldwin. It's good to see you awake. How are you feeling?"

Will stared at him, testing the question. How did he feel?

"Confused," he said at last. It felt like a dangerous confession, but this man didn't even blink.

"That's to be expected," he said. "Can you tell us your name?"

He looked around at the expectant faces, but though he strained his memory, nothing came to mind.

"Your son says his name is Paul Wilson," Doctor Baldwin prompted. "We brought him in to see you, and that's when he remembered."

"Wilson." Will tested the name, and in his mind, he saw his son —the only face that came from his memory—saying *I'm Paul, Will's son*. It felt familiar. "I think my name is Will."

"You think?" Doctor Baldwin looked down at the board in his hand, made a mark with the object in his other hand. Obviously a writing instrument, but Will didn't know how he knew it, when there was no other image to reference. Doctor's voice was neutral, not judging, not friendly, just . . . words.

"It feels right."

"But you don't remember. Do you remember anything? Anything at all?"

"I have a son. Paul. And a . . . wife." He tested the word out, hoping more would come, a name, but nothing did.

"Nothing about what happened?"

The blackness was beginning to feel like an impenetrable wall. "Nothing."

Doctor Baldwin made more marks on the board. "Well," he said at length, "at least we have a name. It's a pleasure to meet you at last, William Wilson."

The name didn't feel exactly right, but Will didn't think there was enough reason to tell Doctor Baldwin he was wrong. He just nodded at the man. Then, "I want to see my son." After another beat, "Please."

Doctor Baldwin looked at the woman, then nodded. "We can wake Paul for this, Ella. He'll want to see that his father is awake."

It was only then that Will noticed the words sewn into her pink cloth tunic. Ella Swartout, NP. Her name? A look back at the man in the white tunic showed the name Derek Baldwin, MD. And

Orderly's blue tunic had the name Russell Black. So, the other words were titles?

"Thank you," he said, as Ella turned to leave the room.

Doctor Baldwin cleared his throat. "It's unusual for two patients to lose their memories, even if they experienced the same traumatic event," he said. "Paul woke from his coma a week ago, and all he remembered was his name, and that you are his father. We were concerned about traumatic brain injury at first, due to his limited vocabulary and apparent total loss of learning. But he's been watching TV and appears to be recovering knowledge at a tremendous rate." He looked at the board in his hand, flipping through pages of paper. "Your son's injuries have healed at a normal rate, but he'll need another few weeks to be completely healed. As will yours, although your injuries were far more significant."

It surprised Will to hear that he had injuries, but then information snapped together and it began to make sense. Doctor Baldwin was a healer, they were in a place of healing, and there had been an event of some sort that hurt him and made him forget his past.

He opened his mouth to ask what had happened, but at that moment Paul ran into the room and jumped up on the bed to throw himself at Will, and Will automatically caught and held him tight. "Paul!" he said, the word tearing from his throat like a sob. And Will realized he was crying.

"Dad!" Paul said. It wasn't a familiar word, but it felt right, like a word Paul chose to convey his love for his father.

"Paul," he repeated, and his son buried his face against Will's shoulder. For a moment, everything in his world narrowed down to the point of contact between them, filling him with a sense of peace. A subtle sound drew attention to the fact that the others had left the room, giving them privacy for their reunion.

After a long moment, Paul squirmed to be released, and Will let him back enough that he could look into the boy's face. His blue eyes, hawk-like nose and thin-lipped smile were blessedly familiar, as was his blond hair, though he remembered it longer than this close-cropped cut.

"It's you," Will said, and Paul smiled.

"Yes, father, it's me. I'm so glad you're awake. And you look so much more better since they took your bandages off. I wonder what

Mama will think about your scars, though." Paul's hand reached up to trace a line from above his eye, across to his ear.

It was only at that moment that Will wondered about his injuries. And Paul's. The loose-fitting clothing on his son prevented a thorough inspection, but Will could see a scar sticking up out of the collar of the boy's shirt. Will moved the material aside and saw the line of a scar disappearing down his torso.

"I've got one here, too," the boy said, and lifted the shirt to show a raw, pink wound in his side.

Anger and fear flashed through Will, though he didn't know the source of it, other than the fact that his son had been injured. He felt as though he ought to know what had caused the injuries, but that blackness stood between him and the knowledge.

He put his hand up to his own head to feel where Paul had drawn his fingers, and found tender skin, raised and puckered, and felt an unnatural notch in his ear. He tried to conjure a memory of his wife, of Paul's mother, but nothing came.

"What do you remember about Mama," he asked, reaching out to ruffle his son's hair.

"Just that she was with us, and now she isn't. She has yellow hair and blue eyes, and I miss her."

"I do, too," Will said, and realized it was true. How could they miss someone they couldn't remember?

I t was some time later when Will woke to the sensation of someone lifting a sleeping Paul out of his arms. He tightened his grip and his eyes snapped open to see Ella looking at him with surprise.

"I just thought you'd be more comfortable if he slept in his own bed," she whispered. Will shook his head, and she released Paul. "Very well. But we need to check your bandages soon, and the doctor will want to talk with you about your injuries . . . and about what happened."

Will nodded, but he wasn't ready to relinquish his hold on his son. Just having him near shook loose vague memories of playing together, running and wrestling, and the feelings he recovered with those memories were a life-line, anchoring him and preventing him from drifting away in the blackness where he knew the rest of his memories should be.

He watched as Ella fiddled with some of the boxes around the room and wrote things on the papers attached to her board, and questions in his mind clamored to be answered. When she passed close enough to his bed, he reached out and tugged a sleeve of her tunic. She turned to him with a smile. "I think I'd like to see the doctor, now," he said. "But I'd like to keep Paul close. Can we make that work?"

She paused long enough to think things through, then said, "Let me move him to the other side of the bed, so the doctor can check your bandages. After you have a talk with him, we can look into getting you both into a shared room."

With a little maneuvering, during which Paul hardly stirred, Will settled with an arm around his son and tried to prepare himself for what the healer would say. When the man came back, drying his hands on what looked like a piece of paper, Will looked at him with a sense of anticipation, and more than a little dread.

"Doctor Baldwin," he said, as much to set the tone as to vent some of his nervous energy.

"Mr. Wilson," the doctor acknowledged with a smile as he pulled on thin, translucent gloves. "It's good that you remember my name. That's a good sign that you don't have a brain injury, as well. Let me check your wounds, then we'll have a chat, all right?"

Will nodded, and the healer immediately moved forward and reached to touch the side of his face, pressing light fingers against the cut on Will's brow. "The stitched skin is holding up, no sign of infection. That's good. The scar should be minimal, too, though it's too large to disguise completely. I'm afraid you'll bear it for the rest of your life."

Will shrugged. It was only to be expected . . . . *Wasn't it?*

The healer did the same test to a cut on Will's left arm, and gave a reassuring smile. "This one looks good, too."

Next, the healer grasped the corner of the sheets and tried to pull them down, but Will stopped him. "What are you doing?"

"Checking your wounds." There was a definite note of surprise in the man's voice. Then he took a breath and a half-step back. "You have more wounds, ones I can only see if we move the blanket."

Wounds. Plural. Hesitantly, Will let go of the healer's hand and let him continue. Beneath the blanket, the doctor lifted the thin shirt Will wore, exposing a wide swathe of bandage wrapped tight around his middle.

"I have to remove the wrap," the doctor said, "and then the compresses. You may feel some discomfort."

Will watched with a kind of morbid fascination as the healer cut the wrap with a small object Will could name as scissors, then pulled back the white squares of bandages to expose a two-inch long cut that appeared to have been very deep but had been stitched closed. Above that, a long slash looked new, with signs of having been stitched closed, but it seemed to be in a different stage of healing than the other, smaller wound. A third wound, a puncture smaller than the other, appeared to be mostly healed. Incredibly, the healer asked him to sit up so he could check another wound on his back. It was several moments of stunned wonder while the healer worked to check and then re-cover the back wound with fresh bandages, during which time Will tried again to remember what happened. When the doctor came back to work on the front again, he re-covered the larger puncture wound with a fresh bandage.

"The laceration and small puncture continue to heal well," Doctor Baldwin said. "But the larger punctures still need to drain. I can see by your face that you want to know the extent of your injuries. Between all six of the wounds, you had four hundred stitches, some of which are inside, holding muscles together, namely on this laceration on your chest. The three lacerations and smaller puncture were straightforward, and we haven't seen any complications with them. The big puncture wound went all the way through, though, and we had to repair some serious damage to your colon. There was a setback and we had to go in again, but we think we caught it all, and there shouldn't be any more complications. Be glad you slept through all of that."

Will had to admit he didn't understand much of what the healer had just told him, but one thing stood out. "How long was I asleep?"

Doctor Baldwin's face went from pleased at the progress he'd seen to a serious frown. He hesitated before he spoke. "Three months," he said at last. "I'm sure that's a shock to you. I can only imagine what it must be like to wake up with no memory of what happened."

Will could hardly take the information in, himself. Three months. *Three months!*

"Our best explanation is that you were in a car accident, up by Suttle Lake," Doctor Baldwin said gently. Something in his expression suggested he wasn't convinced that was the cause. "Some fishermen found you wandering down the road, carrying your son. You were hypothermic, your clothes soaking wet. Your car must have gone into the lake. Divers searched, but no vehicle was ever found.

No one reported any missing persons, so we had no idea who you are, or how to contact your family. Your wife . . . ," the healer stopped, and didn't continue. Will surmised the man didn't want to say out loud that his wife was likely dead, drowned in the lake. It didn't bear thinking about.

"In any case," the healer continued in a brisk tone, "your wounds are healing very well. Now that you're awake, you should make amazing progress. Given your accent, it's highly likely that you are from Great Britain, traveling in America on vacation. It's possible your family is not expecting to hear from you, and they don't even know you're missing."

Something about that sounded . . . if not familiar, at least important. Will tried to focus, but details eluded him. "And my memories?"

Doctor Baldwin drew in a sharp breath and expelled it noisily. "That's difficult to determine. We see no physical sign of brain injury, and even if it's something we can't see, there's still so much we don't know about how the mind works. Your memories could come back tomorrow, in full or in part. Or it could be years. Something might trigger a full resurfacing all at once, or bits and pieces could come back spread out over months or years. There's really no way to predict the process."

Will was silent after the healer faltered to a stop. He put his arm around his son and told himself that as long as Paul was with him, he would be able to move forward with his life. Together, they would deal with their situation.

"You should rest," Doctor Baldwin said. "You've had a big day."

Will nodded and watched as the man left the room, letting the door close softly behind him. He wanted to stay awake and consider everything he'd learned, but it proved impossible. His thoughts wouldn't focus and he couldn't keep his eyes open. It wasn't long before he drifted into sleep, the warmth of his son's body beside him a comfort he cherished.

THE NEXT SEVERAL days fell into a routine. The doctor came and went; other doctors, too. Other women like Ella. He learned to call them nurses. He also learned the healing place was called a hospital, the boxes with blinking lights monitored things like his heart rate and the oxygen in his blood, and others were machines of various functions. A magical thing called electricity allowed the lights to shine, day or night.

The sensors and various tubes were removed from his body—an uncomfortable process—and he was allowed to go to the privy, where Paul showed him how to operate the wonderful fixtures which provided running water at the turn of a knob, and he could easily wash up or fill a glass to drink.

The room they moved into had a window, and Will was fascinated by the things he saw outside. "Cars" flew at amazing speeds down smooth, black streets, and lined up in rows in great black fields, and loud insect-like flying machines called helicopters came and went at intervals, landing, he was told, on the roof of the hospital.

But perhaps the most illuminating activity was watching the television, or TV, that hung from a pole in their room. Paul showed him how to operate it—he seemed to have a knack for pointing the remote at the box and changing what was displayed for them.

Through it all, Will couldn't help but think he should know some of these things, that there should be some spark of recognition, but most things felt brand new.

Paul confessed he felt the same way, but he picked up on the things the TV showed them much faster than Will could.

But oh, the things they learned. News programs showed everything from weather forecasts to fears of nuclear war with a country called USSR. A flying machine called Challenger was launched into space and exploded, killing the seven astronauts on board and prompting a man named Reagan to postpone something called the State of the Union speech. While the world mourned the tragedy, Will and Paul learned about the Space Program and its significant losses and successes—including a man who walked on the moon.

Then there was the entertainment. "Gameshows" where people jumped around in excitement and won money and trips to fantastic destinations. "Cop shows" where killers were always brought to justice. "Kung-fu movies" where men fought each other with hands and feet. And "war movies" featuring terrifying weapons called guns, bombs, tanks, and missiles.

By far the most interesting to both Will and Paul were history programs, where men with serious voices described wars and adventures, men and women who performed amazing feats of intelligence, bravery, and strength. They told of places around the world that Will was sure he'd never heard of before . . . .

But the ongoing fact was that nothing he'd seen so far triggered any of his own memories. Some things felt like they ought to be important, but nothing jumped out and said, "You know this, Will."

Another feeling was growing in him, too. A feeling that something out there held the answer to the mystery of who he was, and he wasn't going to find any answers sitting in a hospital watching TV.

His body healed more every day, and three weeks from the day he woke up, the doctors all agreed that he and Paul were both well enough to go home. The only problem was, no one knew where home was for them. Some people who came to see him began asking questions about payment, and something called insurance, and he overheard heated discussions about charity cases, expensive treatments, and accusations of "convenient amnesia" that saved them from having to pay.

To be fair, not everyone was concerned with money. Several of the hospital staff seemed genuinely sincere in their expressions of happiness that the two of them were healed, but instinct told Will it was time to get out of there.

He had watched enough TV by now to know how much the world revolved around money, and he was acutely aware that unless he and Paul were in truth long-lost heirs to some fortune, they were going to be in debt for a very long time. And instinct told him long-lost heirs only happened on the "daytime soap operas" favored by the nurses in the lounge.

The question of what to do plagued him for a few days, during which time he and Paul walked the hospital grounds to increase their stamina. But it ultimately came down to the fact that he couldn't pay if he didn't know who he was, and he'd never find out who he was if he stayed. It was that simple. No other factors like guilt or morality came into play.

So he hatched a plan, daring to include Russell the orderly, who had loaned Will clothes when he no longer needed to wear hospital gowns all the time, and whose son was Paul's size. As it happened, Russell claimed he was more than a little anti-establishment, and called himself an "old hippie." He insisted he'd come around to hospital work to help people, not to cripple them with debt. When Will carefully expressed the idea of leaving, of disappearing, Russell was keen to help.

And so it was that, at 1:40 AM on March 20, 1986, Will and Paul walked out the back door of the Deschutes County General Hospital and climbed into Russell's waiting VW van. As the orderly drove them the twenty-five miles from Bend, Oregon, to the tiny town of Sisters, he chattered nervously about things that Will could not follow. He was too excited and nervous himself.

Of all the words tumbling out of the orderly's mouth, one thing did stand out.

"There's this psychiatrist over the mountain who published a paper on a theory that some of his patients aren't crazy . . . they're time-traveling! He's seen several patients, some of whom have no memory after these bizarre or un-explained accidents. When he checks back in with them, they tell him about vivid dreams where they're living in the past. Others who still had their memories were having apparent hallucinations of going back in time, and they were insistent that it was real. He started noticing a pattern to their stories, and found it intriguing that they each had so many similarities. If you don't find any answers at Suttle Lake, maybe you should look him up. I heard he got laughed out of his fancy practice in Eugene, and set up shop in Sweet Home."

Something about this struck a chord. "What's the Doctor's name?"

"Simpson," Russell said. "Andrew Simpson, I think." Then he added, "He calls it the Fickle Universe Theory."

Russell dropped them off in front of a cheap motel, where he gave Will fifty dollars in cash and a duffle bag with some warm jackets and socks. "I'd totally take you all the way to Suttle Lake, but my wife will kill me if I'm gone too long. Besides, you can't see anything this late at night anyway. Don't worry about the clothes, man, or the money. I have to pretend I never saw you leave. I just hope you find what you're looking for."

Will hoped they would, too, as they watched the tail lights of the van vanish around a bend in the road. There was definitely something out there, drawing him out into the night.

"I feel it, too," Paul said, slipping his hand into his father's and looking up at him with youthful certainty. "We're closer now than we were before."

Will squeezed Paul's hand. "Yes, I think we are."

Will used the lateness of the hour and Paul's sad eyes to convince the hotel's night manager to give them a room for five dollars, on the promise that they'd leave first thing in the morning and not make a mess.

In the morning, they went to the market across the street and Paul, claiming he'd seen what to do on TV, bought some supplies they put in the duffle bag. Then they stood at the crossroads, wondering what to do next.

ighway 20 shot almost due north out of town, and
Russell had told him that was the way to Suttle Lake,
where they'd been found five months earlier.

Russell had also warned them against hitchhiking, as if Will
knew what that was, citing the danger of getting picked up by the
police to be brought back to the hospital. He stressed that it would
not be a good thing if they came back to the hospital, because
someone needed to be held responsible for the cost of their
recovery—and if they returned, it would likely be them.

A map of hiking trails taken from the brochure rack in the
hotel's lobby also showed two more highways, Highway 126 that led
west through the mountains, and Scenic Highway 242, a byway over
a pass that was closed due to winter snows.

Back when he planned their escape, he'd thought the fourteen
miles from Sisters to Suttle Lake would be an easy day's walk, but
now he wasn't so sure. His mind had convinced him, but his body
had other ideas, given how out of breath he'd become just walking
from the hotel to the crossroad.

He glanced down at Paul, who grinned up at him. He was aware
that they had very little in the way of supplies, but something told
him they'd be all right. Looking at the trees and breathing in the
crisp spring air was the first time he felt comfortable in his

surroundings. It felt right to be outside, with nothing in sight but the forest and the road. Except that the occasional passing vehicles still felt foreign and . . . wrong.

"Ready?"

Paul nodded eagerly and tugged his hand. With one last look at the westbound highway, they headed out, staying to the edge of the pavement.

They soon discovered that having trucks and cars hurtling past them was not only distracting, it was terrifying. Without saying a word, they slipped into the forest together, keeping the road in sight but preferring to scramble over the hillocks and rough terrain.

This felt right. This felt familiar. He scarcely made any noise as they traveled, had to look over his shoulder to be sure Paul was behind him. As they walked, though, he felt in his soul there was more missing besides the memory of why walking in the woods was familiar. When they startled a small group of deer and sent them bounding off, deeper into the forest, his fingers twitched with a muscle memory he almost understood. He glanced at Paul, who looked up at him with wide eyes.

He understood the base of it, too. They belonged out here.

From inside the tree line they followed the road for hours, stopping periodically to rest. Will knew there was a time when he could have run the same distance in half the time without stopping, and it frustrated him. At this rate, it would take days to find anything out, and he was tired of the black fog over his memories. Tired of not knowing what he didn't know. Tired of being weak and feeling helpless.

By the time the sun fell below the mountains in the west, they stood on the shore of a long lake, water lapping at the hard-packed earth and stones. The pink clouds in the sky reflected on the water and instilled peace in his heart. But no memories came leaping forth.

"What now?" Paul wondered aloud.

"We make camp. In the morning we'll have a look around and see what we can see."

"But this isn't the place, is it, Dad?"

"No, I don't think it is. My heart is telling me we must keep going."

"Yes," Paul agreed.

They had deliberately avoided lighted buildings glimpsed through the trees. Music and the smell of cooking food had been a temptation, but Will resisted, knowing that they would have been missed at the hospital, and he didn't want to draw any attention to their whereabouts by being seen. He did not fail to note that this skulking around out of the path of people felt as natural as breathing, and made him wonder what he had been before he lost his memory.

By now it came as no surprise that he knew how to select a good campsite, where fallen logs framed a V of ground where they would have shelter should a breeze pick up. Together, they scraped away the duff on the forest floor and erected a ring of stone where they could build a fire. And building a fire, while not easy given wet wood and nothing but a lighter Paul had bought—they'd both seen characters on TV lighting cigarettes with them—came naturally. He had vague stirrings of memory that told him while the lighter made the job that much easier, he could have started a fire with only sticks of wood.

They sat with their backs to the logs and held out hands for warmth, neither of them ready for sleep. Although the physical exertions of the day had worn them out, Will felt more alive than ever before, and didn't think he'd be able to sleep at all.

He wondered what they'd be doing, saying, if they had their memories back. Surely they'd have tales of hunting and camping trips to share . . . . But they sat in silence, until eventually Paul leaned against his side and fell asleep.

WILL WAS STILL awake when the sky in the east began to grow light. He watched with a peace that settled into his bones, peace like he hadn't felt since he'd awakened in the hospital. From within that peace, he felt a tug, and that tug brought him to his feet.

Paul must have felt it, too, because he stirred awake and stood beside his father as the birds started singing and the first rays of sunshine crept over the horizon to greet them. It was magical . . .

until a stranger's voice rose out of the morning light, a figure obscured by the bright light of a new day.

"Hey there, friends. I hate to tell you, you're camped in an illegal spot."

Will exchanged a glance with Paul, then shaded his eyes against the light. "Excuse me?"

"Your fire. It's illegal," the voice repeated, and they tracked the speaker as he moved to their left, out of the sun glare. A man in a dark green uniform distinguished himself from the light, and Will realized he was some kind of authority figure similar to the cops on TV. The badge sewn on the sleeve of his jacket identified him as a Forest Service Enforcement officer. A badge on his chest declared his name was Harding. "You can't build a fire in the wilderness without a permit, or outside a developed campground. Certainly not this close to the lake."

Will looked around, at a loss. "You're jesting, right?" He couldn't see how anyone could say that this bit of land or that bit of water was not free for the using.

Paul gave the man his most winning smile, the one that had gotten him anything he'd wanted from the staff at the hospital. "We didn't know," he said. "We got here late last night, and this is the best place we found."

"Surely you passed the campground," the man said, giving Paul a tolerant smile. "This time of year it always has open spaces."

"No, sir," Paul said cheerfully, and pointed to the southeast. "We came up that way."

Will took note of the objects secured to the man's belt and, thanks to the hours of TV they'd watched, recognized the pistol as a weapon and the radio as a communication tool, neither one something Will wanted Harding to have reason to use.

Harding glanced in the direction Paul pointed and frowned. "There's nothing that way but forest."

"Right. We were hiking in the woods." Paul ran a few steps and jumped up on one of the fallen logs, taking the man's attention with him. "Can you see our tracks?"

Will blessed his son's ingenuity when the man followed him and leaned over the log to look.

"I don't see anything," the man said after a moment.

"You're not looking hard enough," Paul said, his voice delivering scorn like only a child could. "Even I can see where I scuffed those pine needles."

Whatever the man might have said in response was interrupted when Will brought two fists down on the back of the man's head. Harding slumped to the fallen log, and Will eased him to the ground.

"Are you going to take his gun, Dad?" Paul asked, hopping nimbly down from the log.

"No," he said. "He's still alive. We only take weapons from the dead." He didn't know where that came from, but he could feel it was a personal truth. "Come on." He caught Paul's hand and tugged the boy back to the lake, where they turned left along the shore. He waited until they were well away from the unconscious man before he spoke. "Something tells me we need to head west, and the highway runs on the north side of the lake, so we'll go this way, on the south shore, to stay out of sight."

"What is it, do you think?" Paul asked, hopping nimbly from rock to rock.

"What is what?"

"The *something*. I feel it too, but I don't know what it is. I think it's familiar, though."

"I don't have an answer to that, son," Will said. "There's a lot of answers I don't have. All I know for sure is that we are on our way toward something, and it's good. It's where we belong."

"Yes," Paul said. "And men like that man back there won't want us to find it. That's why I knew we had to trick him."

Will wondered at Paul's certitude on that score, but there were things he knew, too, and he had no explanation as to the why of it, so he didn't challenge the boy. Instead, they followed the shoreline in silence, continuing to make as little noise as they could, and leaving no trace of their passage.

If Harding was an officer of the law, Will wondered if he would try to pursue them. On the surface, what had they done but start a fire somewhere they weren't supposed to? Surely that wasn't a hanging offense. But striking an officer of the law from behind and knocking him out had to be a crime. The question was, would the officer dare to tell his fellow officers that he'd been tricked by a child and his father? Will could only hope that not stealing anything, and not tying him up, threatening him, or using a weapon would be added incentive for the man to just forget he'd even seen them. He was confident that unless they used hounds, Harding and his fellow officers would not be able to track them.

Before they reached the end of the lake, they passed a place that must have been the campground Harding had referred to, and another place where a man was unloading a boat from a trailer hitched to a pickup. Will and Paul hurried by while the man's back was turned, and he never even knew they were there.

Once they reached the west end of the lake they struck out across open ground, trusting the instinctive force drawing them on. They crossed several dirt tracks, finally connecting with a lane that was little more than a pair of graveled ruts heading in the direction they wanted to go.

By noon they reached another lake, this one small, with no buildings on the shore, where they stopped for some food. The sound of traffic on the highway had diminished so much they couldn't hear anything other than the sighing of the wind in the trees, but Will was reluctant to start a fire until it was necessary for warmth.

After lunch they struck out again, until their path ended at an intersection with a larger graveled road that met the path they were on at right angles. Directly ahead of them they could see the snow-clad slopes of a large mountain, and nothing but untracked wilderness in between.

Will pulled out the map and tried to get his bearings. With Suttle Lake behind them and farther back, Black Butte, he thought the mountain before them must be Mount Washington, and the butte to the northwest would be something called Hoodoo Ski Area. They must have passed between Meadow Lake and Torso Lake, putting them on the trail intersecting with the Old Santiam Wagon Road, which went east to a tangle of forest roads and ultimately to Black Butte Ranch, a place they'd skirted the day before. According to the map, the wagon road was a hiking trail built upon an old freight route that headed west, past a lake called Big Lake, and Fish Lake beyond that, before it wound its way through the Cascade Mountains, roughly parallel to Highway 20.

"We go west on the Wagon Road," he said aloud, and hitched their duffle bag higher on his shoulder.

CHAPTER
FIVE

Will didn't know if they were making good time or not. Since they didn't have a destination, it was hard to judge, and the force driving them on was relentless. Every day they both agreed they felt closer to their stopping place, and once, when they took a wrong turn on one of the many forest roads, they didn't get more than a hundred yards before they knew they needed to turn back.

He figured they were making about five miles each day. His instincts told him once upon a time he could have done twice or even four times that much, but they had entered mountainous territory on their second day, and they both felt how far they were from full recovery with every climb. Add to that their need to supplement their supplies with food foraged along the way, and five miles became a respectable distance.

On their third day, they began to find backcountry campsites, with fire rings and signs of other hikers. They even slipped past a pair of hikers setting up camp one night and listened from the trees to them arguing about where to set up their tent, whether the fire ring was too close to the stream, and where they could legally dig their cat-hole.

After that, Will decided it was safe to light fires to cook the food they foraged. He was able to tickle a trout out of a stream, but Paul was better at it, and fish became a staple of their diet, supplemented by soups made with the new shoots of plants coming up from their winter sleep. He recognized and could name blackberry and wild raspberry, and when he spotted new leaves on plants he recognized as lily, he dug up the bulbs and added them to their stew. Once they came across a nut tree and gathered a handful of nuts from the fall that were still edible. Wild roses provided rose hips that still clung to their branches, and he found new growths of mint, nettle, dandelion and watercress, which they ate variously as green salads, or brewed as tea.

There was much more they might have tried, but Will couldn't place all the plant life they saw and didn't want to risk eating anything poisonous until he felt safe enough to test them in small amounts. As tempting as the plentiful mushrooms were, he knew better than to try them without consulting someone local to the area.

He and Paul both seemed to have intuitive skills when it came to cleaning fish and cooking over an open fire. He had taken to fashioning a snare out of his boot laces each night when they stopped, and four mornings they broke their fast on squirrel and rabbit.

The farther they got from Suttle Lake, the more comfortable Will felt about passing other hikers. For the first three days, any time they heard other hikers they slipped off the trail and hid in the undergrowth until the path was empty again. After that they stayed on the edge of the trail as hikers passed them with only courteous nods or warm hellos. Some gave them curious glances, and Will realized how much less gear he and Paul had compared to the other hikers. Where Will carried everything they possessed in a single duffle bag, the others had elaborate packs and hiking poles.

On the sixth night, as they built their fire and prepared to sleep, a gregarious young man joined them. He introduced himself as Dave and exclaimed about their lack of a tent and sleeping bags. He assumed they were survivalists on a training mission, and Will did not correct him, even though he didn't know exactly what that meant.

He didn't need to worry about Dave's curiosity, because while the man asked many questions, he was just as quick to answer them with his own theories, and Will only needed to nod or shake his head to incite another round of speculations.

While Dave's prattle was mildly annoying, it was also informative.

"This is my first time hiking the Santiam Wagon Road trail from end to end," Dave said. "I parked my car at the Mountain House trailhead, ten miles away. I'm training to hike the Pacific Crest Trail, and I thought this would be a great first training hike of the year."

Will broke in to ask a question. "We've been on the trail for several days. Is there anything interesting going on in the world?"

"What do you want to know?" he asked, but didn't give Will a chance to respond. "Susan Butcher won the Iditarod. The second woman to ever win it. A bunch of space probes flew by Halley's Comet and sent back some cool pictures. March Madness is ramping up in college basketball. Oh, and they found some remains of the Challenger astronauts killed in the disaster . . . ."

Dave finally noticed Will's lack of interest and went off on a different trail. "I suppose what you really want to know is if it looks like society is going to collapse soon. Well, let me assure you that the Cold War is still cold. Russia isn't likely to use their nukes anytime soon, but if you ask me, I think Ayatollah Khomeini is more likely to try to nuke America than Gorbachev."

Some of this was familiar to Will from watching TV in the hospital, but he was trying to figure out how to ask whether anything was going on locally without arousing suspicion when Dave gave him the very answer he was looking for.

"But in the end," he said, "I suppose all of that only matters if nobody around here loses their minds and goes crazy. It's a good thing all the crazy people are up in Portland, leaving those of us who won't go anywhere near the city alone."

Will took that to mean there was no search for two patients who eloped from their hospital bill, and no hunt for the man who knocked out an enforcement officer.

Eventually Dave stopped talking and crawled into his tent, leaving Will and Paul to curl up next to each other by the fire to sleep.

IN THE MORNING, they left the camp before Dave even began stirring in his tent, and broke their fast on the move with some trail mix they still had left over from their first and only stop at the store. Thanks to Dave's endless chatter, Will thought he had a destination . . . or at least the next decision point.

When he mentioned the trailhead at Mountain House, that "something" that spurred them on gave an answering thrill of recognition—a feeling Will had learned meant the information was important.

It was tempting to push on when they reached the next camp area, and when Will looked at Paul, the boy's answer was immediate.

"Let's keep going," he said.

Breaking the routine they'd developed, they pushed on, testing their stamina as they doubled the number of miles they normally walked. When they reached a spot where the trail ended at the highway, they found a sign that announced the Mountain House Trailhead, along with several cars parked in the graveled lot.

Will was tired, and he could see Paul's energy flagging as well, but the trailhead was no place to stop and make camp. Besides the lack of shelter, the traffic rumbling by on the highway was an unwelcome distraction. Standing at the roadside, he looked to the right, which was back in the direction they'd been going. When he looked left, he felt the now-familiar tug and put his hand on Paul's shoulder.

"This way," he said, and Paul nodded.

Together they headed west on the highway, keeping close to the tree line so the cars passing them periodically weren't quite as threatening. In less than a quarter mile they saw a big log cabin across the road, and Will wondered if this was the Mountain House itself. It didn't matter, though. He could feel by looking at it that it wasn't their final destination. But it was a waypoint. A single gas pump and its attendant shack looked closed in the evening light, and they saw no one moving around through the windows of the house.

Choosing a moment when they could neither see nor hear any vehicles on the road, they dashed over and headed across a concrete bridge for the intersecting road a few hundred yards farther down. When they reached it, he read the sign on the post.

"Soda Fork Road. This is the way."

"We're so close," Paul said. "But I'm tired."

"Me too, son."

An old building with a metal roof just off the corner of the road beckoned to them. It looked abandoned, with stalls and the whole front wall opened like a barn for horses or equipment, but when they approached and looked inside, it proved to be empty except for some old tires and a couple bales of rotting hay.

Paul crawled onto the hay and curled up, munching on the last of their trail mix. Will covered him with their blanket, then sat beside him in the dust and worried about what they might find to eat the next morning. They had no money left, and there was no telling what they would find up the Soda Fork. But there was no question in his mind that their destination was within reach.

"I think we'll find it tomorrow," Paul said sleepily.

"I think you're right," Will said, and reached out to ruffle Paul's hair. Regardless of what they found, he knew something needed to change. They needed a good night's rest. They needed better food. Most of all, they needed answers.

Eventually he drifted off to sleep, lulled by the sound of his son's soft snores and the infrequent hum of tires as cars and trucks passed by out on the highway.

CHAPTER

SIX

They woke to the sound of wind rattling the metal panels of the roof along with the whisper of pine needles and the occasional cone striking them and rolling down. Outside, gray clouds scudded across sky the color of a fresh bruise and the temperature hovered around freezing. The wind made dervishes of dust, and bits of branches and trash blew fitfully around the dirt lot.

"There's a storm on the way," Will said. Part of him thought they ought to take shelter back in the shed, but the urge to move on was stronger. They were so close to their final destination that he could almost taste it. "We'd better get a move on."

There was no food left to break their fast, so they simply turned up the road and headed out, shoulders hunched against the wind.

Soda Fork Road wound its way into the woods, climbing gradually into the foothills of the mountains. They passed timber in various stages of growth, from areas cleared of every tree—the land scarred and littered with piled branches—to tiny trees planted in rows, to young trees not much taller than Will, and—the deeper they trekked—stands of pines that looked to be a hundred years old or more. Sometimes in the distance they heard the sound of activity. A droning buzz followed by the crashing of trees falling to the earth, or the rumble of engines and horns blaring. Will realized it was the sound made by men harvesting these woods for industry.

The road forked, and forked again, and again, but each time

they only needed to look down one way or the other to know which way to go.

Eventually they left the noise behind and all they heard was the squawk of a pair of black birds with white bars on their wings that kept pace with them, flying from tree to tree along the road. That and the wind whistling in the firs, blowing harder as the day wore on. The cloud cover thickened to solid gray and lowered, threatening rain or even a late snow.

It was close to noon when the first hard rain started to fall, blowing sideways and beating against their backs as though driving them along.

Still they walked on, until at last the shape of a cabin took form in the glooming daylight. No lights shone in the windows and the chimney looked cold, but it looked sound, not run down nor abandoned.

"Here." Paul tugged his hand, pulling him to the door.

There was no answer when the boy knocked, and when he tried the door handle, it turned in his grip. A gust of wind pushed it wide and sent it crashing against the inside wall, and they found themselves looking at a single room, neat and tidy, but empty of any movement.

Another gust of wind spurred Will into motion and he entered the cabin, motioning Paul to follow, then pushed the door shut. The light coming through the small windows was enough to see a lamp on the table near the door, and he fumbled with it until he figured out how to lift the glass to get at the wick, which he lit with Paul's lighter. He replaced the glass and held it up to look more closely around the room.

It was sparsely furnished. A bed. A small closet with hanging clothes visible through a door left ajar. A black bellied stove, open and the makings of a fire laid inside. The table by the door. A footstool by the fire. A chair in front of a desk with some papers atop it.

Opening a door on the opposite side of the room revealed a larder of sorts, where cans and boxes of food lined the shelves and strips of meat hung on drying racks. *Venison*, his mind whispered. There was a stack of folded deer hides and a pile of antlers in the corner. More furs, rabbit and squirrel by the look of them, filled a basket in another corner.

Another door opened out the back of the cabin, and when he opened it to look, he saw a covered woodpile and a tiny shack a short distance away. He stepped back out into the rain to investigate, wanting to make sure the owner of the cabin wasn't inside.

"Hello!" he called as he closed in on it, then the wind shifted and the odor emanating from it identified it as a privy—much more primitive than the comforts they'd grown accustomed to in the hospital, but still more sophisticated than what they'd had available on the trail.

No one responded to his call, so he retreated to the cabin and shut the door against weather turned increasingly wild, the rain now turned to sleet. Back inside, he found Paul putting flame to the kindling in the stove—just as though it was their own home and he had every right to use the supplies laid out by whoever lived here.

And it did feel like home, he realized. That feeling that there was something more still thrummed in his blood, but the force he'd felt driving him so many miles . . . that force was gone, replaced with a sense of homecoming.

"We can replace whatever we use," he said aloud, to assuage any lingering sense of guilt he felt from using things that weren't his. "We can hope the owner understands we needed to get out of the storm."

"It will be all right," Paul said, sitting back on his heels to watch the flames catch. When the wood began to snap he took up a larger wedge-shaped log and put it on the growing fire. The room began to warm appreciably.

"I hate to take without asking," Will began, "but there's enough venison in the larder that we can have some, and when the storm is over, I'll set snares to get meat to replace what we use."

Paul nodded absently, but his eyes were on the wall by the front door, and when Will looked, he saw a pair of swords hanging crossed below a single arrow set on a pair of pegs so that its tip pointed east.

The breath left his body in a rush and all the light in the room gathered around those weapons. Without realizing he had crossed the room, he found himself reaching for the arrow. The shaft was wood, the fletching real feathers, the tip hammered steel . . . all familiar to his hand. He knew without a doubt he'd held hundreds, even thousands of arrows in his lifetime. And this arrow had meaning to the hands that had mounted it there on the wall. It was special.

He replaced it reverently before grasping the hilt of one of the swords. This weapon felt familiar, too, the balance and heft of it comfortable in his grip. He gave it a test swing and muscle memory ignited, so that he knew what it felt like to drive the tip of the blade into a man's body. The thought shocked him so much that he almost dropped the sword. He carefully hung it back on the wall next to its sister and stepped back.

"I'm hungry," Paul said after a long moment during which the only sounds were the crackling of the fire and the sleet lashing against the windows.

Shaking himself awake to the present moment, Will went back into the larder and found a few strips of jerky and a jar of peaches, which he brought back to the stove. He settled on the footstool and Paul sat on the floor at his feet, and they shared the food in thoughtful silence.

When they finished, Paul crawled up onto the bed and burrowed under the blankets, promptly falling into a deep sleep, but Will was too wound up to rest. He prowled the room again, touching various objects, hoping to trigger more memories, but his head was filled with the vision of men fighting with swords and bows and arrows, and a forest that was very different from the one outside the cabin's door.

He found himself at the desk, staring down at a stack of papers, the writing on it cramped but legible. Without thinking, he sank into the chair and began to read. The words immediately trans-ported him to another world, and he didn't notice the passage of time. He barely registered when, several hours later, Paul got up and went out to use the privy, then fed the fire when he came back. On an unconscious level, he heard the storm winding down, felt the aching in his bones from sitting so long, but he couldn't stop reading.

WILL LOOKED UP GUILTILY as the door of the cabin opened. The drenched figure in the doorway wasn't who he'd expected, and he stood quickly.

"Do you live here?" he asked. "I . . . I didn't mean to—"

Steel-gray eyes flickered to the desk where the manuscript lay, the last page exposed. Rage like fire lashed from her eyes, and Will took an unconscious step back.

"I'm sorry. We got caught in the storm and came in to get out of the—" He took another step back as a knife materialized in the woman's hand.

"You've got no right." The woman's voice was low with rage, her British accent as thick as his own. He hadn't heard the like since he'd awakened. When she stepped forward, Will backed up, his heel striking the wall. He held his hands up, palms out.

"It was there. The story . . . . It seemed familiar somehow. I just . . . . I had to read it. I'm sorry . . . ." His voice trailed off as he caught her expression. She had frozen while he spoke. His mind raced back, remembering the word that had stopped her.

Familiar.

So was she, in fact. Without seeing it, he knew her hair would fall the length of her back. He could almost feel the silky tresses running through his hands like water. He *knew* every curve of her slight body. And those eyes . . . . He had once gazed into those eyes.

"Kay?" The name slipped comfortably from his lips.

"Who are you?" she whispered, uncertainty coloring her tone.

"I—"

Before he could continue, the woman swiftly sidestepped to the wall by the door. Her sudden motion startled Will.

"Dad!" The boy shot through the door without seeing her. "I saw deer. A whole herd of 'em."

Will knelt and grabbed the boy's hand, pulling him against his chest. "Paul!" he said, instinctively putting his body between the woman and the boy. He looked up when her knife clattered to the wooden floor.

She stared at his son, eyes wide, her hands over her mouth. Surprised, Will watched her drop to her knees.

"Oh God." Her strangled words conveyed the strength of her emotion. She held her arms out wide, as though to encircle the whole room. "Paul?"

Paul never hesitated. He ran into her arms. They clung tightly to each other for a few moments before the woman looked up at Will.

"Can you be true?" she asked, gently setting Paul back from her. "Both of you?" For a moment, Will thought he saw unshed tears shining in her wondering eyes. Once again, he was caught by the familiarity of those eyes, blue now that her anger was gone.

Paul stood still, studying her with uncanny perception for an almost-eight-year-old.

"I'm William Wilson." He took three long strides forward and put his hands on his son's shoulders. "This is my son, Paul. We got caught in the storm."

"So you said." The woman stood, her movements graceful and sure, like a cat. "I'm Kay."

"I know you." Paul took her hand and she looked down at him. "You've been in my dreams ever since I woke up after the accident."

"Accident?"

"Six months ago." Will supplied. "Neither of us remembered anything from before."

She stared at Paul a few moments more, then moved swiftly around them to the desk. Will followed her with his gaze. She stood with her back to him, looking down at the final page of the manuscript.

"Has it only been six months?" she murmured. Her shoulders began to shake ever so slightly.

"I know you too, don't I?" Will asked, coming to stand beside her.

That sense of searching, of needing to find some place, something, or someone was gone now. The force that had driven him to walk into the mountains with his son was finally at rest.

Gingerly, he put his hand on her shoulder, wondering at her tears—wondering at his own.

Slowly, Kay turned the page over, placing it neatly on the pile.

As she turned to look at him, he knew everything in those pages was her story . . . and his story.

As he took her in his arms, the memories came flooding back.

As he kissed her, he knew he was truly home.

THE END

PLEASE CONSIDER LEAVING A REVIEW.

I love writing stories for you.

One of the best and most important ways *you* can help me continue to write them is to tell other people whether and how much you enjoy reading my work.

Reviews encourage other readers to try an author or a book they might not otherwise take a chance on. It helps an author on so many levels, and we're grateful when readers share their experience with a book.

So, don't be shy. Let the world know how you feel.

Post a dissertation. Post a paragraph. Post a sentence.

Or just post a star rating.

From an author's perspective, the only ineffective way to review is to not leave one at all.

Please consider posting your review with the vendor you purchased it from, and/or anywhere you visit to find the books you enjoy.

www.kristicramerbooks.com

*Visit **WattPad** for opening chapters of published works and sneak peeks at works in progress:* http://kcbooks.us/wpKCpro

facebook.com/KristiCramer.Author

amazon.com/Kristi-Cramer/e/B00HLUEAT4

goodreads.com/kristicramer

pinterest.com/KacyAuthor

patreon.com/KacyAuthor

YOUNG ADULT TITLES BY KRISTI CRAMER

In the Magic of Verridian Series
Fantasy for the Whole Family

   To Make a King (#1)

Time Travel Adventures for the Whole Family
In the Fickle Universe

   Sherwood Rogue

ADULT TITLES BY KRISTI CRAMER

In The Knights of Juneau (Adult Romantic Suspense)

Standalone novels featuring the Knight family, residents of Juneau, Alaska.

Knight Before Dawn (#1)

The Thomas Family Novels (Suspense with a Dash of Romance)

Standalone novels featuring characters connected to the Thomas Family of Syracuse, Kansas.

Last Shot at Justice (#1)

Last Second Chance (#2)

One Last Song (#3)

Last Refuge (#4)

With Elaine Cramer (Adult Dark Humor)

A Sci-Fi short

The Musician & the Alien

FIND THESE (AND OTHER TITLES) AT
WWW.KRISTICRAMERBOOKS.COM

www.ingramcontent.com/pod-product-compliance
Lightning Source LLC
Chambersburg PA
CBHW051437260626
47162CB00001B/141